DEATH FROM THE SKY

From the *Haida's* bridge, Lieutenant Commander Brent Ross stared at the approaching Heinkel. Its 53-foot wingspan looked huge, and he could hear the roar of its powerful Jumo 211 engines.

The Heinkel's bombs came in a cluster. Brent had been expecting a stick, but instead he got a cluster. Loaded tail down, they flipped over as soon as they left the bay and plummeted toward the ship like a handful of thrown darts.

"Right full rudder!" Brent shouted. The destroyer heeled hard into her turn, but the bombs bore down and actually seemed to curve and follow the ship's evasive moves as if they were guided missiles.

"Impossible!" Brent screamed. "Get away from my ship!"

Then he could only stare in horror as the eight black-finned blurs screamed directly down on his head.

ORDEAL OF THE SEVENTH CARRIER

PETER ALBANO

ZEBRA BOOKS
KENSINGTON PUBLISHING CORP.

This book is dedicated to
Max LeVine and Dale O. Swanson,
loyal friends who have enriched my life
for over five decades.

ZEBRA BOOKS

are published by

Kensington Publishing Corp.
475 Park Avenue South
New York, NY 10016

First printing: October, 1992

Printed in the United States of America

ACKNOWLEDGEMENTS

The author gratefully acknowledges:

Master Mariner Donald Brandmeyer, for his advice concerning nautical problems;

William D. Wilkerson, for explaining flight characteristics of fighter aircraft under the stress of combat;

Patricia Johnston, RN, and Susan A. Johnston, RN, who generously contributed their expertise to the solution of medical problems;

Mary Annis, my wife, for her careful reading of the manuscript and her thoughtful suggestions;

Robert K. Rosencrance, who spent long hours editing the manuscript. Mr. Rosencrance also made numerous suggestions concerning characters and their development.

Chapter One

"Target bearing green forty, range forty-one miles, Captain," came up the helmsman's voice tube of the old British destroyer *Haida*.

High on the flying bridge, the warship's captain, Commander Clive Coglan, acknowledged with his usual "Very well."

Comander Coglan opened another tube, his crisp, aristocratic British inflection dropping words like gems from a polisher's cloth: "Electronic Support Measures."

"ESM, aye."

"Is the target ranging us?"

"Negative, Captain," came back. "Very weak signal. Not in my threat library. S-band only. Type of radar carried by small freighters for surface search and piloting. No air search, sir."

"No IFF?" It stood for "Identification Friend or Foe."

The expected answer came back. "No IFF, Captain."

"Very well." Coglan rubbed the sharp bridge of his nose thoughtfully. "Radar, speed and course of target?"

"Speed ten to twelve knots, course two-nine-zero."

"Very well, Radar. Continue tracking. Inform me immediately if the target changes course or speed."

Coglan turned to his navigator, Sinclair Ingilly, a heavy-set lieutenant from Cornwall. "Pilot, cut in the target's approximate position and give me a true bearing."

Ingilly checked his gyro repeater by squinting through the gunsight of the bearing ring, hunched over his canvas-covered chart table, worked his parallel rules. "True bearing of target two-zero-five, Captain," he said, his Cornish accent giving his words a hard, cutting edge.

"Very well, give me an interception course, Pilot. Our speed will be twenty-four knots."

The parallel rules clacked across the chart to a compass rose. "I would suggest an initial course of two-two-five, sir."

Commander Coglan shouted down a tube, "Pilothouse!"

"Pilothouse, aye!" came back from the tube.

"Starboard ten!"

"Starboard ten, sir." There was a pause while the destroyer *Haida* heeled into her turn. "Ten of starboard wheel on, sir."

Coglan glanced at the gyro repeater. "Midships," he shouted.

"Wheel amidships." A pause. "She's holding, sir."

"Very well. Course two-two-five."

"She's steady on two-two-five, sir."

The gyro repeater ticked and the ship swayed. He warned the quartermaster, "Watch your head, QM. Chop! Chop!"

"Minding the helm," came back sheepishly.

Commander Coglan glanced down at the sea. A moderate swell was quartering from the port side. "Two-thirds ahead together. Give me revs for twenty-four knots," he ordered.

Engine room telegraphs jangled in the pilothouse. Then the power of the pair of new General Electric geared turbines was felt immediately, the quickening vibrations of the deck plates tingling the soles of every man on the bridge.

"Twenty-four knots, one hundred eighty revs, sir," a

8

tube announced.

"Very well." Commander Coglan turned back to Lieutenant Ingrilly. "Time of interception, Pilot?"

Anticipating the question, the navigator set his fingers to flying over a small pocket calculator. "Ah . . . a run of about one hour, forty-two minutes to intersect her track," he said to himself more than to his captain. And then, turning to Coglan with one eyebrow cocked, "If the lot holds constant, Captain, we should jolly well ram him at high noon."

Coglan chuckled and muttered, "Good show, Pilot, but I bloody well hope it's not like Gary Cooper's 'High Noon.'"

Ingilly acknowledged his captain's quip with an appreciative laugh.

Commander Coglan turned to his executive officer, Lieutenant Commander Brent Ross, who was also chuckling. His demeanor became serious. "Number One," he said to the six-foot four-inch, 220-pound blond giant, the lone American in the crew of 191 Englishmen, "I plan on closing on the target until we make visual contact and then challenge." There was a quizzical look in his eyes, as if he were measuring a fine cognac while he poured it into a crystal snifter. It was obvious the Englishman wanted an opinion.

Commander Coglan and Lieutenant Ingilly both stared at the American. Even the port and starboard lookouts on platforms elevated slightly above the deck of the destroyer's flying bridge risked censure by stealing looks at the big lieutenant commander, Brent Ross, the "American samurai." This legend had run the gamut in the world's media: he was praised and sometimes nearly deified by friendly nations, but bitterly condemned and compared to Satan himself by the leaders and media of enemy powers.

Thirty years old, Ross still had the massive, well-conditioned build of the all-American fullback he'd been at the Naval Academy. With broad cheekbones and a jaw

9

like an anvil, the man radiated strength. His eyes were his most striking feature. They were blue as polished sapphires, and their depth seemed no less profound than the three thousand fathoms of water beneath the destroyer's keel. They were strange eyes, enigmatic eyes—the eyes of a man equally at home with Tennyson, Pope, Milton, Schiller, Goethe, and Dickens, or swinging the famous Konoye samurai sword which hung incongruously at his side. It was well known that he had beheaded four men and a woman with the vicious curved killing blade. Needless to say, no one every made light of the sword. It was also reported he was a deadly shot and that he always carried a Beretta in a shoulder holster.

The legend of Brent Ross had been born of the hazy mists of a living myth, the great carrier *Yonaga*. An apologue in steel, *Yonaga* was the ultimate World War Two holdout. For the past eight years, the young man's fate had been entwined inextricably with that of the Japanese warship. Flagship of *Kido Butai*, the Pearl Harbor attack force, *Yonaga* had been the largest carrier in the world when it was completed, in 1940. From her yardarm she flew the pennant of the fabled admiral Hiroshi Fujita, who had joined with Minoru Genda and Kameto Kuroshima in planning the Pearl Harbor attack. Fujita commanded the operation which was designated by the Naval General Staff as "Plan Z." All this was accomplished more than twenty years before Brent Ross was born.

Fearing detection by the prying eyes of foreigners, especially embassy personnel, *Yonaga* was sent to the secret cove Sano-wan on the Chukchi Peninsula, in September of 1941. Here the behemoth was to await the sortie of carriers *Hiryu, Soryu, Shokaku, Zuikaku, Kaga,* and *Akagi* from Hitokappu Bay in the Kuriles. *Yonaga* was the seventh carrier of *Kido Butai*. However, an overhanging glacier slipped, blocking the entrance of Sano-wan with a kilometer-thick layer of ice. *Yonaga* was hopelessly trapped, and here she would remain for forty-two years. In 1983 the glacier moved again and the great carrier escaped into the Bering Sea. Without hesitation, her samurai crew carried out their orders and attacked Pearl Harbor, destroying the carrier *Tarawa* and putting the battleship *New Jersey* on the bottom. Then came the return to Tokyo Bay and with it the discovery that the war had ended thirty-eight years before.

The day *Yonaga* dropped her anchor in Tokyo bay was the day Ensign Brent Ross came on board with a contingent of American officers. Not only was Brent on official duty, but he was searching for his father Ted "Trigger" Ross, who had been taken prisoner when *Yonaga* sank his ship *Sparta* in the Bering Sea. However, Trigger Ross had committed suicide the day after *Yonaga's* attack on Pearl Harbor. Like all Americans, Brent Ross had been hungry for vengeance, but then the Chinese had orbited their laser system and the entire world had changed. Orbiting weapons platforms immediately destroyed all communications satellites and not one jet, not one rocket could be ignited without instant destruction. Within seconds, the world's war-making potential was set back a generation and the hegemony of America and Russia destroyed. "You can't kill us all now," the Chinese had chortled.

OPEC raised the price of oil to nearly $200 a barrel. Awash with oil money and armed to the teeth with old fighters, bombers, big-gunned warships, and carriers, Moammar Kadafi organized Libya, Syria, Jordan, Lebanon, Iraq, Iran, and a reluctant Egypt into a *jihad* (holy war) to destroy the hated Israelis. But before the Arab armies could organize, a trivial incident that would grow monstrous in twisted Arab minds occurred over Tokyo Bay: Commander Yoshi Matsuhara damaged a Libyan Douglas DC-3 when the transport invaded *Yonaga's* air space.

Outraged, the arrogant Libyan dictator captured the Japanese cruise ship *Mayeda Maru* in the Mediterranean, forced it into Tripoli Harbor, and garoted over 2,000

11

helpless Japanese. Immediately, *Yonaga* retaliated with airstrikes on Libya and the Japanese-Israeli axis was formed against the Arabs. Surreptitiously, the Americans aided the Israelis and the Japanese while the Russians backed the Arabs. The Japanese-Israeli alliance had endured for over seven years and the tough Israelis had managed to withstand the Arabs' most determined attacks. But for how long could they continue? No one knew.

Assigned to *Yonaga* as a liaison officer, Brent Ross immediately became embroiled in the conflict. Originally from the Naval Intelligence Service (NIS) and a communications expert, he soon found himself assigned to a variety of duties. Admiral Fujita soon recognized the young man's intelligence and ability to learn quickly, never hesitating to assign him to any duty where a courageous, bold officer was required.

Over the years, Brent Ross had engaged the enemy from the decks of *Yonaga* and as a gunner on both Aichi D3A dive bombers and Nakajima B5N torpedo bombers. He had been credited with five enemy aircraft. In his personal war, he had blinded two assassins in bloody hand-to-hand fights and killed five more in gunfights in Tokyo's Ueno Park and in a spectacular gun battle in the main dining room of the Imperial Hotel. He had killed two women, both traitors. Coldly and impassively he had put a bullet through the brain of the terrorist Kathryn Suzuki as she lay helpless at his feet, begging for mercy. The reporter Arlene Spencer had lost her head to his sword in a classic samurai-style execution when she was exposed as a spy. Ironically, it had been reported in the tabloids that he had been romantically linked with both women.

One of his most spectacular achievements was accomplished as attack officer of the old World War Two fleet submarine *Blackfin*. Lying in ambush off the Arab's base in Tomonuto Atoll in the Western Caroline Islands, he had carried out a successful torpedo attack against

Kadafi's big *Majestic*-class carrier *Gefara*, sinking her with three torpedoes. *Blackfin* was later tragically lost in the same area with all hands when depth-charged by avenging enemy destroyers. Brent had never stopped mourning his lost friends.

Lieutenant Commander Brent Ross lowered his personal pair of MIV/IT Carl Zeiss 7×50 range-finding glasses, which he considered the finest in the world, and turned to the captain. The young American's mind was suddenly filled with the insane circumstances that had brought him to the bridge of this antique, resurrected British museum destroyer, which had actually been commissioned in 1939. It was all because of the inexplicable and unpredictable workings of the mind of Admiral Hiroshi Fujita. With the carriers *Yonaga* and *Bennington* badly damaged and their air groups decimated after the terrible battles off Gibralter and the coast of Morocco, Brent had been detached to Captain John "Slugger" Fite's escort command of twelve *Fletcher*-class destroyers. Seven of these sleek ships were *Yonaga's* escorts while the remaining five had steamed into Tokyo Bay with *Bennington*.

Three months of service on the destroyers on constant patrol to the east of the Japanese islands and to the south in the vast, dangerous wasteland that separated Japan from the Arab bases on Saipan and Tinian in the Marianas had quickly made a destroyer man of Brent Ross. He learned with amazing speed. Not only could he execute the duties of the executive officer, but he had actually commanded Fite's *DD-1* in simulated antiaircraft surface gunnery engagements and torpedo attack drills. In these drills, he had conducted himself with great skill and panache. Captain Fite had been impressed. "He's ready to kick ass from the bridge of any 'can,'" Admiral," Fite had reported to Admiral Fujita. "One of the best DD men we have, sir."

Then the British, who had been generous in their help in Japan's war against Colonel Moammar Kadafi's *jihad*,

13

had sent the antique destroyer *Haida* to augment the Japanese forces. On the first night of liberty in Tokyo, two of *Haida's* officers had been murdered by assassins of the *Rengo Sekigun* (Japanese Red Army). One officer, Lieutenant Commander Fraser Simmons, had been the destroyer's executive officer. Immediately, to the surprise of everyone, Fujita had assigned Brent to *Haida* as Fraser Simmons' replacement. *Haida* was desperately needed in the screen. The destroyers and a half-dozen surviving PBYs and PBMs would carry the brunt of scouting and reconnaissance until *Yonaga* and *Bennington* had been repaired and new air groups trained. Then, Brent was convinced, an attack complete with amphibious landings would be made against the festering sore of Arab bases on Saipan and Tinian. The Japanese could never forget that the B-29 *Enola Gay* had taken off from Tinian in 1945 for her atomic run on Hiroshima.

Brent had fit in easily with the British crew. True, the Englishmen did use different terminology in commands to the helm and engine room and they used "red" and "green" coding to define port and starboard in reporting sightings. But, Brent adapted quickly and could move easily from one system to the other. "I'll bet a couple of bob there's a 'limey' dangling from a branch of your family tree," an officer had chided him one afternoon in the wardroom.

"That's silly buggers," Brent had countered, adopting the accent and slang he'd heard used by enlisted men. "Only lime in me comes with my whiskey and sodas." There was a good-natured round of laughter.

Both sea and air patrols had been dangerous. Seven reconnaissance aircraft—two Consolidated PBYs, a Martin PBM, three Douglas DC-6s, and a Lockheed Super Constellation—had been destroyed by Arab fighters operating out of Saipan and Tinian in the Marianas. Although it was reported the Arab force numbered not more than three squadrons of fighters and two squadrons of bombers, its Messerschmitt 109s were brilliantly led and a deadly menace. The bombers were a mixed bag: Douglas DC-3s, DC-6s, a Lockheed Constellation or two, a few Cessnas, some North American AT-6 Texans, and perhaps a dozen Junkers Ju 87, Stukas. The Stukas were the greatest menace. Just two months earlier, one of the *Fletchers, DD-6*, had been severely damaged by air attack when she was caught without air cover 800 miles southeast of Kyushu. The high-flying level bombers had all missed, but the dive bombers nearly sank her with a hit and several near misses.

After *DD-6s* ordeal, Admiral Fujita had assigned two squadrons of fighters under *Yonaga's* Air Group Commander, Yoshi Matsuhara, to the island of Iwo Jima. From here, the Japanese fighters could penetrate all the way to the Marianas. Their TOT (Time over Target) was short, true, but they could provide some cover. All other fighters had to be kept at Tokyo International Airport and Tsuchiura to act as CAP (Combat Air Patrol) for the wounded carriers which were in the yards at Yokosuka. Arab aircraft had been reported in North Korea, and there was always the threat of a surprise attack. In fact, in 1989, just such an attempt was made by enemy bombers. Only an alert CAP had prevented disaster.

Brent eyed the tall, angular Clive Coglan. Fair haired and handsome in a haughty sort of way, the Englishman reminded him of a younger, elongated version of the great actor Sir John Gielgud. Although he was in his early forties and had been at sea for nearly twenty years, his skin was so smooth Brent could not imagine him shaving. His nose was chiseled in an aristocratic fashion, his blue eyes well spaced and thoughtful. Brent had not been surprised to discover the captain's family was of the peerage, with vast holdings in Staffordshire, including an entire village. In fact, he had learned that one day Coglan would inherit the title "Earl of East Rugeley." Although he was quite capable of using the earthy language of the mess decks, Coglan usually projected his words in a cultivated voice, as if he were center stage at the old Globe.

Commander Coglan stared back at Brent Ross, one eyebrow cocked in a curiously individual way, half challenging, half uncertain. Although he was a highly capable officer, he still did not fathom the devious workings of the Arab mind. None was more aware of this than Commander Clive Coglan himself. Now it came home to Brent Ross like a candle in a sealed cavern: although there had been better qualified destroyer officers available for the executive officer post—most prominent among them Lieutenant Sinclair Ingilly—Admiral Fujita had had excellent reasons for assigning Brent to the duty. Anyway, in Fujita's inflexible military mind, with the rank of lieutenant commander, there had been no choice but to give Brent the post of executive officer. A lower posting would have been demeaning.

Brent spoke in a deep, confident timbre, yet appropriate respect for his captain was there. "I would suggest a request for air cover."

Coglan's eyebrow arched even further. "Air cover, you say, Number One?" He waved to the southwest in a baronial gesture. "Why, it's probably only an interisland steamer. You heard the radar report. There are dozens in these waters, the lot of them poking about from island to island. She's probably making for Okinawa, the Bonins, even China." He turned his palms up and shrugged. "We'll make a verification directly as per our orders and carry on with our patrol," he added with finality.

"I know, sir. But she could be a *Gearing*, idling along, radar turned down to low power or even using an inferior set to mislead our threat library, luring us into easy range of the Ju on Tinian and Saipan, or to try us with her five-inch thirty-eights," Brent countered.

The captain's blue eyes squinted to the southwest while a finger and thumb thoughtfully pinched his chin. The *Gearing* was a powerful destroyer, and it was known the Arabs had at least six operating in the Western

16

Pacific. Although they were sometimes spotted in Saipan's Tanapag Harbor, their home base was Tomonuto Atoll in the Western Caroline Islands, where tankers and depot ships were always available and they were out of range of Japanese home-based aircraft. "Very well, Number One. If you're right, we could be in for a real dust-up, by Jove." Coglan turned to Lieutenant Ingilly. "Our position, Pilot?"

"Latitude twenty-one degrees, thirty minutes north, longitude one hundred fifty-nine degrees, twenty minutes east, Captain,"

"Sector?"

The navigator studied his red and blue plastic overlay. "We're in the southwest corner of 'Romeo-zero-nine,' sir."

"Very well." Coglan switched on a microphone mounted inside a small speaker. There was a hum and a hiss like a passing shell. He called for the Wireless Transmitter.

"W-T aye!" came back tinnily.

It was a message for Admiral Fujita. "Send the following signal in our new *Yellow Oscar* code— 'Addressee, Comyonaga. My current position southwest *Romeo zero-nine.* Radar surface contact bearing two-zero-five true, range forty-one miles. Speed of target ten to twelve knots, course two-nine-zero. Am closing on course two-two-five, speed twenty-four. Request air cover.'"

The message was repeated back by the speaker and Coglan acknowledged with his "Very well."

Brent felt a little more confidence. He had been gripped with a sense of predestiny, foreboding, and unease all morning. He knew Coglan was in an uncomfortable corner. No captain wanted to appear overly cautious; on the other hand, recklessness and the taking of undue risks could lead to tragedy. At least six fighters from Yoshi Matsuhara's squadrons based on Iwo Jima were always in the air—primarily to give cover to patrolling PBYs and PBMs. However, distances in the Western Pacific were vast, and air cover could be hours away.

He searched the sky. It was a glorious morning for the tropics; a Pacific day at its very best. He breathed deeply, tasted the salt in the air as the bow shouldered aside the seas like a knife through lace. The sky was overwhelmingly blue, the color of the clean, cool blue of the tropical water beneath it, with a thin drift of herringbone clouds stretched across its vault to provide a greater sense of depth. It was nearing eleven o'clock and the air was still pleasantly cool, an occasional gust of warmth warning of the heat that was certain to arrive by noon.

There was a chance they would all be dead by then. If the contact was a *Gearing*, they would be outgunned—outclassed in all departments except speed. Every man on the bridge was aware of the *Gearings* and feared them. American built between 1944 and 1951, the class underwent FRAM (Fleet Rehabilitation and Modernization) in the mid-Fifties. Fourteen feet was added between the funnels, giving increased bunkerage and stability. Fully loaded, they displaced over 3,000 tons, almost one-third more than that of *Haida*. But most frightening were the six 5-inch 38-caliber guns they carried in twin mount gunhouses. Equipped with electric loading machines, each gun was capable of firing 20 to 25 rounds a minute. They also bristled with 20-millimeter and 40-millimeter AA guns. The wide space between funnels gave room for two quintuple torpedo tube mounts. It was a powerful ship, deadly and capable of 33 knots.

Leaning against the windscreen, Brent ran his eyes over *Haida*. From the bow to the main director overhead, with it lenses jutting out like the clipped ears of a boxer . . . to the Japanese ensign whipping at the gaff . . . to the stern, where greasy black funnel smoke hung over the wake like a black curtain over a widening white band of silk. *Haida* was of the *Tribal* class, the first British destroyer to carry eight guns in twin mounts and

18

the last to be constructed on the transverse framing system. The class was the Royal Navy's answer to the heavily gunned German Type 1934, Japanese *Asahio*-class, and American *Gridleys.*"

Since reporting aboard, Brent had repeatedly heard the story of the most famous member of the class, *Cossack*, which in 1940 had violated Norwegian territorial waters by entering Jössing Fjord, where the German supply ship *Altmark* lay hidden. This ship carried 299 British merchant seaman captured by the raider *Graf Spee*. A boarding party from *Cossack* seized the *Altmark* and, after a brief fight, released the captives, who were transferred to the *Cossack* and brought home. Brent suspected the British enjoyed talking of past glories because their empire had shrunk and faded so steadily since 1945. It seemed the past was all that many of them had to cling to. None ever mentioned the loss of *Cossack* when she was torpedoed and sunk by U-563 west of Gibralter or the sinking of thirteen other *Tribals* during the war.

Although not as fast or boasting the range and speed of the American 5-inch, 38-caliber dual-purpose cannon, *Haida*'s eight 4.7-inch cannons of her main battery could deliver a formidable weight of shot. Brent had been impressed by the gunners' speed and accuracy. In the British tradition, the two forward mounts on the forecastle just beneath the American were designated "A" and "B" mounts, while the third, "X," was mounted on the aft deck house. The fourth, "Y," was bolted to the stern. All guns were shielded instead of protected by gunhouses. This gave the gunners much more freedom of movement, but their rear was completely exposed. Her decks bristled with AA guns: twelve 40-millimeter Bofors in twin mounts and sixteen 20-millimeter Oerlikon machine guns.

In his first briefing with Coglan and his senior officers, Brent had been proudly told of the ship's reconstruction. Completely rebuilt, she had been strengthened and modernized from the keel up, her displacement increased from 1,960 tons to 2,150. New 55,000 horsepower General Electric geared turbines had replaced her old 44,000 shaft-horsepower power plant, and new electronics equipment had been installed. Coglan had concluded with, "Despite the added tonnage, the old girl still can still make her design speed of 36 knots, by Jove."

Brent soon found the captain's remark was not an idle boast. The first time Coglan put the ship up to flank speed just outside Tokyo Bay, she fairly leaped from one shattered swell to the next, forcing Brent to cling to the teak rail of the windscreen to keep his feet while spray pelted his face like cold sand.

Brent was impressed by the British-built radar. *Haida* mounted one of the Royal Navy's best, the Plessey AWS-4 ten-centimeter search radar. Capable of both air and surface search—A and S-bands—it could perform well in conditions of jamming, sea clutter, and rainfall. An IFF signal was transmitted automatically by a D-band radiator in the main feed horn. True, the young American had seen blankets of heavy tropical rainfall clutter the scope; however, the Plessey compared well with the best American radars.

A glint high in the sky caught Brent's eye. Eagerly he focused his glasses. Was it Commander Yoshi Matsuhara's souped-up red, green, and white Zero-sen? Could the air group commander have been nearby and answered their call already? As he ran his thumb over the focusing knob, the superb German lenses brought a seabird into clear view. Planing on outspread wings, the gull swooped in wide circles, using the currents and eddies like a skillful glider, climbing, turning, diving without visible effort. For a moment, Brent envied the creature—such grace, such beauty, but most of all, such freedom. He sighed and lowered his glasses. *Yoshi, my friend, where are you?* he asked himself.

* * *

"Brent Ross, my friend, where are you?" Commander Yoshi Matsuhara muttered into his oxygen mask. He flew at 4,000 meters midway between Iwo Jima and the northernmost of the Marianas, Farallon de Pajaros, and the sea below appeared empty. Pushing the stick to the left and balancing with rudder, he dropped the left wing of the Mitsubishi A6M2 Zero to give himself a better field of vision. Then, with a little rudder, he banked slowly to the south. Nothing but the empty sea.

Centering his controls as his compass settled on a southerly heading, he stretched and twisted his back and shoulders as much as the cramped cockpit would permit. Although he was in superb physical condition, his tan face unlined, his black hair unmarred by gray strands, Commander Yoshi Matsuhara was well into his seventh decade. He was the oldest fighter pilot on earth, and his body was beginning to tell him as much, especially on long, lonely patrols.

He rubbed his neck, turned his head from side to side, pulled his jaw back into a wide grimace like a man screaming in pain, tightened his neck, hunched forward until he felt the restraint of his six-point military harness, and pushed back hard with both feet on the rudder pedals, forcing his leg muscles to bunch and then relax. Then he tightened his stomach muscles, pushed them out with all his power until he felt a tingling discomfort, and gripped the stick hard with both hands until his biceps and triceps bulged. "Isometrics," he snorted to himself. "Enough of these patrols and I'll be Mister Universe by the time I'm seventy."

He laughed out loud at his joke. Over fifty years of fighter duty had taught him to relieve himself of some of the tension of the cramped space by talking to himself. After all, there was no one else around to hear, except, of course, the one time he had forgotten his microphone was open and he had embarrassed himself over ten thousand square kilometers of the Pacific.

A young ensign when *Yonaga* was trapped in Sano-wan, Yoshi Matsuhara had endured the long ordeal with the calm determination of the samurai. There were only a handful of men from the original air crews still flying, and Yoshi was the only one who flew a fighter.

Born in Los Angeles, Yoshi had been sent to Japan when he was in his early teens. At fifteen, the minimum age, he joined Naval Air. After a brief service in China, he was assigned to *Yonaga*. The great ship had been his life, his universe from 1941. He had lived with her, and if Hachiman San (the god of war) turned his back on her, he was determined to die with the warship.

For a long while, he had been *shinigurai* (crazy to die) when he learned his wife and two children had been burned to death in Curtis LeMay's great fire raid on Tokyo on March 9, 1945. *Shinigurai* seized him again when his new love, Kimio Urshazawa, was murdered in Ueno Park by terrorists in 1989. But the gods had denied him, or, perhaps, guarded him. Admiral Fujita had said, "Amaterasu-O-Mi-Kami herself is preserving you for great things—great service for the Mikado. Do not rush through the gates of the Yasakuni Shrine before your time."

He glanced at the fifteen instruments on the panel before him. Most were American made to read the performance of the giant 3,200-horsepower Wright Cyclone R-3350 engine in the nose of the fighter. Called the Sakae 43 or *Taifu* (Typhoon) by the Japanese, most of its gauges were calibrated in clumsy English units: cylinder head temperature 240 degrees, oil temperature 203 degrees, oil pressure 74 pounds, manifold pressure 46 inches of mercury, airspeed 160 knots, fuel tanks full. In fact, he was still operating off his auxiliary tank, which was almost empty. A man could never have enough fuel. He reached to his left and his hand found the throttle quadrant and the short lever of the fuel mixture control next to the large, knobbed throttle. He pulled the small lever back, thinning the mixture until the great engine backfired its objections. It would take no more. He released the lever.

A flash overhead caught his eye. Something metallic? No. Just a sliver of the moon, which was visible in the clear air even in the bright morning sunlight. He nodded grimly. For a moment he thought he had seen a reflection from one of the low-orbiting Chinese weapons platforms. He had seen several at night, moving across the dark blue sky at constant velocities, reflecting the sun like tiny glowing fireflies. "A mistake," the Chinese had claimed. Yoshi snorted. A mistake that had set the world's war-making potential back nearly a half-century and made the Chinese limitless manpower into one of the most lethal forces on earth.

Yoshi had always been amazed and intrigued by the incredible Chinese achievement. "Inscrutable Orientals," he had ironically chuckled to himself many times. In complete secrecy, they had developed a deuterium-fluorine particle-beam system: three command stations in geosynchronous orbit at 36,000 kilometers (22,300 miles) and ten weapons stations in orbit at 15,000 kilometers (930 miles). Beijing had claimed the Chinese government sought only to control the perpetual threat Russia and America posed to every living creature whenever they rattled their atomic sabers.

Theoretically, the lasers would fire only when an atomic missile was launched. However, Chinese scientists claimed a malfunction while the rest of the world sneered and snickered. Because not one jet or rocket could be ignited without instant destruction from the laser lightning bolts, only reciprocating engines could function. The enormous American and Russian arsenals of rockets and jets became nothing but rusting liabilities. Instantly, the world's powers began a frantic search for old World War Two ships and aircraft. There was an abundance of both, and suddenly third-world nations, especially oil-rich Arab countries, became superpowers and the great new wars began. Terrorism was unleashed.

The air group commander glanced to his left and then

to his right. His wingmen were maintaining station perfectly. He laughed to himself. He was the apex of a strange triumvirate indeed—a rebuilt and strengthened Mitsubishi A6M2 Zero-sen with two Englishmen flying Vickers-Supermarine Seafire F.47s protecting its tail. But the two Englishmen were the best wingmen in the world. They had saved their leader's life many times and he had returned the favor. They had become a perfectly matched and blended trio, seemingly functioning with a single mind, anticipating each other's moves and reacting with speed, finesse, and verve. All were crack shots. Over a score of Kadafi's best had fallen to their guns in less than a year.

Captain Colin Willard-Smith was at the controls of the Seafire off Yoshi Matsuhara's port side. The son of a barrister from Barmston in Humbersideton, Willard-Smith had been raised in a prosperous environment, provided with all the advantages a scion of the upper classes could expect. In fact, he enrolled in Eton when only 17, but defied his father and left school almost immediately to join the Royal Air Force. A graduate of the RAF college at Cranwell, he was an instant, natural flyer with the outward gloss of a patrician and the killer instincts of a hawk. He spent 13 years flying every fighter in the RAF inventory and served with distinction in the Falklands, where he was credited with three kills. The Distinguished Flying Medal was bestowed upon him by the queen, herself, and he was made an MBE (Member of the British Empire).

To his starboard side Commander Yoshi Matsuhara could see the head of his other wingman, Pilot Officer Elwyn York. Although the face was almost concealed by an oxygen mask and goggles, Yoshi knew the Cockney was grinning at him. Spawned in the great loop of the Thames in East London, York was a true Cockney. York's father had been a costermonger—a fruit and fish peddler who downed a quart of gin a day. His mother sold lacework and her body in the streets. "Yer mudder rolls 'er

24

arse, rolls 'er arse a penny a pitch," the other boys would taunt. Elwyn soon learned to silence the taunts with his fists. Both parents were dead by the time Elwyn was twenty.

Stealing, pimping, and whoring from the age of twelve, Elwyn ran in the streets with a gang of toughs called the Dog Island Pissers. Nearly killed when caught in an alley by five members of a rival gang, he finally decided to move as far away from the East End as he could. He wound up in Africa, fighting as a mercenary in the endless wars that broke out after England, France, and Belgium pulled out and left the new emerging African third-world nations to fend for themselves.

Here he found his ultimate love, flying. By the seat of his pants, he learned to fly transports from the right-hand seat and then he switched to single-engine. His true passion was fighters. Soon he was flying single-engine aircraft—most of them of World War Two vintage from all powers—and fighting for Chad against Colonel Moammar Kadafi. After his best friend was shot down and tortured to death—skinned and his genitals stuffed into his mouth by the colonel's finest—his consuming hatred for the mad dictator was born. The Cockney sought his personal vengeance by joining Fujita's forces. This had been a fortunate day for the Japanese.

Elwyn York's manners were uncouth, his speech filled with gutter slang and nearly unintelligible, his appearance often careless if not slovenly. However, he was one of the most gifted fighter pilots Yoshi Matsuhara had ever known. He flew as one with his Seafire, as if the manufacturer had designed him in with the rest of the machinery. Once an enemy was in reticle of his electric gunsight, the man was a corpse awaiting his final rites. If Willard-Smith was a killer hawk, Elwyn York was a cobra.

Matsuhara looked around with the short, jerky movements of the experienced fighter pilot. Age had not diminished the power of his eyesight. He depended on detection by the fringe of his peripheral vision instead of the head-on stare that so often missed those tiny specks on the horizon that could materialize into enemy fighters. He saw nothing. However, ominously, on the far southeastern horizon, he spotted the flat smear of a thunderhead like the black head of a great bear beginning to rear up into the crystalline-clear sky. And high-flying gray-white stratus now stretched ahead of the storm in a solid sheet like carelessly washed laundry drying on lines in one of Tokyo's poorest neighborhoods. He felt an anxious pang deep down. Excellent concealment for enemy fighters.

Oberst (Colonel) Kenneth "Rosie" Rosencrance, the renegade American, could be up there with his infamous black-painted killers. Flying Messerschmitt Bf 109s with the new powerful Daimler-Benz "Valkyrie" engine, the enemy fighter was a formidable opponent for the best the Japanese could offer in their fighter inventory: the Mitsubishi A6M2, Supermarine Seafire, Grumman F6F Hellcat, and Vought F4U Corsair.

Flying an unmistakable blood-red fighter, Rosencrance commanded all air groups based in the Marianas. However, he personally led his favorite fighter squadron, *Vierter Jagerstaffel* (the Fourth Fighter Squadron), Kadafi's most proficient killers. In the early years Germans had played a key role in organizing the Arab Air Force. Although it had become highly internationalized since, German designations were still maintained.

Rosencrance had over forty Japanese flags painted on his fuselage. With a million a year American in salary and fifty thousand dollars a kill, Rosencrance was already a millionaire several times over. Yoshi Matsuhara had met him, Brent Ross had fought him with his fists. Rosencrance had given almost as well as he had taken from the American giant before being knocked unconscious. The man was a natural hunter, a killer who could never taste enough of his enemy's blood.

Brent Ross had analyzed Rosencrance succinctly and

with brilliant insight, "If that bastard were a game hunter, he'd shoot deer, quail, game birds—any animal—for the sheer pleasure of killing. He's nothing but a psychopath, the kind of madman who would kill serially, dumping raped and murdered girls along a roadside like garbage. The driving force of his life is the kill. He's lucky he had this war and he's lucky someone will pay him for doing something he enjoys anyway."

And Rosencrance had a new wingman, *Oberleutnant* (Lieutenant) Rudolf "Tiger Shark" Stoltz. Every flyer in Yoshi's air groups had been thoroughly briefed on the sadistic new killer. Stoltz was a strange one. A homosexual who flaunted his aberration, he had the demeanor of the aesthete and the cunning of a sewer rat. From a well-to-do family in Munich, he had become a revolutionary while in his first year in college. He joined the Baader-Meinhoff gang when only seventeen years old. Rumor had it he was a talented pianist, a protégé with great promise. He was also a licensed pilot at eighteen. However, in his second year of college, he killed his male lover in a fit of jealousy, cut him into small pieces, fed him into a shredding machine, and sprayed him over a square kilometer of pasture land. After the police found four teeth and a piece of lower jaw, Stoltz fled to Libya.

According to the dossier Yoshi had studied, Rudolf Stoltz trained as a terrorist at Kadafi's camps at Sirte, Sebha, and Az Zaouiah. In these camps he first met the thugs who would later become his comrades-in-arms in the war against the Israelis and Japanese. They came from all over the world. Especially numerous were Germans, Irishmen, Spanish Basques, French Bretons, Corsicans, Americans, and a few members of the Japanese Red Army. He quickly became an expert with the AK-47 (Kalashnikov assault rifle), Makarov RPG bazooka, SAM-7 (surface-to-air missile), and plastic explosives. He personally murdered a minor American embassy official in the man's own bathroom in Rome.

After he and his two companions bound the diplomat, he skinned him and then cut the man's throat very slowly, a millimeter at a time. At first cutting shallow and slow, he cut deeper and faster with each slash until he worked himself into a frothing frenzy like a rabid dog. It was said he laughed maniacally throughout the entire grisly slaughter. He even sickened his two companions. Kadafi was immensely pleased and personally marked the young man for a brilliant future.

Stoltz's first love was flying. When the Arab *jihad* against the Israeli-Japanese axis broke out, Kadafi saw to the young man's transfer to pilot training at the exclusive Raz Hilal camp near Tokra. He learned with amazing speed and quickly proved to be one of the finest pilots in Kadafi's air force. In 1988 he made his first kill of an Israeli P-51. He added two DC-3s and a Spitfire while fighting on the Israeli front. Then he was assigned to carrier *Magid*.

In the fighting off Gibralter and Morocco, it was reported he had four more kills to his credit. Also, he had been seen machine-gunning two Japanese pilots in their parachutes. He was a small man with big blue eyes, blond hair, and milky-white skin, actually delicate in appearance. But he killed with the instincts of a shark in a blood frenzy. Appropriately, the huge sharp teeth of a shark were painted just in front of the oil cooler intake of his Me 109. But this was not enough for the perverted killer. He added spots to his black paint job, his entire aircraft splotched with big yellow marks. His "tiger shark" fighter was as unmistakable as Rosencrance's blood-red machine. In a sense, Stoltz was saying to the Japanese, "I'm here. Come and kill me, if you can."

"I will! I will kill you, you son of hell!" Yoshi screamed into the thunder of the engine and the undulating roar of the slipstream.

A flickering yellow light on the black baked enamel face of Matsuhara's radio panel jarred his mind back from his accursed enemy. Someone was transmitting in bursts.

Leaning forward, he turned his selector switch through all six radio channels and found nothing. Cursing, he returned the switch through its semicircle, this time slowly, through stop after stop. Then he found it. Ship-to-ship or ship-to-shore. Another oath. Computer generated. He guessed *Yellow-Oscar*. Scrambled. Time and frequency hopping. That was why he had missed on his first search. There was no chance he could decode it. A destroyer must be signaling *Yonaga*. Maybe *Haida* was in trouble. Her patrol was far to the east and slightly south. He could only wait and call on his patience when none of it was present.

Then he heard his call, "Edo Leader, Edo Leader, this is *Hitsuji-kai*" (Shepherd). It was the air control officer on Iwo Jima. Snatching *Yonaga's* signals from the air with its enormous antennas, the powerful station relayed orders from Admiral Fujita to aircraft, and sometimes, if atmospheric conditions were poor, to ships. At times, the installation received, amplified, and relayed the messages directly. But not today. The air control officer was staring at his radar screens where Yoshi knew he could track the air patrols and at least one of the nearby destroyers.

The control officer's voice rasped, "Oshâberi," (Chatterbox). The word brought the Japanese pilot erect, attention newly focused. "*Oshâberi*" was *Haida's* coded call sign. He hunched forward while the voice completed the message. "Patrolling southwest Sector 'Romeo-zero-nine' has found a playmate in sector 'Charlie zero-eight.' Playmate's course two-nine-zero, speed ten to twelve. *Oshâberi* requests little friends. Your vector one-zero-five."

The pilot reached for his pencil, which was attached to the clipboard strapped to his knee. On the clipboard was a plotting sheet with destroyer and air patrols marked in bold red lines on a plastic grid overlay. Sectors were marked in blue. *Haida* was to the east, the contact slightly east of south. He drew his line of interception to the given coordinates of the target. Then, studying the approximate point of interception of the two vessels, he winced with frustration. If the enemy were a destroyer, the two warships could engage at up to 15 kilometers, but probably much closer. He guessed it would take *Haida* about an hour, maybe a little more, to make her run—if she was still in the patrol area marked on his chart. The closest Japanese destroyer was far to the northeast, at least six hours of hard steaming. He slapped the chart with an open palm. Poor support. There was just too much ocean to cover.

A quick check of his plotting sheet brought more frustration and another oath to his lips. At 320 knots it would take more than an hour for *Edo Flight* to reach the area of interception. And that high speed would consume fuel like a parched camel gulping water in the Gobi. But maybe his concerns were for naught. Chances were the contact was just another small steamer plying its trade between islands. Certainly its slow speed would indicate as much. But the Arabs were wily, unpredictable. Brave as lions when they were winning, they could be as cowardly as whipped curs when facing defeat—sometimes clever, sometimes stupid, but always inconsistent and even capricious. Could be a *Gearing* dangling bait.

He set his jaw. Iwo Jima had broken radio silence. In accordance with SOP (standard operating procedures), no latitudes and longitudes had been given, only a reference to sectors on a secret grid chart. However, if the Arabs had copied, they were aware something was up and could probably guess with fair accuracy where. He turned his channel selector to the fighter frequency and switched on the microphone in his oxygen mask. "*Edo Flight,* this is *Edo Leader.* You copied *Hitsuji-kai's* transmission?"

"This is Edo Two," came back in Captain Colin Willard-Smith's refined voice. "Affirmative, Edo Leader. Over."

And then Pilot Officer Elwyn York's voice rasped

through with the Cockney's usual appalling lack of radio discipline. His East London vernacular was almost a foreign language to most people, but Yoshi was accustomed to it and understood immediately, "Right-oh, guv'nur. This is Edo Three. I swot up the bumf. Over."

Matsuhara chuckled into the dead microphone. Then he opened the circuit, "Edo Flight, this is Edo Leader. Remember our vector is one-zero-five. Keep your eyes open. Our buddy 'Rosie' Rosencrance and friends could be up there above that dirty laundry at seven thousand meters. You know we must fly under it if we are to find the surface action. Do not rest your necks or we may march through the gates of the Yasakuni Shrine together. Follow my lead."

"Roger" and "Right-oh" came back. Automatically, the flight leader kicked left rudder, pulled the stick back, reached to his left for the fuel mixture and throttle levers, which were mounted side-by-side on the same aluminum quadrant, and pushed both forward. He released the mixture control after a short travel, but jammed the throttle ahead three full notches. With newly enriched fuel jetting into its eighteen cylinder heads, the great Wright Cyclone engine roared out its newfound power. The Japanese pilot felt himself pushed back and down into his backrest and seat-pack.

As he stared at the southeastern horizon, there was a hard set to his jaw and his lips skinned back into a leer. The clenched straight white teeth were those of the predator sensing the kill.

Colonel Kenneth Rosencrance liked the improved vision the "Galland" canopy of his Messerschmitt Bf 109 gave him. Staring through his right panel, he could see the head of a storm spilling over the eastern horizon like black ink spreading across a blue blotter. His altimeter read 7,800 meters. He nodded his big head. He was well above a layer of cirrus which stretched ahead of the storm. True, his visibility below was somewhat obscured, but he could see the ocean clearly in the frequent breaks in the clouds that lay in rolls like a baker's confection.

Rosencrance generally approved of his new modified Messerschmitt. Originally a late model "G," it had been completely remodeled and strengthened. In its nose it mounted the new Daimler Benz DB 605, inverted V-12 "Valkyrie" engine. Boosted by the new GM-1 supercharger, it could produce 3,150 horsepower. But more important, German engineers had managed to iron out most of the fighter's flight handling and maneuverability problems. Although its wing loading was high and it was still a little heavy in its controls at high speed, most of the resistance had been removed by redesign of its control surfaces, the installation of a large spinner in the fuselage, a retractable rear wheel and modification of the wings with high lift devices. Even a different type aileron had been engineered. One of the most welcome additions was a rudder trimmer which eased the burdens on a man's arms on extremely long flights. And when you were operating in the Western Pacific, all patrols were very long. In fact, the addition of new fuselage tanks and the use of the 300-liter Rustsatz 3 drop-tank had increased the Me's range to over 2,000 kilometers. The high-lift devices and redesign of the wing had reduced wing loading to a small degree and given the Me a shorter turning radius, yet he had serious doubts about the fighter's ability to turn with the Zero.

In addition, the nose-heavy Messerschmitt still had a tendency to stall at high speeds and he had lost two pilots when their slats flicked open and shut in dogfights, causing snatching at their wing tips and loss of pilot control. "*Yonaga's* Butcher," Yoshi Matsuhara and his killers, had pounced on both helpless pilots and blown them from the sky. He had stormed at his riggers and had one crew chief shot. Finally, after much redesign and testing, he had been assured the slats would remain closed.

One of the most welcome new devices had been invented by Rosencrance himself. Inevitably freezing at altitudes over 5,000 meters, the fighter's relief tube could relieve nothing at all. And a pilot could suffer hours of the agonies of hell with an overloaded bladder. Often, especially after power dives and hard pullouts, a man wet his pants. Then the cockpit not only stank of the usual fighter smells of petrol fumes and hydraulic fluid, but the stench of stale urine as well. Worst of all, it was embarrassing and humiliating to see ground crew members smirking and pointing. Now, thanks to Rosencrance's ingenuity, a small heater coil circled the tube, keeping it wide open at the highest altitudes. Now a pilot could piss his heart out anywhere. It was almost as good as a piece of ass.

Along with the tube, the new "Valkyrie" engine had been a godsend. Its great power had made the modifications possible. The Messerschmitt could make over 440 knots in level flight and it was a much better gun platform than the lighter Zero. Its two wing mounted 20-millimeter Mauser cannons, and two cowling-mounted 13-millimeter Rheinmetall Borsig machine guns gave the 109 a devastating punch. Forty-eight times he had caught enemy aircraft in his gunsight, and forty-eight times he had made his kill. The 109 could outdive the Zero, and with the exception of Matsuhara's "freak," outrun it.

The thought of Matsuhara and his strange hybrid "Zero" brought a hot churning in his guts like a whirling *khamsin* born in the inferno of the Sahara. It was said that the Japanese killer had over forty Arab kills of his own. In a space of less than six months, Matsuhara had killed both his wingmen, *Oberleutnant* Ludwig von Weidling and his closest friend *Hauptmann* (Captain) Wolfgang "Zebra" Vatz. And those two renegade English wingmen of his were virtuoso killers. He wanted to kill them all. Not just for the $1 million on Matsuhara's head and the half million on the scalps of those English dogs Willard-Smith and York, but it was something personal—something he owed them. The American punched his instrument panel so hard needles leaped and quivered.

Since the death of Vatz, Rosencrance had adopted the formation called "Finger Four" by the British and *"Schwarm"* by the Luftwaffe. It was an old idea first used by the Condor Legion in Spain and later copied by the British. The Americans used it in their so-called "Top Gun" alignment. It was a simple concept. Flying in formations of four well-spaced planes, in combat the fighters paired off into twosomes consisting of a leader-attacker and his wingman-defender. Since enemy fighter pilots preferred to attack out of the glare of the sun, the wingman flew upsun to be in a better position to intercept any foe heading for his leader. And since the view looking up from his cockpit was much more extensive than the view looking down, the defender flew below and behind the leader to better keep track of him. This released the leader to concentrate on the kill. It was a good system and he had a fine young wingman, Rudolf Stoltz. Maybe he would have a little surprise for Matsuhara and his friends the next time around.

The thought of Matsuhara's souped-up Zero brought a pang of apprehension. It was far more powerful and dangerous than all other enemy Zeros. The engine it packed, the Wright Cyclone R-3350, had been designed originally for the old Boeing B-29 Super Fortress. According to latest intelligence, Boeing and Nakajima engineers had almost whipped the engine's tendency to overheat. But how in the world did they ever mount the twin-banked, 18-cylinder monster in the nose of an aircraft designed for an engine one-third the size? Why, the torque alone should twist the airframe like a corkscrew. According to intelligence, the fighter had been stripped to the bones and new titanium-aluminum alloy members added to, or completely replaced, the main

34

wing spars, ribs, longerons, and formers. Control cables were removed and heavy-duty lines substituted. Control surfaces were strengthened and even the aileron, flaps, elevator, and rudder hinges replaced. A huge new self-sealing fuel tank was supposedly installed back of the cockpit to help counterbalance the enormous engine. It worked. The damned thing flew like a demon out of the gates of hell.

Rosencrance shook his head, muttering, "Fuckin' yellow-assed Jap slant." The whole concept seemed insane. How in hell did the damned thing fly? It violated virtually every law of aerodynamics. He had seen it in two different dogfights. It could climb like a rocket and in level flight could pull away from anything. It reminded him of an old jet of over a decade ago. But word had it the engine still overheated. In fact, he had once seen the Japanese break off a fight, throttle back, and limp for home when he knew the Zero had not been hit. It had been engine trouble, he was sure. And those two "Limeys" protected him like a pair of mother hens.

Grudgingly, he had to admit the Englishmen were two of the most skillful pilots he had ever fought. He could not respect them any more than he could respect a pile of camel dung. But they were good and they flew a fine fighter. Rosencrance knew. He had flown a Seafire F.47 back in Libya. With a new Rolls Royce Griffon 88 engine powered up to over 3,000 horsepower, the Seafire was as fast as the Me 109 but not as maneuverable. The stupid carburetor had been removed and replaced with fuel injection, giving steady engine performance in violent maneuvers. However, forced to clip its big elliptical wings to fit it into a carrier's elevators, they had increased the wing loading. In its favor was the six-bladed, contrarotating propellers which canceled out torque, providing a very stable platform for the fighter's four Hispano-Suiza 20-millimeter cannons. In the hands of Willard-Smith and York, the Seafire was one of the most efficient killing machines in the Western Pacific.

Between them, they had killed at least twenty of his best pilots. "Motherfuckin' Limeys. I'll kill 'em both," he shouted into his mask. He punished his instrument panel again.

A sudden tingle brought the American's hand to his mask. He gathered the rubber and plastic between his thumb and forefinger and pinched his chin. Although he had shaved very close, his whiskers were already beginning to itch against his mask. He always suffered this torture on long patrols. Sweat would make it worse. And his nose tingled like the beginnings of a head cold and his throat was raw, as if he were the victim of a violent cough. Raw oxygen always did that to him. He glanced first at his oxygen pressure gauge and then at the flow indicator. A little high. Could be cut down. He turned the flow valve slightly counterclockwise until the flow indicator dropped a notch. There was no relief whatsoever.

Cursing the oxygen and his stiff neck, he twisted in his seat until he could see his wingman Rudolph "the Shark" Stoltz, slightly below and 50 meters off his starboard elevator. Stoltz was the ideal wingman, a talented pilot and merciless killer. Stoltz liked young boys. Kept two—he called them his houseboys—in his quarters. Rosencrance snickered, wondering about the confusion when they all bedded down together. Or were they organized? He laughed out loud. He preferred women. True, Arab women were unclean. Some did not bathe in a lifetime, and it was actually dangerous to stand downwind from most of them. Chamorro women were not much better. They could be unbelievable in bed if a man could hold his nose while hanging onto a wildly bucking mare. Luckily, he had managed to teach his young housekeeper, Tuolila, the fundamentals of hygiene. Gifted with unbounded passion, the young girl knew some incredibly delightful ways to please a man. And she smelled great. Rosencrance began to squirm with his arousal. His radio interrupted his disturbing thoughts.

"Raka Leader, this is *Salat."*

Rosencrance sat bolt upright. *Salat* was the air control officer on Saipan. The man had broken radio silence. Something serious was afoot. He keyed his microphone, "*Salat,* this is *Raka Leader.* I read you loud and clear."

"*Raka Leader, Hijja* reports a party brewing in sector Juliet Two. You have been invited. Join as soon as possible. Your vector three-five-five."

Rosencrance acknowledged and stared at his plotting sheet eagerly. *Hijja* was the code name for the destroyer *Abu Bakr,* which was trolling for bait at about latitude twenty, longitude one-five-nine. At least the *Gearing* should be in that area and easily- spotted from high altitude. Apparently she had a customer that was moving at high speed. Must be a destroyer. According to plan, bombers should be en route from Saipan and Tinian and the fun and games would begin. And there was a chance—a long chance, true—that he would meet his old friend Yoshi Matsuhara, "*Yonaga's* Butcher."

He glanced at his instruments. Fuel was not low, but he had over an hour's run to the point of interception. A meeting with enemy fighters would devour fuel and then there was the long flight home. He must be cautious or the sea could accomplish what "*Yonaga's* Butcher" had never been able to do. He barked a few orders to his flight into his microphone, increased throttle and banked hard to the northwest and watched his compass swing toward three-five-five.

A quick look to port assured Rosencrance the two black Me 109s of the other half of the *Schwarm* were holding station. Both were piloted by Arabs and both were refined killers—despite their genetics. Between them they had six kills. Very unusual, indeed. Most Arabs had the intelligence of a retarded mule and the disposition of a pregnant camel. Finding most of them contemptible, he assigned the bulk of his Arab pilots to bombers where he hoped their bumbling would not kill too many of their own comrades. In fact, there were only three Arab pilots among the twelve members of his squadron. Counting himself, there were two Americans, the same number of Russians, an Englishman, a Spaniard, a Japanese, an Italian, and an Iranian who harangued everyone, including the Arabs, with the stale fact he was a Persian and not an Arab. In all, he was pleased with his squadron, truly an international band of fighters who were determined to kill as many Jews and Japanese as possible and at the same time make themselves wealthy men.

The Arab leader of the other element of Rosencrance's flight was Oberleutnant Hani Meri from Damascus. He was intelligent for an Arab and an excellent leader. Very unique. Meri's wingman was Leutnant (Second Lieutenant) Hamoud Rogba from Beirut. There were whispers Rogba's grandmother had been a Jewess. Rosencrance disbelieved the rumors, but Hamoud Rogba was very shrewd; very clever, like a kike. All Jews were smart black-hearted crooks. Shylocks, the lot. Everyone knew that. But Rogba looked just like an Arab—big nose, brown eyes, dark hair, and very hairy. But didn't all Jews and Arabs look alike? After all, they were all Semites— in a sense, all related, anyway. Why, some of Adolph Hitler's closest aides had been rumored as having a hebe somewhere in their antecedents.

Most prominent was Reinhard Heydrich. Wolfgang Vatz had mentioned Reinhard Heydrich many times. Heydrich had been a personal friend of Wolfgang's father and as a youth Vatz had known him well. One of Hitler's most trusted aides, he had been security chief of the SS. Vatz had sworn, "Heydrich's grandmother was a *Jüdin*— a matzo-eating, stinking *Jüdin*." But Heydrich was a great Jew Killer. In fact, he organized *Endlösung* (the Final Solution) under direct orders from Hermann Göring. And weren't they all superb hebe-killers, regardless of ancestry? Let the stories fly. Rosencrance was pleased to have Rogba in his flight, even if it were true he lacked a foreskin. After all, a lot of Gentiles had their dicks

38

chopped, too. He chuckled to himself, "Crazy fuckin' world."

Easing onto his new heading, he thought again of Yoshi Matsuhara. Quickly the smile melted into a grim leer, exposing rows of yellow teeth. For a fleeting instant, with his helmet pulled down and his goggles over his eyes, Kenneth Rosencrance looked very much like Yoshi Matsuhara.

Chapter Two

"Target fine on the port bow, Captain," the port lookout shouted, staring into his glasses. "Hull down. Masthead only, sir."

"Very well," Commander Clive Coglan responded.

Commander Coglan, Lieutenant Sinclair Ingilly, Lieutenant Commander Brent Ross, and both lookouts focused their glasses on the sighting. Radar's last report had put the target at a range of fourteen thousand yards. She must have a high mast indeed to be sighted at this range.

"Radar," Coglan shouted into a tube. "I want a reading on the target."

"Bearing red zero-eight relative, two-five-five true, range thirteen-thousand-five-hundred, speed twelve, course two-nine-zero" reverberated back from the copper pipe.

Brent leaned against the teak rail of the steel windscreen, turned his focusing knob gently. The sighting was hull down with only some of her upper works visible over the horizon. He came erect, guts churning; squinted. A director. No doubt about it. "Captain, a fighting top, sir," he managed in a carefully modulated voice.

"Why, those bloody bastards," Coglan spat.

"Captain," a voice, reedy and tense, came up the pipe.

40

"Radar reports target has switched on a powerful new radar. It's the Russian 'Strut Curve' search radar. She has us—is ranging and increasing speed. Our threat library identifies the enemy vessel as the *Abu Bakr* of the *Gearing* class. Her captain is a Frenchman, Commander Henri DuCarme, ex-French Navy, commanded frigates and destroyers, forty-five years old, married . . ."

"Great Scot, man, I don't need a sodding biography. Track the target and give me any changes in course and speed." He turned to Brent and Ingilly. "The knickers are in the twist, gentlemen. Tally-ho." Returning to the tubes, "Action stations. Prepare for gun and torpedo action!"

Sinclair Ingilly's face grew pale, as if it were an image doing a slow fade on a movie screen, and Brent heard him gasp like a man struck in the solar plexus. The navigator dropped his pencil on the chart table and it rolled to the deck unnoticed.

Immediately the clamor of sirens could be heard echoing throughout the ship. Then excited shouts and the pounding of boots on steel decks and ladders, the clang of watertight doors being slammed, the hard sound of steel on steel as breeches received 4.7-inch shells, the fading whir of fans as the ship's ventilation system was shut down. The three officers shrugged into lifejackets, discarded their caps, and pulled helmets from racks attached to the windscreen.

There were two new lookouts. A round young Welshman, Able Seaman Harold Ballew, took the port platform, while a bamboo-thin young stoker named Adam Stanger focused his glasses to starboard. A youthful rating, Leading Seaman Randall Turner, put on the huge potlike helmet of the talker and plugged in his headset, taking his position next to the voice tubes and the captain. Just a boy, Brent thought, securing the chin strap of his own British-style tin hat. If Turner were an American, he would be primping for his senior prom, not standing on the exposed flying bridge of a destroyer.

41

Reports flooded up through tubes and Turner's earphones. "W-T manned and ready, 'A' gun manned and ready, 'Y' gun manned and ready, torpedo director manned and ready, engine room manned and ready, 'A' magazine manned and ready, damage control manned and ready . . ." On and on they went, Coglan acknowledging with his "Very well."

The chant ended, but something was missing. "The gunnery officer?" Brent said.

"Gunnery?" Coglan shouted at Randall Turner. "Blast it, Lafferty's late. He's holding up the whole blasted war."

Leading Seaman Turner spoke into his mouthpiece. Both Brent Ross and Clive Coglan glanced overhead at the old Scott-Vickers director, which was already turning toward the enemy ship. Lieutenant John Lafferty and two rating manned the old split-image optical range finder but had not reported in.

"Director manned and ready," Turner finally reported. Coglan only grunted. He shouted down a voice tube, "Radar! Range?"

"Ten-thousand-five-hundred, sir."

"Very well. All guns stand by." And then, to Turner, a message for Gunnery Officer Lieutenant Lafferty: "'Guns,' commence tracking target fine on the port bow. Open fire at ten thousand yards, it will be port side to." The talker relayed the command.

"Bridge, radar reports enemy vessel has increased speed to thirty knots."

"Very well. All ahead together. Speed full." There was the ringing of telegraphs, the great General Electric turbines whined higher, and the slim warship dug her stern in.

"Starboard ten!"

"Ten of starboard wheel on, sir."

"Steady on two-nine-zero, QM." He turned to the pastry-faced Ingilly. "I want to parallel her course and then close."

"Aye, aye, sir." The pilot hunched over his table.

Slashing through the seas at over thirty knots, the destroyer heeled far to port as she made her turn. Finally, she straightened on her new heading and the voice came up the tube, "Steady on two-nine-zero, sir, speed thirty-two."

"'Strut Curve,' 'Strut Curve'!" Coglan pounded his helmet and stared at Brent. "Any fire control capability, Number One?"

"No, sir," Brent said to his captain. "The Geneva agreements won't allow it. It operates in the E-F bands only. Both sea and air search. Range, maybe sixty miles in air search, one-hundred-fifty max on the surface. Not one of the Russian's best radars."

"Capital! Capital!"

Brent glassed the enemy. Now, most of the *Abu Bakr* was visible over the curvature of the earth. She should have opened fire by now. Either her captain, Commander DuCarme, was totally incompetent or he was supremely confident. In either case, the Frenchman had made a serious tactical error. He had thrown away the *Gearing's* superiority in bigger calibers and range. This was going to be a slugging match. Or was that what DuCarme wanted?

Brent was seized with a familiar assortment of emotions that preceded every battle and fed on all men on the brink of the hell of combat. Excitement charged his veins with racing blood like the rapids in a raging river. There was an augural chill there, too—cold spasms of fear racing through his bones, gripping his heart with frigid tendrils. But he could control it; always had. And the feeling of helplessness, knowing his fate, his life, now hung on the decisions of a captain who had never fought a surface action before, the capricious whims of men on Saipan and Iwo Jima and back on *Yonaga*. Even Washington, Moscow, or Tripoli could decide his chances for death or life. He was a pawn in a mortal chess game, nothing more.

The other men would never know of the turmoil

within; the forebodings, doubts, fears. Brent Ross was the "American samurai." Brave. Stoic. Implacable. He fisted his hands, squared his shoulders, and clenched his teeth, trying to make a rock of himself.

But the navigator's rock was crumbling like weathered shale. "We've got the speed to outrun her, sir," Ingilly blurted out suddenly.

Coglan shook his head. "Just give me our position, Pilot," was his only response.

Ingilly consulted his chart and said with resignation, "Latitude twenty degrees, fifty-minutes, longitude one-five-eight-degrees, forty minutes."

The captain shouted down a tube, "W-T. Addressee *Comyonaga*. Closing on DD *Abu Bakr*, sector 'Charlie Zero-Eight.' Latitude twenty degrees, fifty minutes, longitude one-five-eight degrees, forty minutes. Request support. Will engage."

"But sir," Ingilly shouted, incredulous, face beading with perspiration, "we're outclassed, Captain. She hasn't opened up. We can still break it off—get some support." He stabbed a finger to the east where a storm was building on the horizon, leaden rain slanting into the sea in impenetrable curtains. "We could run for that storm." He indicated Brent while the captain, the lookouts, and the talker stared. "You heard Number One, they don't have fire control radar."

Brent eyed the navigator curiously. Combat always brought out the best and worst in men. He had seen the phenomenon many times. Now, it had started on the bridge of *Haida*.

Coglan fixed Ingilly with eyes as cold as a glacier. "Yes, engage—got to bring him to book. That's what *Haida* was built for, exists for, and may die for." He stabbed a finger at the chart table. "Return to your duties, Pilot."

Jaw twitching, eyes wide with apprehension, the navigator returned to his charts. A lone bead of moisture tracked its way down his cheek.

The bridge crew heard Lieutenant John Lafferty's

voice for the first time. Channeled down from the director by a voice tube that backed up the gunnery circuits, he fed information to all four gun stations. "Range ten-thousand-two-hundred, elevation two-three-five-zero-minutes, deflection thirty-two right."

Then the chant of the gun layers, "Layer on! Layer on!"

The enemy ship was well within range, yet Coglan did not give the order. And the enemy, too, remained silent, steaming parallel, broad on the port beam. It was almost as if the two biggest boys on the block had met to fight it out in an alley and both were loath to take the first swing. Then *Abu Bakr* threw a punch. There was a flash on her bow.

Brent pulled his glasses so tight, the padded eyepiece dug into his flesh and his eyes watered. He could actually see a single glowing red wine bottle rising slowly and arcing toward him. A single round. A ranging shot. The Arabs' favorite method. Either short or long, observe, correct, fire another, hope for a straddle, and then rapid fire with the vicious five-inch thirty-eights. The blue bottle headed directly for Brent Ross, hissed over the superstructure like a great insect, and exploded, the flash of burning lyddite masked immediately by water. They had been fortunate. The fall of the ranging shot had been hidden from the Arab's gunners by *Haida's* hull.

"'Guns'! Range?"

"Ten-thousand-one-hundred!"

"Layer on! Layer on!"

Brent saw another flash from the stern of the enemy. "Another ranging shot, sir," he said.

Coglan could wait no longer and every man on the ship knew it. "Shoot!" he shouted into the gunnery officer's tube.

"Commence! Commence! Commence!" Lafferty shouted. There was a tinny ringing sound like a priest chiming his tiny bell at mass. All eight guns fired simultaneously, lashing out seven-foot yellow tongues of flame. Every frame, every plate recoiled with the shock. The mast vibrated like a tuning fork and the stays twanged and thrummed. The locker beneath the chart table popped open and charts, pencils, and plotting instruments spilled out onto the deck. A loose rivet popped out of the windscreen and struck the binnacle housing the magnetic compass with the clang of a bullet.

Brent staggered and groaned when the thunderclap struck his eardrums. Brown smoke billowed and he was assaulted by the burned solvent stench of cordite that filled his nostrils, coated his throat. Numbly, Ingilly began to scoop up his spilled charts and instruments.

The young American leaned into his glasses, watching for splashes. *Haida* would range by laddering; all guns ladder short, all guns ladder over, down ladder, range found, rapid fire. Brent felt the ladder system was superior to registering by single round ranging. Laddering seemed to find the range faster and it brought a greater weight of shot to bear sooner.

"Enemy round short and astern," the port lookout, Harold Ballew, shouted in a voice so high it sounded falsetto.

"Very well."

A wall of waterspouts rose majestically at least two hundred yards short of *Abu Bakr* and ahead of her, Lafferty shouted, "Up ten, deflection twenty-eight right!"

"Shoot!"

Again the staggering boom and flash and eight more shells hurtled toward the enemy. Ballew's voice bordered on hysteria; "She's opened up—rapid fire!"

Watching *Abu Bakr* suddenly aflame with leaping muzzle flashes, Brent felt a frozen reptile begin to uncoil in his guts. The guns were firing so fast the ship appeared to be burning. It was like peering into a Dantean horrorscape. Her main battery had gone to rapid fire, but without adequate ranging. Orange, green, and yellow towers erupted from the sea, marking the fall of shot from each pair of guns. Short, long, ahead, and astern of *Haida* they rained. Central and local control simultaneously? Brent could not believe his eyes. DuCarme was using shotgun tactics. He would overwhelm his enemy with the sheer volume of fire. His gunners must be mostly Arab and incompetent.

"Long! Long!" Ballew and Stanger both shouted, glassing *Haida*'s shell bursts.

"We've got her bracketed, Captain," Brent said.

Lafferty's voice rang in the tube, "Down zero-five, deflection unchanged!"

Coglan's next command was unnecessary. Lafferty was already bellowing "Rapid fire!" when the captain yelled the same command.

Now *Haida*'s guns fired as rapidly as her gunners could load and fire. Men shouted, brass cartridges clanged to the deck and rolled across the deck plates with the motion of the ship. A cloud of brown smoke began to blend with the black funnel smoke.

"Radar, range?" Coglan shouted down a tube.

"Nine-thousand-five-hundred!"

"Left to two-seven-five." The captain turned to Ingilly, who stood mutely next to the chart table. "Plot it, Pilot, and keep it tight and tidy. We've got to close the range."

"How close?"

"Until we can get grappling hooks over and board her."

Brent was amazed. Coglan could actually find humor with five-inch shells raining all around his ship. The next command startled him even more: "Torpedo Gunner. All tubes train out to port. Stand by to engage! Depth nine-feet, speed maximum!"

"No!" Ingilly shouted. "That's mad!"

Everyone was shocked by the navigator's words to his captain. Coglan shot back, "Mind your tongue and your charts, Pilot!"

Suddenly, Lieutenant Ingilly slouched over his table.

Randall Turner said to Coglan, "Sublieutenant Braithwaite reports he has the enemy on his torpedo director. All tubes ready. Depth setting nine feet, speed fifty. Requests shorter range."

"Very well! All ahead flank!"

Far down in the bowels of the ship, the chief engineer pushed two throttles to their last stops and the powerful turbines whined and roared, their full power unleashed. The two great four-bladed bronze screws lashed the water astern into a boiling white frenzy. They would pull ahead and try to close across the enemy's bow and put four torpedoes into her on the way—if they were not blown out of the water first.

"We've 'it the bloody buggers!" came from a masthead lookout. "We've got 'em taped!" Then, Ballew and Stanger chorused, "He's hit!"

Ballew waved his fist, screamed into the din, "Give the bloody sod what-for!"

Brent saw two shells explode on the enemy's bow, destroying at least four antiaircraft guns. But both forward gunmounts continued to fire. Then two more hits shot off the *Gearing*'s aft funnel and immediately smoke enveloped her from amidships aft.

"Her torpedo officer is blind, sir," Brent said.

"Bully! Maybe the bugger's dead. She's got ten tubes, Number One."

A voice came up a voice tube, "Thirty-six knots, sir."

"Very well. Range?"

"Seven-thousand-eight-hundred, sir."

There was a ripping overhead as if a giant were tearing a piece of canvas directly over the ship. Brent knew that not even Arabs could continue to miss at this range. He hunched his shoulders and tightened his muscles as if he could contract his massive bulk into a smaller space.

A shell exploded close aboard to starboard. Then four more ripped the sea to port, spraying the bridge with blue water and spray. Every man ducked as shrapnel whined and ricocheted off the steel screen. More hisses, warbles, whines, and the first shell slammed aboard with a shock that jarred the entire ship. The aft deckhouse and the

40-millimeter gun crew atop her vanished in a tower of ripped metal, smashed searchlights, flying guns, men, parts of men. The forty-millimeter ready box was hurled through the air like a big gray casket and the ship's boat vanished in a whirlwind of splinters.

Two more rounds struck "X" mount simultaneously, knocking it over on its side at a crazy angle and dismembering every member of its crew. Mangled bundles of bloody rags and broken bones littered the quarterdeck and blood like red syrup spilled across the deck to the scuppers, staining the sides of the ship. Then, all of the upper works from the deckhouse aft almost to "Y" mount burst into flame.

"Flood Number Five magazine!" Coglan screamed at the talker. "Damage Control aft, and I want a report immediately!"

But *Haida* was punishing *Abu Bakr*. A half-dozen shells plunged into her, disabling Number Three gunhouse. Her own ammunition began to explode and flames and black smoke streamed astern of her. But her hull was undamaged and the four guns of the two forward mounts still fired close to a hundred rounds a minute.

Quickly, Damage Control brought *Haida's* fires under control, but high explosives were tearing geysers from the sea all around her. Shrapnel whined, ripped long slashes in the sea, clanged from steel plating. Then, in quick succession, "A" mount took two direct hits that blew the gun shield apart like Christmas wrappings torn by an eager child. The entire crew was killed and the six manning the two twenty-millimeter guns on the bow were shredded by shrapnel.

Then Brent saw an amazing, terrifying sight. A five-inch shell, fired flat, hit the water, skipped and bounced like an amateur pilot attempting his first landing, spun and tumbled end over end, directly at him. Just a few yards from the ship it hit the top of a swell, bounced high into the air, and sailed over his head, hissing like a sack full of diamondbacks. It was clearly visible when it hit the left side of the director, a glowing gray cylinder with two

49

red bands. Dropping to the deck, Brent clapped his hands over his ears.

The explosion was cataclysmic. Locks broken, the director spun on its ball bearings like a child's top. With both legs blown off, the masthead lookout's body plunged onto the forward funnel cover and rolled off, spraying blood on the gray paint. A gay glittering hail of shattered recognition lights rained on the bridge.

Coming to his feet, Brent looked overhead. He viewed a scene of carnage. The director continued to revolve, Lafferty's head and one shoulder protruding through the door which had been blown open. His other shoulder and arm had been ripped off, blood spraying in a wide circle like a crimson haze and raining on the bridge. All the signal halyards had been cut and they flapped and whipped in the wind. Numbly, Brent wiped Lafferty's blood from his face.

Then Brent noticed the port lookout, Able Seaman Harold Ballew. A piece of shrapnel, which must have been the size of a coffeepot, had hit him in the back, smashing his spine and exiting from his abdomen, ripping a huge hole, splattering intestines, stomach, and gore onto the deck. The boy had been knocked from his platform to the deck, where he lay on his back in his own detritus, moaning and twitching, the last vestiges of life draining away. The capricious gods of war had spared every other member of the bridge crew. Not one other man had so much as been scratched.

Eyes like silver dollars, Ingilly stood ramrod straight, staring at the dying lookout. Stoker Adam Stanger began to cry, "Harold! Harold . . ."

"Silence, man!" Coglan shouted. He leaned over the bank of voice tubes and called for the sick bay attendant. "All guns, local control. SBA to the . . ."

Just then, an air burst detonated above the bridge, a few yards off the port side. Either the shell had a defective fuse or the Arabs had begun to run low on AP (Armored Piercing) ammunition and were mixing in AA

50

shells with proximity fuses. There was a brilliant glare like a thousand flashbulbs, the deafening blast of high explosives. The explosion tore one of Brent's hands from the teak railing and spun him around so that his back slammed against the windscreen. His helmet strap dug into his chin as his helmet tried to fly off with the fierce concussion wave. Although his knees gave way, he managed to grip the rail with both hands and remain on his feet, temporarily disoriented and deafened, his retinas starring and flashing with afterimages.

The bearing ring was hurled into the wind, a chart table ripped from its mounts, spilling across the deck onto the corpse of Ballew. Ripped like shredded paper, the binnacle poured alcohol onto the deck. It dissolved some of the cloying blood and ran to the scuppers.

Shaking his head, Brent finally cleared his mind of the paralysis of shock and his retinas of pyrotechnic ghosts. He was in a charnel house. Stoker Adam Stanger lay in the wreckage of the binnacle. However, his head, still helmeted, had rolled across the deck and lodged against the corpse of Harold Ballew. Stanger's jugulars were still pumping blood.

The captain was down, lying on his side. His life jacket had been ripped and he held his bloody chest. He moaned and gasped, spitting blood. Ingilly sat with his back to the windscreen, staring straight ahead, wide eyes glassy with shock and horror. He appeared unhurt; at least physically. And the talker, Leading Seaman Turner, showed no wounds. In fact, the young man pulled himself to his feet and stared around. There was disbelief in his eyes, but he still seemed in control and alert.

Ingilly began to sing, "I've got sixpence . . ."

"Shut up, damn you," Brent shouted, suddenly aware he was in command of a badly wounded destroyer. Ingilly laughed gleefully and continued singing. Reaching down, Brent slapped him across the face with the back of a massive hand. The blow knocked the navigator onto his side. He began to sob uncontrollably.

51

Brent shouted at Turner, "SBA to the bridge—on the double!"

The young man gulped, took a deep breath, and repeated the order.

Haida's superb gunners had not even paused. The two remaining mounts, "B" and "Y," were pouring out a torrent of shells. *Abu Bakr* was hidden by splashes, spray, smoke. Brent could see flames pouring out of her admidships. But she had not slowed. He shouted at the talker, "All layer, lower your sights. Let water into her, not air." He raised his binoculars. They were very close, not more than five thousand yards apart. Only one gun mount on the bow of the enemy was firing erratically and finally some damage must have been done to her hull. She began to slow and swing to starboard. Flames had enveloped her entire amidships section and men could be seen leaping into the water. As he watched, four shells smashed into the destroyer's bridge, demolishing the flying bridge, wheelhouse, and radio room. More fires flared. His British gunners were good; very good. Best shooting he had ever seen.

"Right standard—I mean starboard ten, steer zero-two-zero. All ahead together. Speed full," the American said into the pilothouse tube. Then to Turner, "Torpedo Officer, stand by. You have the show." The talker spoke into his mouthpiece.

"Sublieutenant Braithwaite acknowledges, Commander," Turner said.

"Steady on zero-two-zero, sir. Speed twenty-four," came up a tube.

Suddenly, there was activity behind Brent as two sick bay attendants raced onto the bridge. They ignored the dead and began to minister to the one wounded man, Commander Coglan.

"Sublieutenant Braithwaite is standing by. Ready to launch torpedoes, sir," Turner reported. Brent was pleased with the young man's composure and control under the most hideous conditions.

"Very well," he acknowledged. "Have the Yeoman of Signals report to the bridge," he waved at the corpses, "and remove these bodies." Then he noticed the Arab had slowed even more but the enemy's heading was steady on zero-two-zero. "Give me revs for eighteen knots," Brent ordered.

The turbines pitched down through the crash of the guns. "Eighteen knots, one-three-five revs, sir."

At that moment a shell crashed into the bow, penetrated the chain locker, and blew it to bits. Splinters whined and ricocheted off the steel screen. Immediately, the anchor clattered into the depths, its severed chain following.

"Damage Control—watertight integrity?" Brent shouted at Turner.

"Hull secure," the talker reported back.

"Tell Sublieutenant Braithwaite to launch his damned torpedoes. They'll be hitting us with slingshots soon. And damn it, they have ten torpedoes of their own."

There were four pops like toy guns going off among the thunderous explosions of the 4.7-inch guns. Four long gray cylinders leaped from the tubes amidships and plunged into the sea. The Mark 24, Model 1 Tigerfish torpedo, one of the Royal Navy's best. Shorn of its wire and passive and active guidance systems by the Geneva Agreements, the electrically powered torpedo relied on accurate aim and its contact fuse to make its kill.

Turner turned to Brent. "The torpedo officer reports torpedo run of three minutes, twenty-five seconds, Commander."

"Very well." Immediately, the lieutenant commander rotated the timing bezel of his Rolex Cosmograph to three minutes, twenty-five seconds and pressed the start button. A hand on one of the three subsidiary dials began to revolve. Timing the fish. He had done this repeatedly as attack officer of submarine *Blackfin*.

There were flashes and puffs of white smoke and steam in the hell amidship on *Abu Bakr* and torpedoes sprayed into the water. Obviously fired in desperation, the steel fish were flung at random to the ship's starboard side in hopes one of them would hit *Haida*.

"Right full rudder! All ahead together flank—full emergency!" Brent screamed down the voice tubes.

Acknowledgments were hurled back and the ship accelerated like a frightened greyhound, leaned hard into her turn. "Steady up on one-one-zero!"

The new course would put their stern to the enemy. Ideally, he would have turned bow-on, but he was too close and there was always a chance the Arab had aerial or even warship support on the way. The new course gave the wildly fired torpedoes a narrow target and put *Haida's* bows on a course for the storm which was slipping over the horizon like a great black slug. "B" mount was masked, but "Y" mount continued to fire over the stern.

Brent said to Turner, "All hands on weather decks keep a weather eye for following torpedoes."

For the first time, he noticed that the medical personnel had removed the wounded captain. Then the Leading Signalman and a Yeoman of Signals pulled the still bleeding bodies of Ballew and Stanger from the bridge and lay them aft on the signal platform next to the flag bag. Still, footing in the coagulating blood was very slippery.

The young American forced the horror from his mind. The two boys were just dead meat now. There was a destroyer out there to kill—a dangerous enemy who had fired ten torpedoes at his ship. That was where his concentration belonged. Brent braced himself on the windscreen, glanced over his shoulder as if he could actually see the approaching torpedoes. They were probably Russian Five-Five-Threes. Forty-six knots max. Five-hundred-pound warhead. Electrically driven. No track. He saw nothing. *Haida* was slashing through the mounting swells at 36 knots, only ten knots less than the following torpedoes—if they were set on maximum

54

speed. He knew the chances of being hit were slim and no alarms came through the ship's communication systems.

Ingilly was singing and talking to himself and drawing circles with a single finger in the pools of blood. "Everything's tickety-boo, tickety-boo . . ." the man half sang, half mumbled to himself. Brent felt disgust. The man was not only a coward, he was a mad coward. He shook his head, checked the stainless steel watch. Almost three minutes had passed since they had launched their four torpedoes. *Abu Bakr* was almost dead in the water, burning, listing.

"Cease fire!" Brent shouted. "Damage Control, I want a report!"

Immediately, the guns of "Y" mount fell silent. A sweet silence like the cool water of a mountain brook flowed over his eardrums. Then he noticed his ears were ringing. They always did after heavy gunfire. He shook his head. The ringing continued.

Another anxious glance at his watch. Three minutes, twenty-seconds. He watched apprehensively as the bezel ran out to zero. Then he stared at the black face of the watch, the smoothly revolving second hand adding the seconds inexorably. Never had time crawled at such a slow pace. Three minutes, thirty seconds. Forty seconds. Fifty seconds. He cursed. Punched the windscreen. Gripped the voice tubes and was about to give the order to come about when two great blasts lifted the wounded *Gearing* high up, almost free of the sea. Two torpedoes had struck the destroyer with a one-two punch, one directly under the bridge, the other almost amidships. A great cheer went up from the crew of *Haida*. Scores of boots stomped on the decks. Leading Seaman Turner waved his fist over his head and screamed, "That'll sort your hash, you bloody buggers!"

About one-third of the stricken ship from the bridge forward broke off and floated away as if the destroyer had given birth to another smaller vessel. Flaming fuel poured from both sections. Then both parts of the ship began to settle quickly into the spreading blazing fuel, making a crude burning "V." Men could be seen abandoning ship. A few threw over life rafts while most just jumped into the inferno.

"Damage report, sir," Randall Turner said. "Twenty-millimeter guns One, Two, Three, and Nine destroyed. Aft deckhouse destroyed. Forty-millimeter mounts three and four destroyed. 'X' mount destroyed, aft funnel holed, hull holed above waterline on port side between frames two and four and also between frames twenty-six and twenty-seven. Ship's boat and captain's launch destroyed. Watertight integrity secure. Auxiliary Engine Room Number One destroyed, chain locker and paint locker destroyed. Number Three generator off its mounts. Radar and W-T out of commission. Anchor lost . . ."

"Casualties! Casualties?" Brent interrupted anxiously.

"Seventeen dead, twelve wounded, four missing, but muster is incomplete."

Brent's heart sank. "Good Lord," he muttered.

He stared back over the stern. Only the prow of *Abu Bakr* was visible. The sea was burning, a gigantic black cloud billowing into the sky. Men could be seen swimming frantically away from the spreading conflagration. Some flailed and actually tried to leap from the sea when the flames reached them, bubbling off their flesh, searing their tongues and following their breath to their lungs. There were perhaps a half-dozen rafts in the water, filled with men paddling away from the flames. Others pushed themselves away from the holocaust on barrels, planking, anything that would float. "Must be a hundred of the bastards in the water," Brent said to himself.

He turned to the talker. "Break out small arms. Stand by to come about. Twenty-millimeter machine guns, stand by to kill survivors."

Leading Seaman Randall Turner stared at the American silently, a stunned look on his face. "I say, sir," the enlisted man dared, "that isn't sporting, sir."

"Correct, old boy," Ingilly added, giggling while he continued tracing designs in the blood. "Not cricket a'tall."

Brent felt a familiar uncontrollable rage race through him like lava to the cone of a volcano. His order had actually been challenged by an enlisted man and a lunatic subordinate. Unthinkable! "I don't give a goddamn, Talker," he screamed. "You heard the order. Give it!" Turner's mouth and jaw worked up and down and his face contorted like a man who had just regurgitated a sour meal. He remained silent.

Ingilly looked up, hands and face smeared with blood. "You heard, him, Talker, boff the buggers. Everything's tickety-boo." He waved a fist. Sang in a mock basso-profundo. "Rule Britannia—Britannia rules the waves . . ." He began to laugh. Brent ignored him.

"Give the fuckin' order or I'll do it myself." Brent reached for the headpiece with the intention of ripping it from the talker, but a rumble high in the sky stopped him. He turned his head. Then shouts rose from the AA gunners on the starboard wing of the bridge, "Bombers! Bearing green one-three-zero, elevation thirty!"

Brent raised his glasses. He felt his heart leap, and ice suddenly flowed in his veins. He counted six aircraft flying at about 9,000 feet. They had Arab markings.

Brent shouted down the tubes and at Turner at the same time. "Belay my last order, Talker. Stand by to engage aircraft!" Turner relayed the order.

He had British gunners, the best in the world. But five mounts had been destroyed, AA gunners killed and wounded. *Haida's* firepower had been greatly reduced. He looked at the storm anxiously. Shelter was there. It was still miles away.

Brent shouted at Turner, "Chief Engineer. I want every knot! Tie down the safety valves, if necessary, but I want every knot you can give me!"

He turned, brought his glasses up over the starboard quarter. The planes were closing fast. He brought them

57

into sharp focus. He could not believe his eyes. A Heinkel 111, a twin-engined Cessna, a Douglas DC-3 and three Junkers, Ju 87 Stukas. A strange mix of dissimilar aircraft. A covey of teal, widgeons, and mallards. But these days you put into the sky whatever your money could buy. Without a doubt, the DC-3 was a heavily armed gunship. She led, the point of a "V" flanked by the Cessna and the Heinkel 111. The muzzles of Gatlings stuck out of the side doors of the Douglas and ventral and dorsal power turret bubbles were visible. There were bombs slung under her wings. The Cessna, too, carried bombs under her wings, and Brent knew the Heinkel carried at least two tons of bombs. Her bomb bay doors were opening.

Echeloned above the multiengined aircraft were the Stukas. They, too, flew in a "V." These were the most fearsome, the most deadly. Brent had been under every type of air attack—high level, torpedo, and dive bomber. Nothing could compare with the terror, the accuracy of the plummeting, shrieking Ju 87. During World War Two it demoralized and inflicted crippling losses on the Polish Army, broke the back of the French Army in the Ardennes, and sank hundreds of Allied ships. And it, too, had inflicted terrible damage on Japanese and Israeli forces in the Arab wars.

He scanned the sky hurriedly. Nothing but the bombers. "Yoshi Matsuhara, where are you? In the name of the gods, we need you, old friend," he said to himself.

He was answered only by the rumble of approaching engines.

To Commander Yoshi Matsuhara, the black cloud to the south appeared to be another storm, a minor preliminary to the main event to the east. But it was not light and vaporous. Instead, it was heavy and clung to the water, spreading like a loathsome pox, soiling the clear blue sea and fouling the sky. Burning oil, no doubt about it. A ship was in trouble. Brent Ross and *Haida* were down there. Maybe the old British destroyer had been ambushed—destroyed.

York's voice broke through, "Edo Leader, some of them bullockin' sods is near."

"You have sighted them?"

"No, guv'nor. Me cock's up. A sure sign."

Willard-Smith's refined voice: "I say, York, you're off the rails, old boy. Your digit is always a wicket. You should contribute it to the East Surrey Cricket Club."

"Off the rails my arse, I'm tellin' you, them bloody sods's on the block."

"Edo Flight. Observe radio discipline!" Yoshi barked sharply into his microphone. His wingmen acknowledged with silence.

The flight leader was uneasy. York might be on to something. At times the man's sixth sense was uncanny. But Willard-Smith was right—the Cockney was perpetually randy. Nevertheless, the smoke indicated some kind of sea action. Enemy aircraft should be in the vicinity or on the way.

Yoshi's anxious eyes searched the sky like a man in a strange city hunting street signs. There was a three-tenths cloud cover to the east, where the storm was brewing. Quartering the sky, he examined it section by section. This arena was limitless and full of risk. He had learned long ago that a speck of dirt on your windshield could turn into an enemy fighter in the time it took to glance at your instruments and back again. A little smudge on your goggles could conceal the plane that was hurtling in to kill you. Stretching his neck, he rummaged through the sky from extreme left rear to extreme right rear. The twisting caused his neck and spine to ache all the way from the back of his skull to the base of his spine. It was tension, age, and fatigue.

He wriggled his shoulders to loosen his shirt, now sticky with cold sweat, and pivoted sharply despite the objections of his muscles. He pulled the mask aside momentarily to clear his throat of the metallic taste of oxygen. Instantly, his nostrils were filled with the unmistakable smell of a Zero's cockpit, a blend of oil and dope, leather and webbing spiced with traces of exhaust. It was a good smell, the smell of his workplace, the domain that he alone controlled, where his brain and muscles determined life or death. He pushed the mask back over his face.

As he studied the black smudge of smoke, his uncanny vision spotted the six specks before his younger wingmen saw them. At first they were nothing more than minute dots made by a sharp pencil tip on the blue vault of the sky. But quickly they became tiny vultures circling over a carcass and he could see the sun reflecting from prop-discs like tiny ivory buttons. He unlatched the binocular case and brought his glasses to his eyes. Now he could see them clearly, single-engine and twin-engine aircraft flying in two "vics" of three. Three had spats and gulled wings. He felt a twitch of apprehension. Ju 87s. And the Stukas were breaking away, forming a single line while two of the multiengined aircraft flew high toward an exiguous speck barely perceptible through the smoke on the distant horizon. The third twin-engined aircraft was spiraling down in wide circles. Typical attack formation. They were closing in on a target obscured by haze and smoke. York was right. He had actually sensed them; sniffed them out before they were visible.

York's cry: "Bandits at ten o'clock low! Range long— bloody long. Just fly shit on me windscreen."

"See them, Edo Three. They're enemy bombers." And then Yoshi saw *Haida*. Although it was just a tiny silhouette with most of its hull below the horizon, the pyramidal upper works, the break in the deck line aft of the bridge and the two stacks—the forward stack much larger than the second—were unmistakable. Brent was there, fighting for his life.

The flight leader still hesitated, tapped his helmet so hard he could feel his knuckles through the padding.

Scanned the sky, but saw no fighters. But they could be above the overcast, which was spreading like a bad watercolor. The storm was moving closer and there was four-tenths cloud cover now. It would not be like the Arabs to send out bombers without an escort. They must be nearby, but he had no choice. He must attack. He opened his transmission switch. "Edo Flight, this is Edo Leader. Arm your guns. Engage enemy bombers at ten o'clock. Individual combat. Follow my lead. Keep an eye out for their escort. The *ronin* must be up there above that cover. *Banzai!*"

He replaced the binoculars and secured the lock. Without conscious thought, he pushed the cover from the red button and threw the arming switch. A red light glowed. Then the flick of another switch and the 100-millimeter yellow-orange reticle of his new electric reflector gun sight appeared on the windscreen. Gradually, he pushed his throttle forward, but not into overboost.

"Tally ho, old boy, and York, a 'huzzah' to you. You've got a ruddy divining rod between your legs," Willard-Smith chortled.

Girls call me rod divine, your nibs. Let's give them golliwogs the chop—pull their pissers," the Cockney replied.

Roaring like the wind before the monsoon, the three fighters dropped off into a shallow dive to the south.

Lieutenant Commander Brent Ross shouted at Leading Seaman Randall Turner, "All guns stand by to engage high-level bombers. Main battery engage aircraft when in range. Secondary batteries fire on my command." The captains of the 4.7s had range-finding binoculars; the gunners at the Bofors and Oerlikons had nothing but their eyeballs and tracers. If he allowed them to open fire at their own discretion, they would probably spray the sky uselessly with valuable ammunition. Thousands of rounds of AA ammunition had been lost when Coglan had flooded Number 5 Magazine. Brent patted his MIV/IT Carl Zeiss glasses. He would make the estimates of range.

He had pushed Ingilly's inert form into a corner of the bridge next to the starboard lookout's platform where Leading Signalman George Peterson had replaced Stoker Adam Stanger. The navigator had curled up into a fetal position, lain his head on the crook of his arm, and started softly crooning and talking to himself. At least he was out of the way. Only the talker and Peterson were on the bridge to aid Brent.

Casualties had been heavy. Every man was needed by damage control and at the surviving gun stations. In fact, Brent had sent Yeoman of Signals Robert McVey to replace a dead loader at 40-millimeter mount Number 6. The port lookout platform remained empty. The deck was still slippery with blood and littered with debris. Blood continued to dribble out of the director. Lafferty's head and shoulder and one arm still dangled out the door, the arm whipped by the breeze as if the dead man was waving at his friends below. They must all be dead up there.

Leading Signalman George Peterson was an old professional. At least ten years older than Brent, he had been an eighteen-year veteran of the Royal Navy before signing up with the Japanese National Parks Department. He had proved himself tough and steady in the most trying and grizzly circumstances. Standing tall on his platform, his glasses glued to his eyes, he focused above where the aircraft had broken up into three distinct groups; the two level bombers turning into their final leg of their run, the Douglas DC-3 spiraling down in an ever narrowing radius to bring her Gatlings to bear, and the three Stukas now stacked in a single line at about 7,000 feet and to the north.

Brent was thankful for Leading Seaman Randall Turner. The youngster was made of stout stuff. *British oak*, thought Brent. The talker repeated orders and relayed messages coolly. He also kept a good eye out. The three of them would have to manage.

Elevated at over 35 degrees, "B" mount fired. With the muzzles of the two 4.7-inch guns almost level with the flying bridge, Brent was struck with a stupefying blast and concussion. Then "Y" mount joined in. The four guns were firing on the Heinkel 111 and the Cessna. The Heinkel was leading with its smaller companion following. The Cessna looked ridiculous in the company of the bombers, but the four bombs slung under its wings killed any humor before it started. They were well within the range of the forties, but Brent withheld the order to open fire. He could see the anxious white faces of their gun crews turned toward the bridge. The Stukas had veered far to the north to stand clear of the high-level attack before making their runs.

The young executive officer wondered about the tactics. Falling bombs or not, all of the enemy aircraft should have attacked simultaneously. Split *Haida's* defensive fire and not allow her to concentrate. That is what he would have done. Coordinate all six aircraft into one concentrated attack from all points of the compass. Must be an Arab in charge. A German or Russian would have known better. Still, *Haida* was in very serious trouble.

Brent stared through his binoculars. Knowing the wingspan of the Heinkel was 53 feet, he brought the aircraft down to the horizontal range scale, which jutted up in his vision like the pickets of a fence. Carefully, he matched the wing tips with two of the lines and read the range: 10,000 feet. Still, it was a crude estimate and he knew it. But it made little difference. The forties depended on volume for effect, not just accuracy of aim. He shouted at Talker Turner, "Range ten-thousand-feet. All forty-millimeter mounts that bear, open fire! Commence! Commence!"

The four port-side 40-millimeter Bofors came to life with stuttering blasts. With the loaders working like madmen jamming four-round clips into the breeches, each gun fired 120 rounds a minute. Immediately, the sky beyond and below the bombers was stitched with the small brown blobs of exploding shells. Secured to the fine Mark II Hazemeyer triaxially stabilized mounting and with experienced crews, Brent had expected better results from the Bofors. But the torrents of smoking shells stormed past the bombers to harmlessly self-destruct. Unlike the big 31-pound shells of the 4.7s, the small two-pound shells of the forties needed a direct hit to make a kill. He cursed and pounded his fist into his palm. Radar fire-control was needed, and they did not have it.

"Elevation angle on leading aircraft forty degrees, sir," Peterson yelled over the drumfire of the cannons and Bofors. "Twenty-millimeter gunners request permission to open fire."

The bombers were out of range of the machine guns, but the DC-3 gunship was circling ever closer. "Negative. The level bombers are out of range. Twenty-millimeter batteries are to track the gunship." Brent tried to yawn and rub the thunder out of his ears and leaned over the pilothouse voice tube. The bomb release angle would be at about 50 degrees. "Speed?"

"Thirty-seven, sir," came back.

"Good. Good," Brent said to himself. And then into the tube, "Stand by to give me hard right rudder."

"Standing by, sir."

Brent stared up at the Heinkel as if it were a mesmerizing gold medallion swung by a hypnotist. He expected a stick of bombs that the Arabs hoped to march right through the destroyer. When the first bomb of the stick left the bomb bay, he would come hard to the right. As if reading Brent's mind, the pilot dropped the bomber lower, giving the destroyer less time to maneuver. Brent cursed.

Shaggy black blobs sprouted all around the Heinkel and Cessna. Although the gun captains had to estimate ranges only with the aid of range-finding binoculars and by reading their shell bursts, the British gunners were bunching their shells with amazing accuracy. The two planes bounced and weaved, but still bore in on their bomb runs.

Then Peterson cried out, "Aircraft! Friendlies! Red forty, elevation thirty-five!" He waved. "Just specks out there, sir."

Brent shifted his glasses. His heart leaped with joy. A red, green, and white Zero followed by two Seafires were streaking out of the distant sky like a lance hurled by an angry god. It was Yoshi Matsuhara, Willard-Smith, and York. "Thank God," he said to himself. "Hurry! We need you, old friends."

Despite having used overboost several times in previous dogfights, when Commander Yoshi Matsuhara punched the throttle to the last stop, he was startled by the effect. A great surge of speed jerked his head back and the engine made a raucous bellowing sound, as if someone were torturing it. Everything vibrated. Even the Heinkel was blurred. The temperature gauge began to creep upward. Yoshi said into his microphone, "Edo Two, take the Cessna, Edo Three, the Douglas. I have the Heinkel, but keep an eye on those Stukas."

"Right-oh, Edo Leader."

"Got the bugger, Guv'nor."

A little right rudder and the Heinkel slid into the glowing ring of the flight leader's sight. Its wingspan did not even reach the first sight bars. At least 6,000 meters. He cursed. Pounded the crash pad above the instrument panel. The bomber would probably release before he reached her.

The ferocious dive caused the flight leader's ears to pop and buzz, and he yawned wide to relieve the pressure. With his pair of superchargers shrieking and the injectors pumping water-methanol into his cylinder heads, the Zero surged ahead of its companions. With a worried glance at his instruments he saw the great engine was heating up despite all the efforts of American and Japanese engineers; the cylinder head temperature was 275 degrees, which was only 15 degrees below the red line. Oil temperature was 215, oil pressure 86, manifold pressure 56 inches of mercury, tachometer 2850 and climbing toward its red line at 3100, airspeed 505 knots and winding to the right like a timer's watch peeling off tenths of a second.

With air pouring over her airfoils at a rate far beyond her designers' wildest expectations, the Zero-sen was trembling like a virgin on the verge of her first seduction. Dust rose in the cockpit and the canopy lock clattered; instrument needles vibrated. The bomber was bouncing up and down, across and back through the gunsight. The Zero-sen had become a terrible gun platform.

Pulling back the throttle, Yoshi watched the airspeed indicator drop below 500. The howling and shrieking faded and the engine temperature held steady. Now the bomber was looming bigger and steadier, a new menace. Patches of black shaggy blobs. AA. He began to bounce wildly on the broken, smoky air. He could be killed by his own men. And Brent was down there. No doubt about it, that was the *Haida*. She was damaged but moving at tremendous speed away from a huge black mass of burning oil and debris. She must have sunk an enemy ship. In fact, he could see rafts and men on wreckage frantically paddling away from the holocaust.

Haida had been damaged. She was smoking amidships where she had been obviously hurt and only two mounts of her main battery were firing. Her AA was snapping viciously all around the Heinkel and Cessna and hundreds of 40-millimeter tracers were webbing the sky. Brent must be trying to talk the captain into a cease-fire to protect friendly fighters. But the guns did not cease, or even slacken. Yoshi raced through the bursts, a hellish garden of blooming black flowers of death.

"Our friendly fighters, Commander Ross!" Leading Signalman George Peterson shouted. "They're diving into our fire."

"I know, Signalman." Brent stretched his mouth like someone testing a rubber band. Pounded the windscreen. That was Yoshi up there diving on the Heinkel. The red, green, and white Zero with the gigantic engine was unmistakable. He made the only decision his military mind could make. The ship came first. "Continue firing. Our fighters will have to take their chances!"

He stared at the Heinkel. It was a fearsome aircraft. Fast and durable, it had been called *Spaten* (Spade) by its appreciative crews during World War Two. It was only about 4,000 feet high and Brent could see every detail: a glazed nose blister with a 7.9-millimeter machine gun protruding, another maching gun in a dorsal mount, and a third in a ventral "dustbin." Its 53-foot wingspan looked huge, and he could hear the roar of its two powerful Jumo 211 engines. He could even see the air scoops under the two inverted V-12 engines.

"Fifty degrees, sir," Peterson shouted.

The bombs were dropped in a cluster. Loaded tail-down, they flipped over as soon as they left the bay and dropped like a handful of thrown darts.

"Right full rudder!" Brent screamed. He had expected the bombs to be dropped in a stick, but instead he got a cluster. Either the bombardier was supremely confidant or the pilot was fearful of Yoshi Matsuhara's Zero, which was closing in fast high and from behind.

But Brent had no time to watch Yoshi's run. Instead he could only stare with horror at eight 500-pound bombs as they shrieked down on him—down directly on his head. With hard right rudder and at 37 knots, the destroyer heeled hard into her turn. But the bombs bore down and they actually seemed to curve and follow the ship's evasive moves as if they were guided. "Impossible!" Brent screamed. "Go away! Get away from my ship!"

Eight black-finned glistening blurs plunged directly down on the bridge and then seemed to diverge into a wide pattern at the last second. They were not as closely bunched as Brent had expected and they all struck to the port side of the ship. But close. Very close.

The shock shook the destroyer to her keel and the ship snapped like a bowstring. Eight towers of water rose high into the sky the full length of the ship's port side and then seemed to freeze for an instant before collapsing into the sea, spray and rings of ripples radiating from each impact. Shrapnel whined, whistled, and bounced off the steel sides of the ship. But not all the jagged fragments found steel.

Leading Signalman George Peterson screamed once, whirled like a dervish in a frenzy, and pitched headlong from his platform, adding his own blood to the coagulated sheets on the deck. A piece of shrapnel the size of a chunk of boiler plate had ripped the left side of his chest open and killed him almost instantly. Brent could see his still pulsing heart squirting blood through the ripped remnants of his lung and broken ribs.

Ingilly came to life. "Cannon to the right of them, cannon to . . ."

"Shut up, goddamn you!" The navigator rolled over on his stomach and covered his head with his hands.

The helmsman's voice came up the tube, "Passing one-eight-zero, sir."

"Rudder amidships. Steady as she goes."

"Steady on two-zero-zero, sir."

Turner shouted, "The Douglas gunship, sir!"

Brent whirled. The big transport was closing on their starboard side at a high speed and heading for the bow where *Haida's* Oerlikon mounts 1, 2, and 3 had been destroyed. "The gunship. My God," he said. "They're actually going to try to strafe us, cross our bow—cross

68

the 'T.' I can't believe it!" He said to Turner, "All forty-millimeter and twenty-millimeter mounts that bear, engage gunship to starboard. Commence! Commence!"

Immediately, the Oerlikons added their ravings to the pounding of the Bofors. With gas-driven action, the machine guns could fire over 500 rounds a minute. Trying to satisfy the ravenous appetites, the loaders worked furiously, jamming 60 round drum magazines into the open breech blocks in 11-second intervals.

However, the gunship closed in casually into what appeared to be a blizzard of tracers. It began to turn and Brent could see the four barrels of one of its Gatlings protruding from its port door. No doubt it was the Russian 12.7-millimeter UBK. The Arabs had dozens. A fearsome weapon, it could fire 3,000 rounds a minute at an effective range of at least 1,600 yards.

He tore his eyes from the Douglas and glanced at the storm which was now off their port beam. Down the tube, "Hard a-port." Immediately, the destroyer began to reverse its turn.

"Full left rudder on, sir."

"Return to base course one-one-zero."

Randall Turner began to shout, "The bombers—the bombers, sir. Our fighters are after 'em. And the Stukas are coming in!"

Brent's stomach churned and felt sick, as if it were filled with a writhing mass of cold worms. There was too much to do, too many decisions—and his best men were dead, wounded, or mad. He had never been so alone. He felt like a man who stood alone facing a collapsing dam.

Brent raised his glasses. The Stukas were approaching, stacked up in an oblique line at about 8,000 feet. The leader was painted in a wild pattern of swirls and jagged green, yellow, orange, and purple hues, as if a protégé of Salvador Dali's had drunk too much wine and then splattered the aircraft with paint. Unmistakably, it was the aircraft of Major Horst Fritschmann the leader of *Stukagruppe zwei* (dive bomber squadron two). The old

69

pilot had been reported killed off Morocco, but the report had obviously been wrong. He was up there. There was no mistake. He was the best dive bomber pilot in the world and he was ready to begin his attack: cooling gills shut, propeller rumbling on full coarse, and below the outer wings, slat-type airbrakes down in diving position.

"Main battery, engage dive bombers," Brent shouted at Turner. Immediately, the big guns shifted targets and one of their first rounds struck the third Stuka. With its 2,200-pound bomb detonating, it vanished in a brilliant last moment of glory like a nova that blinked to life in a millisecond and then died. A great wild cheer rose from every deck, every compartment.

But the two remaining Stukas bored on and the gunship's Gatling flared to life with a fearsome orange flash, firing at least 3,000 rounds a minute. Hordes of tracers stormed into the stern of *Haida*, raising huge splashes and killing every member of Bofors mount 6 and destroying Oerlikons 14 and 16. Then the big plane pulled ahead and began to cut across the exposed bow.

The DC-3 had been taking punishment. Its port engine was smoking, and chunks of aluminum had been blasted from its fuselage and tail. But the pilot was determined and courageous. The plane seemed to slow slightly but continued to cut across the destroyer's bow.

Brent stared hungrily at the storm, which was now only a few miles ahead. He wanted that cover, but he had no choice. He must turn away or be strafed from bow to stern. "Port full rudder," he ordered, in his anxiety mixing British and American terminology. "Steady up on zero-four-zero!"

The reply came back and the ship swung away from the bomber, but slowly, very slowly.

But there was help. Yoshi was boring in on the Heinkel, one Seafire was closing on the Cessna, and the other Seafire was in a hard dive on the Douglas.

"For Christ's sake, get the dive bombers! The dive bombers, Yoshi!" Brent screamed, stabbing a finger at the Stukas as if the Japanese pilot could see him. "Kill them! Kill them before they kill us!"

Yoshi Matsuhara did not automatically change targets the moment he saw the Heinkel release its bombs. His duty was not only to protect *Haida*, but to destroy the enemy wherever he found him and as quickly and efficiently as possible. The bomber could return, kill another day. And he had a perfect killing angle, from the rear with only slight deflection. He had to give the big ship a passing squirt before he went on to the two surviving Stukas, which were beyond the bomber and in his line of attack anyway.

Pulling back on the stick, he cursed the frozen relief tube. His bladder was full and a familiar dripping began. Someday, someone would design a heater that would keep the tube free. A man should not be forced to suffer this kind of torture—especially a man over sixty with diminishing bladder capacity.

Fortunately, his dive was not steep and he had throttled back. Still, his speed indicator showed just under 400 knots, and centrifugal force and gravity combined to push him down into his seat. For the first time in combat, he was wearing the new American "anti-G suit" which pressed a bladder against his stomach, thighs, and calves to prevent the draining of blood into the lower body. His peripheral vision faded and the familiar tunnel vision narrowed his eyesight. His stomach felt overfull and heavy and bulged against the bladder as if someone were poking it down with a stick. His nose ran, his jowls sagged, his ears buzzed and popped. Every time they popped, a gaggle of specks showered across his eyes. Blood was being sucked from his brain, but nevertheless the G-suit definitely helped and his head remained reasonably clear even as he bottomed out. Just a little gray fuzziness, no blackout this time. Thanks to the gods, the shallowness of his dive, and the American suit. He blinked his eyes, screamed into the slipstream to clear the gray mists away, and then watched the Heinkel wobble into his sights. He was doing at least 150 knots more than the bomber. One short burst.

He found himself below the bomber and bouncing and rocking in its turbulence. Bright beads were flashing past him, flicking past his wings, under his propeller, over his canopy, and past his rudder. The ventral 7.9-millimeter machine gun in its clumsy dustbin mount was firing, streams of tracers seeming to bend and accelerate as they approached. Throttling back even more, he pulled above the enemy and into the fire from the dorsal machine gun. This gunner was not as good. His tracers dropped off to the right and then sprayed wildly across the path of the fighter and under it like a drunk squirting a garden hose. He snorted in derision at the amateur marksman. *Must be an Arab*, he thought.

The Heinkel had a vast wing, nearly a hundred square meters, and Yoshi's gunsight made the most of it. Already, the wing stretched across the reticle to the second sight bars. The target expanded steadily until its lumbering bulk filled his reflector sight. Feeling the camera pressure first, he pressed down hard on the red button giving the enemy a quarter-length lead for deflection.

The first rounds blew off his muzzle tapes and then the Zero bucked and slowed from the massive recoil of the two Type 99, 20-millimeter cannons in the wings and the pair of 7.7 machine guns mounted above the nose. Harmonized for 300 meters, they shaped a cone of smoking white destruction. Although he had centered the sight ahead of the cockpit, the sparkling tracers passed in front of the bomber's starboard wing. A bare push on the stick brought the stream down. Then it raged across the wing, and hammered through the engine and into the fuselage as the Japanese pilot kicked left rudder and held the fighter in a flat, skidding turn with a hard tug on the stick. Chunks of aluminum were blown into the slipstream like street trash in a gale and black smoke suddenly flooded out of the engine, thick as cream, rich as velvet. A 20-millimeter shell blew most of the gunner's face off and the gun fell silent. Flashing past the yawing bomber, Yoshi fed the last of the burst into the cockpit. Shards of Perspex and glass fleckered and glistened in a glinting trail that was swallowed in smoke. Turning slowly to starboard like a heavy carp, the enemy aircraft rolled into its final dive. No parachutes . . . he must have killed them all.

"Banzai!" Yoshi shouted, glancing into his rearview mirror and turning his head. Miraculously, his back and neck did not ache.

"Tally-ho!" Willard-Smith shouted into the fighter circuit.

Yoshi looked up just in time to see the Englishman fire a short burst from his four 20-millimeter cannons into the hapless Cessna. Built for civilian flying and obviously not strengthened enough for military purposes, the pathetic Cessna dissolved into a corona of debris. The wings flew off at their roots and broke up into at least five pieces. The fuselage broke in half, and the intact tail sailed away on its own like a tiny glider. Both engines broke loose and tumbled, trailing smoke, propellers turning. Two parachutes popped open in the hail of wreckage. One caught a piece of flaming wreckage and flared like a superheated pine in a forest fire, and the man tumbled toward the sea, arms and legs flailing, shrouds trailing and whipping.

"Banzai, Muslim dog! Enjoy your seven rings of hell!" Yoshi spat.

Banking toward the Stukas, Yoshi had time for one short glance downward. York was racing in on the DC-3 gunship. The Douglas was closing in on *Haida's* bow with the Cockney hard on its tail. Tracers were ripping past both aircraft. The gunship's Gatling was erupting like a small volcano and a ventral power turret was firing on the Seafire.

But now Yoshi's entire world was a pair of Stukas ahead. His eyes widened when he saw the gaudy color scheme of the leader. Major Horst Fritschmann, there was no doubt about it. But Fritschmann had been killed. Maybe someone else had adopted his mad design. But not likely. That was not the way of the Arabs or the Germans. Fritschmann was alive—the best dive bomber pilot in the world.

He felt a new surge of confidence. Without a command, Willard-Smith had taken his customary position just off his port elevator. But they were too late. Fritschmann had begun his dive. And the second bomber was nosing over.

Cursing, Yoshi jammed the throttle to the last stop. The Zero leaped forward. But they would be late—too late.

The great glare of the exploding Stuka had caught Kenneth Rosencrance's eye. Then, through the thin overcast, he saw a bare trace of black smoke hugging the sea in the far distance. Sea and air action, no doubt about it. But it was far to the north and east of where *Salat* had vectored him. Actually, *Abu Bakr* was in Sector Juliet 3 instead of Juliet 2. Stupid Arab controllers. They could not read their own charts and scopes.

His engine backfired and he pulled the release cable, dropping his two 300-liter auxiliary wing tanks without even looking. A quarter turn of the tail trim handwheel corrected a sudden heaviness to the right. Now he was on his wing and fuselage tanks. He had maybe three hours of flying time left, much less if he got into a scrap. Not much out here in the vast void of the Western Pacific. He saw tanks fluttering away from the other members of his flight.

After checking the lock on his shoulder harness and making sure his seatbelt was tight, he opened his transmission switch. "Raka Flight, this is Raka leader.

There's some kind of shit storm at two o'clock. Arm your guns. Follow my lead."

Banking to the right with their engines straining, the four Messerschmitt fighters streaked toward the smoke.

Major Horst Fritschmann saw the two Japanese fighters approaching his Ju 87 from below and to the right. He needed fighter support. Had screamed into his radio for help. How could those stupid idiots back on Saipan expect him to carry out an attack without fighter cover? He cursed the surly American and his whole *Staffel*.

This stupid war was not like his time in the Western Desert, where he first flew as a 16-year-old gunner in the rear cockpit of the great Stuka pilot *Hauptmann* Wilhelm Wittenberg. That was a glorious time, flying for the most famous *Sturzkampfflugzeug* (dive bomber) squadron in North Africa, *Stukageschwader ein* (dive bomber squadron one.) They had fighter protection then. Had actually made direct hits on British Matilda tanks with their bombs. Opened some up like sausage tins and blew others sky high.

He learned his trade in the cockpit. Served as a pilot on the Russian front when Wittenberg was killed. Destroyed a half-dozen T-34s before he was shot down by a Yakovlev Yak-3 in 1944 over Minsk. By the time he'd recovered from his wounds, the war had ended, but not his hatred for the Jews who had started it all. Israel was an abomination and he would kill Jews even if Kadafi was not paying him a half-million a year American.

A quick glance at his instruments: air speed 220 kilometers, boost pressure 120 centimeters, altitude 2,500 meters, rev counter 1,800, oil and coolant temperatures in the green, oil and fuel pressure normal. He shouted into his intercom to his gunner, a young Italian named Vincent Trozera, "Watch for those Japanese fighters—climbing from the east."

"See them, *Oberst*," the dark young man said, standing and swinging his twin 7.92-millimeter Mauser MG-81Z machine guns toward the enemy. "And the storm is closing in, sir."

"Good. We may need it." Fritschmann was thankful they were on the intercom and not face to face. The Italian's fondness for garlic turned his stomach. The gunner's overpowering breath could have been put to good use in an Auschwitz gas chamber-saved Zyklon B.

Fritschmann stared out of his side window, ahead and to the left. He had learned long ago the best approach was to let the target slide past his left until it disappeared beneath his left wing root. Steaming hard for the storm, the destroyer was finally obscured by his wing. Then a quick glance through the target view window between his rudder pedals showed him the ship was precisely where he wanted it. He chuckled. The fighters might kill him, but he was going to kill that ship. He was old now; time was running out anyway. There was no better way to go, except perhaps in bed with a young woman. A smile broke through the wrinkles. Putting a bomb into a ship was very much like driving his *nille* into a woman. In both cases, the target writhed and burst in a final orgasmic moment of completion.

It was time to earn his pay. He switched on the auto-pilot assist for the high-G pullout, pushed the stick forward, balanced with rudder, and felt his stomach rise to his throat as the big nose dropped. The horizon shot upward like a dark blue string and his windscreen was filled with the sea. He switched on his sirens (the Trombones of Jericho), whose howl was designed to demoralize the enemy, then had a look at his preset dive indicator. It was approaching 80 degrees, and now the twisting destroyer was visible through his windscreen. He wanted 85 degrees. A glance at the lines painted on his visual dive indicator gave him the angle. He dropped the nose until the 85-degree line coincided with the horizon. A look into his rearview mirror told him the second member of his *kette* (flight) was dropping off into its dive.

Gripping the stick tightly, he could feel the aircraft vibrate as the airbrakes buffeted through the lumpy air. He tested his rudder stirrups, pushed gently on right rudder to counter the bomber's tendency to pull to the left, balanced with aileron and elevators. It was all done automatically, without conscious thought, his whole concentration on the target. It was all manual now, accuracy depending on his judgment and skill. Working his controls ever so gently, he aimed at the bow, actually a lead that allowed the vessel to steam under his bomb and probably take the hit amidships. Break her in half. He must release low so that the captain would not have time for evasive action.

The ship was growing. Long. Slender. Moving at a tremendous speed. Two stacks spouting and leaking smoke from numerous holes. He wanted this kill. It was the British destroyer, no doubt about that. He would kill those Jew-loving limeys, send them to the same hell where they all belonged. He had killed dozens of them during the war and enjoyed every new corpse he created. She had been hit abaft the second funnel and he could see white smoke pouring from the wrecked deck and superstructure. He brought the bridge into his sight. Strange. It was red. A single white face was turned to him. Maybe it was the captain. Waiting to die. He would put his bomb down the *schwein's* throat. "I have a thousand kilograms of H.E. for lunch for you, Jew-loving *Englander scheisse.*"

The deck leaped with flashes—cannons and automatic weapons trying to kill him. The flak was murderous. Heavy bursts and tracers streamed all around. Those gunners were good. Very good. They had already killed one of his bombers. But they were trying to fight off the Douglas gunship, too. He tightened his jaw. The Stuka jarred and swayed from the explosion of a big shell. Shrapnel punched holes in his starboard wing, bright aluminum showing around the vents where paint had flaked off. He fought the controls and kept his angle and the ship in his sight despite the turmoil of tortured air and the drag of the damaged wing.

Gripping the red bomb-release lever, he pulled his lips back into a welter of wrinkles. His eyes were so wide the whites showed like marble above his hollow cheeks. The leer was that of a death's head.

With one hand gripping the voice tubes, Brent Ross watched Fritschmann's gaudy Ju 87 screech down directly on his head. He could clearly see the huge 2,200-pound bomb slung under the fuselage. That one bomb could sink *Haida*. "Right full rudder and hold her in a hard turn until I change the order!" he screamed. The command was repeated and the ship heeled into the turn.

Helped by the turn, the Douglas gunship was cutting diagonally across their bow, Gatling spitting. The big 12.7-millimeter slugs had raked the starboard side, punching through steel plate, both stacks, killing and wounding a dozen men, and smashing the radio room and charthouse. Brent had turned toward the gunship, giving it his bow. But the gunship could not sink *Haida* and the dive bomber could. He had to give Fritschmann the toughest possible target and take his punishment from the four-barrel UBK. The young American assumed the German Stuka pilot would aim for his bow and hope for a hit amidships.

A Seafire was hard on the Douglas's tail, its four 20-millimeter cannons firing, leaving small brown puffs and a glittering hail of brass cartridges in its wake. Flame boiled out of the gunship's port engine, laying down a black ribbon of smoke. Suddenly, the big plane veered sharply away, the fighter cutting across the arc of the turn to bore in to point-blank range. The Gatling was silent. A few men cheered.

The pitch of the Jumo engine above his head changed

and Brent saw the huge black bomb swing low on its crutch, clear the propeller, and hurtle straight down. He was sure it was aimed directly at the top of his head. The first bomber pulled up hard, but another Stuka was close behind it.

Yoshi's A6M2 was pouncing on Horst Fritschmann's Stuka and a Seafire was firing on the second dive bomber. But reality now was the great black glistening bomb shrieking downward. Maybe he should have turned sooner.

"Down!" Brent screamed, ducking below the windscreen. But young Leading Seaman Randall Turner remained erect, staring as if hypnotized at the bomb. Senses overwhelmed by horror and fear, the young man had finally had enough, could no longer react to the slaughter of shipmates, to commands, to anything. The bomb struck close to the port side, just abaft the superstructure.

When Brent was twelve years old his father had been transferred to Mare Island, a base near San Francisco. Brent had experienced a Force 7.2 earthquake. Buildings fell and a freeway collapsed. The explosion of the 2,200-pound bomb made the California earthquake seem as trivial as waves in a child's pool compared to a tidal wave. A tower of water rivaling a dozen Old Faithfuls shot into the air and continued to rise majestically until the whole mass of water seemed to solidify for an instant like a curtain and hang from the sky. Then it tumbled back into the sea in a welter of spray and tortured water.

The ship leaped, twisted, groaned, and rumbled as if someone was pounding great temple gongs in the engine rooms. Shrapnel clanged against steel. Brent looked up in time to see Turner's left shoulder and arm ripped from his body and splattered against the windscreen or blown into the breeze. Most of the left side of his head flew off with his headpiece and helmet. Soft, mushy gore sprayed Brent's helmet, face, and lifejacket. The talker pitched to the deck across Ingilly, loose jaw with broken teeth breaking away and clattering across the deck like a macabre child's toy. The navigator pushed the corpse away until it lay twitching next to Peterson's inert form. Then he curled up in his corner, mumbling something about ". . . a corner of a foreign field forever England . . ."

Numbly, Brent wiped his face with the back of his hand and then looked up for the second dive bomber. Surprisingly, some of *Haida's* antiaircraft guns were still firing. Either his gunners or the Seafire had hit the Stuka. Its left wing folded up like a fighter preparing to be taken down one of *Yonaga's* elevators, the bomb broke loose, and the Junkers, completely shorn of its airworthiness, whipped to the left in an impossible tumbling spin and drove itself into the sea like a locomotive entering a tunnel. At the same moment, the Douglas hit the wave tops, bounced high into the air, and then plunged straight down like a diving gannet. It smashed into the sea like a drunk staggering into a wall. There were a few cheers. To the east, Yoshi Matsuhara was close on Fritschmann's tail, the two planes seemingly connected with ropes of tracers.

"Passing two-six-five," came up from the pilothouse.

Brent shouted down the voice tube, "Steady up on one-one-zero, and, Quartermaster, any casualties?"

"One, sir. The starboard lookout's dead, sir."

"Damn!" Another dead man. And the near miss could have sprung some hull plates. They could be scooping up water like a vacuum cleaner.

"Is your telephone board still working?"

"Yes, sir."

"Get me a damage report—from damage control and the engine and fire rooms. Immediately. My communications are out. And tell damage control . . ."

"Aircraft! Aircraft!" a 20-millimeter loader shouted. "Bearing green one-six-five, high."

Brent raised his glasses. Four Messerschmitt 109s led by a blood-red fighter. "Rosencrance! My God, will it ever end?"

A voice came up the tube. "Engine Room Two reports a foot of water in the bilges. Auxiliary Engine Room Two reports buckled plates. They are taking water through bulkhead Number Three and there is saltwater in some of our freshwater lines. All bilge pumps are operating and can keep up with the leaks. Chief Engineer Townsend requests that we reduce speed to reduce pressure on the hull, sir."

Despite the carnage all around and the still unknown damage to his ship, Brent felt a strange calmness. "Very well. Both ahead together one-third." The ship began to slow immediately. The enemy posed no danger to the ship now, only to Yoshi and his wingmen. "Port ten," he ordered.

"Ten of port wheel on, sir."

"Midships."

"Steady, sir."

"Course zero-four-zero."

"Steady on zero-four-zero, speed twelve, one-one-zero revs."

He would parallel the face of the storm and watch the inevitable clash above. Yoshi had fatally damaged Fritschmann's Stuka and was climbing like a rocket to intercept Rosencrance. The Seafires were hard on his rudders. If more enemy bombers followed Rosencrance's flight, he would duck *Haida* into the storm.

Down the tube: "Where is that report from damage control?"

The reply came back almost immediately. "Lieutenant Stonebreaker reports the plating between frames forty-one and sixty-three on the port side have been forced in. Bulkhead Three has been pierced by a beam. His men are shoring. He suggests you keep speed under ten knots, sir. The bilge pumps are lowering the flooding, but he says we could spring new leaks."

"Any water in the fuel lines?"

"Negative, sir."

81

"Very well. Give me revs for eight knots, and I want continuous reports from the chief engineer and damage control." He gulped a hard knot down. "All stations muster, and I want a casualty report."

The bells rang and the turbines whined down even more. "Speed eight, sixty-two revs, sir. All stations are mustering, sir."

"The bugger's going in!" a gunner on the forecastle screamed. Brent turned just in time to see Fritschmann's Stuka pancake into the sea. It seemed to be in control. Then he saw a solitary figure clamber out of the cockpit.

Yoshi Matsuhara horsed the stick all the way back into the pit of his stomach and pushed the throttle ahead. Four Messerschmitts to the southwest, led by a blood-red aircraft. He could see them clearly in the one area where the sky was clear. Rosencrance. At last. He looked at his altimeter anxiously. Altitude. The lifeblood of the fighter pilot. A man could never have enough. The critical engine temperature was hovering around 278. Still below the red line. His rev counter indicated 2,900. He wanted to open the *Taifu* all the way, use all of the great engine's 3,200 horsepower and damn the temperature. But he would leave the Seafires behind and probably overheat. They must attack as a unit. He knew Rosencrance would attack with his *Schwarm* before breaking up into individual combat. That was his way.

He had used at least eight-seconds of firepower in shooting down the Heinkel and Horst Fritschmann's Stuka. He had twelve-seconds left, more than enough to kill the renegade American.

There was the hiss of a carrier wave in his earphones. It was the control officer on Iwo Jima. "Edo Leader, this is *Hitsuji-kai. Kumá* Flight and *Sumi Hitótsu* enroute Charlie Zero Eight."

Kumá (Bear) Flight, with Lieutenant Kunishi Kajikawa and two wingmen, and *Sumi Hitótsu* (Charcoal

One), with Captain John "Slugger" Fite's DD-1. He acknowledged and then looked around the sky. It was owned by the four Messerschmitts closing from the southwest and Edo Flight. But the storm was enlarging its claim, now occupying at least five-tenths to the east. He saw nothing of Kunishi Kajikawa's "three." However, there was a black speck on the sea, charging over the horizon far to the northwest. Must be DD-1.

For a moment, Yoshi felt the urge to duck into the protective yet dangerous stormclouds, a place where he could hide and gain altitude. But he would lose his wingmen and perhaps his wings in the thunderhead's ferocious down drafts. There was cirrus above. He would use it. He opened the fighter frequency. "Edo Flight, this is Edo Leader. We will climb through this cover and circle south and attack the enemy from above and out of the sun, if possible. First pass as a unit and then individual combat. *Banzai!*"

"Roger, Edo Leader."

"Roger, guv'nor. Let's chivvy the lot."

The fighter plunged into the clouds. Suddenly, Yoshi's windscreen was whipped with vapor and tiny ice crystals began to form. He checked his artificial horizon, kept his trim, but he was blind. The cloud layer was very dense and thicker than he had expected. His American thermometer showed an outside temperature of 60 below zero. Cold penetrated his flight suit and two sweaters and seeped around his silk scarf. His muscles began to stiffen. The small cabin heater warmed his right foot, but his left was growing numb. Tugging with his left hand, he tightened his scarf, pulling its edges above the collar of his flying suit. He wiggled his toes, cursed under his breath, and called on Susano, the storm god, to clear the sky of the clouds and ice. Susano was not listening.

"Susano!" Yoshi shouted in frustration. "Go back to Izanagi's nose where you were born!" There was a flash of lightning and rumble to the east. Susano was displeased.

*   *   *

Kenneth Rosencrance cursed when the Mitsubishi and the two Seafires vanished into the clouds. A glance at his fuel gauges gave him more displeasure. He would get one, maybe two cracks at that Nip bastard "*Yonaga's* Butcher," and then he would have to head for home. He smiled despite the coppery taste of raw oxygen that irritated his throat like the claws of a tiny rake. Maybe he would earn that million-dollar bonus today. But where were that fuckin' Jap and his English killers?

He opened his microphone. "Raka Flight, this is Raka Leader. The enemy is climbing through the cloud cover to the north and east. Let's go upstairs and kill the pricks. Remember, there's a million bucks riding on that Jap's yellow ass and a half-million each on the limeys. Hold the 'finger four' for the first pass and then individual combat—and keep an eye on your fuel gauges. Follow my lead."

"Roger, Raka Leader," his wingman Rudolph Stoltz said softly.

Then the leader of the second element, Hani Meri, acknowledged, followed by his wingman, Hamoud Rogba.

Something shot out of the cloud cover like an artillery shell, trailing vapor like a bride's veil. It was the crazy, souped-up Zero, no doubt about it. Red cowling, green hood, and white fuselage. And, anyway, nothing on earth could fly like that. Rosencrance cursed and hit the canopy with the back of his gloved hand. Then the two Seafires burst through the cover and streaked after the Zero. They were above him and circling high and to his rear. "Sons-of-bitches!" He hadn't expected that kind of climb from the Vickers-Supermarines, too.

"Turning to the right and climbing," Rosencrance shouted into the microphone. The American pushed his throttle forward into full military power, pulled the stick back brutally, and kicked rudder. Another worried glance at his fuel gauges. He would head for Saipan and gain altitude. If Matsuhara wanted to fight, he would have to fight further from his base and on Kenneth Rosencrance's terms.

Yoshi Matsuhara throttled back until the two Seafire fighters resumed their stations. But this slowing had given Rosencrance time to turn away and climb. He was headed away and for the Marianas. Either he was low on fuel or leading Edo Flight into a trap. But the sky was crystal clear to the southwest. He saw no ominous specks. Not yet, anyway, and his vision was good for at least 90 kilometers. He would carry out his attack.

Looking down over his starboard wing, he could see the enemy quite clearly, 500 meters below and perhaps four kilometers ahead and off to the right. "Edo Flight, we should get one good pass. I've got the leading element. Take the second element—Edo Two the leader, Edo Three the wingman," he said into the microphone.

"I say, old boy. Don't be a hog."

"Right-oh, guv'nor. Let me stick one up Rosie's kilt."

"Edo Flight, out!" Yoshi said sharply. The carrier wave clicked off and Yoshi concentrated on the target. A little right rudder, a push on the stick, and he brought the glowing reticle down to the leading element. His dive was too deep. Pulling back on the stick, he brought the "pip" in the center of the gunsight onto the blood-red Me 109. He ignored Rudolf Stoltz's "tiger shark" fighter. He had a good angle, eight o'clock from Rosencrance, and above. He wanted that first burst and then he would deal with both of them. He was suddenly very thirsty, his lips parched. Hunching forward, he dampened them with the tip of his tongue.

Kenneth Rosencrance turned his head to the left and looked back over his shoulder until his neck hurt. He had no choice. The enemy was above and behind and diving like skiers off a mountain. This fight would not be on his terms. When you cannot outdive the enemy or outrun him, you must turn and engage him head-on. That was the first rule of aerial combat.

Pulling the stick back, he kicked left rudder. The horizon spun to the right and dropped out of sight. Without looking, he knew his wingman was with him. The Zero was streaking down on him just like a demon out of the burning jaws of hell.

Yoshi muttered an oath. The enemy was turning toward their attackers just as good fighter pilots should. This would not be an easy kill. Rosencrance and his flight were too good to give up kills easily. And the modified Me 109 with its new powered-up Daimler-Benz *Valkyrie* was turning much sharper than Yoshi had ever seen it turn before. Must be a redesigned fighter with improved wing loading. The old 109s could never turn like this. But he should get a shot before Rosencrance could bring his guns to bear. The oblique angle of the target's wings reached the first sight bars. Allowing a deflective lead of half a length, Yoshi squeezed the button. At that exact instant, almost as if the American renegade could read his mind, Rosencrance kicked opposite rudder and rolled hard to his left and away from Yoshi's turn. Stoltz rolled with him.

The blast of the guns knocked the edge off the Zero's speed. Tracers whipped and snapped past and into the rolling Messerschmitt. He saw tiny flashes, and sparkling butterflies danced from his hits. But Rosencrance's hard roll took him out of Yoshi's turn and out of the gunsight. Yoshi saw his tracers streak off into thin air, but then into the "tiger shark" Messerschmitt, which had rolled from right to left with its leader passing directly into his sight. A hail of 7.7-millimeter slugs blew off the starboard auxiliary cooling intakes, ruptured the coolant header tank, and shot an exhaust manifold faring strip to pieces.

Immediately, the Daimler-Benz streaked a white mist of glycol and Stoltz lashed the wounded fighter into a steep dive, seeking the shelter of the clouds. He was obviously under control, but there was no time to finish off the effeminate killer. He wanted Rosencrance and he had missed him.

Cursing, Yoshi kicked rudder and reversed his turn. He sensed more than saw his wingmen firing.

Hani Meri wanted Yoshi Matsuhara almost as much as his *hajj* (pilgrimage to Mecca.) A million dollars American. Stamping left rudder hard and pushing the stick forward, he turned sharply toward the super-Mitsubishi A6M2 that was streaking after Rosencrance beneath him and ahead of him. He saw a Seafire streaking in from behind in his rearview mirror, but he was still at a long range. A familiar article of faith came to mind and he repeated it over and over. *La ilāha illa-l-Lāh* (no god but Allah). The supplication bolstered his confidence.

Matsuhara had damaged that woman-dog Stoltz and was now intent on killing Rosencrance. But the American flight leader had rolled his 109 into a sharp turn that had surprised even the nose-heavy Zero. There was a thumping behind Meri and several large shells smoked past. He shuddered and uttered more prayers to Allah. The Seafire had immense killing power, but he was still at least 600 meters behind. He jinked to the right and then back to the left. The firing stopped. The Englishman was wasting ammunition.

Where was his wingman, Hamoud Rogba? He was supposed to watch his tail. Give him a shot. Maybe the rumors were true and there was a Jew buried in the roots of Rogba's family and now the slimy-yellow Jewish heritage was showing through. The man was as useless as camel piss. Then he saw Rogba. Far to the west, fighting for his life with another Seafire. He was on his own.

Matsuhara was firing again, catching Rosencrance just

as the 109 pulled out of its turn and brought its guns to bear. The two converging fighters were tied together with ropes of tracers. A glance in his mirror. The Seafire had gained only slightly while he was curving into an ideal killing angle on the Zero. The new Daimler-Benz *Valkyrie* was equal to the Rolls Royce Griffon. He felt new confidence. "Allah akbar" (Allah is most great), he said to himself.

Matsuhara seemed so occupied with Rosencrance, he could not or would not split his concentration. This was foolish, and unexpected from a man who was supposed to be one of the greatest fighter pilots on earth. The Japanese did not see him. He was sure of that. A million dollars was in his grasp. An old fighter pilot aphorism flashed through Hani Meri's mind: "You are killed by the fighter that you do not see." "*Yonaga's* Butcher" did not see him.

He was closing in from the Zero's right and from behind with added speed from his dive. He would get one shot before the enemy's monstrous American engine pulled him out of range. The red, green, and white Mitsubishi at last bounced into his sight. He moved the pip a full length ahead of the Zero for deflection, muttering "*Muhammad rasulu-l-Lāh*" (Muhammad is the messenger of God). And then, squeezing the red button, "Hani Meri is the messenger of death, infidel dog!" His armament exploded to life, hurling a storm of tracers like a desert *khamsin* at the enemy. He saw flashes from hits on the Mitsubishi's cowling and hood and he shouted with joy.

At that moment there was a stuttering crackle like a row of toy balloons being burst and yellow lights streamed past his cockpit. The shout of joy became a gurgle, as if an executioner were tightening a garrote around his throat. He looked back over his shoulder just in time to see the second Seafire charging in from his right at four o'clock with Hamoud Rogba hard on its tail. Fear struck Meri like a death wish.

The Messerschmitt staggered from the great blows of exploding 20-millimeter shells. Hit after hit knocked it about the sky. Dust and fluff swirled up from the cockpit floor. Chunks of aluminum flew from the wings, and a cowling panel bounced off the windscreen and slashed off the top of the rudder. Oil and glycol streamed over the Perspex. The instrument panel dissolved, splattering Hani Meri with daggers of glass, wood splinters, and red hydraulic fluid. A spent splinter ricocheted around the cockpit and smashed his mouth, ripping off the front of his mask and taking part of his lower jaw with it. Blood, bone, and broken teeth sprayed, coating his goggles. The agony of torn lips and tongue was so great he almost passed out. Sickened, he choked on his blood, vomiting blood, broken teeth, and his breakfast down the front of his flight suit. He reached up with his right hand to wipe away the mess when another shell blew out the right side of the cockpit and chopped off the hand neatly as if he had been attacked by a madman with an ax. Arterial blood squirted.

The Arab screamed, spitting more blood and teeth. He felt an immense shock, as if Allah had turned the world upside down and inside-out. His right hand was bouncing about the cockpit, severed wrist spraying. He grabbed his wrist but the bleeding continued. Pain raged through his mouth, his arm, an inferno that flared bigger and hotter until his brain could no longer accept it. His vision fogged, his ears refused sound; the cockpit seemed to fall away beneath him as if he had staggered in a drunken stupor and toppled over a cliff. Weirdly, he was disembodied, his brain seemingly detached from the horror, incapable of comprehending the catastrophe that had ripped his body and saturated everything with his blood . . . all this in less than two seconds. One moment Hani Meri had been the charging, avenging warrior bent on collecting a million dollars, the next he was crippled, bleeding, trapped in the wreckage of his own cockpit.

His brain returned with Rogba's voice, "Meri, bail out!

Bail out!" The horizon was moving rapidly from left to right and there seemed to be no end to the rotation. But there were more explosions and the fighter snapped out of the spin as if it had a mind of its own, rolling, whipping over onto its back, seeming to perform an Immelmann turn of its own design, despite his frantic efforts with the controls. Again Rogba's voice—or was it his own brain?—screaming at him, "Meri, bail out! Bail out!"

Jamming the stick between his knees, he groped wildly for the ball-grip canopy release over his head. The severed hand bashed him in the face just as the front right side of the canopy burst into a thousand fragments. He howled with agony as a shell splinter chopped through his clavicle, broke two ribs, and ripped into his right lung, slicing and rending intercostal arteries and veins in its path.

"Allah! Allah!" His hand was pulling the canopy release when the killing shot struck. A shell exploded just behind the cockpit and a splinter the size of a butter knife and as sharp as a razor slashed into his neck, severing his spine between the second and third cervical vertebrae and ripping open a carotid artery and two jugular veins. With his arms and legs petrified wood and his blood jetting in gouts into the cockpit, Hani Meri soon faded into a red-black haze.

He was dead long before the fighter thrashed to pieces and tumbled into the sea in a rain of fragments.

Yoshi Matsuhara had no time to cheer. He had taken a half-dozen hits to the cowling, hood, and wing roots and the big engine was beginning to overheat. He was forced to throttle back. Elwyn York was in trouble, a white haze trailing his Seafire. Still, the courageous Cockney had managed to destroy the 109 that had had him in its sights. He would have been a dead man if it had not been for the Cockney.

"Turn right! Dive for the clouds, Edo Three!" Yoshi

shouted into his microphone.

"Right-oh, guv'nor. The old girl is gettin' hot as a whore in Soho. Takin' 'er 'ome. But what clouds, guv'nor?"

Yoshi looked down. The clear blue sea glared back like a tray of diamond chips on blue velvet. Like a miracle. The cirrus had vanished like ice cream forgotten in the sun, melted away in minutes. It seemed impossible, but any kind of quirky weather was possible in these latitudes. And the storm had retreated as if Susano had found revulsion in the way men would desecrate the pristine realm of the gods with their obscene machines and the slaughter of each other.

Yoshi watched York's Seafire roll into a graceful turn and head north. Then he looked around. Rosencrance was only a few kilometers to the south and curving back with a black Me 109 hard on his right elevator. Yoshi glanced at his instruments anxiously. The cylinder head temperature was pushing the red line at 280, oil temperature was 229, oil pressure was down to 52. He was losing oil and the engine was firing erratically. He had lost a cylinder or two, or the firing order had been interrupted. Easing the throttle back even more, he turned north. But he would never escape Rosencrance and his wingman.

Then he saw Willard-Smith, high above and diving on the two enemy fighters. Yoshi shouted into his microphone, "Edo Two. Break off. You cannot fight them both."

"Sorry, old boy. Can't hear you. My W-T is broken." Yoshi heard the Englishman chuckle and then the radio went dead.

Rosencrance and his wingman had no choice. They turned toward the diving British fighter. All three aircraft opened fire simultaneously. Willard-Smith concentrated on the blood-red machine. A head-on collision seemed inevitable. Maybe the Englishman wanted this.

The Zero backfired a ragged barrage, leaving a series of black puffs, and the controls became mushy, rudder heavy. Without taking his eyes from the racing fighters, Yoshi feathered the prop slightly, thinned the mixture, and cranked his trim wheel. The backfiring stopped and the controls improved, but there was still a fearsome vibration from the irregular engine beat.

The Japanese pilot stared in wonder as the three charging firing aircraft seemed to blend into a small piece of sky that could not possibly hold all three. At the last instant, Rosencrance banked 60 degrees to his right and Willard-Smith banked the same angle to his right, both without changing course. Yoshi could visualize both men throwing their sticks to the side while just balancing with rudder, maintaining course like arrows and passing each other obliquely at a combined speed of at least a thousand knots. The Englishman shot between Rosencrance and his wingman like a stunt pilot at an airshow. None of the aircraft seemed damaged by the exchange. "Impossible," Yoshi said to himself.

The Seafire curved to the southwest and clawed for altitude. "No! No!" Yoshi shouted. Willard-Smith was deliberately drawing the enemy away from Yoshi's damaged Zero. The 109s banked brutally and raced after the Seafire. The Englishman rolled into a split S and swooped in from the side with so much speed, the climbing Messerschmitts were caught before they could bring their guns to bear.

Rosencrance whipped into a turn away, exposing his wingman. Flame leaped from the wings of the British plane and the black Messerschmitt staggered when at least two shells blew huge chunks from its fuselage and tail. The first shell blew off the aerial mast, D/F loop along with chunks of skin plating sections, exposing frames and U-stringers. The second shell blew off most of the tail structure—the right fixed tailplane, the right elevator, and most of the wooden rudder. Twisting in agony like a demented moth that had flown too close to a flame, the black fighter began a wild, uncontrolled tumble toward the sea, aerial whipping behind it. Then a parachute blossomed above it. *"Banzai! Banzai!"*

In a second, Yoshi's elation turned to horror. The sacrifice of his wingman had given Rosencrance a clear shot. Before the Seafire could complete a quick turn toward the Messerschmitt, Rosencrance had Willard-Smith in his sights. The cannons and machine guns leaped to life with flickering motes of flame. The Seafire staggered, dropped off belching black smoke. Yoshi screamed an oath, pounded the crash pad. Long tongues of flame suddenly fired out of the ejector exhausts and then more flames as big as bed sheets enveloped the front half of the fuselage.

"Bail out! Bail out!"

The Seafire rolled onto its back and a figure plummeted from the cockpit. It tumbled for a few seconds and then a parachute popped open. Slowly, Captain Colin Willard-Smith began to oscillate toward the sea.

Yoshi looked at the sky. "Thank you, *Amaterasu*," he said reverently.

Then a familiar voice in his earphones brought him another start of joy. It was Lieutenant Kunishi Kajikawa. "Edo Leader, this Kumá Leader. Have you in sight, to your northeast and low."

Yoshi peered to the northeast and caught the specks at a range of at least 60 kilometers. "Kumá Leader. Take the red Messerschmitt."

"My pleasure, Edo Leader."

Yoshi lowered his left wing, which was blocking his view of the descending Willard-Smith. Rosencrance had mysteriously vanished. Impossible! Then he saw the white canopy far below and to the south with the red Messerschmitt making a wide turn toward it. Willard-Smith had his pistol out and was pointing it at the approaching fighter.

"No!" Yoshi shouted. Never had he felt so helpless, so

futile and frustrated. Rosencrance was going to machine-gun his helpless friend and there was nothing Yoshi could do about it. His damaged fighter was barely capable of remaining airborne, let alone fight. And Lieutenant Kunishi Kajikawa's "three" was too distant to intercept.

Sobbing, Yoshi watched flame leap from the nose of the Me 109. Willard-Smith's body leaped and jerked like a puppet. The big slugs ripped open his abdomen and Yoshi actually saw the Englishman's intestines stream toward the sea like a bundle of writhing snakes.

Tears pooled in the bottom of Yoshi's goggles and he pulled them up over his forehead. His sobs were uncontrolled. He waved a fist at the fleeing Messerschmitt. "American swine. On the gods and on my name and on my martyred family, I swear the vengeance of the samurai." He punched the canopy so hard it rattled. "With my bare hands, I will kill you."

Rosencrance was now only a speck on the horizon. Kajikawa would never catch him. Instead, the three white Mitsubishis fell in behind and above the damaged Zero. Yoshi set a course for Iwo Jima.

"Thirty-two dead, forty-seven wounded, sir," the voice from the tube said with a slight tremor.

Lieutenant Commander Brent Ross acknowledged with a "Very well" that masked the horror that gripped him. More than a third of the crew was dead or wounded.

He watched as four deckhands carried the bodies of Leading Signalman George Peterson and Talker Randall Turner off the bridge and to the damaged quarterdeck, where canvas covered rows of bodies were already stretched. The usual thoughts that pass through all men's minds after they survive combat gripped Brent's: *It's over and I'm alive* flashed like a persistent neon sign on Times Square.

A cough turned his head. Lieutenant Sinclair Ingilly stood staring silently off to the east. The man's shoulders were hunched, and he seemed to be breathing in short gasps. Brent remained silent. He could not bear the thought of even talking to the cowardly swine. Instead he ran his eyes over the ship for the hundredth time since he had called out, "Cease fire!"

Haida was badly hit but seaworthy. All able-bodied hands not tending to the wounded or assigned to defense stations had been turned out for damage control. "A" mount and "X" mount had been destroyed along with four 40-millimeter mounts and 7 Oerlikons. The radios and radar were out, although members of the communications department were hard at work on the damaged equipment. The two holes above the waterline on the port side and Bulkhead Three had been shored and caulked, and the bilge pumps were keeping up with the leaks in the sprung plates. The two holes in the hull had been shored with mattresses and planking and did not represent a mortal threat to the ship unless they ran into heavy weather. The water had been pumped out of Auxiliary Engine Room One, but the engine was a total loss. The saltwater leak into the freshwater lines had been found and stopped. But the cost had been horrendous: the dead, the wounded, the terrible damage to the ship.

DD-1 had passed them at high speed, headed for the area of the sinking of the *Gearing*. Fite had signaled as the sleek *Fletcher* passed, asking if *Haida* required assistance. Brent had Yeoman of Signals Robert McVey flash back with the one signal light left undamaged, "Can proceed under my own power at eight knots. Damage to hull, numerous casualties, pumps controlling flooding."

"Will escort you after I take care of a little business to the south," Fite signaled back.

Brent assumed Captain John "Slugger" Fite would kill the survivors of *Abu Bakr* and look for downed pilots. The Zeros and Seafires were equipped with life rafts, and it was possible survivors could be floating. A buzz low in the sky and to the west turned his head. A twin-engined

95

gull-winged flying boat. A Martin Mariner headed for the combat area. No doubt it would look for survivors, too. The sea was calm and it could land and take off.

His best friend, Yoshi Matsuhara, was alive. For this he could give thanks. He had seen the air group leader's smoking fighter headed north, escorted by three Zeros. But one Seafire had been damaged and the other destroyed. Either Willard-Smith or York was dead. Maybe Rosencrance was dead, too. He had seen two Me 109s crash and a third limp off. But the air battle had been so distant and he had been so busy with *Haida's* damage, he had not been able to pick out the colors or even watch very closely.

He yearned for *Yonaga*, Admiral Hiroshi Fujita, the security of the great carrier, and his comrades of eight years who waited for him. And he needed the docks and repair shops and the skilled workmen of Yokosuka to repair the grievous damage to *Haida*. He felt like a little boy who had been pummeled in a street fight and needed the succor of his mother. He smiled at the thought. But for the moment, *Haida* was his ship and he had to "mother" her back to safety. There was no disputing that. He was the senior surviving officer. Commander Clive Coglan was still alive but unconscious. Brent had fought the ship and now he would take her home.

Brent was surprised by Ingilly's voice: "I say."

"You say what?"

"I say, old chap, you've done a bully job of it. Absolutely smashing," the navigator said, smiling, face calm, composed, and friendly. "I'll put you up for a decoration myself. You've been a great help. Couldn't have done it without you, old boy." He extended his hand.

Brent could only stare back in disbelief, rigid and mute as a statue.

Chapter Three

At 8 knots, it took the damaged *Haida* over eight days to return to Tokyo Bay. During the run, DD-1 steamed 500 yards ahead, zigzagging because of the threat of Arab *Whiskies* (old Russian-built diesel-powered submarines) that might be stalking them. On the second day, while still over 1,100 miles from their destination, they were joined by DD-2 and DD-5, both destroyers of the *Fletcher* class, as were all of Captain Fite's escort command.

The two newcomers took stations 600 yards off *Haida*'s bows while Fite's DD-1 continued to steam directly ahead of the wounded British destroyer. To Brent, the protecting destroyers appeared beautiful with the graceful sweep of their flush decks, the low flow of the superstructure that seemed to blend with perfect symmetry into the line of the twin stacks and the ten torpedo tubes abaft the stacks, the five gunhouses placed in perfect harmony with the entire silhouette. Crowning each ship was a huge array of radar and electronics gear supported by a sturdy tripod mast that jutted upward between the superstructure and the first funnel. A small forest of 20-millimeter and 40-millimeter AA guns were mounted on every weather deck and on the superstructure. Capable of 37 knots, ton-for-ton these magnificent ships were probably the most lethal killing machines afloat.

From the beginning of the run Japanese aircraft patrolled overhead, further discouraging enemy submarines. In the main, the aerial search was maintained by Martin PBM Mariners and Consolidated PBY Catalina flying boats. But an occasional Douglas DC-3, DC-6, or Lockheed Super Constellation took on the duties. If there were any enemy submarines in the vicinity, the constant patrol on the sea and in the air kept them at bay.

Occasionally Zeros and Vought F4U Corsairs and Grumman F6F Hellcats swept over. They flashed by the patrol bombers like greyhounds passing elephants. Each "vic" of three fighters brought Brent's glasses to his eyes to search for Yoshi Matsuhara, but he experienced nothing but disappointment. The super-Zero was not to be seen, and neither were the Seafires. The disappointment added to the usual post-battle lethargy that affects all survivors of combat. He had known it before, expected it to strike him, fought it but was still victim to it. At times, fatigue combined with this state of drained emotions to drive him to the edge of malaise.

The hideous damage to *Haida* seemed to overwhelm him. And on the very first day, despite being hosed down repeatedly, the bridge began to stink of death. Blood and bits of gore had seeped and been blown into every crack and seam and the sun went to work on it immediately. The stench coated a man's mouth, his nostrils, and his throat and revolted his stomach.

Two of the wounded died almost immediately and the day after the battle Brent conducted services for thirty-four dead on what was left of the quarterdeck. Twenty-seven off-duty men stood in ranks around the rows of canvas-wrapped bodies. Brent started with the Twenty-Third Psalm, which he loved and had used for the dead of submarine *Blackfin* and for his lifelong friend Admiral Mark Allen: *"The Lord is my shepherd, I shall not want. In pastures of tender grass hath thou laid me down . . ."* Then he read Romans 8:36-39, which was befitting a funeral of warriors: *"As it is written, For thy sake we are killed all the day long; we are accounted as sheep for the slaughter . . . Nor height, nor depth, nor any other creature shall be able to separate us from the love of God, which is in Christ Jesus our Lord."* He closed with Psalm 107, verses 23 to 25, which were expected by all hands: *"They who go down to the sea in ships, who do business on great waters. These have seen the works of the Lord, and his wonders on the deep. For he spoke, and he raised the stormy wind, which lifteth up its waves."*

Brent closed his Bible with a snap, as if marking the mortal finality of the moment, unsheathed the Konoye blade, and pointed it at the sky. Lieutenant Anthony Stonebreaker nodded at a squad of seamen who had raised the ship's twelve old Lee-Enfield rifles and pointed them at the heavens. They fired three volleys and the canvas-wrapped bodies, weighed with 4.7-inch shells, were dropped over the side.

Even after Lieutenant Stonebreaker had shouted, "Dismissed," the men stood about, muttering to each other in soft voices and staring back at the wake. Brent sheathed his sword and walked back to the bridge. Only then did the men melt slowly away.

Brent was on the damaged bridge almost constantly. The binnacle could not be repaired, but the gyro compass and the bridge repeater functioned. Both signaling searchlights worked, and the chart table was rebuilt. Damage control did a miraculous job shoring the bent hull plates, stopping most of the leaks. However, the chief engineer, Lieutenant Leslie Townsend, suggested speed be maintained at 8 knots. The damage to the radios and radar was more extensive than at first believed, technicians working furiously around the clock trying to bring the equipment back on line. But even spare parts had been destroyed, and Brent despaired of ever having his "eyes" and "ears" restored.

Commander Clive Coglan refused to die. Despite his concussion, three broken ribs, severe lacerations of the chest and right arm, and suspected internal injuries, treatment by the ship's doctor and Sick Bay Attendants seemed to be working. Plasma was administered continuously, but without an operating room and the personnel, the extent of the internal injuries could not be determined. "Don't you bother your head about me, old boy," the commander had said to Brent on one of his visits to the mess hall which was serving as an emergency sick bay. "Just get this old baggage back to port and into dry dock. There's plenty of fight in the old girl yet, by Jove—mark me."

Brent smiled and gripped his captain's hand and mimicked in his best stiff upper lip, "Upon my word, a man's got to be off his wick to bet against the likes of this old girl, sir."

Both men laughed, Brent for the first time in a week, Coglan with a hint of pain. "Carry on, Commander," Coglan managed, running a hand over his heavily bandaged chest.

"Straight away, sir." Brent left.

Lieutenant Sinclair Ingilly was an enigma. His decorum and control returned immediately after the guns stopped pounding. In fact, during the first afternoon, he managed an accurate estimated position by shooting sun lines and "running them up" and cutting them in on plotting sheets. And this was done in the wreckage of the chart house. He shouted the latitude and longitude up the voice tube from the pilothouse and requested that he be allowed to come onto the bridge—Brent had banished him immediately after the battle. Brent's first impulse was to refuse him. However, after having Yeoman of Signals Robert McVey verify the position with DD-1, Brent found Ingilly's calculations amazingly accurate. Short handed to the point of desperation, Brent allowed the navigator to return to the bridge. Anyway, here he could keep a wary eye on the pilot until he could settle with him on *Yonaga*. Ingilly was not allowed to stand deck watches.

The days passed uneventfully. Luckily, the weather held and the ships wallowed through a relatively calm sea. Sublieutenant August Braithwaite, Lieutenant Leslie Townsend, and Brent Ross stood the OD (Officer of the Deck)watches. Lieutenant Sinclair Ingilly seemed content with his navigator's duty, never questioning his removal from the watch bill. The officers and men regarded Ingilly with a strange kind of silent questioning. Brent could read it in their eyes. Then he realized with a shock that he was the only man alive who had witnessed Ingilly's breakdown into cowardly madness. Ballew, Stanger, Turner, and Peterson were all dead, and Commander Coglan had been hit before the pilot broke down. This might complicate things, because Brent planned on pressing for a court-martial and removal of Ingilly. He was a menace, a mortal danger to the ship, and his conduct must not go unpunished, or, perhaps, untreated in an institution.

The morning of the eighth day was brilliant, with only a few scattered clouds tossed casually about the sky like puff pastries. The first landfall was made on the island of Mikura Jima to port and then in rapid succession in line like a signpost pointed at Tokyo Bay: Miyake Jima, Nii Shima, To Shima, and O Shima. These low lush islands were familiar landmarks to Brent.

He stared through his binoculars. Memories of the many times he had entered Tokyo Bay on board *Yonaga* flooded back, more times than not with battle damage. His friends were only a few hours away now. He was worried, feared for the worst. Not once during the voyage home had he seen a sign of the Super-Zero or the Seafires. Maybe they were all dead. It seemed impossible. Other men died, but not Commander Yoshi Matsuhara. He seemed immortal. And the Englishmen, too. He pounded the windscreen and tried to distract himself by staring at the entrance to the bay looming before him.

Just as the force entered the Uraga Suido, the narrows flanked by Izu Hanto Peninsula to the west and the Boso Hanto Peninsula to the east, the escorts changed formation. There was a flurry of flashing lights from

DD-1 and a whipping of flags and pennants from the halyards of all three escorts. Then, slowly, DD-2 and DD-5 fell astern of *Haida* while DD-1 remained in the lead.

"Sea buoy bearing green twenty, range two-thousand," the starboard lookout shouted.

"Very well."

"I suggest course zero-two-seven, sir," Ingilly said in a businesslike voice, staring through the gunsight of the bearing repeater.

"Very well," Brent said. He knew the course was correct because he had steamed the entrance to Tokyo Bay so many times the courses and course changes almost came automatically. He gave the order to the helmsman.

Still at 8 knots, *Haida* crept through the narrowest part of the channel, where forests crowded down almost to the shore. The sun now quartered the sky to the west, its slanting beams bathing the stands of pine, fir, beech, ash, and oak in cloaks of infinite colors of green while igniting the treetops with gold and silver fire. Only a few houses were visible, low wooden structures with thatch roofs that would do little damage to their occupants if an earthquake knocked them down. Brent knew there were many more, but they were hidden by the trees, placed in the Japanese tradition in harmony with the natural beauty abounding all around.

Usually, these sights raised Brent's spirits, brought joy and nostalgic memories. But not today. He saw no beauty. *Haida* was a ship of death, a floating wreck that had buried thirty-four of her dead and stank of corruption. *A death ship,* Brent said to himself.

Within an hour, they had cleared Uraga Point and Yokosuka was visible broad on the port beam. The two lookouts, Brent and Ingilly, raised their binoculars. Brent focused the magnificent lenses to glaring precision and clarity. The pristine naturalness of the Uraga Suido had vanished. Clearly visible sprawling along the northwestern coastline was Yokohama, Japan's greatest seaport. Kawasaki could be glimpsed further to the north, but the obscene urban sprawl of Tokyo was still invisible over the far horizon.

Over 25 million people live in the Tokyo-Kawasaki-Yokohama conurbation, an area of less than a thousand square miles. In one 160-degree sweep Brent's glasses took in Japan's greatest population center and its industrial zone, its seat of government, and the hub of its largest cluster of universities. Acres of manufacturing plants producing petrochemicals, automobiles, robotics, electronics, precision instruments, and textiles passed through his lenses. The entire area appeared to Brent as blighted instead of developed, typical of the unchecked population growth and industrial cancers that had spread over the entire world and seemed to be consuming the earth like a foul disease.

Brent chuckled to himself sardonically. Automobiles. With the Arab oil embargo and complete dependency on an oil-short United States, the Japanese were hard put to keep their cars rolling. However, despite the gasoline shortage, a foul brown shroud of filthy air hung over the northern horizon.

In the far distance, like a defiant sentinel, the snow-capped peak of Mount Fujiyama wore a circular ring of clouds like a halo. Rearing its head more than 12,000 feet above the Kanto Plain, it soared haughtily above the filth as if to remind the onlooker that purity, dignity, and tradition still existed above the hedonistic chaos below.

Brent lowered his glasses and nodded, remembering a phrase he had heard Yoshi Matsuhara use: *"And the gods look down, sicken, and turn away."*

Brent was brought back to reality by the voice of a lookout. "Escort turning, sir."

Brent watched DD-1 make her turn to port. He leaned over the voice tubes as Ingilly took a sighting and muttered a course. Brent gave the order, "Port ten!"

"Ten of port wheel on, sir."

The young American waited while the rudder gave the ship its head and then, "Midships!"

103

"Wheel's amidships."

"Meet her. Steady up on two-eight-one."

"Meeting her. Steady up on two-eight-one, sir." And then, in a moment, "Steady on two-eight-one, sir."

"Very well."

Now the great naval base was directly ahead of the ship's prow. Glassing the yards, Brent saw an irregular forest of masts, cranes, and antennas. Most prominent were the upper works of the behemoth *Yonaga*. Rising majestically, her vast superstructure towered above the masts, warehouses, cranes, and shops like Fujisan above the Kanto Plain. Slowly, the damaged destroyer approached the naval base. Only a few small boats were in the water and none were close. Apparently, *Haida*'s ETA (estimated time of arrival) had been kept a complete secret. Brent was thankful. It could be bracing to feel the enthusiasm of the welcoming crowds, but all too often Japanese Red Army thugs would circle returning warships with taunts and obscenities shouted through loud hailers and scrawled across crude signs. Today Brent felt he would machine-gun any such vessel and damn the consequences.

Now they were so close to the yards Brent could make out four moored destroyers, carrier *Bennington*, and perhaps a dozen supply ships, tugs, and auxiliary vessels. DD-1 already had her lines over at the far end, warping in to the dock just astern of *Bennington*. The decks of every ship were lined with figures dressed in blue. He shouted down a voice tube, "Quartermaster, steady on the center of the channel, speed four."

The command was repeated and the voice of a stoker came back, "Speed four, thirty-six revs, sir."

"Very well." He eyed the blue-clad men lining the rails of the ships. They were at quarters. He shouted down the voice tubes, "Man harbor stations. Pass the word. All off-duty hands, stand to quarters!" He was about to specify dress blues (Class One) when he realized many of the crew's lockers had been destroyed and it would be impossible to present a uniformly dressed crew. He said into the tubes, "Uniform of the day is overalls and 'stoke hole' boots or whatever work clothes each man is wearing."

There were shouts as crewmen rushed to comply. Men, mostly in blue overalls and boots worn without laces so that they could be kicked off before jumping into the sea, began to man the rails. Brent turned to Yeoman of Signals Robert McVey. "Send the following signal to *Yonaga:* 'To Comyonaga. Request berthing instruction. I have forty-five wounded. Request ambulances at my berth. Ship severely damaged below waterline. Request immediate dry dock availability.'"

There was a clatter of the shutters as McVey sent the message. "Sent and receipted for," he said to Brent. And then McVey said to one of the lookouts, "Stand by to write." Both the signalman and Brent stared at a blinking searchlight high on the great carrier's signal bridge. Brent, who could read flashing light at maximum speed, which was about 15 words a minute for the very best, said nothing as the yeoman of signals slowly pronounced each word of the message and flashed for each group, "Proceed to Berth B-4. Ambulances and auxiliary pumps will be dockside. Drydock 2 will be available in 18 hours. Commanding officer report immediately to Comyonaga. Well done. Well done."

Brent shouted down the tube, "Stand by to moor starboard side to." Immediately, the mooring detail moved to the starboard side. Four men stood next to coiled lines, clutching "monkey's fists."

As the battered destroyer entered the narrow channel, men lining the rails of ships to both sides waved their hats and shouted "*Banzai! Banzai!*"

Brent felt sudden difficulty in swallowing. It was always moving to gain the respect of your comrades. But his mind was with the thirty-four men back on the bottom of the cold Pacific, 6,000 fathoms deep. Had it been worth it?

105

Chapter Four

Dressed in his Number One dress blues and with the Konoye blade at his side, Brent disembarked from *Haida*. The dock was a madhouse, enlisted men frantically connecting pumps, power, water, and sewer lines to the destroyer, trucks unloading dock workmen with their equipment. Everywhere men stood in groups, pointing at the blackened, blasted warship in awe and speaking in hushed tones. A long line of ambulances waited while the forty-five wounded men were carried down two specially rigged gangways and loaded. They would not be taken to a hospital ashore. Instead, they were destined for *Yonaga's* sick bay, which was one of the best equipped hospitals in the world. Also, Brent was convinced that Chief Hospital Orderly Eiichi Horikoshi was one of the best physicians and surgeons in the profession. The old doctor had pulled the young American through serious knife and gunshot wounds. Most of his staff was young, highly professional, and competent. The Arab wars had kept them very busy over the past eight years. They had treated every kind of wound from shrapnel and bullet wounds to severe burns.

Almost at the end of the accommodation ladder, Brent caught sight of Yoshi Matsuhara and the Cockney, Pilot Officer Elwyn York. Brent's joy was immediately tempered by the expression on both men's faces. Captain Colin Willard-Smith was not with them. He was dead.

Brent was certain of that.

When Brent stepped from the ladder, the trio exchanged salutes; Brent and Yoshi bowed. Then convention, rank, protocol be damned, Brent wrapped his arms around the fighter pilot while York pounded Brent's back. "Thank Amaterasu you're safe, Brent-san," Matsuhara said, stepping back.

"You're appearin' bloody fit, sir," the Cockney said, standing at a shabby semblance of attention. "I would'a bet a twopenny shit agin' a good bullockin' from a Soho 'ore you 'ad copped a ticket to blighty." He waved airily at the twisted wreckage of *Haida's* upper works.

Brent expected little military discipline from the Englishman and cared nothing about what onlookers might think. The man was one of the finest fighter pilots in *Yonaga's* air groups, had saved Yoshi's life on numerous occasions, and certainly helped save *Haida* when he attacked the bombers. What tighter bonds could hold men together?

Brent jerked a thumb over his shoulder at the destroyer. "I was lucky. We took a lot of casualties." The two flyers stared at him silently, eyes unusually bright and wide. The line of Brent's jaw altered and he popped his lips before continuing, "You saved our butts, Yoshi-san."

The pilot shrugged and remained silent. Over the years, Brent had seen Yoshi Matsuhara's air groups take frightful casualties. Although Brent knew that his friend died with each man, Yoshi always took his casualties with the stoic, implacable exterior of the case-hardened samurai. But not today. Brent could read an ineffable grief in his eyes. And the flip cockiness was missing from York's demeanor. "You lost Willard-Smith," Brent added simply.

Yoshi's jaw worked, his eyes glared in a frightening way. "Rosencrance murdered him in his parachute."

"Oh, Christ—Christ."

"Gutted him with twelve-point-seven ball. Butchered him like an animal."

"Damn! I should've killed him two years ago when I had the chance."

Yoshi shook his head. "There are regrets only in the past, Brent-san. Look to the future and you will find none." A slight smile flowed down from the incipient wrinkles crinkling the corners of Yoshi's eyes. "I will kill him—personally. Find my revenge of the Forty-Seven *Ronin*." Yoshi's reference to the tale of classic Japanese vengeance brought a knowing smile from Brent and a perplexed look from York.

"Sorry, guv'nor. Bugger the *Ronin*. The sod'll be boffed by one fuckin' Cockney." Brent and Yoshi exchanged a smile and then chuckled with the Cockney.

Quickly Yoshi's serious demeanor returned and he pointed at Dock B-2 where the gray hulk of *Yonaga* was moored. "Admiral Fujita is waiting for your report."

"I know. I got the order by flashing light."

The Japanese began to wave at a staff car. "No!" Brent said. "Let's walk. I need to feel something solid under my feet."

The two pilots nodded understanding and side-by-side the three officers walked toward the waiting giant.

Admiral Fujita's cabin was spacious by warship standards. Located in the center of the flag bridge, it contained a large solid oak desk, five plump leather chairs facing it, two bookcases securely bolted to the bulkhead behind the desk, and a small table with two telephones in a corner for a communications man. The deck was thickly carpeted and the bulkheads were pierced with two portholes. Charts of the Pacific Ocean, the Marianas Islands, and the Japanese Islands were attached to the bulkheads on both sides of the bookcases. An equestrian picture of the late Emperor Hirohito in uniform hung next to the room's single door while a picture of Emperor

Akihito in mufti adorned the bulkhead on the other side of the doorway. A small wooden paulownia shrine hung from a prominent place next to Hirohito's photograph. It contained both Buddhist and Shinto icons. Overhead, four shielded lights glowed among the usual jumble of conduits and cables. The soft hum of a blower could be heard.

When Brent first entered the room, Admiral Hiroshi Fujita was seated behind the desk. The huge desk, glowering arrogantly with layers of polish and wax from generations of busy hands, should have dominated the room. But as usual, the small withered figure seated behind it captured Brent's attention instantly. The tiny man's stature belied the power of his persona. It was a singular presence unlike any Brent had ever experienced before or would come to know in the remainder of his life. It not only riveted his attention, but seemed to capture his mind, his psyche, with the empyreal aura the old man wore like a cloak. The power was concentrated in his piercing black eyes—eyes of a magus that seemed to penetrate with laser-like power, reading a man's thoughts like a speed reader flipping through the pages of a child's storybook. This arcane force ensnared everyone in its presence, commanding respect, and at times of extreme stress and danger, servile obeisance. Men would rush to their deaths for the old admiral. And, indeed, hundreds had already made that journey.

Brent had felt it over the years, expected it, on occasion even fought it, but had never been able to escape it. Sometimes, a man felt like a fish caught in the enveloping nets of a purse seiner which dragged him from his own personal depths to places to which he did not wish to go. But none could argue with the genius, the master military stategist and tactician who time and again had anticipated his enemy's moves and struck with speed and daring to destroy him.

Over a hundred years old, Fujita had withered as every old man does, now appearing much like an icon that belonged in its own shrine. Less than five feet tall and weighing perhaps ninety-five pounds, the old sailor had a face that was seamed and wrinkled like barren slopes in a desert ravaged by millennia of flash floods. He was nearly bald, his shiny pate crowned by wisps of white hair. His sagging flesh was not yellow. Instead, an amber white tinted his cheeks, as if he had been standing in an Arctic gale for most of his life. And, in fact, he had been locked into the frozen wastes of Siberia's Chukchi Peninsula from 1941 to 1983. At times, when the old man sat still, deep in thought, eyes focused straight ahead and unblinking, he reminded Brent of Egyptian mummies he had seen in New York's Metropolitan Museum.

The man was more than a legend; he was a fable that lived and breathed. And he was living history, too, a bridge to the past. He had been a classmate of Isoroku Yamamoto's at Eta Jima, Japan's Annapolis, and fought the Russians at Tsushima in 1905. Both men saw service in the Pacific during the Great War. After that, Fujita enrolled in graduate English courses at the University of Southern California, while Yamamoto attended classes at Harvard. Both men were impressed by the awesome industrial power of the United States. This respect would cause them grave problems later in their careers.

Posted as a military attaché after his graduation, Fujita attended all important naval conferences that followed the Great War and served in embassies in the United States and Europe. He met Winston Churchill, who had served as First Lord of the Admiralty in 1914. On several occasions, he had long personal conversations with Franklin Delano Roosevelt—a rare politician he liked and respected because of the man's strong belief in the importance of naval power—and had become well acquainted with Adolph Hitler, Hermann Goering, Benito Mussolini, and a host of their underlings. He renewed his friendship with Churchill, met Neville Chamberlain, whom he considered a spineless coward, and established a friendship with Viscount Alanbrooke,

110

who would become Chief of the Imperial General Staff when Fujita had to fight them. He had known them all, had learned their strengths and their weaknesses.

But above all there was his love for Japan, for his Emperor, for the code of *bushido* and the Imperial Navy. It was Hiroshi Fujita who'd convinced Isoroku Yamamoto of the coming importance of air power. Fujita and Yamamoto were the driving force in the development of the great carrier strike forces. Fujita and Japan's most talented naval architect, Vice Admiral Keiji Fukuda, designed the first two great carriers, *Kaga* and *Akagi*— *Kaga* a converted battleship of the *Tosa* class, *Akagi* an incomplete battle cruiser. A decade later, they would design *Yonaga*.

Climbing the ranks swiftly, Yamamoto and Fujita spent nearly two decades fighting the army and the navy's "big-gun admirals" for funds for more aircraft and their carriers. The two developed the techniques of torpedo and dive bombing, honing the finest naval air striking force in the world. Then, with strong objections, Yamamoto, who had become Commander-in-Chief of the Combined Fleet, ordered Fujita to plan an attack on the American base at Pearl Harbor. Fujita, too, objected, feeling a war with "the sleeping giant" was unwinnable. But the orders came down again and again, along with veiled threats, and as military men and to protect their families, Fujita and Yamamoto had no choice. Fujita, Commander Minoru Genda, and Commander Kameto Kuroshima formulated the plan—Plan Z, to the Naval General Staff. Then came *Yonaga*, the entrapment in Sano Wan, the breakout, the attack on Pearl Harbor, the return to Japan, and the Arab wars.

The astonishing eyes were focused on Brent's face. There was a rare softness there as if the old man were looking straight through him and into the past, seeing another time and another place. And, indeed, Yoshi Matsuhara had many times told Brent of Admiral Fujita's family, his wife Akiko and sons Kazuo and Makoto. They

111

had all been vaporized at Hiroshima. Kazuo had been a giant for a Japanese. Yoshi was convinced Brent reminded Fujita of the immolated Kazuo, and in a very real way, Brent had achieved all the greatness and glory the old admiral had dreamed for in both his boys.

Brent bowed. The old man nodded tersely and waved Brent to a chair and said, "You have seen the seven rings of hell, Brent-san."

Brent was not surprised by the oblique reference to *Haida's* ordeal. Instead, he had become accustomed to the oriental's fondness for circuitous allusions. He picked up the thread and wove his own fabric, showing his profound knowledge of Buddhism. "Yes, Admiral. Revival and reanimation of the damned by the terrible winds, the Black String where they are cut to pieces, concussion, weeping, great weeping, heating and heat beyond endurance."

The old parchment cracked and the deep lines framed what Brent interpreted as a smile. Then the cracks rearranged themselves into their usual inscrutable pattern and the ancient mariner tugged meditatively on a single white hair dangling from his chin. "*Haida* found them all, Brent-san."

"*Haida* was lured through all seven, sir."

"Lured?"

"Yes, sir." He described the slow speed of the target, weak radar, and lack of IFF, all of which indicated a merchantman or possibly a cruising *Whiskey* that had worked to bring the British destroyer within gun range.

The old man hunched forward, scanning the young man's face intently as if he was searching for facts not yet disclosed, words not yet said. He probed, "The captain, Commander Coglan, then, was indiscreet, could have improved his judgment."

"Not in my opinion, sir."

"No?" Fujita arched the few white hairs that defined the remnants of an eyebrow.

"No, Admiral. I was on the bridge. I would have

112

reacted in the same way. The target warranted an investigation. It could have been a steamer carrying contraband or a *Whiskey* charging its batteries." He turned both hands up in a gesture of futility. "He followed your orders, sir. Patrolled his station diligently. The ruse was clever. I believe he did the right thing—the military thing." The old man nodded while tendril-like fingers tugged on his chin, but Brent was not sure he was convinced. He read doubt on the old face.

Brent gestured at the desk top where a leatherbound copy of the *Hagakure* (*Under the Leaves*, the handbook of the samurai) rested near Fujita's right hand. He quoted it, "'Above all, the Way of the Samurai should be in being aware that you do not know what is going to happen next, and in querying every item day and night.'"

The old man chuckled. "You have been studying, Brent-san—throw *bushido* in my face."

"You gave me my copy and gave me the order to study."

"Sometimes, you are more Japanese than American."

Brent nodded at what was intended as a compliment while Fujita continued in a serious mien. "Commander Coglan was severely wounded. At this moment Chief Hospital Orderly Eiichi Horikoshi is operating on him. One of his lungs was punctured by broken ribs, and he has some abdominal bleeding. He may pass through the gates of the Yasakuni Shrine before his day is out." A thumb and forefinger grasped the lobe of an ear like a small raisin and tugged thoughtfully. "You were second-in-command. You must have fought the ship."

"I commanded her for part of the battle, sir, and the return voyage."

"You sank *Abu Bakr*. Fought off bombers. An extraordinary achievement, Brent-san."

"Thank you, sir. But I had no extraordinary crew, and Commander Matsuhara and the Englishmen attacked the bombers. I would not be here if they had not intervened."

113

"We lost Captain Willard-Smith."

Brent nodded. "A terrible loss of a good man."

The old man sighed. "We have lost so many good men these last eight years, Brent-san." Then, suddenly, his mood changed with its usual mercurial swiftness and he was all business. "Commander, your report."

Without missing a detail, Brent described the engagement, the enemy's coordination of sea and air units, *Haida's* excellent gunnery, the terrible damage, and the outstanding performance of the crew.

"The English have the world's greatest tradition of naval warfare. Why, battleship *Mikasa,* on which I served on at the Battle of Tsushima, was built in British yards. All four of our battleships were." He waved over his head in a circular encompassing gesture. "We were British trained, British equipped. I helped build Eta Jima with bricks actually brought from England. We used their tactics, adopted English as the language of the Imperial Navy, modeled our uniforms after theirs."

Brent knew it all, had heard it many times not only from Admiral Fujita, but the other senior officers as well. If the years had affected the old mariner's mind adversely, it was in the strange way of the aged in recalling distant events with vivid clarity while seeming to forget recent happenings, sometimes immediately after they occurred.

Fujita continued, tapping the desk with bony knuckles for emphasis, "The English are all fine seamen and dedicated warriors."

Brent squared his jaw. "Not all, sir."

"Not all?"

"No, Admiral. I have not completed my report." Then, bitterly, he told the old sailor of Lieutenant Sinclair Ingilly's appalling conduct, the breakdown and sickening cowardice. "As acting captain of destroyer *Haida,* I recommend a court martial, Sir. He should be out of the service, either in prison or in an institution."

The lines curved down the parchment, all harsh and

angry. "I cannot understand this, Brent-san. He impressed me as a fine officer."

Brent nodded his agreement. "Until the guns began to fire and we took our first casualties."

The old sailor stared straight over Brent's shoulder. "Yes. Battle is the great catalyst. It brings out the true nature of men." He leaned back, stared at the overhead and put his hand on the *Hagakure*. "'The samurai constantly hardens his resolution to die in battle, deliberately becoming as one already dead.'"

Brent sighed at the familiar aphorism and said, "The *Hagakure* is filled with wise words, sir. Ingilly violated every imperative of command. He was scared out of his mind."

"There is truth in your words, Brent-san. All men feel fear when the guns begin to fire, but the brave men control their fear and give battle even when their guts become icewater and fall through their bowels."

Brent smiled at the admiral's metaphor. He knew war, he knew battle, and he knew men.

The old mariner's fingers drummed the desk like withered roots. "You have witnesses?"

Brent shook his head. "They're all dead."

"Commander Coglan?"

"He was wounded before the navigator broke down and I had him carried off the bridge." Now it was Brent's turn to tug on his chin thoughtfully. "But the captain did witness Ingilly's near-panic when he ordered the torpedo attack."

"I believe you implicitly, Brent-san. There are no doubts, no challenge to your integrity. I would convict him on the strength of your words alone. But it is not only the military aspect at work here, Brent-san. We Japanese have a wise saying: 'Even those who share the same bed will have different dreams.' So we must hear his dreams, honor Lieutenant Ingilly's right to a hearing where he can confront you, his accuser, face-to-face. You have actually accused him of a capital offense. I would behead him."

"Please, sir. I believe he is ill—he has suffered a mental breakdown. He recovered immediately after I called a cease-fire."

The drumming fingers relaxed and then began to war with the fingers of the other hand, which had crept across the desk. "That is precisely when the cowards get off their stomachs and change their undergarments. He reached for a telephone. "I will send for him immediately and we will have this out here and now—let him tell his side, if he has one. Then, we will convene the court-martial, give him a fair trial and execute him." He spoke into the phone.

Because he was in the sick bay visiting Commander Clive Coglan, it took Lieutenant Sinclair Ingilly only a few minutes to reach Admiral Fujita's cabin. Impeccably dressed in his freshly pressed Royal Navy dress blues complete with "monkey jacket" (or reefer), Ingilly entered the room. In appearance, at least, he was the consummate naval officer. Two woven yellow rings circled his cuffs and two more crossed his shoulder straps, showing his rank. His peaked cap with rank badge was pressed to his side by his right arm. The "DOP" (Department of Parks) shoulder patch, which was now worn by all officers and men of Fujita's command, was stitched to the upper sleeve of his right arm. Because the bridge was considered belowdecks, he did not salute, but instead marched smartly to center front directly opposite Fujita, snapped his heels with a sharp report that would have made a Prussian wince with envy, and stood at attention. "Lieutenant Sinclair Ingilly reporting, sir," he said briskly.

"At ease, Mister Ingilly," Fujita said, gesturing at a chair.

Seating himself, the Cornishman turned to Brent Ross, smiled, and said, "Good to see you, Commander."

Brent nodded once, pursed his lips into a hard circle,

and remained silent.

Fujita continued, "Commander Ross has made his report."

Apparently completely composed, Ingilly said to Fujita, "It was a bloody awful show, sir. And, I daresay, Commander Ross took over gallantly after Captain Coglan was wounded and did a smashing job of it. Saw it all myself, sir."

Brent felt a small fire flare deep inside him, as if someone had put a match to his stomach, "How could you?"

"How could I?"

"Yes. How could you see anthing? You were groveling on the deck."

Ingilly's eyes sparked. "I say, old boy. You can't . . ."

Fujita interrupted, "Commander Ross can and did give me a complete report concerning your conduct during the action against *Abu Bakr* and the enemy bombers. He reported that you displayed cowardice so consuming you were in a state of paralysis."

Eyes wide, Ingilly turned to Brent in astonishment. "I say, old boy, that's a not cricket."

"I'm not your 'old boy,' Lieutenant. I am Lieutenant Commander Brent Ross, your superior officer and acting captain. Don't abandon your discipline as you did your courage back there on the bridge of *Haida*."

"I resent that, Sir."

"Resent anything you damn well please," Brent shot back.

"You have no witnesses to these false charges," the navigator said with new confidence.

Brent chuckled. "Remember when the captain ordered the torpedo attack?"

Ingilly nodded, lips turned under, jaw twitching.

"What was your comment?"

The Cornishman remained silent, eyes searching the deck. "I'll tell you," Brent added, the suppressed rage of days finally venting. "You said, 'That's mad!'"

"It was."

"Our torpedoes sank her."

"It was still mad—we got too close—took a bloody awful weight of shot." His eyes were glinting feverishly. "We were almost sunk. We took terrible casualties."

Brent shot back, "War is an exchange. You cannot achieve anything without paying the price. Let me remind you again . . ." His lips tightened like blades; he chopped off each word as he spoke. "We sank *Abu Bakr*."

Ingilly's Adam's apple worked hard. It was as if a wad of words were stuck in his throat like a fish bone. The Englishman shifted his gaze to the communications center. Fujita's eyes were riveted on the navigator, but he said nothing.

Brent was not surprised by Fujita's silence. He watched as the admiral sagged back, a curious, almost pleasurable expression now on his face. His eyes moved to the overhead. Many times in the past, Brent had seen the old man apparently relax and in a very real sense withdraw when subordinates fell into heated arguments in his presence. Brent often thought it was a carryover from the long entrapment in Sano Wan, a way to drag brewing hostilities out into the open and let them air instead of festering and growing insidiously like cancers. But Brent suspected other, more personal motivations: the old man also derived pleasure from the clashes. He was sure of that. He had seen it in his face and in his eyes. And the exposure did not always work to reduce hostilities. In fact, on several occasions, the exchanges resulted in fights to the death in the confines of the ship's largest shrine, "The Shrine of Infinite Salvation," located in a corner of the hangar deck.

Brent stared at Ingilly and moved on, his voice acid with sarcasm, needling, "Everything's tickety-boo, tickety-boo . . ."

The navigator's eyes widened and a patina of moisture covered his face.

Brent twisted the needle. "A corner of a foreign field that will be forever England."

"What does that prove?" Ingilly demanded, half rising.

"You remember? You remember what you said, what you said while you cowered on the deck? I'll never forget."

"I was frightened." He sank back and stabbed a finger at the American, "And so were you."

"I wasn't flat on my face, cringing in my own puke."

Now perspiration beaded like strings of frozen pearls across the lieutenant's brow. Cutting like an assassin with a knife, Brent sang, *"I've got sixpence, jolly, jolly . . ."*

Brent had finally hit a nerve. Ingilly shot out of his chair, waving a finger that shook like palsy under Brent's nose. "You Yanks think you're so damned high and mighty. And who are *you* to talk about courage? We've always fought your bloody wars before you got off your dead arses. Twice this century . . ."

"Sit down, Mister Ingilly!" Fujita shouted, hands on desk, half rising.

The Cornishman ignored him. Brent rose and came nose to nose with the navigator. Again he slashed at him with his own cruel memories, using Ingilly's words from that terrible day on the bridge of *Haida* as if he were driving daggers into Ingilly's soul. *"Rule Britannia, Britannia rules the waves . . ."*

The lieutenant screamed "Swine," then threw a wild punch at Brent's head. The American rolled away from it casually and brought up a massive fist that caught the squat 200-pounder squarely on the chin. The blow knocked the lieutenant over his chair and onto the deck, where he lay facedown, sobbing. He curled into a fetal position.

Both Brent and Admiral Fujita could hear him softly muttering, *"God save our gracious queen, long live our noble queen . . ."*

Fujita pushed a button and immediately two burly seaman guards entered. He stabbed a finger at the form on the deck. "Take that garbage to the brig."

119

"Sir!" Brent interjected, feeling a change of heart. "The sick bay, sir. Confinement, Admiral. He's mentally ill."

"All cowards are mentally ill. There is no better excuse."

"Please, sir—have him taken ashore to a mental hospital. He's out of his mind."

Fujita turned his thin lips under. "Very well." Then, to the guards, "Take him to the brig and put him in irons." He looked at Brent Ross, and explained, "I will keep him there, where he cannot cause any problems, until we can arrange to have him transferred to a mental facility ashore."

"Then send him home, Admiral. I withdraw my request for a court-martial."

"Yes. I agree. There will be no court-martial. I will send him home."

Each guard grasped an arm and pulled the blubbering Ingilly to his feet. The demented navigator was not finished. Ancient national pride, hatred, and terrible racial memories were suddenly unlocked. Events that had happened long before his birth poured out of his twisted brain like venom from the fangs of a cobra. He stabbed a finger at Fujita and screeched in a spray of spittle, "We built your bloody navy, trained you, taught you tactics, even gave you our uniforms, and what for? You stabbed us in the back when we stood alone against Hitler, stole Malaya, Hong Kong, Singapore, herded thousands of our lads into Indochina and Japan, and killed them like flies in your prisoner-of-war camps."

Brent and the admiral looked at each other. Fujita's expression was as implacable as stone. He expected to hear the admiral call a halt to the outburst. But again he was fooled by the old man's unexpected silence. It was almost as if he wanted to hear the Cornishman unload his full burden of enmity.

Ingilly turned to Brent, eyes wide as silver dollars, wild as the churning rapids of the Niagara. "And you, Yank.

Have you forgotten Pearl Harbor? It's been fifty years since the first attack, eight years since *Yonaga* . . ."

Now Fujita felt the sensitive nerve grate, had his fill. "Enough!" he shouted. "Take this garbage to the brig and put him in irons!"

As the two guards dragged Ingilly through the door, he was chanting Nelson's famous signal, flown before the battle of Trafalgar, "England expects every man will do his duty . . ."

Hiroshi Fujita and Brent Ross stared at each other silently. Brent felt awkward, almost embarrassed by the navigator's attack. He had heard old animosities unleashed many times on board *Yonaga,* but usually between old warriors—men who had actually fought against each other in World War Two. He knew the English still harbored great resentment at the way British prisoners of war were treated during the war. In fact, the British prime minister refused to attend Hirohito's funeral. Instead, an underling was sent. Sinking back into his chair, he tried to put the vicious words out of his mind. He directed his thoughts at the collapse of the Cornishman. He said softly, "I didn't enjoy destroying him." And then, with genuine remorse, "It was too easy."

Fujita shook his head. "You cannot destroy a man easily or with great difficulty unless that man has already destroyed himself."

"And the hatred, Admiral? It didn't make sense. Most of the things he was raving about took place before he was born."

"But not before his race was born, nor before I was born, Brent-san."

"True."

The old admiral stared up at the overhead and said, "Some hatreds are etched in tribal memories. Never die. Can endure beyond the memory of those who carry them. Are suppressed only behind a dam of reason. You broke that dam, and it flooded out like a foul affluent." He

121

sighed, looked at the young American, and said, "It is the way of mankind. There have been hatreds and warfare ever since the day two men trod this one planet." His eyes seemed to bore through the young man. "Your Western philosopher Immanuel Kant said, 'Out of the crooked timber of humanity no straight thing was ever made.'" He knuckled his forehead and continued, "A very wise man, Brent-san."

Brent turned his lower lip under and rubbed his chin thoughtfully. "So very true, sir. So very true. He knew the nature of man." He glanced at his watch and stirred uneasily with a new concern. "With your permission, Admiral, I'll return to *Haida*. There is much work to do."

The old man smiled. "I have relieved you of the command."

Startled, Brent came erect. "Relieved me?"

"Yes, Brent-san. You are a valued member of my staff. Your primary function is here, on *Yonaga*, in communications and intelligence. You are also one of my best deck officers. We need you back on the watch bill."

"But *Haida*, Admiral?"

"I have temporarily assigned the chief engineer, Lieutenant Leslie Townsend, to the duties of commanding officer." He patted a dossier on his desk. "His qualifications are excellent, and in the destroyer's damaged condition, he would be an ideal choice."

Brent hunched forward. "But he couldn't steam her—fight her. Give her back to me when she's seaworthy, Admiral."

The old man shook his head. "When she is combat ready, Commander Coglan can resume command."

"He may not be ready."

The old mariner nodded concurrence. "True. Replacements are en route from England, including an experienced destroyer captain."

"Then I'll never command her again."

"I did not say that, Brent-san."

Brent's right fist impacted his left palm. "But it

doesn't look very good."

The old man sighed. "Each man, each officer in my command will be used where he can function with maximum benefit to this force."

"So, I return to *Yonaga*." Brent surprised himself with the sharp tone of his voice.

"You find that repugnant?"

Brent smiled. The old man was trying to put him on the defensive. "Of course not, Admiral." He gestured at the overhead. "*Yonaga* is my life, but I owe something to the men of Haida. I—I . . ." For one of the few times in his life, Brent was at a loss for words.

The old man chuckled. "I know, Brent-san. I have commanded for over a half-century." He hunched forward. "You are not only part of that crew, you actually feel you are part of the ship itself— I know, I know. You steamed into hell and back together, took terrible wounds." He sighed and sank back in his chair. "There are inviolable truths to be found in the imperatives of command, and you have shown the finest."

"An officer lives with many imperatives, sir."

Fujita ran a thumb and forefinger down the single hair curling from the end of his chin. "You have shown the strongest qualities of three of the most critical. The imperative of kinship—showing you care for your men. The imperative of action, that is, knowing when to attack and doing so with dash and daring. And the imperative of example, which, of course, is your willingness to share danger with your men."

Brent felt himself nearly glow in the warmth of the praise which was such a rare commodity with the old samurai. Fujita was a legend, one of the world's great mariners and commanders. The praise was incongruous and unprecedented, yet Brent knew in the samurai's eyes he had earned it. If Fujita had been on the bridge of *Haida*, he'd have commanded in exactly the same manner. In a way, Fujita's yardstick was himself.

123

"You are very generous, Admiral," Brent managed in a hushed voice.

"You are a fine officer, Brent-san." Gnarled fingers tapped the desk like bent roots. "Return to *Haida* whenever you wish. Mingle with your men—they will always be your men."

"That is my intention, sir." Brent began to rise. "I'd better return to her now and get my gear together . . ."

Fujita waved him to silence. "I have sent a detail. Your gear is being moved to your cabin at this moment."

Brent was not surprised. As usual, the old man had made all the arrangements to fit his plans, which had been laid far in advance.

Fujita continued, "You are dismissed, Commander."

"Thank you, Admiral." Wearily, Brent began to push himself to his feet.

"Commander Yoshi Matsuhara is waiting for you in his cabin."

"I know, Admiral."

"He is no longer in command of the Iwo Jima fighter group."

"No longer in command?"

"He is needed here in our training command. We have many new pilots to train." The old man ran a hand over his pate and smiled wryly. "As you know, Brent-san, I am quite capable of changing orders." He caressed the *Hagakure,* spoke from memory. "'When matters are done leisurely, seven out of ten will turn out badly. One should make his decisions within the space of seven breaths.'"

Brent stared down at the little admiral. "The last sentence of the passage, sir?"

"The last sentence, Brent-san?" Fujita knew, but he would play Brent's game.

Narrowing his eyes, Brent looked over the admiral's head and completed the quote, "'A warrior is a person who does things quickly.'"

Fujita was beaming when the young man left.

Chapter Five

Commander Yoshi Matsuhara's cabin was only a few doors down the passageway from Admiral Fujita's and just forward of Brent's. Although all cabins in "flag country" were designed for flag officers and their staffs, they were no more equal than their inhabitants, varying in size and appointments with the importance of their occupants. Yoshi's cabin was twice the size of Brent's. Still, there was no desk. Instead, built into a corner was a "study center" equipped with an NEC computer, a file cabinet, and bookcases. In fact, bookcases dominated the room. Bolted to every bulkhead, they were crammed with an eclectic assortment of Western and Oriental writers of every period. During the long years of entrapment in Sano Wan, the opium of the printed word had helped the pilot preserve his sanity. He had become addicted to books and whenever off duty could be found with a volume in his hand.

A small table with four chairs occupied the center of the room. The compartment was so spacious, the bunk was actually in a separate alcove and the head was large and boasted a full-length mirror. To Brent, the quarters were opulent and lavish.

"Welcome, Brent-san," Yoshi said, waving his friend to the table, where a bottle of Chivas Regal and two glasses waited.

The two men settled themselves and Yoshi poured two generous drinks. He topped Brent's with soda. He raised his glass, "To *Haida*."

Brent shook his head. "No!"

"No?"

"First Willard-Smith, Yoshi-san."

The Japanese nodded grimly and the two men drank. Then *Haida* was toasted.

"I will miss the Englishman," Yoshi said grimly.

Brent stared at his friend's somber face. Yoshi felt the loss very deeply and very personally. "One of the finest," Brent said. They drank again and Brent told him of his changed orders.

The aviator nodded his approval and replenished their drinks. He spoke to the table top, "You lost many good men."

"Thirty-four of them are six thousand fathoms down." He pounded the table with a closed fist.

"These past eight years have cost us hundreds of the bravest, the brightest."

Brent nodded. "And yet they come to fill the ranks."

"Good men all, Brent-san. In fact, I expect Captain Willard-Smith's replacement at any time. One of the RAF's finest, Flying Officer Hooperman, I have been told." He pinched the bridge of his flat nose thoughtfully and said, "The scourge of wickedness cannot prevail while such men fight."

Brent felt sudden new life. Despite the somber mood, his friend, an inveterate reader and thinker, was eager to joust philosophically. He could see it in the set of his jaw, the brightness of his eyes. It was a way to shake the depressing memories and, perhaps, actually explore the periphery of the meaning—if there was any—behind their violent lives. "White whale hunts," Brent had called them in the past: arguments and discussions where each man sought answers to why they did the things they did. Why they seemed to be following in the footsteps of countless thousands who had preceded them. Why there

126

had always been men like Kadafi and the men who fought them. They even speculated on what was reality and what was illusion. He studied Yoshi's face over the rim of his glass, sloshed the amber liquid around its circular well with small movements of his wrist, sipped it, and said simply, "You've been meditating."

"Of course. You know I am a follower of Zen."

More precisely, Yoshi was a follower of the first patriarch of Zen Buddhism, Bodhidharma, the Indian monk who had introduced Zen (a Japanese term for meditation) to China in the sixth century. Bodhidharma had founded a purist sect that rejected ceremonies, scriptures, and trappings of other Buddhist groups. Only through intuition could enlightenment be found. "First intention, then enlightenment," Yoshi had said many times. And he further insisted, "One must attain *Munen mushin,* the state of no thoughts, no mind, where one is truly free of worldly thoughts." For each man, this was an individual quest, insight arriving in intuitive flashes. This Spartan approach to the quest for the meaning of life appealed to the samurai and particularly Yoshi, who had been devastated by the incineration of his family in the great Tokyo fire raid of 1945 and the murder of his beloved Kimio Urshazawa in 1989.

"You have studied Bodhidharma?" It was a rhetorical question. The Oriental knew Brent was a student of all religions; he read incessantly.

Brent took a small, thoughtful drink. He enjoyed the dry, musty taste of the whiskey, sloshing it through his teeth before swallowing it. Slowly and exquisitely the glow came on him, starting deep down inside and spreading out warmly to the very tips of his fingers. His delivery was deliberate. "Most Buddhist practice *Tariki* —emphasizing reliance on the strength and compassion of the Buddha." Yoshi nodded his approval. Brent continued, "But Zen teaches *Jiriki,* demanding self-reliance on the path to enlightenment." Yoshi watched his young friend with near awe in his eyes. Brent tilted

127

his head back, stared up at the overhead, riffling through the sheaths of memory. "According to Zen, we take it for granted that you and I are essentially lumps of meat with a mind in our head. But the perception is nothing but illusion. Our belief that we are like that creates each other." He waved his glass at his approving friend, "Your ability to fly, your skill as a pilot, your commitment to *Yonaga*, your pilots, your friends are essentially an illusion, a fabrication of consciousness, which, of course, is an illusion. There is no reality, no universe existing eternally, absolutely, and independently of our own observations and thoughts . . ."

"Very good, Brent-san," Yoshi interrupted. "Then you concede that the answer is to be found in the meditative techniques of Zen which allow us to transcend the illusion of ego and reality—free for brief moments, living fully in the world, free from the barrier of preconception, free from the 'known,' which is nothing more than imagination, memory, and the past . . ."

It was Brent's turn to interrupt. "And free, Yoshi-san, from the 'unknown,' which is the future and projection of the past into the future."

Obviously impressed, Yoshi beamed and charged both glasses. "Yes, indeed, you've been studying, Brent-san. But do you believe?"

Brent shrugged and thumped his huge fists on the table like a drummer striking kettledrums. "I don't know what I believe, Yoshi-san, but it's as good as any." Brent took another drink and then rolled his massive knuckles over the table, making small popping sounds. He threw out his own opening gambit, "You've tried inner perception?"

Yoshi brightened. "This differs from meditation?"

"Not really. To me it's just a matter of semantics."

The young American spread his fingers like a giant tarantula. The thick legs of the huge spider began to drum on the table. "Then have you sensed that you are one with all men and all men are one with nature?"

Chuckling, the pilot sank back. He grabbed the bait and

ran with it, "You forgot that nature is one with God."

"Right, Yoshi-san."

"You've been reading Emerson—transcendentalism," the pilot observed.

Brent was not surprised by his friend's knowledge. In fact, he rather expected it. Shrugging, he turned his hands up in a noncommittal gesture. "Why not?" He leaned back and searched the overhead with half-closed eyes. "'That which shows God in me fortifies me. That which shows God out of me, makes me a wart and a wen,' Emerson wrote." He waved at the books. "It's as good as any of the rest, and there's a touch of Zen there."

For the first time, Yoshi showed confusion. "A touch of Zen?"

"Yes. Ralph Waldo Emerson, Henry Hedge, George Ripley—the 'Transcendental Club'—believed that although the existence of realities were beyond the reach of the senses and the ability of man to understand, the mind could still apprehend by direct intuition. They believed truth was the expression of spiritual or personal insight rather than a deduction from premises provided by history and science." He dropped his eyes to his friend. "There is your touch of Zen."

"Yes, my friend. I see. But you must throw out God. And remember, the proof of the power of Zen is everywhere, in everything, if one is perceptive enough. The pilot tapped his glass with a single fingernail, making tiny chiming sounds that reminded Brent of the firing gongs on *Haida*. He looked up suddenly. "This world is in chaos, Brent-san."

"Can't argue with that."

The pilot dampened his lips with the tip of his tongue. "Then Zen is the best means of coping with chaos, because it does not rely on the reality of an ordered universe."

"Like Christianity?"

The pilot emptied his glass with a sharp toss of his head and refilled both drinks. "Right. I know you were brought up in a Catholic family, Brent-san, and I do not mean to offend, but Christianity borrowed heavily from other religions and insists on order where there is none."

Brent laughed sardonically before taking another stiff drink. The glow had spread further and he was feeling relaxed, warm, mellow. "You do not offend, old friend. Yes, I was brought up a Catholic. But I know Christianity did not borrow, Yoshi-san." Matsuhara raised an eyebrow in surprise. Brent ran on, "Actually, Christianity *stole* its dogma from every religion that preceded it and insists the universe was assembled by the 'great Swiss watchmaker in the sky.'" He moved the drink back and forth, watching the amber liquid peak until it was on the verge of spilling. "You know, Yoshi-san, there I must disagree, there I must break. Sometimes I think there is nothing—nothing out there, no rhyme, reason, purpose . . ."

The Japanese spoke eagerly, "You agree. Chaos!"

"Yes, Yoshi-san. I cannot completely reject the idea of a God, but this is where I find power, redemption in Zen and . . ."

Yoshi halted him with a raised palm. "Of course I agree, my friend. You are a mixture of the Occident and the Orient. But none can argue—clearly good and evil do exist."

"True. They are not illusions—not in our world, not in the way we perceive it. And we are on the side of good."

"Have you ever doubted that?"

Brent shook his head. "No. On that I am clear. There is no equivocation. On that score alone there is purpose in what we do—some order in the chaos. I don't need a theology to find justification—to point the way."

The Japanese smiled broadly and touched Brent's glass with his. Brent, feeling a spreading warm glow, took only a small sip. Yoshi continued, "I have nearly a hundred new pilots to train, Brent-san."

130

"I know. The admiral told me he had changed your orders."

"They come from all over the world—America, England, France, Germany, Greece, Turkey, and I even have one from Russia."

"But the majority of our air groups are still Japanese, Yoshi-san."

"True. But it is heartening to find good men flocking here from all over the world to take up our fight."

"The Arabs aren't having any trouble finding recruits, either."

A look of disdain crossed the pilot's face. "They serve for money. Nothing but filthy mercenaries."

"And damned good pilots, Yoshi-san."

Matsuhara nodded grimly. "True. But I have the men to beat them . . ."

A knock interrupted him. Brent opened the door and found a tall young man dressed in the blue-gray woolen serge uniform of the RAF, standing at stiff attention. Single rings of black and light blue lace on his cuffs and shoulder straps indicated the rank of flying officer. Embroidered in silk over his left breast pocket were white-drab wings with a crown over the RAF monogram and a brown silk laurel wreath. His shoes shone like mirrors and his peaked cap was squashed under his right arm. A bright new DOP shoulder patch was sewn high on his right sleeve. It was Hooperman; Brent was sure of it.

Brent's suspicion was confirmed with the stranger's first words. "Flying Officer Claude Hooperman reporting, sir. I'm Captain Willard-Smith's replacement."

Brent noticed an obscure, unobtrusive accent: a light twang, just a broadening of the vowels and a light touch on *h*. Not from the streets, but not from the gentry, either.

Yoshi waved him in, introduced him to Brent, and insisted the Englishman have a Scotch. Obviously ill at ease, the newcomer sipped his drink and sat stiffly. Brent studied him over his glass. The Englishman's square jaw

131

was sharply chiseled, his nose long and angular, ending strangely in a sharp wedge like an arrowhead, and his eyes were curiously wide spaced. At first sight, Brent had guessed his age at about twenty-four, twenty-five, maybe. But quickly the American realized he had been fooled by the boyish jawline, the shock of blond hair, the wide blue eyes, and the gentle hollows in the cheeks. When he looked more closely, he could detect fine-etched lines in the brow, incipient creases trailing down from the corners of his eyes, and a curious distance in his eyes, a self-confidence that came only with experience, time, and hardship. He saw a formidable man, a strong man, a man to be reckoned with, and Yoshi's expression told him the air group commander saw the same thing.

"I was told by the duty officer that I was to report to you immediately upon boarding this ship, sir."

"That is correct, Mister Hooperman."

"I do not mean to be presumptuous, sir, but are you considering me to be your new wingman?" Hooperman asked.

Yoshi nodded. "True. But that remains to be seen, of course."

"Of course, sir."

"Your aircraft?"

"Seafire F-47. Absolutely sterling condition—ready to do her bit, sir."

"Experience?" Brent was certain that Yoshi had already studied Hooperman's record. But the new man had to be tested, and Yoshi's approach was the best. Studying the Englishman, Brent felt confident Hooperman was quite aware of his commanding officer's intentions.

"Jets, Commander, until the Chinese made a filthy muck of things with their bloody laser system. And then some old 'Spits,' a Hurricane squadron for a few months, and then Vickers Armstrong came out with their new version of the Seafire."

"Hours?"

132

"Three thousand six hundred twenty, sir."

"In Seafires?"

"One thousand two hundred twenty four."

"Combat?"

"I was too young for the Falklands, but I served on *Invincible*."

"She was sunk in the Mediterranean when Margaret Thatcher decided to attack Libya."

Bitterness crept into Hooperman's voice. "I was flying CAP when she was sunk along with *Illustrious* and *Ark Royal*. They strafed our chaps in the water."

"Your kills?"

"A North American P-51, two JU 87s, and an Me 109."

The Japanese balled his fist, made a stanchion of his arm, and rested his chin on his knuckles, his eyes riveted on Hooperman. "Why do you wish to serve with me, fly into mortal danger? You will probably be killed."

"I know that, sir." Instead of answering, he shifted his eyes boldly to Brent. "Why do you serve, Commander Ross? You're the 'American Samurai.' You've been fighting the bloody Arabs for eight years."

Brent smiled and sipped his drink. "I fight them because our cause is just and the freedom of the world depends on our victory." His eyes bored into the Englishman's. "Sounds dramatic, but it's as simple as that."

"Completely altruistic," the Englishman observed.

"There's no money in this business," Brent replied.

"I'm not here for money," Hooperman retorted hotly.

"I didn't say that."

The flying officer tossed off his drink and leaned forward. A sanguine hue colored his cheeks. "I'm here for the same reasons and more."

"And more?"

"Yes. I saw my comrades killed in the water—helpless men, murdered."

"You want revenge?" Yoshi interjected. He recharged the Englishman's glass.

"Does that cheapen my cause?"

Yoshi chuckled and looked at Brent, who smiled back. "Not to the samurai. Vengeance is one of the most precious motives that drives the samurai. It is mandatory—sacred." He took another drink and his jawline hardened. "You talk of the murder of helpless men—Captain Colin Willard-Smith was murdered in his parachute by Kenneth Rosencrance." Yoshi slammed his fist down so hard Brent had to steady his glass. "I saw it! Saw it! Swore revenge, and I will have it as the forty-seven *ronin* had theirs." He stabbed a finger at a copy of the *Hagakure*, which was propped up, cover out, in one of the bookcases. "It is written, and I firmly believe, 'The warrior who forgets the Way of the Samurai and does not use his sword for vengeance will be forsaken by the gods and Buddha.' No, Flying Officer Hooperman, I would never depreciate revenge. Seek it. Find it. Rejoice in it. Wallow in it." He sank back while his two companions maintained a respectful if not self-conscious silence. For a moment only the ship sounds of whining blowers and rumbling auxiliary engines could be heard. Matsuhara took several deep breaths, a large swallow from his glass. Then he glanced at his watch and his mood changed with amazing swiftness. Suddenly, he was the senior officer, all business, all professionalism. "I have a meeting with some of my new fighter pilots in Ready Room Two in twenty-minutes. You are to accompany me, Mister Hooperman." He turned to Brent, "Why don't you come along—meet them?"

Another thought had intruded into Brent's mind, and suddenly he forgot Hooperman was seated next to him. Instead of answering Yoshi's question, he asked his own. "Rear Admiral Whitehead? I haven't seen him. And Colonel Bernstein?"

An Annapolis classmate of Brent's dead father, Ted "Trigger" Ross, Rear Admiral Whitehead had known Brent since the young man's birth. Very close to Ross, he was a father figure to the younger man. His career in the

134

U.S. Navy spanned a half-century, and he was permanently posted to *Yonaga,* along with Brent in communications and intelligence—actually, liaison with NIS. His career in World War Two as an air operations officer had been distinguished by fourteen battle stars, the Navy Cross, and the Purple Heart. Yet at the same time his record was appalling. He had been sunk five times. He had been on carriers *Lexington, Yorktown, Hornet, Wasp,* and *Princeton* when they'd received their death blows. Behind his back, he was referred to as "Sinker" Whitehead and sometimes "Deep Six Whitehead." Near the end of the war, dozens of officers would request transfers whenever he was assigned to a new ship. His one singular achievement was planning the attack that sank battleship *Yamato.* This was done when he was chief of staff to Admiral Marc Mitscher, who'd commanded Task Force 58. Discreetly, this accomplishment was never discussed in the presence of Admiral Fujita, who'd helped design *Yamato* and counted many good friends in her 3,000 dead.

Colonel Irving Bernstein was another man who had earned Brent's respect, and, although he would not admit it, his affection. In fact, over the years, he had become very attached to the Israeli Mossad (Intelligence) officer. A Polish Jew and survivor of Auschwitz, where his mother, father, and sister had been killed, Bernstein was in the habit of wearing the sleeves of his Israeli Army desert fatigues rolled up, exposing the blue tatooed numbers on his right forearm. "Jew number nine hundred sixty two thousand four hundred twenty one," he would say matter-of-factly to anyone who happened to stare. After the war, he immigrated to Israel, where he fought in the Arab-Israeli wars of 1947 and 1948, the Six-Day War, the Yom Kippur War, and innumerable skirmishes and ambushes. His hatred for Arabs was ineffable. An expert in codes and ciphers, he had been attached to Fujita's staff from the moment the Japanese had become allied against Kadafi and his *jihad* in 1983.

"Admiral Whitehead and Colonel Bernstein are ashore and have been for two days," Yoshi explained. "Something's afoot. Big meetings at the Israeli and American embassies and at the headquarters of the Self Defense Force. And Admiral Whitehead and Colonel Bernstein have been interrogating the new prisoners personally."

"New prisoners?"

"Yes—the survivors of *Abu Bakr* and a few air crews."

"I thought Fite killed them," Brent said, straightening.

Yoshi shrugged. "Admiral Fujita wanted prisoners—all he could get."

Brent shook his head. "Why the switch? He always killed the vermin."

"Hear! Hear!" Hooperman injected.

Smiling at the Englishman, Yoshi shrugged. "Who can fathom his mind? But there is a purpose."

"I know."

The air group commander glanced at the brass clock mounted on the bulkhead. "Time to meet my pilots, Brent-san. Are you coming with us?"

Brent tossed off his drink and stood. "Let's go, Yoshi."

The three officers strode the length of the passageway in order of rank: Commander Yoshi Matsuhara leading, Lieutenant Commander Brent Ross on his heels, and Flying Officer Claude Hooperman trailing. Actually, Hooperman's rank was equivalent to lieutenant. Willard-Smith had always disliked the clumsy RAF designation of "Flight Lieutenant" and had given himself the equivalent army rank of "Captain." No one had objected. In fact, most of *Yonaga*'s officers found "Captain" far more convenient and familiar.

They passed through the chart house, where a chief quartermaster was carefully winding the ship's chronometer. Set to Greenwich Civil Time, the delicate, gimbal-mounted timepiece was never reset. Instead, twice daily its error was checked against "time ticks" broadcast from

136

the Japanese Naval Observatory and carefully recorded. The delicate instrument was wound the same number of turns at exactly the same time every day. Another quartermaster was seated at a large chest-high chart desk, correcting charts. Both enlisted men snapped to attention and bowed.

The officers nodded and Yoshi said, "As you were."

The rating returned to their work, but as Brent stepped through the forward door, the chief said, "Great work, Commander Ross. Good kill."

Brent nodded silently.

They hurried past a room filled with radar and ESM equipment. It was a dark place, glowing with a weird blue-green light from scopes, radar screens, and the cathode-ray tubes of computers. "I say," Hooperman said waving, "you have state-of-the-art equipment in your combat information center."

Brent nodded. "A and S band search, ESM, computer-generated codes and ciphers—the latest and the best. I'll take you on a tour sometime."

"Right-oh."

They entered the ship's lone elevator, which was just abaft the pilot house.

As the small car descended, Yoshi turned to Hooperman. "Do you know much of the construction of *Yonaga?*"

"A converted battleship of the *Yamato* class."

"Yes. Designed by Admiral Fujita and Vice Admiral Keiji Fukuda. She was lengthened to one thousand fifty feet and is powered by sixteen Kanpon boilers instead of twelve. She has a triple bottom, one thousand one hundred seventy-six watertight compartments with a double bulkhead dividing her from stem to stern. She still has her antitorpedo 'blisters' below the waterline, and inside of them her main hull is made of eight-inch plate. The hangar deck is actually the battleship's main deck."

"Must be armored," Hooperman offered.

"Right. Up to seven and one-half inches," the Japanese

said, casually remaining with English units. "Our flight deck is nearly four of your English acres in size, and Fujita decided it had to be able to withstand the impact of one-thousand-pound bombs."

"I say, quite a trick."

Yoshi nodded. "It was built in layers—nearly four inches of steel was laid down on the flight deck, then nearly a yard beneath it, another layer of one-inch steel was installed. This formed a box that was filled with beams, cement, sawdust, and latex." The Englishman whistled. Yoshi hurried on, face flushed, as if he were describing a beautiful mistress. "An eight-inch steel plate box was built around the heart of the carrier—the engines, boilers, steering equipment, and magazines."

"Like a citadel," Hooperman offered.

"That is what we call it. In all, *Yonaga* has nineteen thousand six hundred tons of steel for defensive purposes alone."

"Good heavens! That's a hundred tons more than *Invincible* displaced." Brent and Yoshi chuckled at the Englishman's astonishment. Not many men were aware of *Yonaga's* awesome statistics. Admiral Fujita was not one to advertise the power of his command, information that could prove useful to his enemies.

"What I have just told you is secret, Mister Hooperman."

"Of course, sir." The Englishman rubbed his hollow cheek and stretched his lips with a hard push of his tongue. Something was troubling him. "Commander, the Arabs attached *Invincible* with bombs tipped with depleted uranium. They went through her like butter."

"We took one in the Mediterranean."

"Did it penetrate the flight deck?"

Yoshi and Brent exchanged a grim look. "Yes. It exploded in the hangar deck. We took a lot of casualties." The opening of the elevator doors on the gallery deck halted the conversation. Exiting just forward of amidships, the trio stepped onto the gallery deck, a long

138

platform that ran along the starboard side of the ship above the hangar deck. Doors opening off it led to pilot briefing rooms and pilots' and junior officers' quarters.

Hooperman moved to the rail and looked down on an awesome sight. Brent and Yoshi stood at his sides. Stretched beneath them was one of the largest compartments man had ever put to sea. Just under 1,000 feet long and 140 feet wide, the hangar deck was swarming with activity. At least thirty aircraft were in various stages of repair and maintenance. There were fighters, dive bombers, and torpedo bombers clustered by type. Green-clad mechanics and crew chiefs swarmed over their charges. Reflected and reverberating from the steel deck, bulkheads, and overhead, the noise was overwhelming. Pneumatic tools fired in machine-gun bursts, steel-wheeled bowsers and tool carts rumbled and ground over the deck, and every man seemed to speak in shouts, adding to the cacophony that assailed the officers' ears.

The dive bombers were all Aichi D3As, unmistakable with slatted fixed undercarriage, graceful tapered canopy, radial engine, and bomb trapeze secured to the fuselage. Yoshi waved, "That plane looks antiquated, but it is one of the most efficient dive bombers ever built. In fact, during the war it sank more Allied fighting ships than any other aircraft." Hooperman glanced at Brent, pursed his lips, and said nothing.

Yoshi pointed at a group of 6 Nakajima B5N torpedo bombers. With long three-man canopies and wide wings tapering sharply almost to points, the torpedo bombers appeared clumsy. Brent knew that at Pearl Harbor the B5N had done most of the damage to the American battleships. Later, the tough torpedo plane had sent Rear Admiral Whitehead home on three survivors' leaves by torpedoing carriers *Lexington, Wasp, Hornet,* and *Yorktown.*

"The Nakajima B5N," Yoshi said matter-of-factly. "In all respects better than your Fairey Barracuda and the Grumman TBF Avenger. Great war record." He tactfully avoided mentioning the battleships and carriers the Nakajima had sunk. "They are all powered with the new Nakajima Sakae Forty-Two, two-thousand-horse-power engine. We are installing new high-compression pistons that should improve the power rating to twenty-two hundred. Even with two thousand horsepower, their performance has been vastly improved."

He gestured at the fighters which represented three different nations: 7 Mitsubishi A6M2 Zeros from Japan, 5 Grumman F6F Hellcats from America, and 4 British Vickers-Armstrong Seafires.

Before Yoshi could continue, Hooperman pointed and said, "My fighter's at Tsuchiura. I had a chance to inspect it after my transport landed."

"Right," Yoshi answered. "Most of our aircraft are there and at Tokyo International. We use both fields as training bases." He waved a hand in an arc over the deck. "Most of these are newly arrived reserve aircraft. They are being completely overhauled." He stabbed a finger at an oddly shaped red, green, and white Zero with its hood, cowling, and canopy removed. "Except that one."

"That's your fighter," Hooperman offered.

"You've heard of it?"

The Englishman grinned. "Only that it's souped up—defies the laws of aerodynamics. Has as much right to fly as . . ." he chuckled, "the *Royal Scot* or the *Queen Mary*."

Yoshi laughed. "I know. I was accused of being *shinigurai* when I first test-flew her."

Brent nodded. After Yoshi's beloved Kimio had been murdered in Ueno Park, the Japanese had shown every evidence of being precisely *shinigurai*.

A puzzled look crossed the Englishman's face. Yoshi read it. "*Shinigurai*," the Japanese explained, "means 'crazy to die.' It's an old samurai expression. I'm not *shinigurai* now."

Brent was pleasantly surprised; he raised an eyebrow but remained silent. The Englishman looked long and hard at the Zero's gigantic engine with its twin banks of cylinders, the delicate appearance of the airframe and the numerous bullet holes that crewmen were patching. He smiled wryly. "Are you sure about that, old boy?"

Brent and Yoshi both laughed. The air group commander slapped Hooperman on the back and steered him toward a door. "This way, Flying Officer Hooperman. I have a dozen green pilots to brief before they begin their training at Tokyo International and Tsuchiura. I am going to put you in charge of the detail."

"In charge, sir?"

"Yes. You are senior and will see to it they are all transported to Tokyo International Airport."

"I've never seen the bloody place."

"The lorry driver knows the way and you will be accompanied by four armed seaman guards who are familiar with the route and billeting procedures at the airport."

"Well, sir," the Englishman said, head back, shoulders squared, burlesquing rigid military bearing, "be assured I'll be a ruddy tyrant and herd the lot into their proper stockades."

"Jolly good," Yoshi said, mimicking an English accent.

They all laughed. Then Hooperman asked, "Will Pilot Officer Elwyn York be at the briefing?"

Yoshi shook his head. "He's at Tsuchiura on a training assignment. You can meet him there."

The three officers entered the room.

Chapter Six

The briefing room was a long, narrow compartment with twenty-seven chairs. Twelve were occupied, all with very young pilots: seven Japanese, three Americans, and two Englishmen. All wore DOP shoulder patches. "Christ. They look like they just graduated from high school," Brent whispered into Hooperman's ear as they found seats but remained standing at the rear of the room.

"Quite so, quite so," the Englishman agreed. "I'll stand you tuppence to a quid some of those faces haven't been graced by a razor."

The young pilots snapped to attention as Yoshi Matsuhara strode to the front of the room and mounted a small platform equipped with a lectern. For a moment Yoshi stood silently, his black eyes searching each face of his new pilots. They stared back eagerly at *"Yonaga's Butcher"* as if a mystical legend from the dark ages of mythology had suddenly come to life before them. Brent could feel an electricity in the room, a palpable amalgam of excitement and anticipation. In all these years he had never attended one of Yoshi's meetings. He was eager to hear just what an experienced pilot could teach his novices in a classroom.

The air group commander opend with the expected "I am Commander Yoshi Matsuhara, your air group commander." He stabbed a finger at the end man. "From left to right, your name and rank."

Voices pitched high with youth and nerves, the twelve young men screeched out their names. All the Japanese and the Americans were ensigns, while the two Englishmen were pilot officers. One of the Japanese stood out—a youngster named Hitoshi Kitajima, who was taller and broader than the others and much darker. And Brent thought he detected a strange inflection in his voice. Then Yoshi introduced Brent Ross and Claude Hooperman. Heads turned and Brent heard whispers of "the American samurai."

The command "Gentlemen, be seated" sent the pilots and Brent to their chairs. Brent noticed each pilot had a pad and pencil. Some even had small tape recorders.

"I welcome you to the fight," Yoshi said. He patted his DOP patch, "And I welcome you to the Department of Parks." There was a nervous titter. "In the event you are not aware of why you are employed by the Department of Parks, you must become acquainted with the Japanese constitution—especially Article Nine." He half-closed his eyes and looked up at the overhead. He quoted, "'Aspiring sincerely to an international peace based on justice and order, the Japanese people forever renounce war as a sovereign right of the nation and the threat and use of force as a means of settling international disputes. Land, sea, and air forces, as well as other war potential, will never be maintained.'"

He looked down at his new men, his eyes wide and gleaming, his face a study of revulsion. "This idiotic article is still in effect simply because the Diet is made up of spineless women. Fortunately, Admiral Fujita had close cooperation with Emperor Hirohito from the very beginning, and it continues to this day with Emperor Akihito. In 1984, with the Emperor's insistence, *Yonaga* and all forces under Admiral Fujita's command were declared national monuments, which put them under the Department of Parks. In this way, the Diet could vote appropriations for the support of the carrier along with

143

other monuments such as battleship *Mikasa* and some of our most sacred temples and parklands. It is legal and it works. That is why you are all park employees." A weak wave of laughter rippled through the room.

"You may wonder about the Maritime Self-Defense Force," the air group commander noted. "It was a high-tech fleet of frigates, destroyers, and submarines made virtually useless by the Chinese laser system. And then you all know of the Arabs' sneak attack here on the bases Kure and Sasebo in 1988. What the enemy bombers did not destroy, *Rengo Sekigun* traitors sabotaged." His scowl was as black as thunder. "All thirteen submarines were lost. These were the vessels we needed more than any other." A sigh relaxed the tight countenance. "But we have two survivors that have provided valuable radar picket duty—frigate *Ayase*, and destroyer *Yamagiri*. They have the most modern radar and have been equipped with new AA batteries." His restless eyes surveyed an audience that was so rigid and quiet it appeared to be made of stone.

Yoshi squared his shoulders, altered the set of his jaw, and lashed out at a new topic with both fists. "You must understand the odds against us are high and our enemy is skillful and well equipped. Within a year, most of you will probably be dead." He paused, staring at his new men. His expression was absolutely inscrutable. He continued, "The media thoroughly reported our last carrier battle off Africa." Some of the men nodded, others stared with wide, unblinking eyes. "All of you know *Yonaga* and *Bennington* fought carriers *Daffah* and *Magid*—sank *Daffah* and damaged *Magid*, while both our carriers were damaged."

The terrible memories that all fighting men suppress flooded back into Brent's mind: *Yonaga*'s deck made inoperative to her own air groups by sixteen North American B-25 Mitchells lashed down from amidships aft; the long voyage to the coast of Morocco with *Bennington*'s F4U Corsair and F6F Hellcat fighters

144

providing air cover; the suicidal attack on Kadafi's poison gasworks at Rabta by the unescorted B-25s, a 1,400-mile run-in; Colonel Latimer Stewart, the gallant bomber commander, and his brave crews betrayed by the drunken CIA man Horace Mayfield, who talked too much during drunken drug and sex orgies with the enemy agent Lia Mandel and her dupe, the reporter Arlene Spencer; Colonel Stewart and a dozen of his men captured after the B-25s were ambushed and massacred. Then the horror of the bloody battle: both Japanese carriers hit, but *Daffah* sunk and *Magid* heavily damaged; the return to Japan; Fujita hanging Horace Mayfield from *Yonaga's* yardarm; Yoshi shooting most of Lia Mandel's head off. And finally, the hiss of the Konoye blade as Brent personally beheaded Arlene Spencer, the woman he had once loved passionately.

Yoshi's voice broke through the web of memories with more harsh rhetoric spiced with bloody statistics. "In our last battle off Africa, *Yonaga* lost thirty-four fighters." There was a rumble of voices and heads turned. "That's not counting *Bennington's* losses and the losses to our bomber groups. What you must realize is that we face hard, costly battles and that any one of you can resign his commission and return home. But this must be done immediately. See me privately if you so decide after this meeting." He was met by a mute audience. Brent felt some of the young men were in near shock.

Quickly and in a businesslike voice, Yoshi launched into *Yonaga's* early history, specifications, and speed, and the aircraft repair and maintenance facilities. He spoke of other great battles, the terrible losses, continued to deliver hard punches of bloody facts. It was obvious to Brent he was trying to drive any weaklings out. "She can operate a hundred fifty-seven aircraft," he indicated. There was a whistle from one of the Americans and gasps from the others. "Fifty-four of those aircraft are fighters; thirty-six Mitsubishi A6M2 Zero-sens; a squadron of twelve F6F Hellcats; six Seafires which are not used

145

independently. In fact, my own wingmen fly Seafires. The remaining one hundred three aircraft are split almost evenly between our torpedo and dive bomber squadrons. They are *Yonaga's* broadside, her punch, and we must protect them—see to it they deliver their ordinance. This is the only reason for *Yonaga's* existence."

He stopped again, his eyes searching each man as if he were a sorcerer trying to read the fate of each bright young face turned up to him. Brent thought he detected a hint of sadness in his friend's face.

Yoshi pressed on. "And now, listen carefully, if you are to remain alive." Every man straightened, including Hooperman. They all stared at him with the keen eye of a high-stakes gambler watching his cards fall. "Here are my rules of combat, what I have learned over a half-century. You are to take notes, but more important, when we are in training, you are to employ what you hear here today. Remember, in combat, you are allowed one mistake— never two. The enemy will see to that." An oppressive silence filled the room in which the faint whine of blowers, the barely audible clatter of tools on the hangar deck, and the subdued rumble of engines deep in the bowels of the ship intruded like sledgehammers on empty oil drums.

Yoshi waved to a yeoman who had sat unnoticed in a corner of the room. The young man walked to a chalkboard which was mounted to one side and behind the air group commander. There were a computer, keyboard, projector, and screen on the other side of lectern. Ignoring the electronic equipment, the yeoman picked up a piece of chalk and stared expectantly at the commander. "Always stay with your sections until released by your leader," Yoshi began. "*Never* break radio silence until your leader transmits or you are ordered to do so. No lone-wolf heroics or you will just be another fifty-thousand dollar American in some enemy pilot's bank account. Keep the sun behind you and maintain as much altitude advantage as possible. Always check your back when popping out of clouds; you could run out in front of an enemy fighter and give him the easiest kill of his life. Be wary of cumulus clouds; they are like big slabs of rock and you can be easily ambushed. And just as dangerous are thin, high cirrus. The enemy can look down through them and see you, but you usually can not see up through them. *Always* carry out an attack once you have started it. Fire only at close range, under two hundred yards, if possible, in short bursts. Long bursts will overheat your guns and there is a good chance they will jam, and remember, they are harmonized for three hundred meters." The switch to metric units did not seem to bother any of the men. "Firing at ranges of five hundred meters will only spray the sky harmlessly with your bullets and shells. Be very careful about overshooting your enemy. This will put you in front of his gunsights. You will be shooting yourself down." His eyes roamed over the young faces.

Brent thought the session was nearly finished. He was wrong. There was more; much more.

Matsuhara pounded the lectern. "New pilots always seem to fire at long ranges and too often try for the impossible full-deflection shot. Do not make these mistakes." He punished the lectern again for emphasis. "Remember, fire at short ranges and with minimum deflective lead." He held up both palms, one chasing the other, the unavoidable sign language of the fighter pilot. Brent was convinced no fighter pilot could utter more than two sentences without one palm dogfighting the other. "Hit them from behind, close, minimum deflection, and look out for debris—a damaged aircraft can shed aluminum like a tree losing its leaves in a gale." The two palms closed into fists and hit the lectern together. The pilots wrote furiously and the yeoman scribbled numbered rules across the board. He was at least two sentences behind the commander.

Yoshi's next statement took both Brent and Hooperman by surprise. "I have noticed over the years that when I close from behind and get in my first burst, nearly every enemy pilot turns his head to the left."

"The left?" several surprised voices chorused.

"Yes. The fact is, most people when looking behind them will turn to the left. Maybe the muscles in the right side of the neck are stronger, resist, make it easier to turn to the left. I do not really know why, but it happens, so be prepared for it."

Brent was amazed. He had never dreamed there was so much to learn about this bloody trade. Yoshi had discussed dogfighting with him in the past on many occasions, but had never hinted at the depth of detail he was now expounding to his new men.

"I'll be buggered," Brent heard Hooperman say in awe. "Who in creation would know that bit?"

Yoshi pressed on. "Never fly straight and level in a dogfight unless you have made peace with your god. Jink, weave, turn your head, keep an eye behind you. The Arab who kills you will be the one you never see. Never rest your neck, stretch it incessantly, look from extreme right to extreme left, and then do it again and again. You will become bored on long patrols with the complete absence of anything to look at. Your eyes will weary of trying to focus on objects that are not there." Sarcasm crept into the timbre of his voice. "Then slacken your search, rest your neck," he paused, "and die." He sighed in the weighty silence, drummed the lectern with his fingers, and continued, "If an enemy dives on you, *never* turn away. Always turn into him. Attack head-on. Remember, the Messerschmitt has great diving ability." He fell silent. Brent felt Yoshi was tiring.

The commander hunched his shoulders, grimaced, and bore on. "Keep in shape. We have training and weight-lifting equipment on board and at all our training facilities. Dogfighting is very hard work, and you need strong arms and shoulders. You know your controls are not hydraulically boosted, and at combat speeds they can become extremely heavy. None of us has cabin pressurization, so high-altitude flying will wear you out much faster than operating at ground level. And pulling sharp turns, loops, and dives will fatigue you. Remember, a two-hundred-pound man will weigh a thousand pounds during a five-G turn or pullout. I can assure you, after a few minutes of dogfighting, your arms and back will feel like you have been dragging a bull up a flight of stairs." Straightening his hunched shoulders, he took a deep breath. Then he licked his lips and said, "I have seen enemy pilots tire in front of my gunsight. I can tell by the way he turns and maneuvers. He becomes cold meat." He stabbed a finger at his men. "Do not let this happen to you!" There was another charged silence.

Again Brent thought the air group commander was finished, and again he was mistaken.

"Watch the wind," Matsuhara exhorted, waving both hands in sweeping, whirling motions. "Before a mission, note the prevailing winds in your latitude—you will always be briefed. From the equator to thirty north you will find the northeasterly trades. We fly there often." He stabbed a finger down at the deck. "In these latitudes, they are westerly. If you operate east of these islands, get into a fight, run low on fuel, are damaged, you will fly back to base into the teeth of the wind. Then the wind can drain your tanks and kill you where the enemy has failed." He slapped the lectern. "A stupid, useless way to die."

Yoshi tugged at his ear thoughtfully and stared at the far bulkhead. Then he asked almost casually, "Are there any questions?"

"Commander Matsuhara, Ensign Marvin Rubin here, sir," a young redheaded American said, voice low and leisurely with the unmistakable tones of Texas in it. A burly young man, he had a face that looked as though it had been roughly chipped our of granite.

Yoshi made an approving gesture and the young pilot said, "I done paid close mind to your valuable information, sir." He held up a yellow pad covered with scribbles. "But I have a question about the enemy aircraft we're fixin' to meet." Yoshi encouraged him with a nod. Rubin drawled on, "Besides the Me 109, what other enemy aircraft are we aimin' to tangle with, and what are their strengths and weaknesses?"

Good mind behind that ruptured English, Brent said to himself.

Leaning on the lectern, Yoshi explained, "In this theater, the enemy uses the Messerschmitt fighter exclusively. He apparently has several squadrons of Ju 87s, Heinkel IIIs, a few Douglas DC-3s, and even a few Cessnas all based on Saipan and Tinian. The Me has been modified and is a dangerous adversary. We have reports its Daimler Benz "Valkyrie" engine has been reworked and supercharged and produces over three thousand horsepower. I clocked one at four hundred forty knots in level flight before I shot him down." A nervous giggle swept the room. Yoshi ignored it. "However, it still has a weakness in its wide turning radius and could have its wing-loading improved."

"They'se talk they've done installed high-lift devices and redesigned the wing including the ailerons, sir," Rubin said. "I reckon that'll give 'em better turnin'."

"True, but it cannot turn with the Zero."

"Not even a hummin'bird can figure on that, Commander. Everyone knows the Zero can turn faster'n a cow in heat lookin' for her bull."

There was laughter from the men, and Yoshi chuckled. "Correct again, Ensign Rubin." And then with a sly smile, "And that's no bull." More laughter, deeper, longer. The men were delighted to see a spark of humor break through their commanding officer's stern demeanor.

"But the Me can turn with the F6F . . ."

"And the Seafire," a young pale, blond Englishman interrupted Rubin nervously. Then he added, "Pilot Officer Gerald Ransom here, Commander Matsuhara."

"Yes," Yoshi agreed. "But it is not as stable as either fighter in a high-speed turn, Ransom. Remember that. It still tends to waffle, and I can tell the controls become mushy, making it hard to control. As for the Ju 87, hit from below. It's cold meat. Attack the Heinkels from above or head-on. They can only fire back with seven-point-nine mgs. Be very cautious around the DC-3s. Most are gunships and are armed with as many as four Russian UBK twelve-point-seven Gatlings mounted in side doors. The UBK can fire three thousand rounds a minute and has an effective range of sixteen hundred yards. That weight of shot can turn a fighter into confetti—even sink a destroyer."

"How do we attack them, sir?" Ransom asked.

"From below or head-on, but remember, the pilot will turn to bring his armament to bear. Get in a burst and dive out of there." Yoshi smiled. "Or as you Englishmen would say, 'Bugger out!'" There was appropriate laughter.

Allowing his breath to escape in a long sigh, the air group commander almost sagged against the lectern. "Are there any more questions?" he asked.

Flying Officer Claude Hooperman came to life. "Commander Matsuhara, may I respectfully suggest you discuss gunnery? Some of the lads may not be aware of the full implications of their gunnery problems."

Yoshi thumped his forehead with a closed fist. "Why, of course—thank you for reminding me, Mister Hooperman." The hand dropped to his chin and he pinched it thoughtfully. Then he spoke, but seemed to be reprimanding himself, "Yes. Yes. Gunnery, of course." Then he reached into his pocket and withdrew a single bullet. Obviously, gunnery and more had been on his mind when he had entered the room. He held up the bullet. "This is not a magic sword," he said. "You can have your pip on the enemy pilot himself and miss for many reasons. One," he nodded at Hooperman, "is bullet-drop. You must keep in mind the instant the bullet leaves your gun, it begins to fall. Obviously, the further it travels, the more it falls. And it tumbles. Every bullet and shell wobbles slightly, and the further the travel the greater the wobble. And you must remember recoil. All of you know recoil shakes your gun platform. But you may not know that vibration is good for an error of thirty, forty feet at a range of three hundred yards." Hands braced on the lectern, he leaned forward, eyes burning with new energy. "Think," he said. "Think of the combined effects of deflection, bullet-drop, and bullet-wobble. If your target is not only crossing in front of you, but climbing, too, it is useless to just aim ahead of him." He stabbed a finger repeatedly at his new pilots to emphasize each word. "You must calculate how far ahead and above his line-of-flight to aim your ordnance, because shells and bullets will fall faster when you fire upward than when you fire level." He stared at the silent faces. "Do you understand?" he shouted.

"Hear! Hear!" and *"Banzai!"* rang through the compartment.

Hooperman said into Brent's ear, "He's as keen as mustard."

Matsuhara smiled. "Well, in training you will have ample opportunity to solve these problems. Learn your lessons well. You will have only one opportunity once we engage the enemy."

A young Japanese shouted, "Commander Matsuhara, Ensign Hitoshi Kitajima here." Brent recognized the young man from the introductions that had opened the meeting. He was the broad-shouldered, dark young man who stood out with the very dark skin and fine yet strong features and strange accent. And now, Brent thought he placed the accent. Incongruously, it seemed Spanish. *Weird.*

Yoshi nodded and the young Japanese continued, "Is *Yonaga* ready for action? We all know she was damaged. And what about *Bennington*? She was badly hit. The whole world knows that." Spanish inflection was there, no doubt about it. Everyone stared curiously.

Yoshi answered, "And there are many things the

whole world does not know. Some things are best held in confidence. You will be briefed in due course—when the time is right." He scratched his chin and stared at the young man. "You are not from the Japanese Islands, Ensign Kitajima?"

"No, sir. My grandparents emigrated to Brazil immediately after the Great War. That was where I was born. Then, in 1980, my family emigrated to Japan." And then, self-consciously, "I was raised in the city of Oizumi. However, I attended Tokyo University and started my flying lessons when I was eighteen."

To a man, the other six young Japanese pilots threw glances at Kitajima. Brent saw undisguised hostility in some of their eyes, heard *yadonashi* (tramp) and *ie-nashi* (homeless) whispered by one. From his position, he could not tell who had made the derogatory remarks. He seethed with anger and frustration.

Hostility toward Brazilian-Japanese was deep seated. Theirs was a strange story with overtures of tragedy. Kitajima's family was part of the wave of 100,000 Japanese-Brazilians who had emigrated to Japan during the halcyon years of the high-tech explosion. Labor had become very scarce, and native Japanese disdained some of the poorer paying jobs and their wretched working conditions. Japanese-Brazilians, Pakistanis, Nepalese, Bangladeshi, and Koreans had all flocked in to take the jobs and at the same time face the prejudices of a homogenous, intolerant society. Many times Brent had heard hoodlums shout at foreign workers, *"Tanitsu kokka, Tanitsu minzokuy!"* It translated, 'One nation, one race."

Thousands of the foreign workers settled near or in the manufacturing town of Oizumi, where even the Japanese-Brazilians were forced to live in segregated communities. A bastard group who spoke a ruptured dialect, they were considered by most natives no more Japanese than a tabby cat is a tiger. Brent had seen this prejudice directed at other minorities—ironically, including the Eta, who were native Japanese of the lower classes. And racial slurs had enraged his black friend and fellow American Lieutenant Reginald Williams. Later, off Tomonuto Atoll while fighting for the Japanese, Williams had died horribly with his entire crew on submarine *Blackfin*. Brent felt anger and frustration swell. His stomach became a hot knot that seemed to be creeping toward his chest.

Yoshi Matsuhara despised the prejudice as much as Brent. He had seen the looks, heard the whispers. Waving a hand at the Japanese pilots, he declared forcefully, "We are here to fight the enemy, not each other. I will not tolerate hostility toward our own or toward our foreign pilots." He punched the lectern so hard it rocked. "It makes no sense, with the fate of Japan in the balance, and perhaps that of the entire free world—that we should have ignorant squabbles among ourselves. I have seen it in the past and will not tolerate any of it now. We must fight together or die alone." He stabbed a finger at the group of Japanese pilots. "If I see or hear anything of a disciminatory nature from any of you, you will be immediately court-martialed and dismissed from this command."

"Sir," Kitajima said. "True, I have experienced some disagreeable moments at home," he waved, "and elsewhere." He turned to his comrades and eyed a surly pilot with an arrogant smile on his face. Brent recognized Ensign Yasujiro Mizoguchi. Nearly as large as Kitajima, Mizoguchi had a narrow face, eyes like black beads, and a sharp nose and chin that gave him the aspect of a mouse. Staring at Mizoguchi, Kitajima straightened, suddenly appearing bulkier, shoulders wider, neck thicker. He said softly, "Commander Matsuhara, with your permission, there is nothing here I cannot handle myself."

Yoshi roared back, "You do not have my permission!" He pointed at Yasujiro Mizoguchi. "Stand, Ensign," he commanded, his voice strident enough to fill the Royal Kabuki Theater.

Fearfully, Mizoguchi came to his feet. Every man

154

stared. "Do you feel you will have any difficulty serving in my command?"

"No, sir."

"Or with any of your fellow pilots?"

"No, sir."

"You made derogatory remarks concerning Ensign Kitajima?"

The young man swallowed hard, as if most of his lunch was still wedged in his throat. "That is true, sir. It was unconscionable, and I deeply regret my remarks." He turned to Hitoshi Kitajima. "I apologize, Ensign Kitajima."

"Get out!" Yoshi bellowed. "Only weaklings apologize." He jabbed his finger at the door. "Off this ship now, before I have you thrown off!"

Eyes down, lips turned under, the young man left. Silence, viscous, like cold syrup, flowed through the room, filling every corner, coating every man.

After a long moment a persistent voice broke the silence. It was Lieutenant Marvin Rubin. "Commander Matsuhara, may I ask a question?" The voice was calm and cool, exuding confidence.

His face still reddened by a sunset flush, and breathing in short gasps to contain his anger, Yoshi stared at the young man. Brent expected a blunt refusal and dismissal of the meeting. But instead, the air group commander nodded his approval.

"Commander," the Texan said in a strong voice. "It's no secret the enemy *Essex, Al Kufra,* was repaired at Surabaya and has been seen puttin' to sea hell-bent for election. Also, carrier *Magid* has been reported ready for bear in the yards at Tripoli. Can we expect to dry-gulch these critters soon?"

Everyone was staring at the young ensign. He had certainly distracted the air group commander and altered the tense mood in the room. Maybe it was deliberate. In any event, Brent was amazed by the young man's verve, panache, and confidence. He also almost laughed at the

Texan's idiom. Yoshi placed both hands on the lectern and stared down at Rubin. He was cooling and appeared to be collecting himself well after his rage. The ensign stared back unflinchingly. Brent was surprised by the restraint in Yoshi's voice. But, he, too, was favorably impressed.

"Yes, Lieutenant Rubin," he said calmly. "We can expect to engage those vessels." He tapped the lectern with a single finger. "Yes, we will engage them simply because our business is to destroy them. But I do not know when or where." He pinched the bridge of his nose with a thumb and forefinger and closed his eyes for a fleeting instant. The Mizoguchi incident had upset him, but the air group commander was under control despite his recent rage; he wanted to end the meeting on an upbeat note, not an air of acrimony. He would do it with Rubin.

Matsuhara again leaned against the lectern. "I know you are anxious to engage the enemy. Not only is it your personal war against tyranny, terrorism, and evil, it will be the ultimate test of your manhood. Combat does that and we all seek it." He shifted his eyes to Rubin. "But remember, a good warrior engages the enemy in a place and time of his choosing—if this is at all possible. All I can tell you now is that I do not know when or where we will engage these carriers. These strategic considerations are beyond the responsibilities of the air group commander." His eyes roamed over his pilots and settled on the Japanese. "And underlying it all, you must remember there are scores to be settled, the comrades butchered, our Emperor insulted." With the force of his scowl, his brow was suddenly as corrugated as a plowed field. He waved a fist. "We will find the vengeance of the forty-seven *ronin.*"

"*Banzai! Banzai!*" rang through the room, and the Japanese half-rose from their chairs. Puzzled, the Americans and Englishmen looked at each other. Brent wanted to explain to Hooperman, but it was impossible in the bedlam.

Yosh's eyes wandered over the young faces staring up at him. The anger was gone. Again, Brent thought he saw sadness in the black eyes. Yoshi took control with a loud voice. "Many years ago a wise man said, 'Neither fear nor courage can save us, only skill and the smiles of the gods.'" He shifted his weight from one foot to the other. "We samurai believe in *bushido*, and the code of *bushido* is found in our sacred book, the *Hagakure*. The *Hagakure* teaches many lessons. One of the most valuable, and one all men should remember, is, 'If I do not know the way to defeat my enemy, I have found the way to defeat myself.' Remember those words."

Again his eyes wandered over his new pilots as if he were trying to imprint each face in his memory. "When I dismiss you, you are to report to a lorry which is waiting for you on the dock. You are to report with all your gear. You will be taken to Tokyo International Airport, where you will be billeted and assigned to training squadrons. I will be there tomorrow to see personally to your training." He stopped as if he were catching his breath and nodded at Hooperman. "Flying Officer Hooperman will be in charge." Then, curtly, "You are dismissed."

Before a man could rise, Flying Officer Hooperman's voice held them in their chairs. "By your leave, sir, twice I have heard you mention 'the revenge of the forty-seven *ronin*.' I know this is an important bit of Japanese lore." He gestured at the Americans and the Englishmen. "Do you have time to explain it to us, Commander?"

"Yes. You should know this tale," Yoshi answered, apparently pleased by the request. "The story of the forty-seven is sacred to all samurai, helps explain the hunger for vengeance that is so dear to all Japanese." He took a deep breath and began the tale. Brent had heard it many a time, but it never failed to challenge his imagination and intrigue him. "It was in the fourth month of the thirteenth year of the Tsunyoshi shogunate . . ." He caught himself, "Ah, that is seventeen-oh-one on your calendar—when an honorable samurai, Lord

Asano of Ako, was a guest at the Imperial court at Edo—now Tokyo. A scoundrel named Kira insulted Asano and tricked him into baring his sword in the palace." Matsuhara dampened his lips and continued, "This was a mortal offense. Immediately, Lord Asano committed *seppuku—hari kiri* or 'belly slitting' to Westerners—and his estates were confiscated and his samurai automatically became *ronin*—masterless vagabonds or tramps."

"Masterless vagabounds? Tramps?" Hooperman asked fascinated. "But why?"

Brent was sure the Englishman was no longer aware of anyone else in the room except Yoshi Matsuhara. It was a two-man exchange.

Yoshi shrugged. "Tradition. When a man's estates were confiscated, his samurai became *ronin*. However, forty-seven of Asano's *ronin* plotted vengeance." The commander's eyes sparked with new life and his cheeks took on a sanguinary hue. "For more than a year the forty-seven lived drunken lives of debauchery, all the while plotting their vengeance. Exactly one year passed and on the same day of the month on which Lord Asano had died, the forty-seven struck. They cut their way into Kira's home, found him hiding in a woodshed, and hacked him to pieces." Yoshi paused as if he were savoring the tale like a gourmet dinner enjoying a superb cuisine.

"Splendid tale of classic revenge, indeed, sir," Hooperman said.

"It is not finished."

"Not finished?"

Yoshi shook his head, a sardonic smile twisting his lips. "No," he said. "According to *bushido*, the *ronin* had no options. They all committed *seppuku*, preserving their honor for immortality."

"Banzai!" echoed from the Japanese contingent.

Yoshi silenced the young men with raised palms. He directed himself at the Englishmen and Americans. "Now do you understand the sacred nature of vengeance to the samurai?"

The pilots mumbled approval and understanding, although Brent believed most of them were preplexed by the many strange twists to the tale. One thing was certain: they now appreciated the importance of vengeance to the Japanese.

The commander smiled and leaned against the lectern. "Now it is time to bring this meeting to a close." He stood erect and in a military voice commanded, "You are dismissed."

The pilots stood as one, the Japanese bowed, and then the eleven new pilots filed through the door behind Hooperman. Brent Ross remained standing next to his chair. He expected his friend to say something about the meeting, especially about Ensigns Hitoshi Kitajima and Mizoguchi. But the air group commander obviously wanted to put that disagreeable topic out of his mind. To Brent's surprise, Yoshi asked with the hint of a smile, "Do you have liberty tonight?"

"Both port and starboard."

The pilot's big hand fell on the American's shoulder. "Good, Brent-san," he said with new energy. "I have a new lady-friend." Yoshi's eyes were dancing with a gleam Brent had not seen for years.

"A new woman?" Brent repeated. Now he understood why Yoshi was no longer *shinigurai*. A new woman. Love must be creeping back into his barren life. At least the hope was there.

"We are having dinner together, Brent-san. It is our second date—I just met her last week." He saw the unseen question in Brent's eyes. "We are friends, Brent-san—just friends, nothing more."

"I'd be honored."

"She had a lovely young friend who is very eager to meet you."

Brent felt a long latent excitement suddenly spring to life. "Honor be damned, just try to stop me," he said smiling.

Both men were laughing as they left the briefing room.

Chapter Seven

Brent liked what he saw in the mirror. His blue wool tunic stretched without a crease, without a wrinkle across the expanse of his broad chest, and his shoulders appeared wider than ever. Perfectly tailored, the tunic tapered sharply like a wineglass to his small waist and narrow hips. He was proud of his physique and kept his 220 pounds of muscle hard and in high definition with a rigorous daily regimen of exercise.

Eyeing a slight bulge in his left armpit, he smiled. With a single quick motion, he pulled his Beretta M951 Brigadier from its holster. It was only eight inches long and weighed less than twenty-nine ounces, and he held the black automatic in his hand like a small boy eyeing a new toy. Brent was convinced that ounce for ounce the pistol was the finest hand weapon in the world. The first locked breech model to appear under the Beretta name, the vicious little killing machine's action was still based on the usual Beretta configuration of open-topped slide and external hammer. A thumb to the latch in the grip released the ten-round magazine, which was propelled into his hand by the force of its spring. Then a tug on the slide worked the action, which slid through perfectly fitted oiled surfaces like newly waxed skis skimming a fresh layer of powder. A slight pull on the trigger and his thumb eased the hammer back into its chamber. He rolled a finger over the top oiled Parabellum cartridge, especially designed to destroy tissue, and palmed the magazine back into the spring-loaded grip and locked it into place. Then, carefully, he returned the weapon to its holster.

He leaned closer to the mirror. His weeks at sea on *Haida* had deeply tanned his face and bleached his hair out so that it was a mixture of golden hues: the color of ripe Iowa corn streaked with strands lightened to the white of Alpine ski slopes, a marvelous contrast to his tanned face. There were a few new lines there, imprinted by time and the sea and defined by the sun which could not penetrate some of the creases trailing off from the corners of his eyes during those long hours when he was forced to squint in the glare. "The mark of the sailor," he said to himself.

He rubbed his freshly shaved chin. With whiskers wire-hard, no razor could ever give Brent Ross a skin-close shave. Fortunately, his whiskers were fair and the perennial stubble did not show, at least for a few hours. He put on his cap and squared it. He was ready for his big date. He smiled. Yoshi had refused to tell him anything about the girl. He had only grinned and repeated, when asked, "She is lovely, beautiful, intelligent. You will like her, Brent-san."

Brent filled his lungs like a smoker enjoying his first cigarette of the morning. He exhaled it slowly through clenched teeth so that it hissed and whistled. It had been a long time since he had even spoken to a woman and nearly a year since he had touched one. He had known many beautiful, hot-blooded women. "You have an effect on a woman's libido—like a giant, walking aphrodisiac" the clever, articulate Arlene Spencer had teased solemnly, laughter deep down in her voice. And after their first night of lovemaking she had giggled, "You're nothing but two hundred twenty pounds of superheated sperm."

Arlene Spencer had been the last. Long-limbed and

with a coltishly elegant body, she had been both lovely and extremely intelligent, with an investigative reporter's inquisitive mind. And she loved classical music. He was pleasantly surprised, almost shocked, by her eccentric carnal appetite. An animal in bed, she insisted on making love to the "Spartacus and Phrygia" love theme from Kachaturian's *Spartacus* ballet music. Also, she was a traitor who he had calmly beheaded in her own apartment. He could never forget how her jugulars had squirted a mad design on the white wall, running to the floor, puddling. He stood rooted, gripping his bloody sword, not believing what he had done. It was Yoshi who had finally pulled him away, wiped off the Konoye blade and returned it to its jeweled scabbard. Then he had led Brent out of the apartment like a father taking his stunned, injured son home.

Brent shook his head, cleared all thoughts of Arlene. Dale McIntyre replaced her. Poor Dale. He was twenty-seven when he met her and she was nearing forty. She could not cope with the difference in their ages. Hot memories of her inventive gymnastics in bed flashed back. Maybe it was his youth that had stimulated her so. Or maybe it was an innate libidinous force that, once unleashed, engulfed a man like a ravenous beast. Most women yielded their bodies submissively. Dale attacked with near savagery. Rolling, butting, thrashing, shouting incoherently, she made love viciously. Scars were left on his ears from her teeth, on his back from the frantic pull of fingernails. And she was insatiable. "They couldn't have had it better in Sodom and Gomorrah," she had murmured the first night as they both sank back in exhaustion. "Well worth a rain of fire and brimstone." They both laughed wildly, drunk on their spent passion.

Then there was beautiful young Mayumi Hachiya; the only woman he had loved who had been younger. With glossy black waist-long hair, she had skin as vibrant and luxurious as the petals of a newly bloomed rosebud. Her body was perfection: rounded, firm breasts that hardened under his kisses, tiny waist flaring to sculpted hips and buttocks, and long, slender legs that felt like hot satin under his hands. And she was passionate, a raging onanistic heat that enveloped him with its demands, fogging his mind like a storm-driven cloud, erasing reality. But she was torn from him by *yuino* (arranged marriage) to a cousin she did not love.

The first one came back. Pamela Ward, the intelligence officer. He had been a 22-year-old ensign newly assigned to the NIS Seattle office when he met her back in 1983. He chuckled. A lieutenant and 37-years-old, she outranked him, but not in bed where he drove her into ecstatic exhaustion.

Then, there had been Sarah Aranson, the Israeli Mossad agent. She had lost her fighter-pilot lover over the Sinai when he and his *Mystère* had been blown to bits by an SAM (surface-to-air missile). Filled with hate and bitterness, Sarah had devoted her life to fighting the Arabs. But from the beginning she had been attracted to Brent. Their fierce attraction was finally consummated in her apartment in Tel Aviv in a wild night of lovemaking. She marveled at his inexhaustible stamina. In fact, she experienced a little trouble walking when she finally eased herself out of bed in the morning to prepare breakfast. He asked her if she was sore. "A little," she giggled back like a schoolgirl. "But it feels great." They both laughed. And then she added, with her wry sense of humor, "Let's let the sequel wait for a few hours."

"What about syndication?" he quipped.

"I'll be ready for every rerun," she laughed back.

Tucking his lips under, he stepped back from the mirror, his mind suddenly filled with cruel memories of Kathryn Suzuki. A clever terrorist, she had duped him with his own desires. No man could ever forget that torrid night in Hawaii. She danced the hula for him in a scant costume that made her magnificent body maddeningly attractive. She rotated her perfect hips in the timeless motion of the aroused woman, broke through

163

the *ti* leaves with her marble-like legs, thrust the half-moons of her heaving breasts at him until he ripped the flimsy halter free and began to kiss them frantically. Then the bedroom and a full night of thrusting, clawing, and cries of ecstasy. The wild convulsive orgasms, her hands pleading at the small of his back, and his own explosive, draining climaxes that left him weak and limp between her raised knees. And it had all been part of a plan—a scheme to lead him in a weakened condition into the hands of an assassin waiting in ambush just outside the apartment. "You fucked yourself to death," Kathryn jeered as she ran off and the assassin closed in.

The fight had almost cost Brent his life before he'd smashed the Arab's face with a wrench. He still remembered with satisfaction the moment months later when he finally trapped Kathryn and pulled the trigger, sending a bullet crashing into her brain. He had actually enjoyed standing over her, watching her arms and legs twitch and spasm in the final grasp of death.

A knock closed his book of memories. When Brent opened the door, a grinning Yoshi Matsuhara was standing there. "Are you ready?" the pilot asked.

"For almost a year," Brent answered.

Laughing, the two officers walked down the passageway.

"We'll meet them at the *Chōjō Seiyoken* restaurant," Yoshi said as the two officers stepped from the accommodation ladder. "It is a charming old place. You will love it."

"We won't pick them up?"

"Negative. My date had to work late. The women will drive to the restaurant. It is better this way. We will have more time together."

The two fell silent as they walked in single file along a narrow path that led to the main gate through staggered concrete barriers. The maze reminded Brent of pictures he had seen of World War Two tank obstacles erected by the Germans in front of their Siegfried Line. There were twelve sandbagged Nambu machine gun emplacements strategically placed among the barriers. Brent could see the helmeted heads of their crews jutting just above the sandbags. In addition, four more Nambus could be seen on top of the giant warehouses and machine shops surrounding Dock B-2. Admiral Fujita had ordered the barriers and guns emplaced after Kathryn Suzuki and a confederate had smashed through the main gate with a truck loaded with explosives and charged toward *Yonaga,* which was on her blocks in the great graving dock. They had been stopped by one of only two Nambus and Brent Ross's accurate fire. It was here that Brent had executed an injured Kathryn after she had been thrown from the overturned truck.

"You've told me absolutely nothing about the women," Brent complained as they emerged from the maze and could walk side by side. The gatehouse was very close. "What's the big secret? Why are you being so damned coy?"

"All right, Brent-san. The surprise will not be as good, but I will tell you something about them. The rest you will discover for yourself." Yoshi placed his hand on his friend's back. "My friend is Tomoko Ozumori. She is a widow and very beautiful. She is personal secretary to the chief of the Maritime Self-Defense Force's supply office in Tokyo. That's where I met her."

"My date? My date?" Brent demanded impatiently.

"Your date is Garnet Shaw."

"Garnet Shaw? That's a theatrical name. Is she an actress?"

Yoshi exhaled audibly. "She's a writer."

Brent stopped in his tracks. "Jesus Christ, man. Another Arlene Spencer?"

"Come, come," Yoshi chided. "You cannot distrust all female writers because of Arlene Spencer." He grasped Brent's shoulder. "Anyway, Garnet is not a reporter.

165

She's a novelist."

"Novelist! I've never heard of her."

Yoshi shrugged. "Eight, nine historical romances published back in the States. She has a reputation with the female audience—no Barbara Cartland or Danielle Steel but successful." And then with new enthusiasm, "I told you she is lovely, and she is intelligent, too, Brent-san—you'll see."

Yoshi tugged and Brent resumed the walk toward the main gate. When they reached the gatehouse, an old chief machinist mate, Chief Masatoshi Nomura, saluted with short, jerky movements. Four seaman guards standing to either side in pairs and armed with 6.5-millimeter Arisaka Type 38 rifles snapped to attention, their weapons at order arms.

Tall for a Japanese, Chief Masatoshi Nomura was white-haired, gaunt, and slightly stooped. He was an original member of *Yonaga*'s crew, and the weathered face like the leather of an old glove showed it. Scuttlebutt had it he suffered the agonies of hell from severe arthritis—a fact he kept carefully concealed from the crew, especially the medical staff. Similar to most of the old "plank owners," he refused discharge and retirement. In fact, the old chief appeared fearful of this prospect. "I was a young unmarried seaman when I reported aboard *Yonaga* in nineteen forty-one," he had explained to Brent and Yoshi one afternoon in the hangar deck as he'd looked up from a dismantled engine. "When we broke free of Sano-Wan, my mother and father were long dead and my only brother had disappeared in Siberia when the Kwantung Army was overrun by the Russians in nineteen forty-five. I have some cousins living on Hokkaido." He shook his head. "But they do not want me. I am a creature from another age, like a dinosaur." He turned up his hands. "Who would want a dinosaur? Where would I fit? In a museum? And this is not the Japan I left. This is a different world." He gestured in a wide circle. "*Yonaga* is my life." And then the words that

166

would forever earn Brent's respect: "I have followed Admiral Fujita into hell and back many times. It is what I know, all I know, and the admiral needs me. One way or another, I will die here, on or with *Yonaga.*"

Beaming and with his hand held rigidly to the bill of his cap, the old chief greeted both saluting officers with a broad smile that incongruously turned the lean, wrinkled face into a death's head. "Good evening, Commander Matsuhara, Commander Ross," he said, dropping his salute when Brent and Yoshi dropped theirs. Nomura remained at attention. "Your staff car is waiting." He gestured at a Mercedes SEL 560 sedan parked just outside the gate. The seaman guards raised the barrier.

As Brent and Yoshi walked to the Mercedes, Chief Nomura shouted after them, "Great kill, Commander Ross!"

And then the seaman guards added spiritedly, *"Banzai,* Commander Ross! *Banzai, Haida!"*

Smiling self-consciously and waving his acknowledgment to the chief and his men, Brent Ross entered the sedan. Yoshi slipped into the driver's seat.

"Remember, old friend, this isn't a Zero," Brent said, fastening his seatbelt.

"Do not worry yourself. I promise to cruise under two hundred knots." Then the engine roared, the wheels spun, and the big sedan was off with a squeal of tortured rubber, leaving a trail of blue smoke in its wake.

The *Chōjō Seiyoken* restaurant was located at the corner of Kototoi-dori and Kappabashi-dori streets in the charming old Asakusa area of Tokyo. A temple town throughout Japanese history, Asakusa was known as the *shitamachi* (the downtown of the common people). However, its pride was the oldest temple in Tokyo, Sensoji Temple. The restaurant was just west of the temple's lush grounds. However, in the darkness, Brent could see only a few colorful lanterns hanging in the temple's parklike setting. Slowing, Yoshi began to search for a parking place.

The long drive to Tokyo had been uneventful. A year earlier they would have been accompanied by seaman guards. In fact, twice Brent had had fist fights just outside the gates to the dock area with picketing Japanese Red Army terrorists masquerading as peace marchers. And there had been gun battles and assassinations in Tokyo, most in the Ginza. Fujita's rage had inspired the Tokyo police and two motorized battalions of Self-Defense Force troops into aggressive, vigilant patrols.

However, the most decisive force was a 300-man contingent of seaman guards especially recruited by Admiral Fujita. In addition to belligerence and a hunger for physical violence, Fujita required that every man pledge his belief in *bushido* and *Kokutai*—the ancient doctrine that the national essence was embodied in the Emperor, the one hundred twenty-fifth direct descendant of the goddess Amaterasu-O-Mi-Kami. Divided into ten-man crews, the new guard units patrolled the city in trucks equipped with a Nambu on the cab and another over the tailgate. The first month of the patrols, eleven terrorists were killed and ten captured. Three of the dead had been beaten to death.

There were the usual editorials condemning brutality, stern denunciations in the Diet, and a few angry attacks by television commentators. But the Emperor was firmly behind Admiral Fujita, and support in the Diet managed to squelch the opposition. "After all," Admiral Fujita had said during a staff meeting, "they want petrol for their Toyotas, and as long as *Yonaga* is a viable force, supplies from America will get through." And, indeed, there had been an abundance of automobiles on the road on the drive into the capital.

To Brent, raised in America and a product of Western civilization, and speaking a fundamentally Indo-European vocabulary, Tokyo was massed confusion and contradictions and in a very real way a synthesis of the world's religions, philosophies, and technologies. Every time he entered this strange city he marveled at its singular uniqueness.

Here met over twenty civilizations and a dozen or more religions and uncounted races and subraces. And here, in this ancient crossroads of the world, could be found the most modern electronics plants on earth, the fifty-six ways of making love of the Kama-sutra, the two great principles of *Yin* and *Yang*, dozens of mundane steel and concrete towers, the beauty of elysian gardens, miles of garish neon signs, innumerable exotic perfumes, 100,000 stinks, a financial center where corruption was the rule, virtues of esthetic holy men and uncounted vices of pimps, whores, and thugs.

It was all to be read in the streets: women and girls in kimonos either brightly colored or subdued, according to their age, young women as fashionably dressed as Parisian models, girls in tight-fitting jeans, others in Indian saris, men in finely worsted three-piece suits, others in dirty work clothes or the ragged uniforms of dead armies, many carrying children on their backs, wearing fine leather shoes, straw sandals, boots, baseball caps, derbies, and bowlers. And in their midst a sprinkling of sumo wrestlers, Sikhs in tall pink turbans, Americans, Germans, Latins, British, French, Portuguese, Chinese, Korean, Pakistani, Nepalese, Bangladeshi, and more from the four corners. The pastiche of religions was on parade, too: Buddhist monks, Catholic priests, Protestant pastors, Shinto priests, Muslim imams, and Hindu sadhus. The variety was staggering, infinite.

Brent had tried with other Americans to describe it. "Hybrid, multifarious, preposterous, transcendent, paradoxical, dissolute, monstrous, phenomenal, puissant, noisy, quiet, garish, simpering, and Olympian freak," were just some of the words all agreed applied. But they also agreed that they had failed to do justice to this stupefying city.

Yoshi's voice interrupted Brent's musings. "Here we

are," he said, whipping into a parking place on a dark side street. As Brent stepped from the Mercedes, he felt a tingle of excitement. *Lovely, intelligent* ran through his mind. He suddenly felt very impatient.

The *Chōjō Seiyoken* reminded Brent of the *Kabayaki-ya* restaurant where he and Sarah Aranson had dined in 1984. It, too, was built in the old-fashioned way, with individual small huts arranged in a random pattern. Each small house was built in the traditional way, with walls of weathered pine and roofs of gray tile, scattered over a large, irregular plot of ground; a low wooden fence completely surrounded the buildings. Above the entrance suspended from bamboo poles, a large paper and bamboo lamp covered with ideograms advertised the restaurant in flawless calligraphy.

The two officers pushed their way through the bamboo door and were immediately confronted by two young men in dark business suits. It was immediately apparent one was the manager and the other his assistant. Both men bowed. "Ah, Commander Matsuhara, it is so good to see you again," the manager cooed in a high, soft voice. Short and slender, he waved a limp white hand at a hut at the far end of the compound. "The ladies just arrived."

The assistant, a tall, portly young man with an uncomfortable smile frozen on his face, clapped his hands for a waitress. "*Jochu! Jochu!*" he called authoritatively. Looking at the pair, Brent was reminded of Laurel and Hardy, whose old comedies he had loved to watch on television when he was just a boy.

A short young woman with glistening black hair piled high on her head and held in place by an assortment of jeweled combs, willow sprigs, and silver hairpins approached. The fragile beauty of her face reminded Brent of the masterful work of the famous dollmaker Ryujo Hori. Her fine silk kimono was spectacular. Brent had never seen one quite like it. Brocaded with iris, roses, and camellias, intertwining in an enchanting pattern, it appeared to be the work of an artist, not a seamstress. A thin white *obi* tightly tied emphasized her delicate waist.

She had been waiting in an alcove next to a small structure that was obviously the kitchen. "Take Commander Matsuhara and his friend to their dining room," the assistant ordered. There was the usual male superiority in the timbre of the voice. The fact that the woman was a waitress had nothing to do with the attitude. Women were inferior—it was as simple as that. It still permeated Japanese society. Brent hated it.

The waitress bowed, smiled shyly after stealing a look at Brent, and gestured to a hut at the far end of the compound. The two officers followed her, footfalls crunching on the carefully raked gravel path. Her progress was slow, her steps made short by her tight kimono. Watching the twin ovals of her buttocks moving in perfectly balanced harmony beneath the flowing silk brought a tightness to Brent's throat and a warmth much further down. His impatience grew, but he managed a facade of nonchalance as the trio walked down the narrow winding path. *Randy bastard!* He upbraided himself silently.

Even in his slightly irritated state, Brent was impressed by the grounds. The weak light of overhead paper lanterns cast an eerie glow that produced shadows and at the same time seemed to enhance colors like the dying light of twilight. Everything was miniaturized, as if they had entered a fairyland designed for elves.

There was no homage to Euclid here, no rigorous geometric patterns like those that dominated Western gardens. Brent had once heard an old monk say, "The Western garden is the child of the intellect, the eastern garden the child of love." How true. Brent had learned long ago that no single connecting thread could ever be found in Japanese gardens. The eastern garden was man-plant, sun-happiness, water-mused. Mosses, trees, shrubs, flowers, boulders did not just fill space, they seemed to infuse it with life, with soul. And water was used to frame it all, subtly, playfully reflecting stone, grass, boulders, and flowers.

The life and vitality of nature was all around Brent. All was in *wa*, perfect harmony, the very center of life to the Japanese. To the right, a waterfall tumbled from the top of a small hill covered with *bonsai*. The water bubbled and splashed gaily over red and green rocks to a riverbed of volcanic stones where it swirled like a slender blue-white serpent to a small pond, *de rigueur* for a Japanese garden. A bridge guarded by two stone lions crossed the pool. In the center of the pond a small island glowed with the riotous colors of blooming roses, lilacs, and camellias. Looming tall there a cast-iron crane stood boldly like a palace guard. Dotting the banks a half-dozen stone lanterns added their light to those overhead.

To Brent's left was a long pergola covered with blossoming grape and lilac. Surrounding it all were rocks, shrubs, moss, and growing in porcelain pots, dwarf trees perhaps a hundred years old, and as twisted and gnarled as thousand-year-old giants of the forest. All seemed cast about aimlessly, yet each element seemed to be in its natural place, its natural order. "Beautiful. Magnificent," he murmured.

The waitress gestured and the two officers turned off the path and mounted some low stairs to the door of the last hut. Above the door were the words *Tsŭkí Haná* (Moon Flower). To the right of the door neatly resting side by side were two pairs of high-heeled shoes. Glancing at the shoes, Brent felt the warmth started by the waitress build to a small fire. The American thought, *If I can get my kicks from a waitress's butt and women's shoes, I must really be horny*. He was chuckling to himself as he and Yoshi placed their shoes next to the women's and pulled on paper slippers provided by the waitress. Before they entered the hut, the waitress looked up shyly into Brent's eyes and said, "My name is Sashi."

"Sashi-san," Brent said, generously adding "Miss" to the girl's name. Then he followed Yoshi through the door. The waitress's eyes never left the big American's tiny waist, and detectable under the close-fitting uniform, the tight, synchronized movements of his rock-hard buttocks.

The room was what Brent expected. Everything about him was of wood, paper, straw, and smooth, unpainted surfaces, nothing that concealed the grain of the planed wood surfaces; and no metal. Every plank, every post had been chosen with care, fitted with precision, and polished with devotion. Woven rush *tatami* mats covered the floor; *shoji* screens opened onto the garden. Brent guessed the room to be a six-mat room, about 9 by 12 feet. The only furniture was a low table surrounded by *zabútons* (cushions), a cast-iron heater, a small chest of drawers in one corner with a china tea service, and a dozen more *zabútons* casually piled in against one wall. Brent knew these were reserved for guests who wished to finish their meals with sex. *Futons* would have been too obvious.

In the far corner in its usual alcove was the obligatory *tokonoma*. The *tokonoma* was reserved for a few beautiful things—a poem, a vase, a piece of sculpture—and a handful of cunningly arranged flowers. The *kakemono* (backdrop) was the showpiece of this one, a long *sumi-e* (scroll) with black ink on a white silk landscape done in the simple style of the great fifteenth-century artist Sesshu. No doubt it was selected by the management for Yoshi's party because of the strong Zen influence in the work. The flowers were arranged in a Heian vase to suggest love, romance. Next to the vase was a miniature of the great Daibutsu of Nara, a fifty-three-foot-high bronze Buddha that Buddhist believe radiates divine light to the farthest precincts of the universe. No other wall decorations appeared in the room except for carvings

173

above the *shoji*.

But Brent's eyes were not for the unique beauty of the room, the clever workmanship, the exquisite *tokonoma*. Instead, his eyes fell on two women standing to one side of the table. The first was an attractive middle-aged Japanese with black hair, long and soft, flowing to her shoulders. Her skin, flawless as the most expensive jade, and the slant of her eyes gave her that exotic quality that so enchanted Western men. Deep dark, they were doe eyes touched with all the mystery and intrigue of the East. Her blouse bulged with large breasts for a Japanese and her skirt hugged the voluptuous, accommodating hips of a woman who had loved many times, fully and completely. Brent could understand why Yoshi had been so attracted to her.

The second woman was a stunning blond Caucasian who appeared to be in her mid-twenties. "Commander Brent Ross, Tomoko Ozumori and Garnet Shaw," Yoshi said, gesturing.

Brent mumbled the usual salutations, grasped hands, but could not take his eyes from Garnet. When he enveloped her tiny hand in his, he felt excitement tingle up his arm and lift the hair on his neck. Her coloring was vivid: golden hair reflecting the light as if precious stones were strategically placed in the strands, creamy skin with the purity of a ripe peach tinted slightly brown by the sun, lips and cheeks blooming with the rush of fresh young blood beneath the surface, and blue eyes, the dark indigo-blue of a mountain lake shadowed by passing clouds. Her body was superb. Slender like a long-distance runner's, its firm round breasts thrust out defiantly against the restraining black silk of her tight dress and her tiny waist tapered alluringly to Junoesque hips that appeared to be the work of a Michelangelo or Rodin. Cut just above the knees, her dress revealed extraordinary legs with long planes of perfectly shaped muscles that appeared especially enticing in black hose. Her eyes drew him, held him. There was a baffling winsomeness in their depths enhanced by a hint of provocative irony—the look of rigid moralist, the perennial virgin, or a woman who had seen it all; perhaps too much.

With sudden embarrassment, Brent realized he was still holding Garnet's hand. Flustered and feeling like a schoolboy on his first date, he dropped it and jerked his eyes to the *tokonoma*. Muttering something about the beauty of the display, he moved toward the table. A smirk exchanged by Yoshi and Tomoko heightened Brent's discomfort. Luckily, Sashi entered at that moment carrying a tray with four *sakazukis* (small handleless porcelain wine cups).

"Brent-san," Yoshi said, gesturing to the *tokonoma,* "you have the seat of honor." Sashi stopped in her tracks. Tomoko and Garnet stared silently.

"You're senior officer, Yoshi-san. It's your place."

"I did not sink *Abu Bakr*, Brent-san. It is yours for tonight. You have earned it."

"My whole crew earned it," Brent muttered. Then, conceding with a smile, he moved to the place of honor, which placed his back to the *tokonoma*. As the foursome seated themselves, the waitress leaned over the table and placed the four cups in front of the diners. Brent felt the nipple of a hard breast brush the back of his head and trace a hot line down past his ear as Sashi placed his *sakazuki* on the table. The girl was not wearing a brassiere. He caught his breath.

Carefully, the two Japanese and Brent turned the cherry blossom design on their cups outward in the traditional, courteous fashion of the Japanese. Garnet's eyes caught the movement and she, too, turned her cup. *Alert, smart,* Brent said to himself. Yoshi held up his cup and said to Garnet, "Hot, spiced saké."

"I know, Commander."

Yoshi kept his cup extended. "A toast to our lovely guests," he said, eyes slipping to Brent.

"Hear! Hear!" the American responded. "Give us some of your *haiku*, Yoshi-san." Yoshi loved to write

175

poetry. Brent was certain he had prepared something for the occasion.

The pilot nodded and the women saluted with their cups. Yoshi spoke softly, almost reverently, "Darkness enshrouds the vast universe, In an illimitable night; Only the warmth of a woman's heart Can erase the gloom." They all sipped the hot liquor and then tabled their cups.

"Your *haiku* is beautiful," Tomoko said.

"Lovely," Garnet added, voice low and a little husky with shyness. "And you wrote that, Yoshi—ah, Yoshi-san?"

The commander nodded modestly. "But it was not really *haiku*, Garnet-san."

"No? Not *haiku?*"

"That is true. *Haiku* is unrhymed verse of three lines containing five, seven, and five syllables." He shook his head. "It is impossible to translate without losing the meter, and too often, the meaning."

Garnet's smile revealed perfect white teeth, timorousness giving way to growing confidence. "I understood, and the meaning was clear—lovely, sweet."

Yoshi nodded and smiled. "I am happy you enjoyed it."

"To a beautiful evening," Garnet said, eyeing Brent from the corner of her eye. They all drained their cups. "Whew," Garnet said. "I can't get used to this."

"To what?" Brent asked.

"The Japanese habit of doing their serious drinking before dinner."

"It is only hot wine," Tomoko said.

"With the kick of a hand grenade," the writer countered. There was a round of polite laughter.

There was a flash of a colorful kimono and the cups were replenished. Yoshi gestured toward Garnet with his cup and quoted an old Japanese saying, "'Never let the cup be full and never let the cup be empty.'"

There were more toasts, and with each sip Garnet

176

became even more beautiful. Brent found it increasingly difficult to tear his eyes from her. And she looked back, warmth deep in the limpid pools of her eyes.

More saké and tongues became loose. Tomoko explained how her duties had brought her into contact with Yoshi when he'd roared into the Maritime Self-Defense Forces' office to personally claim long overdue supplies of ammunition. "It was like trying to stop a *tsunami* with your hands," she laughed, eyeing the pilot with obvious affection.

"And how did you meet Garnet?" Brent asked.

"Three weeks ago she came into my office looking for brochures, literature, anything that would help her build a library on Japan." She looked at the American woman warmly. "We immediately became friends."

Brent eyed the writer over his *sakazuki*. "I thought you wrote historical romances."

"I do. I look for information everywhere, try to soak up the culture. You must, if you are to write convincingly about a culture foreign to your own. Libraries, museums, corporate offices, armed forces," she waved and smiled, "and restaurants," she held up her cup, "and booze."

Laughing, everyone raised cups and touched them, and before anyone could drink, Brent said, "To history and a lot of romance." More chuckles, and then they all drank. Garnet held Brent's eyes briefly over her cup. It was more than liquor that ignited a flame in his stomach and groin. Again Sashi flitted around the table like a hurrying butterfly and the cups were recharged. This time the nipple of the hard round breast traced a hot line up Brent's neck all the way to the crown of his head. He caught his breath and downed half his drink in one gulp. Two women, both exciting. It was torture—a divine kind of torture, but torture still. He took a deep breath and managed in an even voice. "Your current work, Garnet. What historical period? What is it about?"

Garnet's eyes were not on Brent. Instead, hard as

polished sapphires, they followed Sashi as the waitress closed the door behind her. "Ah, yes, my work." And then a baffling half-smile, half-frown. "Are you sure you want to hear?" And before Brent could answer, "It's dangerous to ask a writer about her work."

"Dangerous?"

"Yes. Once writers start talking, you can't stop them."

Everyone laughed, drank. "Please, tell us a little—a bare outline, if that is all you want to tell us."

Garnet tabled her drink and suddenly became serious. "My novel concerns itself mostly with Japanese women—nineteenth and twentieth century. It begins in the nineteenth century, just before the Meiji restoration. I have the opening chapters well in hand, but I still don't know where it will end or how." She captured Brent with her eyes. "Does that surprise you?"

"Not really." He glanced at Yoshi and returned to the blue pools as if drawn by a magnet. "In our business, you learn never to predict the end to anything." He rubbed the faint stubble on his chin thoughtfully. "You must do a lot of research—study history constantly."

She nodded agreement and sipped her drink. Then she held up her cup and examined the cherry blossom design as if she were reading a secret woven into the pattern. "History—yes, history. Funny thing about history," she said as if she were speaking to the secret of the cherry blossoms. "It's really fiction."

"History is fiction?"

Her face was twisted by a strange smile, a disconcerted look that bordered embarrassment. "You're going to think I'm drunk," she blurted.

"No. No," Brent insisted, fascinated by the obvious intellect behind the beautiful face. "Please go on."

She took a large drink, sighed, and pressed on into very private ground. "I believe any attempt to capture the past is doomed simply because experience can never be resurrected and packaged."

"You've found this in your work."

"Over and over."

"Then you mean we reinvent it?" Brent offered.

Challenged by his interest and quick mind, she smiled, a slow captivating movement of the full lips that was enhanced by the line of the perfect white teeth. Brent felt like a man looking at a jewel dangled by a hypnotist. "That's what I believe, Brent-san, and you have an imaginative mind." She hunched forward, emboldened by the handsome young officer, the saké, and the inquisitive eyes of Yoshi and Tomoko. "It seems to me it's reinvented according to the whim of the historian, who is actually the inventor." She thumped the table with a tiny white hand. "Where the past lies is not found through the magnifying glass, in the ten-pound tomes, documents, or fragments of pottery and scrolls, but in ourselves. History is nothing more than the historian." She turned up both palms, "It's got to be completely relative and subjective."

Everyone stared at the girl. Brent was completely captivated. She looked down at her cup like a woman who knew she had talked too much. "You all think I'm crazy or drunk or both," she rued softly.

"No! No!" the others chorused.

Brent had to keep her thoughts rolling. "Your new book—about Japan. What's the plot, the subject?" he prodded, leaning toward her as much as the low table would permit.

"Yes," Yoshi said. "Your new work?" Tomoko nodded encouragement.

Pleased by the interest of the group, the girl answered with one word: "Whores."

"Whores?"

"Yes. Whores, not *geisha*. Generations of whores who have earned their living in Japan's 'soaplands.' After all, this is the world's oldest profession."

The men sat coldly, not daring to offer information. Tomoko came to life. "You mean the massage parlors. They're part of Japanese tradition. Perfectly acceptable.

179

Don't forget, Garnet-san, Japan is free of the Christian notion of sin."

"But there are Confucian codes of conduct," Yoshi declared hotly. "The samurai follows them." His look at Garnet was cool and somewhat reproachful.

Inspired by her own thoughts, Garnet raced on, her words made careless by the liquor. "My women are masters at the massage and soapy body-to-body lather dance. I found this takes maybe forty-minutes, and then they have intercourse and this is followed by an hour of oral . . ."

"I understand," Brent interrupted. The young American was shocked. He had expected a flimsy romantic tale of perhaps a Japanese Cinderella breaking the shackles of centuries of bondage, or a variation on "Little Red Riding Hood." In his mind, all romances were built on one of these two themes. But instead, he had heard a philosophical discourse on history and a plot description of a novel about whores. This girl was full of surprises, and her eyes were definitely not those of the perennial virgin. No, indeed. He knew now they were the eyes of a woman who had seen everything. But how much had they really seen of Japanese sexual mores and practices, which were as ambivalent and contradictory as the rest of Japanese society?

Although Brent had never patronized "soapland" or any other commercial sex parlors—volunteers were too easy to find, and the thought of paying for sex was demeaning to his manhood—he had seen one live sex show with his shipmates and learned much of this underworld of Japanese eroticism in his eight years in Japan. On his one trip to the *nudo gekijo* (nude theater) he had been drinking and was taken there by some young new officers. It was disgusting. After the players onstage actually performed sex acts, the audience was invited to have intercourse with women on the stage. That was when Brent left.

Over the years, Brent learned that the Japanese

attitude toward sex was paradoxical, reflecting a society that was both licentious and puritanical. Everyone acknowledged the Confucian codes of conduct with profound piety, yet men flocked to "love hotels," porn video parlors, fertility orgies, and no-panty coffee shops. Brent had seen crowds of businessmen devouring sex-and-splatter comic books while riding the commuter trains. Nevertheless, it was common knowledge hundreds of censors covered breasts and removed pubic hairs from the thousands of foreign porno magazines that arrived each week.

Brent was convinced the two sexes lacked the ability to communicate with each other. Men seemed to view women as either housewives or mistresses while women saw their workaholic, absentee, prostitute-patronizing husbands as burdens to be tolerated when they collapsed on Sunday and demanded attention. Home was for procreation, passion lay beyond the threshold. The whole structure was conflicting and ambiguous. At first the contradictions were illogical, however, over the years Brent learned to accept the ambiguities as typically Japanese.

"When in Rome do as the Romans do," one young pilot had suggested to Brent one night when the American had politely refused an invitation to attend a "fertility festival." "I can never be a Roman," Brent had smiled back.

Brent tabled his drink, rotating the cup aimlessly, staring at Garnet. The eroticism of their discussion had made her even more exciting. She had obviously amassed a considerable amount of information. How much did she really know? "You've learned a lot since you've been here," he queried casually. "And how long have you been in Japan?"

"One month."

"One month?" Brent repeated, unable to conceal his astonishment. "You've learned a lot?"

"I've been to a dozen libraries and five of these

parlors." She read the surprise on the faces of her companions and laughed deep down, a laugh that shook her entire slender frame. She added breathlessly through her laughter, "My research did not involve participation."

The men and Tomoko added their laughter to the girl's. Brent proposed a toast, "To soapland, may there never be a shortage of suds." Everyone laughed boisterously and drained their cups.

The door opened and Sashi entered carrying a tray with four rectangular black lacquered boxes. While Sashi placed a box in front of each diner, Yoshi eyed the American woman and said, "I hope you like Japanese food."

"I'm learning."

"Tonight you will have a good lesson. Our food is like our language, it takes some study and practice."

"I'll try to be a good student," Garnet said, lifting the lid from her box. Her eyes widened, "It's beautiful, but what is it?"

Yoshi chuckled. "Good food should please the eye as well as the palate. You are looking at raw fish garnished with seaweed and bean curd." He nodded to a small bowl in the center of the table. "And there is a mixture of soy sauce, radish, and red pepper. You may enjoy dipping your fish in it."

Brent thought he saw a pallor creep through the flush of Garnet's cheeks. She picked up a pair of wrapped sticks. "*Hashi,* not chopsticks," she said, unwrapping the two wooden sticks.

"Four-oh," Brent said.

"Four-oh?"

Brent grinned. "That's navy for an 'A.'"

The conversation died as Sashi brought course after course: fish-and-mushroom soup; a well-proportioned salad of pumpkin, fish, cucumber blossoms, and chestnut leaves; boiled eel and halibut roasted with onions, cherries, carrots, and ginkgo nuts, followed by a spectacular basket of baby crabs the size of spiders. "The basket is seaweed," Tomoko said to Garnet. "The restaurant is famous for it. You can eat the basket, too."

"What about the table?" Garnet asked as serious as a priest saying mass. "It looks delicious."

Laughter. "Oh, no," Tomoko said. "We leave that for the termites."

After a melon was served for dessert, the diners all relaxed while Sashi cleared the table. Garnet eyed Brent. The serious look was back. Brent steeled himself. He was not disappointed. "You're making history," she said matter-of-factly.

"History? You mean our actions against the Arabs?"

"Yes."

"I don't think of it that way, but I guess you're right. One thing is certain, it's not fiction."

"No, but it will be lied about in the future when we are all gone and it is reinvented."

Tomoko entered the conversation, her eyes on Yoshi, "Can you tell us if you will you be leaving us soon, Yoshi-san?"

"I do not know," the pilot answered. He gestured at Brent, "Our fates are in the hands—are at the mercy of men on the other side of the globe."

"If they act, you must react," Garnet suggested.

"Sometimes. But Admiral Fujita prefers to have the enemy react to him."

Garnet stared at Brent, "He is like a legend—no, a myth from the pages of Homer."

Brent stared back. "He has the greatest military mind I have ever known."

"Such a strange situation," Garnet said.

"In what way?"

The keen perceptive mind was fully alert and at work. "The United States and Russia stand in the wings, and supply you and the Arabs with the means to kill each other while professing their love for peace."

"Hypocrisy is not in short supply," Brent said. "But

183

oil controls it all. You know that."

The young woman sighed sadly. "And you must fight them, maybe die for that thick gooey stuff that sells for two hundred dollars a barrel."

"Few men control their own fates," Yoshi said. "Ours is truly the oldest profession, not the one you write about."

The girl smiled slowly, almost sadly. "Perhaps you're right." She tapped the table with a manicured nail and then looked up at Brent. "Can you answer a question about *Yonaga?*"

Suddenly, the traitor Arlene Spencer was back. The same look, the same tone of voice. "It all depends," he said calmly, concealing his apprehension.

The question was innocuous. "How does *Yonaga* operate? The media are very confusing." She paused to organize her thoughts. Brent felt relieved; she was not probing for sensitive information. "I mean, your carrier is not part of the Self-Defense Force." She gestured at the DOP patches on the officers' shoulders. "You're park employees."

Brent laughed and tapped his patch. "Well, we don't rake leaves and mow lawns. This was made necessary by the Constitution."

"I know. But who does Admiral Fujita answer to?"

Both men chuckled. "That's one good question," Brent acknowledged. "To a great extent, *Yonaga* is independent, its missions controlled by one man, not the Maritime Self-Defense Force, the Diet, a cabinet officer, or even the emperor."

"Yes. That's what I don't understand. At home everything filters down from the president, his cabinet, the Pentagon. But *Yonaga,*" she shrugged and turned her palms up to show her frustration, "is almost as independent as a sovereign state. True?"

Yoshi ceased his role as a spectator. "True, to a point, Garnet-san. But we have the cooperation of governmental agencies. It would be impossible to operate without this support." The pilot tapped his temple while Brent nodded approval. "And we have good men and support coming from all over the world. This is truly an international assault against terrorism."

Tomoko sighed and sagged, eyes cast down. "Why," she asked in a hushed voice, "does evil always flourish—always force good men to fight and die to stop it?"

A cathedral hush filled the room. Yoshi broke it. "Tomoko-san," he said softly. "You could ask why germs propagate and why the men of medicine must eternally fight infection."

She looked up at him, the blackness of her eyes heightened by moisture to the intensity of newly mined coal. "The fight against infection can never end."

"Nor against evil. It is the way of mankind." He nodded at Brent, "It has been our calling since time began."

"I lost my husband on destroyer *Shirayuki*."

"I know, Tomoko-san," Yoshi said gently.

She waved a hand in an encompassing gesture. "It's insane. Never stops."

"We are fighting madmen."

"Madmen. Ha!" She fixed wide, unblinking eyes on Yoshi. The look was frightening. She rasped from deep in her throat, "When the whole world is insane, who knows where madness lies?"

Brent recognized the quixotism, but said nothing. However, Yoshi responded to it, "We do not tilt at windmills, Tomoko-san."

She dropped her eyes. "I know, Yoshi-san. But since the Arabs sank *Shirayuki* and killed my husband, there has been a terrible emptiness—like a vacuum." She moved her eyes to Brent and Garnet. Her look softened and a feeble smile touched her lips. "Forgive me. I have ruined the party."

"No. No," Brent and Garnet protested. And then Garnet took the lead, "Tell us about your son."

Tomoko drew herself up pridefully. "My son, Ryo, is a

185

graduate student in computer science at Kobe University." She looked first at Brent and then at Yoshi. "But his first love is flying." She drummed the table. "He wants to fly for you."

"For me—for Japan? You never told me this."

She shrugged. "He is still in school and it is his destiny. Only he can seek it."

"True. True," Yoshi agreed.

Turning to Garnet, Brent broke the mood. "Have you been to the *Kabuki*, *Bunraku*, the *Noh* theater, or seen sumo wrestlers, Garnet-san?"

The girl took the cue. "None of it, Brent. I've been spending all my time in libraries and, ah . . . 'soaplands.'"

Brent waved a hand through a semicircle. "Why, right here in Akasaka are some of Tokyo's most famous attractions—the Suntory Museum, which has some of Japan's greatest art, the Hie Jinja Shrine, the Sensoji Temple." He felt a rush of excitement as he stared at the smiling, receptive face. He had to see this exquisite creature again. "May I be your guide?"

"Of course." She reached into her purse and pulled out a card. She scribbled a number on it. "I'm staying at the Tokyo Prince. Please call me." He pocketed the card while Yoshi and Tomoko exchanged a smile.

Then they talked of the theater, the museums, and the magnificent parks of Tokyo. Everyone seemed energized by the change in topics. But deep down, Brent knew they were all, to a certain extent, acting. The weight of the fighting, the bloodshed, and Tomoko's loss had been too heavy to shrug off. Finally, Yoshi glanced at his watch and said, "It is late. I have early duty at Tokyo International. I hate to suggest this, but I am afraid it is time to go."

They all stood, the women gathered their purses, and they moved to the door. Yoshi slid the *amado* aside and the foursome stepped out onto the porch. Quickly, shoes replaced the paper slippers, and with Yoshi leading, they

186

descended the stairs to the path.

Something was not quite right. It was too quiet. Not one waitress was visible, and there were no patrons. Brent felt a familiar disquiet, a sense of foreboding that caused him to take Garnet's shoulder in one hand.

The moon was full, the sky clear, the stars big and low, illuminating the garden with a strange stagelike quality, almost as if the shrubs, rocks, and trees were two-dimensional cutouts decorating the stage of a *Kabuki* theater. Brent could see the length of the compound quite clearly. The manager and his assistant were at the gate, but they were not quite Laurel and Hardy anymore. It appeared that another "Hardy" had materialized, and Laurel had disappeared. Yoshi, too, with instincts of both the hunter and the hunted, pulled Tomoko close to his side and stopped.

"What is it? What is it?" both women asked, voices hushed by apprehension.

"Quiet," Yoshi hissed.

Brent felt an old enemy return. Fear, a cold heavy thing, seeped like oil through his guts. Then a sound of pain, a demented hysterical shrieking that froze his blood and made his skin prickle. He turned his head. Then, a staggering, crashing movement to one side caught his eye. It was Sashi, weaving her way out of a clump of bushes. She lurched onto the path. The color of her beautiful kimono had changed, the bright red of roses dominating. But the pattern was not of roses, but of streaming blood. She had been cut from her throat down to her chest, her left breast nearly severed. She clutched it in her right hand as if she were trying to reattach it. Her face was ice-white with pain and frozen horror. She cried out, "Commander Ross!" then reeled on legs of rubber and tumbled off the path into the stream. Both Tomoko and Garnet screamed.

The two officers reacted in identical fashion. Pushing their women off of the path, they pulled pistols from their shoulder holsters. Brent heard Garnet cry out as the force of his shove propelled her head-first into the water, now reddened by Sashi's blood. She tried to rise.

Brent leaped in behind her, pushing her down and shouting "Get behind a boulder! Stay down!"

He heard her gurgle as she obeyed him and hid behind a large rock. Yoshi had pushed Tomoko into the foliage and behind a small pile of rocks on the other side of the path and was racing for a large boulder. The two men at the gate crouched, scurried to opposite sides like large crabs, and blended into the garden. They opened fire.

The reports were thunderous, muzzle flashes lighting the garden with flashes of infernal light like St. Elmo's fire. The eerie streaks of yellow flame turned the beautiful grounds into a Dantean garden of hell; branches became the twisted tendrils of the damned, rocks the carapaces of long-dead creatures. Bullets fluted and cracked like bull whips, lashed billows of water and storms of stone fragments, ricocheting with the sound of tearing silk and angry hornets. "Magnums!" Brent shouted at Yoshi. "Probably three-fifty-sevens. I've got the one on the right." The weight of fear in his viscera turned into a cold, indigestible lump, dried his throat. He ignored it as he had dozens of times in the past.

"There must be more of them, Brent-san. Probably *Sabbah*. They use only the knife. One got the waitress. Tomoko, Garnet, keep a watch to the sides and behind us!"

Sabbah! Kadafi's most feared killers. Brent had fought them hand-to-hand three times before. Named after the legendary "old man of the mountains," Hasan-ibn-al-Sabbah, they still practiced their craft exactly as it had been taught by the "old man" nine centuries ago in his Persian fortress. Invariably, they were wild on hashish; smoked it, chewed it, even made potions of it, and then hunted their victims. They attacked recklessly and with unbelievable strength, like rabid dogs maddened by the heat of summer. Only death could stop them.

Brent shuddered. The gunmen were probably Japanese

Red Army. Apparently, they were being stalked by men of two of the most merciless and fanatical groups of killers on earth.

There were cries of fear from inside some of the huts, but no one dared leave.

Garnet was sobbing, "No. No."

"God damn it! Shut up!" Brent hissed. "They already know where we are. Don't give them more help. Watch behind us."

The girl shoved a clenched fist into her mouth and bit down on it. She was still shuddering but silent. Brent waited patiently. He knew his muzzle flashes would give him away. He must hold fire. Yoshi was doing the same. The assassins had revealed their positions when they fired at least ten rounds, but he knew they had moved. He had heard them. Now there was silence. They had been careless for *Rengo Sekigun*; perhaps overconfident. Efficient killers would have cut them all down on the path.

Every sense tuned to its limit, he strained his eyes into the darkness, searching for something that refused to be seen. He cursed, pounded a fist on the rough surface of the rock. Suddenly there was a hissing rustle to the right, as if a python were slithering toward him through the garden. He shifted the Beretta. It seemed that time slowed. Instantly his vision was concentrated to brilliant clarity, his hearing magnified, and even his sense of smell so clear he could pick up the taint of moss on the rock, the scent of the flowers. A splashing of water, a sob, and Brent's head snapped to the left as if his neck had become a tightly wound spring. His left hand shot out for Garnet. It was not Garnet. Sashi had risen and was standing fully erect.

"No! Down!" Brent shouted. Too late.

The python became a pistol that boomed off five quick rounds. Striking with a force of nearly 400 foot-pounds each, the powerful slugs annihilated the young waitress. They seemed to strike almost simultaneously. There was the unmistakable taut drumlike sound of bullets slapping into living flesh, muscle and bone, spreading, ripping. One sliced across the muscles of her stomach, unzipping it like a purse, entrails bursting out like the eels she had just served. Another split her head open like a ripe melon dropped on a stone floor. As she fell, two more hit her in the shoulder, spinning her like a child's toy, spraying blood in a circle, splattering Garnet and Brent with brains, gore, blood, and shattered bone. Before she could pitch into the stream, the last struck home squarely in the chest, splintering her sternum as it entered and breaking her spine as it exited, blowing out chunks of lungs, pieces of vertebrae, tissue, and gouts of blood. The tremendous energy of the magnum load hurled her completely out of the stream and onto the side of the path. She lay still, a hideously ruined doll cast aside by its master. It had all happened in less than two seconds.

Garnet screamed. Brent cursed, fear replaced by hatred and rage that came on him like a ravening beast. He felt his muscles charge, felt the tension build in his sinews and nerves until he was like an arrow notched against the curve of a longbow. His only thought was to avenge the butchered girl.

Sashi's slaughter had given Brent an advantage. He had the Beretta almost on the target when the killer's muzzle flashed. Shifting his aim slightly to the left and moving the weapon from right to left so that he covered at least five feet of ground, he squeezed off six rounds so fast the sharp cracks sounded like an automatic weapon, spent cartridge cases spewing from the breach in a glittering stream. The muzzle flashes left afterimages flashing back from his retinas like novas, and the pungent, thick smell of cordite filled his nostrils, coated the back of his throat. There was a hoarse cry of pain. A dark figure rose and staggered back toward the gate. He was limping. One out of six in the leg. Lousy shooting. Cursing, Brent squeezed off two more rounds. With lead and antimony cores, cupro-nickel coatings and snub-nosed, the bullets were superb killing machines. Both struck, tumbled, spread, fragmented. There was a high, shrill scream of an animal struck its death blow, and the man dropped as if his bones had turned to jelly.

Brent tried to get as low as possible behind the rock. But at least a foot of water forced him to remain higher than he wished. He knew the other assassin had seen his flashes. Now it was up to Yoshi.

Far to the left and behind the corner of a hut a pistol barked. Three slugs struck Brent's rock, showering him with pulverized granite. He pushed himself deep into the water and held the Beretta above the surface. Then he heard Yoshi's Otsu. The wicked little "Baby Nambu" got off five 8-millimeter rounds almost as fast as the Beretta. There was a scream. A man staggered out from behind the hut into a well-lighted section of the garden. Brent could see him clearly. He was a burly man, big in the shoulders. Lung-shot, he bent over, clutching his chest. He staggered and screamed again, spraying frothy red blood. Then the screams became squeals, the hemorrhaging blood spraying in a scarlet spout from his mouth and nose.

Brent and Yoshi fired together. Hit by four bullets, the big man spun around and toppled over, rolling to his back, limbs flung out, pistol sliding across the ground. His arms and legs twitched and jerked spasmodically as death tightened its grasp.

"You all right, Brent-san?" Yoshi shouted.

"Yes." Brent ejected the empty clip and rammed home a fresh magazine.

"Stay down. There are more."

"I know."

Flames erupted from a muzzle about midway between the gate and the kitchen. Brent squeezed off four rounds, Yoshi five. "One, maybe two!" Yoshi shouted.

Brent bit his lips. Tension coarsened his breath. There had been no screams, no crashing sounds of a falling body. They had missed the man or men. And where were the *Sabbah?* Where were the police? Where were *Yonaga*'s patrols? Then he realized the gunfight had lasted only two or three minutes. It had seemed like two or three years.

He heard Garnet sobbing. "I've got to leave!" she screamed, and began to rise. Brent leaped to the left in a wild grab to push the girl back down. The movement saved his life.

There was a snarl behind him and a hungry leopard landed on his back, claws extended—but to the right side instead of squarely between the shoulder blades. There was the tooth-grating sound of a steel blade striking rock as a knife aimed for his heart struck the boulder instead. But the handle of the knife clutched in a massive fist impacted his right hand, knocking the Beretta out of his grasp. Pain shot up to his shoulder like a strike of lightning, and the momentum of the impact sent both men tumbling into the water, the assassin's left arm clamped around Brent's throat like a steel trap.

Garnet cowered behind a rock screaming "Brent! Yoshi! Help! My God!"

But there could be no help. Yoshi was apparently pinned down by clever gunmen who slithered and fired, continuously changing positions.

Brent landed on his back on top of the *Sabbah.* His windpipe was being crushed. In a panic, he pushed hard against the boulder with both feet, forcing the killer's face beneath the water while managing to grip his right wrist and force the knife away from his body. The man twisted frantically, heaved up his stomach with unbelievable force, propelling Brent against the boulder and rolling away. Both men leaped to their feet, water swirling around their legs. They both ignored the gun battle roaring behind them.

Brent rubbed his throat, breathing deeply, filling his lungs with sweet air. Even in the dim light, he could see the man quite clearly. He was shorter than Brent, but just as wide. His black hair was shoulder length, his skin swarthy, his nose that of a brawler, wide and flat. His thick red lips were pulled back into a frightening grimace revealing uneven yellow teeth. His heavy breathing came out like snarls, spraying water and spittle. Glowing as if backlit, the black eyes held Brent. It was as if he were looking into the fierce, pitiless eyes of a stalking lion, a fierce bird of prey, a poisonous reptile ready to strike. Hell was there, burning in the dim light. Brent felt like a naked man suddenly dropped into the wildest African jungle, facing a stalking wild animal.

The man advanced, knife extended, making a small circle, catching the light and glistening. Brent stepped back, eyes glued to the point as if he were watching a cobra. Then, with the experience of a man who has brawled many times, he shifted his eyes to the man's feet. *Watch for a change in balance*, he told himself.

"I'm going to circumcise you, Yankee dog, like those Jews you fight for. Cut your balls off, great American samurai." The *Sabbah* gestured at the woman. "Then your whore will not like you anymore." He giggled and saliva foamed and ran off his chin. "And when I finish with you," he waved the blade, at the girl, "I'm going to stick this up her cunt, gut her from crotch to tits like a goat." He rocked with laughter at his own wit.

Garnet could only sob and cry out, "No! No!"

Brent needed a weapon. But what? He gave ground, stepped on a piece of volcanic rock. Rough, jagged. He reached down and scooped up a piece of rock the size of a small club. He revolved it until he found a comparatively smooth spot to grip. It still pricked and cut. But he felt nothing. He had a weapon.

More gunshots in the other side of the garden. Screams. Someone was hit, but if it was Yoshi, there was absolutely nothing he could do about it. Garnet was crouching, staring at Brent and the killer with wide glazed eyes filled with terror. He could hear her praying.

Brent saw a slight shift in balance, the Arab's feet take a quick, short step. Anticipating the lunge, Brent leaped

193

up onto a wide spot in the path in front of one of the huts. The Arab's knife caught Brent's tunic below the chest, slicing through it like a razor through a wisp of silk. Brent felt something sticky and warm trickle down his side. He had been nicked but felt no pain. The Arab shouted *"Allahu Akbar!"* ("Allah is most great!") And then leaping up onto the path, "You are quick, great American samurai," he spat sarcastically.

The two men began to circle each other, looking for openings. Brent decided to goad the man, try to enrage him, perhaps, to a point of carelessness. High on hashish, his emotions must be screwed up to the highest tension. Smiling, Brent said casually, "Your mother's crotch was home for a thousand lizards, an oasis for thirsty camels, mighty *Sabbah*." The Arab roared his anger, feinted with the knife, Brent countering with the jagged stone.

"Come on, oh mighty *Sabbah*. Let me help you rush into paradise where you can have all those maidens to yourself, roll in milk and honey for eternity. And maybe you'll find your mother there, in heat, servicing goats."

This time there was no feint. The Arab charged like a corrida bull, swinging wildly in a wide arc at Brent's taunting face. The American did not give ground. Instead, he dropped almost to his knees while the blade hissed just over his head. He grabbed a handful of gravel and loose dirt. In one motion, he threw a rolling block into the Arab's knees and threw the dirt and gravel into his face. The impact knocked the rock from Brent's hand.

Tumbling over Brent, the man did a complete somersault and landed on his back, knife splashing into the stream. Both men were temporarily winded by the impact, but both, charged with adrenaline, recovered quickly and leaped to their feet. The Arab blinked, brushed dirt from his face. Brent had missed his eyes. Now the odds were even. No weapons. Only fists, experience, and guile.

The space was confining, no place for Gentleman Jim Corbett, but ideal for Jake LaMotta. It would be settled by the brute force of two raging bulls and their staying power. Finesse was out the window.

The Arab's first swing came in a wide semicircle from the left. Brent ducked, and felt the big fist impact the top of his head and glance off. The American brought up his right, punching into the man's midsection. It was like hitting bedsprings made of tempered steel. His big fist actually bounced back and more pain shot up his wrist. But the assassin grunted, breath exploding with the blow.

Brent leaped back. The Arab followed. A fist lashed out, then another. Brent stood his ground, counter-punching. He felt his fists drive home into the man's face and body, blows that would destroy an ordinary man, but this was no ordinary man. A rock-hard ham caught the American squarely on the side of the face. The blow made a tremendous roaring sound in his ears, and comets and whole constellations raced across his retinas. Oozing from his lacerated cheek, the blood tasted thick and metallic. He had been hurt, but so had the killer. They clung together for a brief moment, two reeling drunks trying to steady each other, Brent striving desperately to blink and shake out the celestial shower. He could smell the Arab's filth, his foul breath. His head began to clear, but there was pain in his jaw, and his ear had been bruised. He spit blood on the assassin's shoulder and neck.

Then the Arab stepped back. His left eye was a swollen slit and bright rosettes of blood blossomed from his nostrils. More blood streamed from the corner of his mouth. He spat mucous and gory detritus, cursed, stopped his retreat, and held both clublike fists chest-high.

Brent jabbed twice with his left, waited for the counterpunch, dropped below it, transferred weight smoothly, and threw the third punch of the combination, a right hand delivered with all his power to his enemy's chin. The Arab twisted and Brent felt his fist catch the man on the side of the jaw instead of the point. It was a

195

pole-ax of a blow, delivered from the toes with the combined might of his arm and legs behind it. It would have punched a hole in the fence, broken bricks, stunned a horse. Brent felt the Arab's jaw collapse, actually heard bone break with the sound of snapping kindling.

The killer staggered back, fists dropping to his waist. But miraculously, he remained standing. His mouth was pouring blood. It looked as if he had chewed a mouthful of blackberries and the jagged line of his front teeth was bright red with the juice. Brent followed his advantage, punishing the man's head and body with lefts and rights, short, hard hissing blows that cracked his skull backward, exploded air from his lungs. Garnet shrieked, "Kill him! Kill him!"

The man caught his heel on a small boulder on the edge of the path and fell backward, landing flat on his back. Brent was on him like a predator making its kill. But the Arab was not finished. Showing an amazing reservoir of strength, he pushed hard on Brent and rolled over on top of the startled American. Then Brent pushed, and the two rolled like passion-maddened lovers off of the path and back into the stream. The Arab was screaming, punching, scratching, spraying blood into Brent's face. Brent bellowed back, punching, but at short range, both men were at a disadvantage. They rolled over the hard rocks, screaming into each other's faces. The Arab tried to bite, caught Brent's collar with his teeth, and ripped it like jackal devouring carrion. Pushing with all his strength, Brent forced the Arab against the bank, punched him until he sagged weakly. Groping at the edge of the stream, he found a piece of jagged rock and gripped it in his right hand.

Holding the *Sabbah* down with a left forearm across his chest, a red curtain dropped down over the American's eyes and he felt a familiar atavistic lust grip his soul, take command of his body. He must not only kill, he must obliterate. It had happened many times before; there was no control, no hesitation, no conscious thought. He swung the jagged rock in a big arc over his head and felt it impact the Arab's forehead with the sound of a meat cleaver chopping through a shank. The man screamed. Brent brought the rock down again, this time squarely onto the man's nose. Blood and mucus sprayed. The Arab sagged like a wax doll forgotten in the sun.

"He's finished!" Garnet screamed.

Brent heard an animal snarl. It was himself. The rock tore away part of the man's lower jaw and teeth flew in a brown-red hail of shattered enamel and blood. A dozen more blows to the face turned the Arab's countenance into an unrecognizable pulpy mass of pulverized flesh, broken bones, and torn cartilage. Eyes were no longer visible, instead the man had two bloody indentations just below his forehead that oozed clear liquid into the gore.

A familiar voice broke through the roaring in his ears. It was Yoshi. "Brent, in the name of the gods, stop. Enough! Enough!"

"Never enough!" Brent snarled and smashed again with the rock.

Strong hands gripped Brent's arm and pulled the weapon from his hand. Other hands pulled him away from the *Sabbah* and hauled him up onto the path. Hunched over, fists balled, a snarl baring his teeth, Brent stared at Yoshi Matsuhara, a powerfully built young chief petty officer and four equally formidable-looking seaman guards. "He's finished," Yoshi said.

"But I'm not," Brent shot back. He tried to leap on the Arab, but the seaman gripped him and pulled him back.

Yoshi grabbed Brent's tunic, shook him. "Enough! Enough!" the commander shouted into his face. "Come to your senses! We will take care of him—quicker. Get hold of yourself!" Brent's labored breath hissed and rattled, mucous and blood running to his chin. Staring into his friend's eyes, he felt his sanity begin to creep back, slowly pushing the blood-lust aside.

Garnet climbed out of the stream on unsteady legs and approached Brent. She seemed to be the only one who

197

understood. Perhaps it was because of the terror she had shared with Brent in the stream when the bullets were whipping over. The flashing knife. The foul threat to her sex. She touched his neck, rubbed gently. Her hand was wet and cool from the stream and she was surprisingly composed. "You had no choice, my darling," she said, voice as calm and restful as an evening breeze off the sea. "He would have killed us both in the most hideous way."

Brent suddenly felt the hot oil in his guts drain away, rage fade like a brush fire under rainfall. True, he had lost control again, but the enemy was defeated, probably blind, he was alive and Garnet was safe. He tried to smile, found it impossible. Then he took Garnet's hand and turned toward the gate. There were at least six seaman guards standing on the path with their Arisakas at the ready. Outside, Brent could see the revolving lights of police cars and he could hear the murmurs of the crowd which had collected outside the restaurant.

A seaman guard approached, handed Brent his Beretta. "It is dry, sir. It was on the bank, Commander Ross," he said. Mumbling his thanks, he holstered the automatic. He felt complete again, as if a severed limb had been restored.

Yoshi gestured at the gate. Taking Garnet's hand, Brent followed. Yoshi stabbed a finger at the kitchen. His voice rumbled thick, deep like distant thunder. "It's a slaughterhouse. The manager, his assistant, two chefs, and three waitresses all dead. Throats cut."

Garnet cried, "Oh, no! And poor Sashi, too." Brent put his arm around her. She crowded close, her hip rubbing against his leg.

The pilot pointed to three bodies barely visible in the weak light. "Two *Rengo Sekigun* and a *Sabbah*. They tried to rush me—cared nothing about their lives."

"There must have been more."

"I do not know, Brent-san." He stopped, turned, as if he had overlooked a minor item, and spoke to the chief, who was standing near Brent's mangled opponent, Otsu

198

gripped at his side. "Take care of him, Chief Nakahashi," Yoshi said, "and then come with us."

"Aye, aye, sir. My pleasure, Commander Matsuhara." The chief pointed his pistol at the injured man, who was now blowing red bubbles with each breath and rattling grotesque sounds through a smashed larynx. A single bullet through the head stopped the rattling and the bubbles vanished. Far from giving him a second bullet, the chief hardly gave him a second glance, only turning to spit in his face as he followed Matsuhara down the path.

Garnet recoiled, gripped Brent's biceps with both hands. Then she begged in a tremulous, plaintive voice, "Take me out of this place, Brent, while I'm still sane. Please take me home."

"Seaman guards will escort you, guard you," Yoshi said.

"No! No!" she said, gripping Brent's arm with both of her hands. "I want Brent! He must take me home! Can't you understand?"

Yoshi sighed at her intransigence and yielded. "All right. Brent will escort you home, but you will be accompanied by two seaman guards." He stopped, and Brent and Garnet moved close. He said to Brent, "Take the Mercedes. I will take Tomoko home in her car and use it to drive to my duty. I will leave a guard with her." He waved in frustration. "You might be right, Brent-san. There may be more." He scratched the side of his head. "Maybe they are out there. We must be cautious."

Garnet said to Yoshi, with new alarm in her voice, "Tomoko? Where's Tomoko?"

Yoshi gestured to the gate, where a shadowy figure huddled on the manager's chair. A policeman was leaning over her, talking into her ear. "There. She is fine. Suffering from a little shock, but she is made of sturdy stuff, that woman," he said with pride.

Brent pointed at the policeman, "The police? They'll want long, detailed statements."

"I will take care of them, Brent-san," Yoshi said, hand on the American's shoulder. "I will give them their statement. You take Garnet home."

Followed by the chief, who still held his pistol at his side, the trio walked to the gate. Tomoko rose slowly and embraced Yoshi.

The Tokyo Prince Hotel is located near the waterfront and across from Shiba Park. Although not as deluxe as the Imperial, Palace, or Hilton, the Tokyo Prince boasts a prime location. In fact, from Garnet's eighth-floor apartment there was a clear view of the gaudy lights of the Ginza to the northeast, Shiba Park spread like a dark mat not more than a hundred feet directly in front of the hotel, and the sparkling panorama of Tokyo Bay filling most of the eastern exposure. The bright lights of the Ginza, the lights of a dozen anchored and moored ships, and the amber lamps of the waterfront gave the entire area a festive air. It was all lost on Brent.

Seated next to Garnet, Brent saw nothing of the view. Instead his attention was focused on his second Scotch and soda, which Garnet had just placed on the low, highly polished oak table before him. The whirlwind of bloody events still swirled through his mind. The vision of the butchered waitress and the wanton killing of the entire staff of the restaurant were cruel haunts that would fade with time but always remain alive in the archives of his memory. At this moment, it was all too vivid and he had had an upsetting experience with a policeman; one of many.

The ride from the *Chōjō Seiyoken* restaurant had been uneventful. Chief Nakahashi drove with Seaman Guard Nyogen Senzaki at his side. Brent and Garnet sat silently in the back, the girl still clinging to his arm and huddled close like a frightened kitten trying to burrow her way into safety. He could feel her thigh against his, her hard breast pressing his arm. He felt no reaction whatsoever.

He felt as emotional as a stone temple icon.

When they arrived at the Tokyo Prince, a police car followed close behind. By the time Brent alighted on the sidewalk, a police sergeant was approaching. "Sir," the policeman said. "May I have a word?" Short, plump and sweaty, he waited expectantly.

Brent glanced at the anguish on Garnet's face. "Make it quick."

The policemen handed Brent a card. "I am Sergeant Takashi Ishinabe and you are . . . ah, Commander Brent Ross, 'the American samurai.'"

"Please, Sergeant. Commander Matsuhara already gave you a statement. I don't have time to give you an autobiography."

"I am sorry for what happened."

"Not nearly as sorry as I am."

"Our antiterrorist unit has been very active."

"Not active enough."

"We need your statement."

"I'll send it."

"At the station—now."

"Sorry. I won't do that."

The sergeant turned as if he were going to gesture to two more officers waiting in the car. Chief Nakahashi and Seaman Senzaki stepped to Brent's side. "I wouldn't do that if I were you," Brent warned.

Sighing, the plump little policeman dropped his hands to his sides. Voicing the frustration and the friction that had existed for the past eight years between *Yonaga's* personnel and the Tokyo police, he said, "I know your motives are unimpeachable, but you are not a law unto yourselves. You cannot just wage gun battles in the heart of Tokyo and ignore the authorities."

Frustration and rage exploded a flood of spiteful words from Brent's lips. "Where were the authorities when the entire staff of *Chōjō Seiyoken* were butchered? Where were the authorities when *Rengo Sekigun* opened fire on us? Where were the authorities when that *Sabbah* jumped on my back and tried to stab me? Did you expect me to call the cops?" His laughter was utterly devoid of humor. Then he stabbed a finger into the sergeant's chest and spat, "Stay out of my goddamned way or I'll squash you."

The man was no coward. "This is not finished, Commander," he shot back.

"Stay out of my way," Brent growled, brushing the policeman aside.

Sergeant Ishinabe glared at Brent's back as the foursome entered the hotel and walked to a bank of elevators.

All four entered an elevator together and rode up to the eighth floor. Seaman Senzaki barred four other guests who tried to board. Brent allowed the chief to enter the apartment ahead of the rest of the party. Pistol drawn, Nakahashi thoroughly searched the modest bedroom, the cooking alcove, the drapes that stood open next to the picture window they framed, the bathroom, the shower, the closets, under the bed, and even a small storage area above the linen closet. Satisfied, he holstered his pistol and reported, "All clear, Commander Ross." And then, somewhat awkwardly, "Ah, Commander Matsuhara ordered us to remain—to escort you back to the ship."

"The woman?" Brent said. "She cannot be left alone."

"If we are not relieved by the time you wish to leave, sir, Seaman Senzaki will remain here until his relief arrives."

Now with Nakahashi and Senzaki standing guard just outside the door, Brent felt a warm sense of security begin to grow; or was it the liquor? Probably both. Garnet emptied her glass and replenished both drinks from a bottle of Johnnie Walker which she had placed on the table. She added soda to Brent's, took hers neat. For a moment her mind was off the slaughter. "You feud with the police?"

"Sometimes. They feel we infringe on their authority." He was pleased by the control in her voice. "That pompous little ass was typical."

"You were hard on him."

"He asked for it."

"The report?"

"I may send it."

She sighed, eyes wandering over the strong face of the young officer. Inevitably, her mind came back to the horror in the garden. "You've been going through this for eight years," she said, her voice suddenly husky.

"You mean the killing—the ambushes?"

"Yes."

"Worse than tonight."

"Worse?"

"Yes. Yoshi lost Kimio Urshazawa—the woman he loved—in Ueno Park." He drank. "A Red Army ambush—an AK-47. Six slugs in the chest. And I've fought them at the dock, in an alley where they cut me across here." He made a slashing motion across his chest.

She shuddered. "Oh, God." Then, for the first time, she seemed to notice the stain where his tunic had been gashed, the bloody hands. "You've been hurt." She touched the tunic carefully. "You're bleeding and your hands are cut."

He shook his head. "Only a nick, and I have a few scratches on my palms from the volcanic rock." He raised the two big fists. "And I bruised my knuckles on that *Sabbah's* face." He smiled for the first time. "He had sharp teeth, but it was a pleasure."

She took a gulp from her glass, rose, and hurried into the bathroom. In a moment she returned with a basin filled with warm water, soap, washcloth, towel, and a bottle of alcohol. "Strip down to your waist," she ordered.

"I'll live, Garnet. Just scratches."

"Nonsense. It'll only take a few minutes—I owe you this. It was only my life, you know."

Brent sighed and removed his tunic, shirt, and undershirt. He placed the Beretta on an end table within

203

easy reach. There was a large red stain on the white undershirt and dress shirt. For a moment, the girl stared at the thick neck, powerful shoulders, muscular arms, and matted chest. A soft flush like the first glimmer of sunrise banished the pallor from her cheeks. She said somewhat breathlessly, "Good lord. You're put together just like the All-American fullback."

"How did you know?"

"There's been a lot of copy written about 'the American samurai', you know—even TV." She began to wash the cut in Brent's side. "It's clotted—not deep."

"I told you."

She washed his hands in the warm water, cautiously dabbed alcohol on the torn knuckles and palms. Carefully, more alcohol cleansed the wound in his side. "Almost finished," she said.

"Then I'll put my clothes back on and leave," he said. For the first time, they both laughed.

Some of the dried blood had seeped down and disappeared beneath his waistline. She washed lower and lower, cleaning the coagulated blood from his skin. He held his breath as she reached under his beltline and wiped lower—lower than necessary, cleansing the flat abdomen. Then she withdrew the cloth and ran it across his stomach and chest. Suddenly, she stopped. Traced a finger through two hairless grooves that ran across the mat of blond-brown hair. "Strange," she said. "Are these from those knives?"

"No, Garnet. Tracers. Phosphorous kills the hair follicles."

"My God. My God. Such violence—for all these years."

"No one ever gave a nonviolent war."

She grabbed his hand. "Don't leave me tonight!"

He came erect. "But my men?"

"They can't leave until relieved—you heard the chief."

"The chief is to return with me—you heard him.

204

You'll be protected. You don't need . . ."

She began to cry, grabbed his arm like a baby clinging to her mother's leg in a panic of fear. "Please," she sobbed. "Just for a while—a little while."

She stood, pulled him to his feet, and led him to her bedroom. Fully clothed, she threw herself on the bed and rolled to her back. She raised her arms. "Come to me. Stay with me."

In spite of the slaughter, the horror, Brent felt the first stirrings of arousal. There was no way he could avoid it. She was so desirable, so blatantly sexy, so vulnerable. Too vulnerable. It would be betrayal, a loss of honor, not an act of affection. He dropped the Beretta on a nightstand and stretched out on the bed. She immediately crooked one arm under his neck, pulled his head close, and grabbed his bare arm with the other. Holding him close, she snuggled her face against his chest and kissed it. He held her, kissed the side of her forehead, her temple, her cheek. He avoided her lips and she did not offer them.

"Thank God, my darling, I'm safe. I'm safe," she said softly.

"Yes. Garnet. You're safe."

For a long while they held each other, and then she began to sag and her breathing became deep and regular. Gently he eased her onto her back and then stood. He looked down. She was a baby, content and shielded from the world. And then she was a woman, sensuous, irresistible with the power of her sexuality.

He pulled on his clothes, took one last look back, and left the apartment.

Chapter Eight

Brent was to report to Admiral Fujita's cabin by 1000 hours. Shaving gingerly, he skimmed lightly over the bruises, especially a purple splotch marking the lacerated left cheek. His right eye was slightly swollen and the tanned flesh beneath it had a plum-colored tint. He pulled his lips back and examined his straight white teeth again. He reached in, gripped a tooth next to the torn cheek, and felt it move under his fingers. "That son-of-a-bitch had a punch," he said to the mirror. He brought his teeth together gently, felt the teeth clamp shut and lock. Just one loose tooth. He was lucky. Rubbing his chin, he loosened the grip of his jaw, recalling the moment he had stepped onto the carrier's quarter deck.

Reports of the fight had reached *Yonaga* long before he had returned. Immediately upon saluting the duty officer, he was ordered to report to the sick bay. He thought of protesting, but the orders had come down from Admiral Fujita himself. In the sick bay Chief Hospital Orderly Eiichi Horikoshi had cleansed the cut on his side and bandaged it. As he began treating the wound, the old man had chuckled with his usual subtle irony, "Killed a few more, Commander?"

"Two that I know of," Brent had responded, alert and ready for the sardonic barbs sure to follow.

"Slow evening," the ancient chief had said matter-of-factly, stabbing a disinfectant-laden swab into the shallow cut with far more pressure than necessary. Brent did not even wince. "Will not need stitches," the old man observed. "And someone has already sterilized it."

"A friend, yes." The old chief grunted a noncommittal sound.

A young medical attendant when *Yonaga* went into commission, Horikoshi had survived the ship's doctors, who had all died during the entrapment in Sano-Wan. Before the last one died, the young Horikoshi had mastered their combined skills and then added a few that he developed on his own. Fujita recognized his genius and made him the head of the medical department. Disliking officers, he had refused a commission and kept his enlisted rating. He was aloof and arrogant, and ruled the sick bay as his private domain. All men were less than equal here, despite the number of gold stripes they wore on their sleeves. He was accepted by all for what he was; a medical genius and a boorish eccentric. Admiral Fujita's ears were deaf to any complaints that came his way.

When *Yonaga* returned to Japan, Eiichi Horikoshi built the sick bay into one of the most modern medical facilities in the world. Treating the torn and burned bodies of war and, Brent suspected, the ravages of accumulating years, had done strange things to the chief's mind. But not to his hands. He was still a highly skilled surgeon, but was wisely passing those responsibilities on to younger members of his staff. He hated war and the quintessence of his soul was torn by the streams of ripped, seared bodies that poured into his wards after each engagement. Yet he refused to leave *Yonaga*. Like most of the old "plank owners," the carrier was his whole life and Admiral Fujita was a deity. Without the ship, without the admiral, without his sick bay, there would be no purpose in life.

His attitude toward the crew was schizophrenic, one of love-hate, sometimes the concern of the mother hen with her feathers spread protectively, and at other times the stern, ruthlessly chastising father. In the early morning hours, he was ready to chastise Amaterasu herself.

"I hear your last woman, that Miss Spencer, lost her head over you," he said like a close friend exchanging idle gossip.

It was a low blow, and Brent felt a hot swelling of anger and resentment ignite deep. He refused to be goaded into an outburst. "She is a few inches shorter," he said with equal candor. "Now, she's about your height."

The deep wrinkles arranged themselves into a pattern that passed for a smile. "I could not stay in business without you, Commander," he said, wrapping gauze around Brent's massive chest and midriff.

"Glad to accommodate you, Chief," Brent responded casually. "Wouldn't want to see you in bankruptcy."

"You know something?" the old man queried almost wistfully.

Brent knew the needle was being prepared for a jab. However, his curiosity led him into the "straight man's" expected response. "What's that?" he asked with exaggerated naïveté.

The old man's smile bared uneven yellow teeth and he let the needle fly. "If you notched your pistol for each kill, you wouldn't have a grip now, would you?"

Brent answered the question with a question of his own, "You're good at head wounds, aren't you, Chief?"

"Head wounds?"

"Of course, Chief. Without a grip, I could club their heads in, now, couldn't I?"

The old man snorted and silently completed his job.

Now, staring into the mirror, Brent touched his side cautiously. It was slightly sore to the touch, but would not impair his movements. He smiled despite the aching cheek and jaw. The cut had been treated by Garnet and Horikoshi. One who regarded him with obvious affection and the other with cordial loathing. He would phone Garnet as soon as the day's meetings were concluded. A staff meeting was scheduled in Flag Plot for 1300 hours.

He wanted to see her, had to see her. He turned toward the door.

Admiral Fujita was seated behind his desk when Brent entered. Brent bowed; the old man nodded and gestured to a chair. Brent seated himself and his commanding officer stared for a moment with silent concern on his face. "You have been injured." He gestured at Brent's face, "Beaten."

"Beaten, but not defeated, sir."

"Well said. And I understand you made a *jerachin* of the other man's face," referring to gelatin. He stared at Brent silently for a moment. "You lost control."

Brent pinched the bridge of his nose. "Yes. The animal possessed me. I wanted only to destroy him."

"You are much like your father."

"I know."

"You must fight with more discipline, Brent-san— fight *yourself* as fiercely as you fight our enemies. This strange ungovernable rage must be brought under control or it may lead to your end."

"I know, sir," Brent said resignedly. "I'm trying."

Fujita patted a document on his desk. "My reports are sketchy, incomplete. You fought five or six."

"I counted six."

"Any survivors?"

"To my knowledge, they're all dead. In fact, when our seaman guards were closing in and the police arrived, the last three made a suicide charge right into Commander Matsuhara's muzzle. He sent them to their *Sabbah* paradise, Admiral."

"Like many more we have sent before them, Brent-san." The old sailor leaned back, folded his hands across his chest, and showed the incredible power of his mind by quoting the Koran: "Allah hath awarded them for all that they endured, with Paradise and silk attire, reclining therein upon couches. Naught shall they know of hot sun

209

or bitter cold. Its shades shall close upon them, and low shall its fruits hang down. Vessels of silver brought round for them, and goblets like flagons, flagons made of silver whose measure they themselves shall mete . . ." Stopping, he fixed Brent with a warm stare. "According to their beliefs, you served them all well, Brent-san."

Brent answered with his own quote: "Naught befalleth us save that which Allah hath decreed for us."

"Their fate was fixed and you were that, Brent-san."

"These beliefs make our enemies more formidable, sir—more dangerous."

"True. But over the years we have learned much about our enemy's character, his drives, the power of his fanaticism."

"Know your enemy or be his victim," Brent said.

Fujita smiled. "Said like a samurai."

"Thank you, Admiral."

"It was a well-planned ambush, Brent-san?"

"Yes, sir." He swallowed back a sudden bitter taste in his mouth. "They slaughtered the staff silently, with knives. Set up their ambush cleverly and the gunmen were armed with three-fifty-seven magnums."

"One of the most powerful hand weapons in the world."

Sashi's butchered body stormed into Brent's mind. He winced. "Unbelievable hitting power, sir."

The old man placed both palms down on his desk and sat upright. "I actually believed that with our new seaman guard patrols, the additional Self-Defense Force patrols, and the renewed efforts of the Tokyo Police, we had brought this terrorism under control."

"This was an isolated incident, sir. We haven't had one in over a year."

"I know. You and Commander Matsuhara are our most attractive targets. You know, Kadafi has put a million American bounty on Commander Matsuhara's head, and I understand he has assigned the same value to your neck."

210

Brent chuckled. "He's raised the ante. I'm flattered, sir."

The two palms raised and the twisted fingers began to beat out a tattoo on the polished oak. "I do not wish to cancel all leaves—restrict all personnel to the ships."

Brent's mind conjured up Garnet's face, beautiful and smiling. "We would be conceding a victory to them—play into their hands."

The old man missed nothing. "You have a new woman, Brent-san."

Brent felt pink join the purple of his bruises. "True, I have met a very interesting young lady, sir."

"You would like to see her again?"

"Of course, sir. I was hoping to have dinner with her tomorrow night."

The fingers stopped warring with the desk and formed a temple instead. Fujita hunched forward. "We will continue with liberty as usual."

"Good idea, sir."

"But the Ginza is off-limits."

"The enlisted men love that place."

"It is too hard to police." The old admiral ran a finger over his pate, searching for the strands that had vanished decades ago. "I will have a list of eating places and other places that the men can patronize and station seaman guards in each one."

"And the officers?"

"Seaman guards will accompany every officer who leaves this ship."

"Could be awkward, sir."

"Funerals are even more awkward, Brent-san."

Brent sighed. "So true, sir."

The old man toyed with the single hair hanging from his chin. He was suddenly the rigid professional. "And how would *you* handle this situation, Commander?"

Brent would not patronize—not even Admiral Fujita. However, he could not disagree, "In exactly the same way, Admiral."

"Good. You are dismissed, Commander." And then, as an afterthought, "I have recalled Commander Matsuhara from his training duties. He will be at the staff meeting this afternoon." He gestured toward the door. "You may leave."

Brent stood, bowed, and left the room.

Chapter Nine

The last compartment in "Flag Country," Flag Plot was the largest room on the bridge. Long and narrow, it contained a long oak table that had seen lavish care by the same generations of busy hands that had polished Admiral Fujita's desk and the rest of the furniture in flag country. Its mirrorlike sheen reflected the overhead lights with an eye-aching glare.

The bulkheads were put to good use. Charts of the Western Pacific nearly covered one side, while at the head, just behind Admiral Fujita's chair, a large picture of Emperor Akihito in mufti hung next to a paulownia wood shrine.

The shrine—a miniature cabin-like structure built with the typical roof of rafters protruding in the shape of a Saint Andrew's Cross *(chigi)*—was painted red and lacquered like a piece of furniture. It was cluttered with icons. Some were new, some were old. Tora the tiger, who wandered far, made his kill, and always returned home, had been there as long as *Yonaga* had been in commission. Other perennials were a small exquisite gold "Buddha from Three Thousand Worlds" and a precious jade representing the "Eight Myriads of Deities." In the place of "the Seven Gods of Good Luck" there was a new deity. It was a camphor wood miniature of Kwannon whose 36-foot original resided in the celebrated Buddhist

213

temple of Hase. Even for the Japanese, unusual powers were ascribed to Kwannon. The heavy, soulless figure in the shrine was actually a composite of Kwannon, Jizo, and Amida. In this way, in one person, the icon represented the present, the past, and the future.

In one corner were two more new deities. Representations of Shinto *kamis* are rare, and it was curious to find two in the shrine. The first was Inari, the Shinto god of oats and of good fortune. Inari was a simple figure, an aged sage bent under the weight of two sheaves of rice. The second was Atago, the god of archery. A fierce warrior, he was done in bronze inlaid with gold. In his traditional posture, his bow was strung, arrow drawn.

And finally, the admiral had added a large jade horse with eyes of tiny diamonds. A common symbol in Japan, the horse signified success and the attainment of goals. Brent smiled. *Yonaga* was certainly well armed with *kamis*, gods, icons, and helpful animals. If shrines won battles, *Yonaga* would certainly be the favorite in any future engagement.

Mounted opposite Brent on the bulkhead was a spectacular new *nishiki-e* (full color woodblock print) which the admiral had selected as an inspiration for his staff. Done by the famous nineteenth century artist Mizuno Toshikata, it depicted a naval battle fought during the Sino-Japanese war of 1894. Central to the 3-panel print was a gallant captain waving his sword, urging his crew on to victory over a Chinese warship clearly visible in the background. Smoke billowed, air bursts cluttered the sky, and crewmen worked their guns. The sea swelled and frothed in graceful arabesques. There were no corpses, no shattered bodies. To Brent, it was a pyrotechnic exercise in comic-strip panels that grew up to become a scene from an old Cecil B. DeMille epic. *Off the wall*, he said to himself, staring at the print. Then he chuckled at his inadvertent pun.

Tiring of the print, Brent turned his head. From his place next to Yoshi Matsuhara and almost midway down the table from the admiral, Brent eyed the staff which waited patiently while Admiral Fujita conferred with his ancient scribe, Commander Hakuseki Katsube. Old and bent, Katsube was so withered he reminded Brent of a dehydrated corpse that had been baked in the desert sun for decades. With a permanent bend in his spine, he hunched over his pad and brush, sometimes cackling to himself, sometimes drooling into his notes. He and the admiral disdained modern recorders. At the moment, he was stabbing his brush at some ideograms and whispering into the admiral's ear. Brent was sure the admiral's ear was being sprayed.

On the other side of Admiral Fujita sat his executive officer, Captain Mitake Arai. A destroyer captain during World War Two, he had sunk cruiser *Northhampton* off Guadalcanal with a daring torpedo attack. Brent knew the man had to be over seventy years old, yet he still maintained his ramrod military bearing. He was intelligent, efficient, and highly respected. He was the best navigator on the ship.

Next to Arai sat Captain Paul Treynor, the commanding officer of carrier *Bennington*. Of average height and powerfully built, he gave the impression of towering height. Although he was over fifty years old, his brown hair was very dark, very thick and close cropped, standing on end like a stiff-bristled comb. The head was big-nosed and gaunt-boned, with a heavy jaw brownish now with afternoon whiskers hinting at a beard as persistent as Brent Ross's. An Annapolis man, he had had years of experience on carriers *Coral Sea*, *Eisenhower*, and *Nimitz*. He had proved himself, shrewd, tough, and resourceful in the great battle off Gibralter. In fact, his seamanship and miraculous damage control had not only saved his ship, but his fighters had arrived over *Yonaga* just in time to drive off twenty Stukas that were queuing up to deliver a death blow to the Japanese carrier. He was favored by every man in the room. Most of them owed him their lives.

215

The dive bomber commander, Commander Takuya Iwata, occupied the chair next to Treynor. Young and arrogant he was huge for a Japanese. Over six feet tall, he easily weighed two hundred pounds. From pure samurai stock, he had the attitudes and prejudices of an eighteenth century *daimyo*. Perhaps, this was why the Emperor had personally recommended him to Admiral Fujita.

Brent had felt instant antipathy for the man the first moment they had met nearly two years before. The feeling was mutual. In fact, when Brent first looked into the baleful eyes he had found hatred dwelling there. Perhaps it was the old beliefs, the traditional distrust of foreigners, the distilled essence of xenophobia which was still strong in Japan. Or maybe it was the instant jealousy the man felt for Brent's best friend, Yoshi Matsuhara. It was no secret Iwata considered Matsuhara far too old for the post of Air Group Commander—a post he felt he should fill himself. The virus of his dislike had encompassed both men, erupting into a bloody fistfight with Brent Ross on the hangar deck. Brent had beaten the proud samurai senseless in front of a wildly enthusiastic group of enlisted men. The humiliation could not, would not ever be forgotten. "He was born two hundred years too late," Brent had whispered to Yoshi once during a staff meeting. Nodding agreement, Yoshi had said, "He should be astride a war horse, not an Aichi, charging his enemies with his bared sword."

But there was an incongruous mix of respect in this baffling samurai's blood. He admired Brent's uncanny prowess with the machine gun. In fact, once Brent had flown as his gunner against carrier *Ramli al Kabir*. The best dive bomber pilot Brent had ever seen, Iwata had attacked with great courage and skill, hitting the carrier with all three of his bombs. Brent had shot down an Me 109 and the carrier had been sunk. Despite the sharing of mortal dangers together, the implacable samurai still carried the grudge, waiting for the day when scores could

216

be settled. Staring across the table, Brent could see it in the man's black eyes, relentless and hungry.

Next to Iwata sat the new torpedo bomber commander, Lieutenant Shinji Hamasaki. He was the replacement for Lieutenant Commander Iyetsuma Yagoto who had hit the Arab carrier *Daffah* with his torpedo, disabling her starboard screw and jamming her rudder. Then, apparently wounded, he had crashed into the carrier's flight deck, his Nakajima B5N vanishing in a long streak of burning gasoline and tumbling wreckage. Circling and burning *Daffah* had been an easy kill for Iwata's dive bombers.

Not quite forty years of age, Hamasaki was of good samurai stock, tracing his antecedents back to the Mori family of the fabled city of Hagi. Typical of the aristocracy, his forebears had conspired and fought to ward off Western domination. They battled zealously to restore to the Emperor power that his forebears had lost to the Tokugawa shogunate. Their struggle was successful and they used this newfound unity to drag Japan kicking and screaming into the modern age. A new young emperor named his rule Meiji, and what Hamasaki's ancestors accomplished has been called the Meiji restoration.

Lieutenant Shinji Hamasaki was rightfully proud of his heritage. Tall and slender, he held his head high but without the arrogance of Iwata. His forehead was wide and intelligent, eyes bright and alert, nose rather large and ridged, more like an Anglo-Saxon than a Japanese. He was the consummate samurai in appearance, the personification of *bushido* and *Yamato damashii* (Japanese spirit).

Brent shifted his eyes to the escort commander, John "Slugger" Fite. A World War Two destroyer commander, the passage of years had done much to his appearance but nothing to his aggressive, daring, fearless attitude. All were requisite to a destroyer man. His big rounded body, white hair, and square pugnacious face gave him a bearlike aspect. Despite terrible losses over the eight years he had served under Admiral Fujita, the man still had a laugh that would shake the Astrodome. Brent not only liked him, he admired him.

Turning his eyes further down the table, Brent saw Chief Engineer Tatsuya Yoshida seated next to the gunnery officer, Commander Nobomitsu Atsumi. Both were plank owners and both were over seventy years of age, yet the contrast was incredible. Like the scribe, Commander Hakuseki Katsube, Chief Engineer Yoshida showed every day of his great age; gray thinning hair, skin of dry parchment riven by wrinkles as if it had been combed by a cultivator, back bent, hands twisted by arthritis. But gunnery officer Nobomitsu Atsumi was much like Yoshi Matsuhara, one of those unique men who refused the years. Most of his hair was still a glistening black; his face was clear, showing only a few lines in the brow and trailing off from the corners of his mouth and eyes when he frowned. The chief engineer and the gunnery officer were an astonishing pair who seemed more like father and son than the two senior officers they were.

At the far end, facing the admiral, was Lieutenant Tadayoshi Koga. A representative of the Maritime Self-Defense Force and sometimes conveyer of information from the Emperor, he was a fat, round man who reminded Brent of a dumpling dipped in brown sugar. The admiral disliked Koga and the crippled force he represented. To the admiral, the Self-Defense Force had not put up a fight worthy of the samurai tradition. "Too many televisions, movie machines, and cars," Brent had heard the admiral mutter one day. "And traitors, sir," Brent had added. The admiral had nodded his concurrence. But Koga was a pipeline to the Chrysanthemum throne. This alone warranted his presence.

Fujita stopped talking to Katsube and stared down the length of the table. Everyone stared back expectantly. The admiral said, "Colonel Bernstein and Admiral

Whitehead have been ashore for three days conferring with the Israeli, American, and British ambassadors." He waved at a bulkhead-mounted brass clock. "They are late, however; we will begin without them." He turned to Captain Paul Treynor. "Your report, Captain."

Coming to his feet, Treynor spoke in a soft but firm voice. "As you know, gentlemen, *Bennington* took four bombs. All were five-hundred-fifty-pounders and all struck from the quarters aft. Two were tipped with depleted uranium and went right through the flight deck," the Japanese exchanged a knowing look, "and exploded on the hangar deck. The other two exploded on the flight deck amongst a squadron of SBDs." He sighed, obviously suffering the agonies of hell as he relived the horror. "Bombs and gasoline were ignited on both decks. The aft elevator was not blown out, but it was warped by the heat and the hydraulic pump destroyed. In fact, both decks need major replacements of plates from frame one-five-six aft, and we need a new elevator." He sighed again and ran his fingers through his hair. "One hundred seven dead, one hundred twenty-six wounded. And my air groups were decimated—thirteen fighters, twenty dive bombers and twenty-two torpedo bombers were lost with most of their crews." He looked at Yoshi Matsuhara. "Replacement crews are in training under Commander Matsuhara." He hunched his shoulders up and turned up his palms in a gesture of futility. "But I don't have a viable ship for them to operate from, even if they are ready."

"You're in dry dock," Fujita said.

"Yes, sir. Three more days of availability."

"Your hull is intact."

"Correct, sir. Number five bulkhead was slightly warped by one of the bombs, and two of the fuel oil tanks ruptured, letting water into some of our fuel lines. These have already been repaired. It's the two decks and the elevator that sustained most of the damage. Nakajima is building a new elevator and most of the damaged plates have been replaced."

"How much time will you need?"

Treynor palmed his chin. "If we had the elevator, we could put to sea in a month."

"We may not have a month." Every head turned to Fujita and startled eyes widened. But the old man did not provide more information. Instead, he nodded at Chief Engineer Tatsuya Yoshida. Treynor found his seat.

The old engineer struggled to his feet, stared at a few documents spread before him, and spoke. It was the usual agenda of boilers, auxiliary engines, bearings, evaporators. He reported boilers one and six down for descaling, but all the others were capable of 750 pounds of pressure.

"When will they be on line?" Fujita asked.

"Two days, sir."

"Fuel?"

"All tanks topped off, Admiral. We could put to sea now, sir. I could give you twenty-eight knots."

"Very well." Fujita shifted his stare down the table to the gunnery officer, Commander Nobomitsu Atsumi. Atsumi rose and gave his report. A dozen new 127-millimeter gun barrels had arrived and were being installed. Twenty new 25-millimeter barrels were due tomorrow. "And all magazines are full, sir," he concluded. Atsumi sat.

The old admiral glanced at Lieutenant Tadayoshi Koga. "Your report, Lieutenant."

The little round Maritime Self-Defense Force officer struggled to his feet. He had put on more weight since Brent had last seen him, layered fat overhanging his belt and collar. He seemed to have problems dragging his huge buttocks out of his chair. His beady black eyes stared only at the admiral. "Sir," he said, attempting a military bearing but appearing ludicrous with his paunch overhanging the table and obscuring his own notes, "*Tenno* has been upset by the recent bloodshed. I heard him say as much in his own honorable words." He was referring to the "heavenly Emperor." The black eyes flicked to Brent and then Yoshi.

Mention of Emperor Akihito mandated an exchange in the peculiar honorific form that Brent found risible and clumsy. In an attempt to create an other world aura of reverence to ultimate superiority, the usual three forms of politeness of speaking down, or up, or on a level of equality was avoided. Instead, Kaga and Fujita always observed the flowery fourth level of ultra-subservience, where every noun and verb changed form. On this level, both men resorted to honorifics and the passive voice. They stumbled into ridiculous extremes to avoid the commonplace. Brent had even heard them avoid saying the Emperor "went to" or "came from." Instead, it was *oide ni naru*—literally, "the honorable going or coming." Brent considered the whole charade preposterous. Fortunately, both men remained in English, where much of the clumsy form was lost in translation.

Fujita was obviously upset. "*Tenno* has been informed of the ambush?"

"Of course, Admiral. He has been wishing that less blood would be flowing—places no blame on you or your men." Again, his eyes moved to the young American and the air group commander. "He has been wishing for more caution—his honorable word was 'restraint.'"

Brent almost laughed, and Yoshi squirmed. Fujita continued, "Please inform *Tenno* that I will do my utmost to comply with his wishes."

"My command, sir," Koga acquiesced.

A new, military timbre crept into Fujita's voice. "Your report on the amphibious vessels?"

A murmur swept the room, glances exchanged. Amphibious craft could only mean an invasion. "Saipan—Tinian," Brent whispered into Yoshi's ear.

"The best way to remove a cancer is to do it with a scalpel," Yoshi said.

Koga leaned and peered over his stomach at his notes. "The four LSTs based at Sasebo are now operational."

"The *Motobu, Miura, Yura,* and *Yusotei,*" Fujita said."

"Correct, sir."

"The other five?"

Koga shook his head. "The Arab air attack left them beyond salvage."

Fujita's tiny fist struck the table top. "Not enough! Not enough! We need assault transports, small craft, amphibious tanks . . ."

"I'm sorry, Admiral." Koga looked down the table at Brent Ross. "The Americans have those vessels in great abundance."

Brent shook his head. "I am not aware of any negotiations on that matter."

Fujita said, "Admiral Whitehead has been working in that area and will have a report for us."

There was a knock. Fujita nodded and a seaman guard opened the door. Rear Admiral Byron Whitehead and Colonel Irving Bernstein entered. Both men looked as if they had aged a year in the past month. Whitehead had also lost weight and added lines, and the last vestiges of blond hair had yielded to white. Bernstein, too, looked thinner, his Israeli Army battle fatigues hanging from his spare frame in disheveled folds and wrinkles. His haggard face seemed to reflect the disarray of his clothes.

Then Brent saw the third man, standing behind Whitehead and Bernstein in the passageway. He seemed reluctant to enter, almost as if he were hiding behind the rear admiral and the colonel. Finally, he stepped through the doorway. Younger than Bernstein and Whitehead, he was portly, with snow-white hair, a ruddy, avuncular face, and bloodshot blue eyes. He looked like Santa Claus not yet dressed for the holidays, but one who had already dipped into the wassail bowl. Brent was sure he was looking at the CIA replacement for Horace Mayfield. Considering that Fujita had hanged his predecessor from the yardarm, the man's recalcitrance did not take Brent completely by surprise.

Fujita stopped the stranger and nodded at Brent Ross

and Captain Paul Treynor. "Our new CIA liaison man, Alfred Gibney," he said, introducing Gibney to his fellow Americans. Nodding, Gibney smiled fleetingly and muttered greetings. The officers stood and said their greetings in return.

The newcomers bowed to the admiral and then walked to their chairs. Each carried an attaché case. Whitehead sought Brent's hand and grasped it in both of his, "I heard about *Haida*. Well done. Thank God you're all right."

"Thank you, Admiral. I had a good crew."

"Shalom," Bernstein said, greeting his friends. Brent grasped his friend's hand. It felt like bones wrapped in loose plastic.

Crowding close behind, Alfred Gibney shook Brent's hand and then Paul Treynor's. The grip was firm. He sat next to *Bennington*'s captain. Fujita said to Whitehead, "Your report, Admiral. You have word on the amphibious craft?"

"Yes, sir." Whitehead pulled a dossier from an attaché case and placed it on the table. He began to open it.

Fujita stopped him. "It is not necessary to read it. I will read it. Did you get the equipment I requested?"

"The amphibious craft's committed, Admiral Fujita, including the small craft, transports, and even a control vessel. You can have it anytime you want it."

"The Russians?"

"No problem. The stuff's been in mothballs for decades—the U.S. Navy will sell it to the East Asian Scrap-Iron Works for junk." He scratched his bulbous nose. "And, sir, most of it is just that—been laid up since World War Two. That's why no one objects."

"East Asian Scrap-Iron Works?" Captain Treynor asked, entering the exchange.

Whitehead explained to Treynor, "Yes, Captain. It actually exists at Yokohama. It's our front." He chuckled. "It doesn't fool anyone—the Russians know, the Arabs . . ." He shrugged.

223

Fujita stared the length of the table. "It is obvious to all of you that I have been planning an invasion of the Marianas." Every man nodded. "That is the only way we can escape," he waved a hand in circular gesture, "this threat of enemy LRAs"—long range aircraft.

Brent Ross said, "Admiral, Admiral Whitehead said nothing about big-gunned ships."

"That is correct."

"But Admiral, we would need big-gun support." He gestured at Captain Fite. "Our escorts only have five-inch guns. The Arabs have taken over old blockhouses left over from World War Two and built more of their own. Our five-inch shells would bounce off them like ping-pong balls. They'd cut us to pieces, sir."

"I know, Commander." Fujita looked at Whitehead.

"Still no luck there," the rear admiral said. He paused while a disappointed rumble filled the room. He almost pleaded, "As you know Admiral, I requested the *New Jersey* months ago—it's back in mothballs." He turned to the other officers. "But they turned me down—claimed the Russians would walk out of the Geneva talks."

"The Russians are coming apart," Captain Treynor said.

"True, but they're still helping the Arabs and, don't forget, they still have four carriers in commission—two nuclear carriers of the *Breznev* class and two more *Kievs*, the *Novorossiysk* and the *Baku*. The Navy Department is convinced that if they gave us *New Jersey*, the Russians would give the Arabs the *Novorossiysk* and the *Baku*." Angry mutters filled the room.

Everyone knew the Arab bases in the Marianas posed a mortal threat to Japan, and Fujita was determined to destroy them. After all, in 1945, B-29 *Enola Gay* took off from Tinian with her atomic payload for Hiroshima. No Japanese, regardless of age, could ever forget that— would ever be allowed to forget. The islands must be taken and the threat removed forever. But, again, Americans and Russians in the hypocritical collusion

224

they both called *Glasnost* had stopped such an attack in its tracks. Antique assault craft could not attack those beaches without the support of big-gunned ships.

Fujita stared at Gibney. All other eyes in the room followed his. The CIA man locked his eyes with the admiral's. "And what has the CIA done to assist in this situation?"

Gibney rose slowly, like a man mounting the stairs to the guillotine. However, he spoke in a surprisingly strong, well-modulated voice like a 1940s radio announcer. "Admiral, as you must recall, I advised you that attempts to acquire any of the *Iowa* class—*Iowa, New Jersey, Missouri,* or *Wisconsin*—would be useless. The navy feels it needs these vessels and their transfer to your forces would almost be an open declaration of war by the United States."

"What's wrong with that?" Bernstein shot at the CIA man.

"Everything," the CIA man retorted with aplomb and control that surprised Brent. It was obvious that both men reflected the generic antipathy the two competing intelligence agencies felt for each other. Gibney continued, "You would open the gates to full Russian support for the Arabs—most dangerous, modern subs, not these antique *Zulus* and *Whiskies* they're giving them now." He waved at the Japanese at the head of the table. "And Japan is getting our full Alaskan oil production now. Not one tanker leaves Valdez that is not bound for Japan. That supply could be cut off."

Bernstein was fatigued, his patience worn to the bare bones by a lifetime of warfare, sacrifice, and loss. The blue numbers tattooed on his forearm seemed to glow along with the anger building in his eyes. "We've been doing your dying for decades. Four million of us holding back nearly two hundred million of those Arab fanatics," the Israeli spat. Then he waved at the Japanese. "And *Yonaga*'s men have been dying for the past eight in wholesale lots—for what?" Everyone froze at the outburst, not daring to enter the bitter exchange. But Fujita hunched forward, the usual hungry look of intense interest he always showed when members of his staff fought out their animosities. Surely, such exchanges could act as catharses, but Brent had seen them lead to feuds which were only resolved in bloodshed. Fujita would not intercede; not yet, anyway.

"For the whole free world."

"Free world, bullshit!" Bernstein fired back. "You and those Russian bastards pull your *Glasnost* strings in Geneva while your puppets tear each other to pieces."

"I won't take that. Fight your own fuckin' war!" Gibney began to gather his papers. Brent was shocked. He had completely miscalculated the man. He had guts. It was time for Fujita.

"Gentlemen," the old admiral said, pushing himself to his feet. "Seat yourselves."

"I'm leaving," Gibney said.

Fujita gestured at two seaman guards flanking the door. They took a step toward the American intelligence officer. "No, you are *not*."

Gibney eyed the two guards under hooded lids. "I remain under protest."

"Protest all you like, Mister Gibney. But you will remain and give us your complete report. You have intelligence on the Arab forces at Tomonuto, in the Marianas and more. Is that not correct?"

Gibney gritted his teeth and stretched his lips back as if he were testing an elastic. "All right, sir." He stabbed a finger at Bernstein like a dagger. "But keep him off my ass."

"Choose a better vocabulary—a military vocabulary," Fujita warned.

The edge came off the CIA man's voice, but the irritation was still there, "Off me! Keep that Israeli quiet while I speak, Admiral."

"Very well." Fujita turned to Bernstein, "You will remain quiet, Colonel, or I will have you removed."

Dropping his head, Bernstein sighed audibly, like wind through dry branches. "My word, sir."

Fujita waved at the CIA man. "Proceed."

Gibney's eyes scanned the entire room, finally coming back to Admiral Fujita. "Sir, I decoded some transmissions just before coming aboard. I have the latest information on the Arab strength in Tomonuto Atoll and the Marianas and . . ."

"Proceed, please," Fujita said, waving impatiently.

The intelligence officer pulled some documents from his attaché case. "The Arab strength at Tomonuto has been increased." The blue eyes traveled the room. "As you know, our SSN (nuclear attack submarine), *Glenard P. Lipscomb,* has been on station off Tomonuto. *Lipscomb* reports three depot ships, a tanker, two yard oilers, twelve destroyers, the carrier *Al Kufra,* and two cruisers at anchor."

"Have they built an airstrip yet?" Commander Iwata asked.

"Negative. They've been bulldozing a strip on a small spit of land called Barry Island, but it's not finished and they don't have the fighters, anyway. But a constant patrol is maintained in the area between the Marianas and the atoll by LRAs based on Saipan and Tinian."

"The cruisers?" Lieutenant Koga asked. He dared a glance at Admiral Fujita. "You have not kept the Self-Defense Force apprised of these vessels."

"Humph!" Commander Takuya Iwata snorted. "What will you do, sink them with a cavalry charge?" A snicker went through the room. Koga glared at the dive bomber commander.

Fujita halted the outburst with a wave and nodded to the CIA man. Gibney glanced at Koga and then his notes. "The cruisers are the *Babur,* ex-HMS *London,* which Kadafi bought from Pakistan, and . . ."

"Pakistan!" Koga exclaimed. "They sold him the cruiser *Dido.*"

"We sank her four years ago with fish," Captain Fite

227

offered. "I lost two DDs doing it."

Gibney continued. "As most of you know, *Babur* has been upgraded." He looked over the attentive faces. "Length five hundred seventy feet, displacement seven thousand four hundred forty tons. She now mounts six five-point-five Armstrong-Vickers Mark 26 rapid-fire guns instead of the four four-point-five main battery for which she was originally designed. She is heavily armed with forty-millimeter and twenty-millimeter secondaries. she can do at least thirty-two knots." He riffled through some documents. "The other cruiser is the *Umar Farooz*, the ex-HMS *Llandaff*, bought from Bangladesh. She's small by American and Japanese standards—three hundred sixty feet, thirty-eight hundred tons. She was completed in 1955 and was diesel powered. But the Arabs have reengined her with Parson-geared turbines giving her a flank speed of thirty-four-knots. She is heavily armed for such a small ship—four four-point-five cannons in two gun houses, and, perhaps, twenty forty-millimeter guns and about the same number of twenties."

Fite's voice was solemn with his most critical concern, "Radar! Have they installed fire control radar?"

The CIA man shook his head. "*Babur* has none and *Umar Farooz* had her Mark Six M, I-band fire control removed as per the agreements reached at Geneva. But our reports indicate both vessels have one of the oldest but still very efficient British air and surface search radars in the British inventory—Type Nine-Six-Five combined warning type." He glanced at his notes. "The Nine-Six-Five operating frequency range lies in the metric wavelength band and output power in the megawatt range, and it does have target designation capability."

Fite pressed on into the one topic that could spell doom for his entire command. "Their *Gearings?* Have they changed their radar?"

Gibney said to the worried American, "Our latest

reports indicate all enemy destroyers are equipped with American equipment. The SPS-10 surface search radar and the SPS-40 air search. No fire control radar. It's all optical."

Fite nodded, but his eyes were narrow, lips tight with concern.

Fujita said, "And gentlemen, remember, their *Essex*, *Al Kufra*, is in Tomonuto." He squinted at the CIA man. "But, according to my calculations, her air groups cannot be complete."

Gibney smiled at the old man's perceptiveness. "True, sir. You destroyed most of her aircraft. At the moment she is a fighter without fists." Everyone chuckled, more with relief than at the clumsy attempt at humor. "But we have word that a transport is underway for Tomonuto with complete air crews and replacement aircraft for *Al Kufra*."

There was an angry rumble. Even Fujita appeared surprised. "When should they arrive?" the admiral asked.

Gibney shrugged. "Five days, a week."

"They will need to train," Iwata said. "Flying from a carrier on the high seas is much different from flying from a rectangle laid off on the desert."

"True," Gibney agreed. "But we have word that the bulk of these replacements are surviving pilots and crewmen from *Ramli al Kabir*, *Daffah*, and *Magid*. They are highly experienced."

Lieutenant Koga spoke up, face alight, as if he had discovered a hidden gem. "Then if *Yonaga* moves against Tomonuto, the enemy patrols from the Marianas will spot her and report her location to the enemy forces at Tomonuto, and then the enemy can sortie to fight or flee." He smiled all around, as if he were the master strategist. However, every man in the room was aware of the problem and it had been discussed many times.

Brent and Yoshi applauded lightly and chuckled. "Brilliant," Yoshi laughed.

"Now, see here . . ." Koga sputtered.

Fujita hacked off the exchange with a harsh, "Enough!" Then he nodded at the CIA man. "We know the Arab's Fifth Special Combat Battalion occupies Saipan and the Seventh Parachute Brigade occupies Tinian. Any reinforcements?"

Gibney nodded. "Yes, sir. They've been running a steady stream of troops in by submarine. We count at least eight *Whiskies* and four *Zulus*." He shifted his eyes to Tadayoshi Koga. "These are diesel-electric boats based on old German World War Two designs."

"I know."

"How many troops and artillery? Tanks?"

Gibney sighed. "They may be in division strength on Saipan." An ominous rumble filled the room. "And may have as much as two regiments of their best infantry on Tinian."

"Fourteen to fifteen thousand men on Saipan and perhaps ten thousand on Tinian."

"That's what we figure."

"And tanks?"

"It's hard to transport their T-54 and T-72 MBTs by sub. Must be done by transport. We figure the armor is weak."

"And Tinian is not as heavily defended as Saipan."

"That is correct, Admiral."

"Their aircraft strength is weak on Saipan and Tinian?"

"True, Admiral. You've chopped them up pretty good. But they still have at least three squadrons of fighters and maybe ten to twenty Ju 87s, six to ten Connies and DC-6s, a few DC-3s, and maybe a dozen HE-111s, twin-engined Cessnas, and North American AT-6 Texans." He looked around, then spoke to all the officers. "You must understand, these are estimates. I could be way off. They are capable of bringing in disassembled aircraft by sub, you know."

Fujita said, "They must bring transports into Tanapag

Harbor to bring in massive reinforcements, heavy artillery, tanks, and aircraft in large numbers. This they have not dared while *Yonaga* waits just to the north. They have bled before."

Cries of *"Banzai! Banzai!"* filled the room. Brent half-rose with his own *"Banzai!"* Gibney stared at the young American curiously.

"But, sir," the CIA man interrupted, "the Pentagon has given us the word that that is precisely what the Arabs intend to do."

"Even with their cruisers, they don't have the strength. *Al Kufra* is no match for *Yonaga*—cruisers or not."

More cheers. Alfred Gibney held up his hands. "They could match you if *Magid* joined *Al Kufra*."

Silence. *"Magid* is in the Mediterranean," Fujita protested.

"True. She's been stripped of her air groups which were sent to *Al Kufra*. But she is training new flyers."

Yoshi Matsuhara entered the exchange, "It would take months to train them—make them ready to meet my eagles."

Gibney rubbed his chin and stared down at the table. "Two months. That's all we have."

The remark jolted Fujita into one of his instant decisions. He stood, moved to a chart of the Western Pacific and picked up a rubber-tipped pointer. He stabbed Tomonuto. "Then we will make a preemptive strike—hit Tomonuto, and we must be under way within a week."

An uproar filled the room. Treynor objected. "*Bennington* won't be ready."

"I know. We will leave her."

Fite spoke up: "I have three DDs laid up for major repairs."

"We still have nine *Fletchers*."

Yoshi Matsuhara said: "Half of my pilots have never landed on a carrier. They are green, inexperienced."

"They must learn their trade while under way."

Iwata added his objections: "We are expecting new engines for my dive bombers. The Sakae 42 is underpowered."

The torpedo bomber commander, Lieutenant Shinji Hamasaki, supported Iwata with his objections.

"They have power enough to carry their bombs and torpedoes." Fujita stabbed the chart. "We must strike before the enemy reinforces—concentrates his forces." His black eyes swept the now silent room. "We have no choice."

The long-silent executive officer, Captain Mitake Arai, broke in, "They will know we are coming. If LRAs from the Marianas do not spot us, submarines stationed off Tokyo Bay will."

"I know."

"Then it is possible we will be under attack from both carrier-based aircraft and aircraft based in the Marianas," Arai warned.

Fujita shook his head, then raised the pointer and traced a wide sweeping arc. "We will swing far to the east." The rubber tip swung east of Wake Island, curved southwest, past Eniwetok Atoll, then west and north of Truk to a point about 200 miles northeast of Tomonuto and stopped. "We will launch here," the old man said with finality.

"They will still know, sir."

"True. But we will be out of effective range of their fighters and Ju-87s based in the Marianas." He pounded the atoll. "And they will come out and fight or flee."

Captain Arai was not finished. "If they have their strip completed on Barry Island we could face land-based fighters and bombers, too."

"There are no guarantees in war, Captain Arai. You should know that." His glance encompassed the entire room. "All of you have studied the great Prussian Carl von Clausewitz. He said, 'The element in which war exists is danger. The highest of all moral qualities in time of danger is courage. Daring, boldness, rashness, trusting in luck are only variants of courage, and all these traits of character seek their proper element—chance.'" He paused for a moment as if waiting for the words to seep into the minds of his men. "We must depend on courage, chance, and the blessings of the gods."

Brent was not surprised by the admiral's verbatim quote from the nineteenth-century military genius. An inveterate reader whose library jammed the cabin of a long-dead flag officer, he read continuously and his knowledge of military and naval matters was encyclopedic.

Arai replied, "There is no shortage of courage in this room, Admiral."

"I know," Fujita smiled back. And then, in a businesslike tone, "Now, it is understood. All departments will be combat ready and prepared to get under way in seven days." There were some grumbles, but everyone nodded.

Fujita dropped the pointer into its tray but remained standing. He clapped twice to attract the attention of the gods. Every man rose. Brent and the Japanese also clapped twice—odd numbers of claps were considered unlucky. Fujita turned to the shrine and pointed at the "Buddha from Three-Thousand Worlds." He began his prayer with Buddha's given name, "Oh, Siddhartha Gautama, show us the way to defeat the devil, Mara, who has cloaked himself in Arab robes and kills like a snake and lead us to the noble truth of the path that leads to the cessation of suffering—the eightfold path of right view, right thought, right speech, right action, right livelihood, right effort, right mindfulness, and right concentration. Thus our arms will carry our blessings and lead us to victory over the hosts of Mara."

A cathedral silence filled the room. Brent knew Fujita would not neglect *bushido*. All eyes followed the old Japanese as he picked up a copy of the *Hagakure*. "And here, in this sacred book," Fujita said, holding up the leatherbound tome, "it is written, 'It is a cleansing act to throw away one's life for the Mikado. For the man who would cut off his life for the sake of righteousness, there is no need to call on the rewards of sacrifice. All the gods of heaven will polish his karma and send him on the road to his reward.'"

"There were shouts of *"Banzai!* and *"Tenno heika banzai!"*

Fujita's raised palms halted the shouts. "Admiral Whitehead, Captain Fite, Captain Treynor, Commander Katsube, Commander Matsuhara, Commander Ross, Mister Gibney, please remain. The rest of you are dismissed."

There were mumbles of surprise and then Captain Arai, Commander Iwata, Commander Atsumi, Lieutenant Yoshida, Lieutenant Hamasaki, and Lieutenant Koga filed out of the room.

After the door closed, Fujita gestured with his fingers and the officers moved down the table close to their commanding officer. Then Fujita addressed the group. "The prisoners, we must discuss ours and theirs. Thanks to Captain Fite, we should be able to make excellent progress there."

Now Brent knew why most of the Japanese officers had been dismissed. The topic of prisoners was one of great delicacy and controversy indeed. After all, *bushido* did not even acknowledge the concept of surrender. Repeatedly the *Hagakure* exhorted the samurai to maintain his honor by fighting to the death. In a hopeless situation, the warrior would make a final death-seeking charge against the enemy. If the enemy did not dispatch him, he was obliged to do it himself. There was no option.

Although Japan had signed the Geneva Convention in 1929, with the outbreak of war in 1941, the Japanese government announced it would comply *mutatis mutandis*—a legalism meaning, "necessary changes have been made." And indeed they were. This abhorrence of surrender led to the savage abuse of prisoners. By allowing themselves to be taken captive, Britons, Americans, Canadians, Australians, and New Zealanders were beneath cowardice and warranted the most brutal and inhuman treatment. They were starved, beaten, and sometimes beheaded. Nearly 30 percent of the 95,000 Allied prisoners perished.

Every man in the room knew of these horrifying statistics, but Fujita had skillfully managed to avoid most of the old festering wounds and maintain the camaraderie of a force that was now truly international. But *bushido* had influenced the old man's handling of prisoners, too. Many captives had been summarily executed by beheading; two were hung from the yardarm. Now, however, the enemy held a large number of prisoners including the brave Colonel Latimer Stewart and at least eleven of his men. Brent suspected that despite the dictates of *bushido* the old man would make every effort to save them.

Through the corner of his eye, Brent looked at both Captain Fite and Rear Admiral Whitehead, who had both fought in World War Two. Their faces were stark, stoic, free of emotion. If memories of the ghastly treatment of Allied prisoners were troubling them, their faces revealed none of it. Then he saw Fite nod and stare at Admiral Fujita knowingly. The old man nodded back almost as if the pair were exchanging secrets telepathically. Now Brent began to suspect why Fujita had commanded the escort commander to take prisoners after *Abu Bakr* was sunk. Bargaining chips . . . he was sure of it.

Whitehead pulled some sheets of paper from his attaché case. He waved them. "I have a complete list of our prisoners held by the Arabs. I got it from the Swiss ambassador this morning." Fujita waved the American rear admiral to his feet. Whitehead glanced at his notes. "As you know, Colonel Latimer Stewart was taken prisoner along with eleven more pilots and crewmen when he attacked the Rabta gasworks with his B-25s.

Also, Arab destroyers picked up twelve more of our pilots and crewmen after the battle off Gibralter."

"That makes twenty-four POWs," Treynor said.

Both Bernstein and Whitehead shook their heads grimly. "Twenty."

"That doesn't add up," the captain of the *Bennington* argued.

Whitehead's eyes found the table. He spoke from deep in his chest, "It does if you execute four."

There was an uproar, curses, waved fists. "Gentlemen! Gentlemen!" Fujita shouted, the power of his voice restoring order. He waved down the table, "Captain Fite please."

The escort commander stood, white face ruddy from the hot blood pressing close beneath. He was obviously agitated. "I took forty-one prisoners from the crew of *Abu Bakr* and I picked up four Arab pilots and five crewmen."

"That totals fifty," Treynor said with finality.

Fite shook his head. "Forty-two. I executed eight!"

A confused murmur filled the room and hasty glances were exchanged. Katsube—half-rising and shouting *"Banzai!"*—staggered, and would have pitched to the deck without support from Rear Admiral Whitehead, who caught him like a sack full of twigs and guided him back into his chair.

"We're no better than they are," Treynor exclaimed bitterly.

Fujita reentered the conversation. "Not true, Captain Treynor. I have sent word to Kadafi that I will execute two of his men for every one of ours he kills. That is all those savages understand."

"What happened to the Geneva Convention? This is a jungle."

"The Geneva Convention was stillborn." The old Japanese drummed the table. There was irritation in the withered fingertips. Then, with a voice that singed, "You can be transferred, Captain Treynor."

The American captain tucked his lower lip under and bit down. Perspiration beaded on his forehead. Several deep breaths seemed to calm him. "No. I don't want that." He waved at the bulkheads. "I just don't understand these rules."

Fujita smiled, reached under the table and withdrew a copy of the *Hagakure*. The officer passed it down the table to Treynor. "Here," Fujita said, "here is our rule book. Study it and study the *Koran*." Treynor glanced at it curiously and shoved it into his pocket. Fujita returned to Captain Fite, "You brought some of the senior prisoners with you?"

"As per your orders, sir. I have the captain of the *Abu Bakr*, Commander Henri DuCarme, the commanding officer of *Stukagruppe Zwei*, Major Horst Fritschmann, and a fighter pilot, Lieutenant Hamoud Rogba, in the passageway." He waved at the door. "The remaining prisoners are in *Yonaga*'s brig."

The old Japanese rubbed his hands together as if he were anticipating a gourmet meal. He spoke with a benign smile. "Before we greet our new guests, I would like to hear from Colonel Bernstein." He hunched forward, eyes narrow. "Mossad must have the latest intelligence on our B-25 attack. We know Colonel Stewart inflicted some damage."

Brent suspected Mossad had operatives within the Rabta works. But that topic was always discreetly skirted. Nevertheless, it was obvious that some of Bernstein's reports could only come from eyewitness observers. This always irritated CIA men. Gibney was no different. Brent could see the resentment in his eyes. *Like a ham actor upstaged by a stand-in*, Brent thought. He laughed inwardly.

Bernstein rose. He had notes but did not refer to them. "True, sir. the B-25s destroyed at least twenty-two enemy fighters, blew up two warehouses at Rabta, and may have inflicted damage on the main works themselves." The men looked at each other and exchanged excited whispers. This was much better than anyone had expected. Up until now, the raid had been considered a complete failure. Bernstein glanced at Gibney, a triumphant, baleful look. "Let me emphasize," the Israeli officer said, "they were under attack by at least four squadrons of fighters for at least four hundred miles—only three planes got as far as Rabta. Two were shot down there."

"The third?"

The Israeli sighed. "He made it to the Mediterranean, then crashed, and the four survivors were shot in the water." A funereal silence gripped the room. Brent could hear Treynor whispering, "No! No!"

"Where are the prisoners being held?" Fujita asked.

"We have reliable reports they are in the camp at Al Aziziyab, which is about fifty-kilometers south of Tripoli."

"Heavily guarded?"

"A fortress—three electrified barbed wire fences, machine gun towers, minefields, laser sensors."

An attempt to release the prisoners by force was out of the question and everyone knew it. All eyes moved to the admiral as he tugged on his chin thoughtfully. "What cannot be conquered by force of arms sometimes can fall through diplomacy."

Captain Fite interrupted, showing his depth of military theory and thirst for action. "You mentioned von Clausewitz, sir. Clausewitz also said, 'War is merely the continuation of policy by other means.'" His knuckles drummed the table. "You would reverse this?"

"Of course," Fujita said. "Anything that will serve our purpose."

"You can't trust an Arab," Fite insisted. "You can't deal with them. Good faith, honor, and integrity just don't exist when they bargain."

"We must try."

Brent could hear Fite rumble deep down, "Kill the bastards—kill 'em." Brent gave the escort commander a pat on the back.

Colonel Bernstein moved on impatiently, "You are thinking of a prisoner exchange, Admiral Fujita?"

"You have done it many times."

"True, Admiral. However, we often trade in the ratio of a hundred Arabs for one of ours. A real bargain. You cannot hope to match that ratio."

Fujita turned to Whitehead. "When we conclude this meeting, call on the Swiss ambassador and have him send word to Kadafi that we would like to have a parley to discuss the exchange of prisoners." He tightened his jaw and tapped the table with the tiny white knuckles. "And tell him we will observe the Geneva Convention as long as he does."

Brent saw Treynor smile and nod his approval. Bernstein looked skeptical but remained silent. Fite shook his head. Whitehead seemed pleased. "Good idea, Admiral. I will request a neutral site," the American rear admiral said.

"Good thinking," Fujita said. "And then, to a seaman guard, "Bring in Commander Henri DuCarme."

Chapter Ten

Commander Henri DuCarme was a fairly tall, slender man with a spadelike beard much like Colonel Bernstein's, but DuCarme's was black. His abundant hair and eyes were black, too. His face was long and lean, his prominent nose twitching. His eyes shifted uneasily, darting from man to man. His whole aspect reminded Brent of a sewer rat—one that had been trapped in a corner and was ready to bite back. But as Brent was soon to learn, this rat had no teeth.

"*Monsieur*, you are Admiral Fujita," DuCarme blurted in a quivering high voice, heavily accented. His black eyes were wide, staring at the admiral as if he had encountered a three-headed Cerberus at the gates of hell. Brent could not restrain a contemptuous smile.

The old Japanese stared back at the Frenchman standing before him, eyes running from head to toe and back. DuCarme threw back his shoulders and presented his most military bearing. However, his shoulders sagged suddenly, and he leaned forward, eyes riveted to the admiral's sword, which hung from its brackets behind the old man. His expression changed as if a Halloween mask of terror had been suddenly pulled over his face, his lower lip quivering, and his nose twitching and sniffing as if he were suffering an asthma attack. He gestured at the sword. "*Mon Dieu, e'epée.* You would execute me?"

"I ask the questions here, *Monsieur Capitaine*," Fujita retorted. A slow smile crinkled the old lines. He gestured at Brent Ross. "Meet Commander Ross. He sank you."

The squinting black eyes found Brent. The Frenchman bowed stiffly, a clumsy attempt at gallantry. "*Félicitations, Monsieur Commandant*. You fought with *éclat et humeur belliqueuse*."

"Commander," Fujita said impatiently, "the language of your fleet is English?"

"True, *Monsieur Amiral*."

"Well, then, please confine yourself to English. It is the language of my forces, too.

"*Oui*—Ah, yes, Admiral." He stumbled badly on the English and turned his hands up in a gesture of futility. "But, *s'il vous plaît, mon anglais* is not good."

"It will be good enough." Fujita gestured at Brent. "He congratulated you and said you fought with brilliance and fighting spirit."

"I know, sir. I understand French," Brent said. He studied the Frenchman. Before him he saw an amalgam of clenched hair and perverse mediocrity. The man had no more right to command a destroyer than Mary Poppins. Brent said, "I cannot say the same for you, *Monsieur Commandant*. Your gunnery was terrible and your ship handling appallingly poor. You should've sunk *Haida* long before we were within torpedo range."

The Frenchman drew himself up indignantly. "My crew was mostly Arab and you had *Anglais* . . ." he looked fearfully at the admiral. "I mean, you had Englishmen."

Brent said to DuCarme, "You had a handicap, no doubt about that."

Fujita slapped the desk impatiently. "Your base?"

"The Geneva Convention?" the Frenchman dared.

"You have it."

"I need not answer that, *Monsieur Amiral*."

"And I need not observe the Geneva Convention." Fujita gestured at his sword.

241

The Frenchman tried to swallow and failed, as if his Adam's apple had turned into a steel ball and lodged in his esophagus. "Tomonuto," he blurted. Then, without prompting, he described the ships and number of each type. His count fit exactly that provided by Alfred Gibney. The CIA man turned to Bernstein and smiled triumphantly.

"You were trying to lure and sink one of our patrols," Fujita said.

"True," DuCarme said. "But those *imbéciles* on Saipan did not give us the aerial support they promised." He stabbed a finger at Brent Ross. "You should be on the bottom, *Monsieur*."

Brent chuckled. "The best laid plans, *Monsieur*." He shrugged, mimicked the Frenchman's gesture of futility and, imitated the near falsetto of his voice. "*C'est la guerre, Monsieur Commandant*."

Everyone laughed. DuCarme glared at the American with a face rippling with anger and hostility.

Fujita gestured to the guards. "Take this scum back to his cage."

The Frenchman stiffened, suddenly rigid with rage and humiliaton. "*Monsieur, Amiral.* I am an *officier.* As an *officier . . .*"

"Out!" Fujita shouted, pointing to the door. "You are nothing—offal not fit for command. You have earned the noose, not the sword. Out!"

A pair of guards grabbed the Frenchman's arms and dragged him through the door. As a final attempt at bravado, he shouted "*Bâtards! Bâtards!*"

Fujita said to one of the guards as the shouts faded down the passageway, "Bring in the Arab."

Second Lieutenant Hamoud Rogba slouched at a sloppy burlesque of attention, staring at Admiral Fujita. He was a short, stocky young man with a large nose and black eyes that glowed like smoldering charcoal. Brent sensed that unlike DuCarme, this man had a spine. He would be insolent, difficult. "Second Lieutenant Hamoud Rogba," the Arab announced before a question could be put to him. Bernstein raised an eyebrow and stared at the young pilot curiously.

"Unit?" Fujita asked.

The Arab laughed and gestured at the sword. "You are going to chop off my head. That is all you get, old man."

The admiral nodded and a seaman guard slapped the Arab across the face so hard that he staggered back against the bulkhead. "It's Admiral Fujita or sir," Fujita said. "You will observe military discipline."

Wiping blood from the corner of his mouth, the young Arab straightened. Nevertheless, defiance was still in his demeanor. "You will get the Geneva Convention, if you earn it," Fujita added.

"I don't understand."

"Your understanding is not requisite to these proceedings." Fujita palmed the few hairs remaining on his pate. "Just answer my questions."

"I reserve the right to restrict my answers in accordance with the Convention."

"Reserve anything you like," Fujita said. "But remember, I am not bound to adhere to the Convention." The Arab's eyes found the sword and Brent saw the lips tighten. He wondered if Rogba's stiff spine would begin to bend. "Unit?" Fujita repeated.

"With all respect," Rogba said, grimacing like a man who had bitten into an apple full of worms, "I am not required to answer that question."

Brent expected more punishment from the guard. However, Fujita did not signal the seaman, who stared expectantly and eagerly. Instead, the old man said, "You fly from Saipan. You are a member of Kenneth Rosencrance's Fourth Fighter Squadron . . ."

"And, sir," Yoshi Matsuhara said, "he was a wingman to Lieutenant Hani Meri." He chuckled. "Now deceased."

"Since you know so much, why do you ask me these questions?"

Again Brent was surprised by the admiral's reaction. He suspected Fujita's samurai background influenced a modicum of respect for the young pilot's courage. "It is our privilege, and I remind you, Lieutenant, we ask the questions."

Rogba said to Fujita, "I fly for the finest squadron on earth. Someday we will kill all of you." He glanced at Bernstein and focused on the blue numbers tattooed on the agent's forearm. "And we will complete what Hitler began." He stabbed a finger at the Israeli, "Complete the Holocaust—drive those Hebes into the sea."

Colonel Irving Bernstein said in a surprisingly calm voice, "You are from Amman?"

"Yes. I was born in Jordan."

Bernstein tugged on the tip of his beard and said thoughtfully, "The Rogbas of Amman." He looked up, face brightened by a half-smile. "Your father was Salim Saleh Rogba." It was a statement of fact, not a question.

Everyone stared at the pair silently. Brent knew the Israeli was on to something, something big, something explosive. The look of rapt concentration had crept back into Admiral Fujita's eyes.

"Haj Salim Saleh Rogba," the Arab pilot said with pride. "He has made his journey to Mecca, kissed the Black Stone at Ka'aba. He has earned *Haj.*" He stared at the Jew curiously. "How did you know about my father?"

"He is in the import-export business?"

"True. When young I traveled with him. I learned English, German, French, and a little Italian. But you did not answer my question."

"I used to deal with him."

"Deal with my father? A kike dealing with my father? Ha!"

Brent expected an explosion. But the slur slid off Bernstein like butter off a hot knife. He was suddenly

244

very animated, "Yes. He sold arms to the Haganah and the Stern Gang."

"Lies—*Jew lies!*"

"Ha! I knew your family well. Your grandmother was Reba Wehbeh of Haifa." Bernstein rocked with laughter. "She was a German Jew. We were on the same boat together from Germany in nineteen-forty-five. Her name was actually Rebecca Webberman. Your grandfather, Shafeek Ghabra Rogba, made her change it." He held out both arms in a mock gesture of affection. "Welcome, brother 'kike.'" Then he laughed, a deep, full sound of genuine mirth Brent had never heard before.

Rogba's face clouded bright red, rippling with ineffable rage. He sputtered, choked on unutterable words. Bernstein was not finished. Brent wondered how the Israeli could top the affront. Bernstein managed. Smiling benignly, he spoke with concern in his voice. "I must say this about your grandmother. I had an affair with her, and you will be pleased to know she was the best piece of ass I ever had." And then, as if struck by a sententious new thought, "Why, I could be your grandfather! You could come to our next reunion during Hanukkah . . ."

The young pilot's emotions finally exploded like trapped magma bursting from a volcano. "Lies! Lies!" he shrieked, waving a fist at Bernstein, who had come to his feet. "You lie about my grandmother as you lie about everything. My heritage is pure—my family goes back to Ishmael, who founded the Arab race and his father Abraham, who gave him the mission. They were Arabs, not Jews, as you allege in your Torah." He looked around at the uplifted faces, pleading. "See! See! Those kikes lie about everything." He pounded his chest. "I am an Arab—pure, a Sunni, the only true Arab."

Fujita nodded at a pair of guards who grabbed Rogba's arms. "Well, pure Arab, you will be returned to your cell and I will send you a meal of matzo balls and gefilte fish." Everyone laughed at the admiral's humor.

"*Allahu Akbar,*" Rogba shouted as he was pulled through the door. And then a parting shot at Bernstein, "Jew! A thousand maggots feasted on your mother's cunt!"

"I'll make sure your meal is kosher," Bernstein shouted after him.

Laughter filled the room. After it died down, Brent said softly into the Israeli's ear, "Did you actually lay his grandmother?" Curious heads turned; eyes stared.

The Israeli laughed quietly. "I was lying."

Brent nodded. "I thought so," he said, looking around at the other men, who were smiling knowingly.

"Actually," the agent said, tugging on his beard, "she was a lousy lay, I've had much better."

Brent had never heard such thunderous laughter.

"Bring in Major Fritschmann," Fujita shouted over the bedlam.

Major Horst Fritschmann's appearance completely belied his fearsome reputation. Short, with thinning gray hair, a wrinkled face that appeared preserved in spirits, a neck that would shame a turkey, a hollow chest, and a concave belly, the man gave the appearance of one who belonged in a geriatrics ward, not the cockpit of a dive bomber. Brent wondered how this harmless looking senior citizen could have the reputation of being the most feared dive bomber pilot in the world.

"Major Horst Fritschmann, *Stukagruppe Zwei,*" the pilot announced without prompting, standing at rigid attention in front of Admiral Fujita. His hazel eyes focused on the admiral. "You are Admiral Hiroshi Fujita," he said.

"True," the admiral affirmed. "You still use German designations."

"We Germans, with the help of a few bumbling Russians, built Kadafi's air force."

"But you are international now," Yoshi Matsuhara said.

246

"Who is this man?" Fritschmann asked, gesturing to the air group commander.

Brent expected the admiral to stop the German in his tracks and take over the interrogation. Instead, Fujita seemed fascinated by the man and allowed him his head.

"He is Commander Yoshi Matsuhara, the man who shot you down," Fujita said.

"Your gunner was not very good," Yoshi said.

"He was an Italian. What did you expect?"

"He is dead."

"Good. He was less than useless."

Now Brent was beginning to understand the Stuka pilot. He was a killer without heart, without conscience. Brent could see through the arrogant facade as if the man were made of plate glass. Fritschmann could see everything but feel nothing. The killer incarnate. When others saw roses, he saw clotted blood.

"When will you kill me?" the pilot asked as casually as a man inquiring about the weather.

"We may not," Fujita responded.

Fritschmann shrugged indifferently. "I have killed men in France, England, North Africa, and Russia." He smiled, an expression as emotionless as a Greek bronze. "I am ready for death." And directly at Fujita, "Why would you deny me?"

"It pains me to disappoint you," Fujita chided. "But you may be of greater service to me alive."

"Prisoner exchange?"

"Perhaps."

Fritschmann laughed. "It will not work, Admiral. Arab integrity is as foul as the smell of their women. I can't stand either."

"You fly for them."

"For money." He waved at Bernstein, "And to kill them—those without foreskins." For the first time he smiled.

Bernstein spoke, "Is the money important?"

"Not really. I would fly just to kill you, *Judeischen*

247

scheisse." He stabbed a finger at the blue numbers. "You were our guest?"

"Auschwitz. Class of forty-five."

"You're lucky, *Juden.*"

"My mother, father, and sister are still there."

"Baked *Juden* make good fertilizer."

"We have something to settle, you and I," Bernstein murmured.

"Any time, *Juden.*"

"Enough!" Fujita shouted. "You flew from Saipan, Major?"

The old pilot shrugged. "That's obvious."

"Number and types of aircraft in the Marianas?"

"I refuse to answer."

Fujita nodded at a guard who slapped the German across the mouth so hard that spittle and blood flew in a crimson streak and smeared the bulkhead. The major staggered, bringing both hands to his face. Brent expected the prisoner to cry out for the Geneva Convention. Instead, he straightened, wiped his mouth on his sleeve, and laughed. The guard punched him in the stomach with so much force he doubled over and vomited. Brent could smell the sour odor of half-digested rice, cheese, bread, and milk. It took the gasping German several minutes to straighten. His eyes were running and his gasps shook his frame. "I'll tell you nothing, *du altes arschloch*. Kill me!"

Brent knew Admiral Fujita understood German and realized he'd been called an old asshole. However, the leathery face remained inscrutable except for a slight twist to the thin lips that hinted at a smile. Fujita said to the major, "I will be happy to oblige you at a later date and I assure you, I will think of something inventive."

"Do your best, *Japanisch schwein.*"

Fujita pointed to the door. "Take him back to the brig. He is to have bread—unleavened bread—and water. Nothing more." Fritschmann was dragged from the room. Brent could hear the old man's laughter reverberating down the passageway.

Everyone was sobered by the interview. The first prisoner had been a coward, the second a fool. But Fritschmann, like Kenneth Rosencrance, was the insatiable killer who enjoyed fighting just for the sheer pleasure of the kill. These were the dangerous adversaries. And the enemy forces were growing in strength with them as Kadafi's bounties increased and thugs from all over the world flocked to his banners.

A solemn group of officers filed out of Flag Plot. Brent was stopped just outside the door by Yoshi's hand on his sleeve. His mood brightened with his friend's voice. "You have liberty tonight, Brent-san?"

"Negative." He waved forward toward CIC. "Admiral Whitehead and I are going to work with some new communications personnel. I'll go ashore tomorrow night."

"To see Garnet Shaw?"

"Yes. I've already phoned her. And you, Yoshi-san?"

The pilot smiled. "I will see Tomoko tonight. She claims she will prepare me a meal fit for the gods." He sighed. "With the new restrictions and two seaman guards following us like guard dogs, it is difficult to take a lady out—anywhere."

"How true. Garnet will do the same at her apartment. She promised me Caesar salad, filet mignon, potatoes au gratin, and chocolate mousse."

Yoshi slapped his hands together and smacked his lips. "You know something, Brent-san?"

"What?"

"The gods may claim your meal."

The last of Brent's depression vanished with his friend's smiling jest. He grasped Yoshi's arm and leaned close to his ear. "They'd better leave the girl alone or you'll be searching for new deities."

They were both chuckling as they walked to their cabins.

Chapter Ten

Tomoko Ozumori lived in the Itabashi suburb of Tokyo, in the northeastern part of the great sprawling metropolis. Her house was just south of the Arakawa River. Compared to most of the homes nearby, it was large and showed strong Western influence in the arrangement of the six rooms, kitchen, and bath. However, the walls were wood and paper *shoji*, and the furnishings were mostly traditional.

Yoshi was driven to the house by two seaman guards who were to take stations in front and in back of the house. They would remain on guard until the commander left. They had their own rations of rice and fish. Both carried thermoses of hot tea. As Yoshi walked to the door, he noticed a police car parked at the far end of the street. He pointed to the car, the two guards nodded, shouldered their slung Arisakas, and took their posts. They would keep a weather eye on the police car. Not all things were as they appeared.

After removing his shoes, Yoshi knocked. The door opened and the flyer was greeted by a breathtaking sight. Tomoko's hair was upswept into swirls and peaks held in place by jeweled combs and red ribbon which was wound around her head. Tucked into one lock was a sprig of cherry blossoms. Her dress was a traditional kimono, and it was the first time Yoshi had ever seen her so garbed.

The effect was spectacular. A soft-lined winter kimono, it was orange, decorated with the delicate outline of plum blossoms. A yellow silk obi, tightly wound, pulled in her small waist and enhanced the flare of her womanly hips. Spirit-toed socks covered her tiny feet.

Her face was flushed by the excitement she felt at the sight of him, adding to the power of her erotic appeal. With both hands, she clutched Yoshi's and pulled him into the room. Closing the door, she wrapped her arms around him. He found passion and hunger on her lips, and for the first time he reacted with equal emotion. Then, breathing heavily, he broke the embrace and stepped back.

"The brave samurai is still afraid of me," she mocked.

"It is not that, Tomoko, and you know it."

She sighed and led him to a low table where two *sakazukis* and a porcelain pitcher waited. They seated themselves and she filled the cups with hot, spiced *saké*. "To *Yonaga*," he said. She nodded and they drank.

"The last time—the night at *Chōjō Seiyoken* was horrible," she said. "That poor waitress and all those others."

"I know. I hated to put you through that."

"The police have been watching me."

"I know. I'm sure Admiral Fujita made the arrangements."

"I'm afraid, Yoshi-san. They made *Shirayuki*, a tomb for my husband."

"I know," he said. And then, looking up, "Your son, Ryo, is in Kobe and you have other family there."

"Yes. An old aunt and some cousins."

"Go there. Leave Tokyo."

She recharged both cups. "I am not that afraid. That would be cowardly and," she held up her cup and saluted him, "I would not be able to see you."

Yoshi returned the salute. She was a bold woman, a new breed that challenged and excited him. She broke the stereotype of the Japanese woman as the willing domestic servant, the fawning courtesan who bowed to male supremacy. A college graduate, she attended plays, listened to fine music, wrote stories, and even dabbled in local politics. She knew what she wanted out of life and charged after her goals with courage and determination. He not only liked her, he respected her, a rare commodity in men of his generation. "You are kind, Tomoko," he said, tilting his *sakazuki* to his lips.

She drained her cup and refilled it. Her cheeks began to flush. She poured more of the liquor into Yoshi's cup. "Your American friend, the American samurai, is brave and very vicious."

"Brent Ross is a very unusual man. He is a mixture of both East and West."

"Christianity and Buddhism?"

"With a dash of Shinto."

She laughed and a mountain brook sang over pebbles, a change of mood that pleased him. He felt more than the warmth of the liquor penetrate deep down. He emptied his cup and she poured more of the hot saké. "He has studied Zen and Bodhidharma with me."

"He can believe it?"

He shrugged. And then, thoughtfully, "In a way, I am his *roshi*. But teaching a foreigner, taking him to Zen is much like showing him Fujisan at a distance when it is wrapped in mist. The mountain is beautiful and appealing. But up close, they see nothing but hard rock."

"You are a poet, Yoshi-san."

He laughed. "You are generous, Tomoko-san."

"Can your friend crack the rocks? Foreigners find many ambiguities in us—the ascetic living with carnality all around him, the clash between the spirit and the flesh. As Garnet Shaw has found out so soon, it is everywhere."

"True, but Brent-san not only has great physical strength, he has enormous intellectual powers."

"You did not answer my question."

He sighed. "Yes. His mind is open. He understands and

252

I know he meditates and follows the Noble Eightfold Path."

"But there is no god, no soul; nothing is permanent, only cause and effect. Can a Christian live with these beliefs?"

He shrugged. "He tries. He has an amazing ability to perceive, accommodate, reconcile."

She stared at her cup thoughtfully. "You know, Yoshi-san, if you wish to enjoy new tea, you must pour out the old tea that is in your cup first, otherwise your cup just overflows and you can have nothing but a wet mess." She looked into his eyes. "The heads of all men are like that cup."

Impressed by her intellect, he pondered her clever metaphor. There was much truth in it. "I am sure Brent-san has the unique ability to mix his tea and savor the result."

She quoted an ancient concept: "The more the contradictions, the stronger the man. He is a giant."

"I think you are right."

"And you, Yoshi-san, have you found peace in Zen?"

"Yes. At times. I do follow the Four Holy Truths."

She sipped her drink and then showed her own deep knowledge: "Existence is suffering, suffering springs from desire, desire can be extinguished by following the Buddha's path of truthful and chaste behavior."

She stood. He thought she was ready to bring the meal. He could smell the savory odor of hot food seeping from the kitchen.

Instead, she spoke in a thick voice. "How long will you mourn, Yoshi-san. Mine is over. How long this chastity? You are like a man with your arms and legs bound by your own grief." She gestured at him. "And you are a fine specimen of a man—youthful, fit, intelligent. You are alive but not living, peep at heaven through the eye of a needle. Do not let yourself wither into nothing."

Sipping his drink, he eyed her magnificent form. "It is not only grief, Tomoko-san."

253

"Then what?"

He emptied his cup and rose, stepped toward her and took her hand. "My love has brought death to those most dear."

"Your family? That Kimio—ah . . ."

"Kimio Urshazawa. All died horribly."

"But not because of you."

"My karma must be flawed."

"No! No, you cannot know." She stepped close, ran a hand over his cheek. He could smell her, womanly with the gentle scent of perfume. He ached to hold her.

She moved closer, and ran her hands over his back, her lips only inches from his. "I am not afraid, Yoshi-san. I will not flee *Rengo Sekigun*. Why should you be a fugitive from your own fears?"

"If you want my love, you may find your end."

She eyed him with unblinking, piercing black eyes. She quoted an old poem: "'You have yet to know, this soft flesh, this throbbing blood, are you not lonely, my fierce samurai'?" She covered his mouth with hers. Yoshi felt her tongue seek his. The earlier sensation of control slipped away and he kissed her back with a fury of emotions unleashed. Her hard breasts were against him, hips pressing. His hand cupped a breast, toyed with a nipple through the silk. She moaned. His other hand slipped down her back, dipped at the waist, and ran down to her buttock and pulled her hard against him. Gasping, she pushed him away.

"What is it?"

She answered him by untying the obi and allowing the kimono to part. She wore no brassiere, only white panties trimmed with lace. With trembling hands he pulled the kimono open until she shrugged and the garment slipped from her body and fell to the floor, revealing her flesh, honeyed ivory in color, textured like cream-colored rose petals. He eyed the breasts capped with large red areolas like rosettes, the tiny waist, flat stomach, flare of the hips, dainty line of the long legs. He kissed her neck, tongued her finely shaped breast, ran his hands over bare skin like hot silk. He felt her hands on the back of his head. Her hips began to rotate against him in the maddening twist of the aroused woman.

She pushed him back again, pointed at her panties, and managed through hard, deep breathing, "For you—you must do it."

With trembling fingers, he reached down, hooked his fingers under the elastic, and pulled down. He dropped to his knees as he slid the silk garment down her legs. She kicked it off. He kissed her fiercely on her abdomen, cluthing a buttock in one hand while the other crept up her leg until it found the short hair, the hot, wet center of her that opened for him like the petals of a rosebud. She cried out incoherently as he began to explore her and then pulled him to his feet.

"Not here." She gestured to a *shoji* and then led him to her bedroom, undoing her hair and allowing it to tumble in black folds around her shoulders.

She stretched out on a wide futon and watched him undress. He pulled his clothes off frantically. Finally, he stood nude before her and stared down at her. He had never seen anything so beautiful, so appealing. She raised her arms and he lowered himself onto her.

The kisses were savage, deep, their hands frantic. They locked together, breathing each other's breath, their tongues twisting together, kneading, pressing. He rolled on top of her and she parted her knees. He slipped into her easily and she cried out, hands pressing against his buttocks and pulling him deeper into her. "Ah, wonderful—ah . . ." she cried out.

He was lost in her, swimming in a hot sea he had never known before. He kissed her mouth, her eyes, her cheeks, her neck, thrusting to meet the surge of her hips which rose to his onslaught with surprising force. She clamped her mouth over his and her hips began to move in a rhythmic rising and falling. He was lost, his mind filled with only the feel of the hot flesh against his, savoring the sensations that flowed up from the depths of her like waves of a storm surf, growing higher and higher with the approaching storm.

Swept beyond their sense of self, a magical *kami* seemed to possess both of them. His body deep in hers, she enfolded him and blended with him so that their very blood seemed to mingle, and their hearts to beat together. They shared the same breath, thoughts that gleamed and glimmered. "I love you, my darling," she cried. And his voice replied, crying through the cavern of her throat, words upon her lips, "I love you." They were no longer two.

She butted, thrashed. Her hips began to move more quickly, legs entwined around his back. The magical, devastating moment hit her suddenly like a bursting damn and she screamed out, "Yoshi! My love—ah, ah!" She convulsed, twisted, drove her hips upward with astonishing power in a burst of short, frantic movements, screamed again, threw back her head, covered her face with her hands as if she were trying to muffle her cries. And then he joined her, crying her name, calling out, "In the name of the gods," groaning and gasping as his very life seemed to spurt out of him like a rocket within her. It was the most complete and devastating moment of his existence.

Then they lay locked together for a long time, weak, unable to move, stunned by what they had felt and shared. "I love you, Yoshi-san," she whispered into his ear. "Do you truly love me, or was that just the moment?"

"Yes, Tomoko-san. I love you."

She shuddered and began to cry.

"I was too rough. I did not mean to hurt you."

She shook her head and choked back her tears. "No, you did not hurt me. That was the most beautiful, wonderful . . ."

"Then why do you cry?"

"Because everything that is good is so fleeting. The

more beautiful it is the shorter its life, while the cruel, vile things seem eternal."

"There is truth in what you say, but you must try not to think like that, my darling."

"I know, Yoshi-san. You are right. I will try. I will live for these moments." She kissed him. "I cannot live without you."

"And I cannot fly away from you."

"You will come back to me. Promise?"

"I promise."

Then, still locked in each others arms, they rolled to the side. He felt her breath in his ear slow, then become even and measured. He thought of the guards outside, the forgotten meal, and tried to move. But one leg around his and both arms locked around his neck kept him trapped. Quickly, a sleep of great depth overcame him. He had never known such peace, such happiness.

Chapter Twelve

It was a long day for Brent. He had phoned Garnet again and she seemed depressed but eager to see him. "Dinner at six," she said.

"Eighteen hundred hours," he countered.

"Just be here, sailor-boy."

"Nothing short of Armageddon could stop me," he said.

She laughed and he felt encouraged by her brightening mood.

He longed to talk to Yoshi Matsuhara. But Yoshi was at Tokyo International Airport, training his new pilots. All departments were working at a frantic pace to meet the admiral's deadline for getting under way. Brent hoped that Tomoko Ozumori had helped pull his friend from his personal "Slough of Despond," his mood of *shinigurai* that had gripped him since Kimio's murder. It would take a woman's love. All men were incomplete without it. Yoshi was no different. But Yoshi was afraid of love, afraid of the evil *kamis* that dogged him and killed those most dear to him. In his Asian mind, he was a walking bad omen that destroyed the best, the beloved. Maybe Tomoko had made some inroads last night. Yoshi would never reveal anything of an intimate nature. There was too much chivalry and honor in him for that and Brent would not ask, anyway. However, Brent could read his moods; would know immediately if the appeal of the beautiful, intelligent woman had finally claimed his heart.

Brent was in the CIC by 0800. A half-dozen new men were being trained and all of the gear was in operation, officers and technicians hunched over glowing CRTs, clattering printers, humming computers, and radar screens with the bright sweeping beams and jagged waterfall displays. With the ship's lights rheostated down, the long compartment was filled with its usual blue-green light. The results were macabre. Skin was green, lips were purple; and veins stood out on men like blue lines. Brent turned to Rear Admiral Whitehead. "This place always looks like a lousy job of colorizing Doctor Frankenstein's laboratory."

Whitehead laughed. "Seen better on the late, late show." He waved, "And we're all monsters."

Brent laughed. "Well, at least Kadafi thinks we are."

"I can live with that, Brent."

The thought *"and die, too"* came to mind. However, Brent just smiled and with the rear admiral at his side, walked up silently behind a pair of technicians seated before the six-foot-wide console of a new AN/WLR-8 tactical electronic warfare and surveillance receiver.

The first man was the experienced, reliable cryptographer second-class Stan Fleishman, a short, fair athletic man in his late twenties. The second was one of the new men, electronics technician Theodore Tedzweski. With tousled black hair, wide green eyes that had a weird yellow tint in the eerie light, and a boyish grin, Tedzweski appeared far younger than his twenty-one years. A replacement for the highly competent electronics technician Martin Reed who had been killed off Gibralter, Tedzweski had been on board only three days. Already he had been playfully dubbed "Ted-Ted" by his shipmates, who immediately tired with grappling with his name. These two men were the key enlisted personnel in the ship's intelligence and cryptological department. In addition to coding and decoding, they were expected to be competent with all of the complex equipment in CIC.

Oblivious to the officers, Fleishman was speaking to Tedzweski. "This new mother is a talented baby, Ted-Ted." He waved at the two CRTs, rows of switches, buttons, and keyboard, spoke proudly like a man boasting about his talented mistress. "Automatic measurement of signal direction of arrival, signal classification and recognition, simultaneous scanning over its entire frequency range, automatic detection for threat warning, analyzes signal parameters for frequency, modulation, pulse width, amplitude." He tapped the first cathode ray tube. "This one's a two-trace system for display purposes and this other one," he finger moved to the second, "is a five-trace panoramic display, displaying signal activity data . . ."

Tedzweski interrupted, revealing a bright, inquisitive mind. "Azimuth, threat library, Stan?"

Fleishman waved at a computer next to the console, "On line with the UYK-19, Ted-Ted. Three-hundred-sixty-degree azimuth, fifty-megabyte threat library which can identify Kadafi's fart at three hundred miles, access time thirty-two milliseconds . . ." He turned, saw the officers and began to rise. Tedzweski followed.

"As you were," Rear Admiral Whitehead said. Then, to Fleishman, "You're doing a fine job, Cryptographer Fleishman."

"Thank you, sir."

Whitehead waved at a corner of the room. "Commander Ross, would you take electronics technician Tedzweski to our secret little alcove and brief him on coding and decoding?"

"Ay, aye, sir."

"I'll stay here with Fleishman and he can check me out on our new miracle baby—ah, 'mother'." Everyone laughed at the senior officer's quip. Then Brent and Tedzweski walked to the end of the compartment. Whitehead took the empty chair next to Fleishman.

Entering the alcove, Brent and the enlisted man were confronted by banks of electronics equipment. They sat

260

side by side. Brent indicated a computer. "That's our Control Data CYBER One-Seven-Six. It's the heart of our system." He patted the machine fondly. "Its language is 'Ada.'"

"Of course, sir, military."

"Right. It has a six-hundred-megabyte hard-disk memory." Tedzweski whistled. "Its ROM has built-in softward that automatically encrypts and decodes signals. It's formatted to interface main-frames in Washington and Tel Aviv." He waved at a small box. "You know what that is?"

"An encryption box, Commander, interfaced with the CYBER."

"Right. It's hard-wired by the CIA and Mossad for CISRA and COMYONAGA transmissions. It's seeded with a new pseudorandom sequencer, PCM, and it time-hops transmissions in compressed random bursts, some in milliseconds."

"Pulse Code Modulator, frequency hopping, Commander."

Brent was very pleased with the young man. He slapped him in the back. "Right, Technician Tedzweski."

"Sir," the young man said, "how do I recognize CISRA? It must be keyed."

"It certainly is. The first group will always be five Ys, followed by four groups of numbers. The Greenwich Civil Time of transmission will be in plain language. You will immediately call Admiral Whitehead or me."

"I understand." The young rating scratched the side of his nose and pulled on his chin. "Then there's another sequence of decoding which cannot be accessed here."

"Correct." Brent sighed, thinking of the complexity of the system: the first eight-figure subroutine, based on random combinations and permutations of a ten-figure master; the feeding of the subroutine and signal into a laptop computer along with an eight-figure digital control code predicated on the phase of the moon and the Greenwich Civil Time of the message plus three; the striking of the "Enter" key and the appearance of the text on the CRT in plain language. This was all done in the privacy of his cabin or that of Rear Admiral Whitehead. In the event they were both killed or wounded, Colonel Bernstein was the only other man on board capable of decoding CISRA. It still seemed a near miracle that the whole intricate system worked. And it had become an even denser electronic jungle.

Because of the brute-force attacks of computers in Moscow and Tripoli on intercepts, the subroutine had been increased to twelve figures and the ten-figure master had become sixteen. The combinations and permutations of the master now exceeded an astonishing 2 to the ninety-sixth power. But the enemy computers were still "chewing" relentlessly.

"You must change codes often, sir. The enemy have some powerful main-frames of their own."

Brent sighed. "You're very perceptive. It's been a bitch. What can be encrypted by computer can be broken by computer."

The young man nodded. He toyed with the keyboard. "I should be able to handle it, sir. After all, this little beauty does most of the work."

Brent nodded. "I want to check you out on the CYBER, and then there's much more to learn." He waved at the room. "I'll program in some dummy messages and we'll see what you can do with them."

The young man rubbed his hands together. "I'm ready, sir."

"Good!" Brent threw a switch and immediately the rising hum of a hard disk coming up to speed could be heard. He gave the computer time to warm up and then began to type.

Time moved fast for the engrossed young men. At 1230 hours they were still at the CYBER 176 when they were interrupted by the ship's PA system. "Admiral Whitehead and Commander Brent Ross, report to Admiral Fujita at thirteen hundred hours," the hollow,

262

tinny voice commanded.

Brent pushed himself from his chair, patted Tedzweski on the back, congratulated him on his quick learning, and left the room on Rear Admiral Whitehead's heels. He must clean up, put on a fresh shirt, and grab a bite of lunch—if he had time.

When Brent entered Admiral Fujita's cabin, he was surprised to see Yoshi Matsuhara and Colonel Bernstein seated in front of the desk with Rear Admiral Whitehead and the CIA man Alfred Gibney. Brent bowed and seated himself. Yoshi looked fatigued. Either he had been working too hard or Tomoko Ozumori had pumped the life out of him. Brent hoped it had been the latter.

Fujita said, "Gentlemen, I have received a communication through the good offices of the Swiss ambassador." He held up a yellow dispatch form. "It was hand-delivered to me this morning." He removed his steel-rimmed glasses and rubbed the bridge of his nose. "Kadafi requests a parley to discuss a possible exchange of prisoners." He looked at Whitehead. "You were successful with your request, Admiral."

Alfred Gibney said, "He can't expect us to come to Libya. It's his seat of power. He would play conqueror to us, the vanquished. We would lose our honor, our dignity as fighting men, and . . ."

Whitehead interrupted sharply, "We are all aware of these things. I requested a neutral site as per the admiral's orders."

Fujita said, "He has agreed to Formosa—ah, I mean Taiwan. it is within easy range of our four-engined transports and it has tried to maintain neutrality." Gibney's face was tinted with obvious embarrassment. He had spoken too soon and knew it.

Receiving most of its oil from China, Taiwan had managed to maintain a strong posture of neutrality despite the bloody fighting raging in the Western Pacific. In fact, Taiwan had been pulled back into a close alliance with communist China, which had softened its posture

263

with the National Government of the Republic of China, which in the past had always been considered a renegade government.

Yoshi Matsuhara said, "Kadafi must be sending his delegation from the Marianas."

Fujita waved at a chart on the bulkhead and spoke without rising. "As you can see, Taiwan is in within range of LRAs based in the Marianas."

Whitehead said, "He's sent a mission to Saipan by sub?"

"Negative, Admiral. He will send personnel already attached to his forces in the islands."

Brent felt an ominous suspicion begin to grow. Why were he and Yoshi summoned to this meeting—Yoshi from his duties at Tokyo International Airport? Where was the rest of the staff? Rosencrance must be involved.

Whitehead asked, "Will they send some of their top army officers?"

Fujita shook his head and Brent knew what was coming. "The head of the delegation will be Colonel Kenneth Rosencrance."

"Damn!" Brent slapped his knee.

"Sacred Buddha," Yoshi muttered.

"Madness!" Whitehead joined in.

"Doesn't make sense," Alfred Gibney offered.

Colonel Bernstein turned to the CIA man. "But it does make sense. According to our intelligence, Kenneth Rosencrance has adopted the Moslem faith and is one of Kadafi's most trusted officers. The Colonel would prefer to have him back in Tripoli as a member of his staff—chief of air operations."

"Why doesn't he recall him?" Alfred Gibney asked.

"Because Rosencrance would quit. His one love is flying, and he has become a millionaire with his kills." Yoshi growled deep in his throat and Brent saw his knuckles turn white with the power of the grip he had on the armrests. He knew his friend was reliving the death of the Englishman, Colin Willard-Smith. The Israeli glanced fleetingly at the air group commander and continued, "He places great trust in Rosencrance."

Fujita and the rest of the officers watched silently as the CIA and Mossad fell into another of their disputes. Gibney said, "The commanding officer of all Arab forces in the Western Pacific is General Ibrahim Mohammed Awad, based on Saipan."

"We all know that. You wouldn't expect him to head the delegation," Bernstein chided.

"No. But his chief of staff is Lieutenant General Habib Shihadeh." Gibney turned to Admiral Fujita. "Respectfully, sir, why don't you request Lieutenant General Habib Shihadeh head their delegation? He should have more clout than Rosencrance, and you could counter with your executive office, Captain Mitake Arai."

Fujita looked at the CIA man silently. For a long moment only the sound of the auxiliary engines, the whine of blowers, and the tick of the old-fashioned brass clock on the bulkhead could be heard. The old man said, "Because the Arabs insist on Rosencrance and they have also requested Commander Matsuhara, Commander Ross and Colonel Bernstein represent us. We would not be outranked."

Bernstein said, "Sir, you remember we met with him once in the UN offices in New York in nineteen eighty-nine. He has the Byzantine mind of an Arab. He deliberately made a shambles of the meeting. We wound up in a fistfight."

Whitehead said, "The man's completely untrustworthy."

"The man is incorrigible, inflexible, obstinate, prejudiced beyond belief," Brent Ross added.

"You would prefer not to represent me?"

Brent was shocked. The old man had already made up his mind to accept the offer. He suspected the Emperor had intervened. It was not like Fujita to accept the enemy's terms so completely, so casually. "You wish a replacement?" Fujita persisted.

"Of course not, sir. I'm ready."

Fujita's eyes flicked from Brent to Yoshi Matsuhara. "And you, Commander?"

"I welcome the assignment, sir." The flyer tapped his palm with a closed fist. "But Admiral, if Rosencrance attacks me, makes a move toward any of our delegation, I reserve the right to kill him."

"You are to be unarmed."

"I can do it with my hands."

The old Japanese sighed. "You owe him a debt—many debts. Of course, in the event of physical threats to our delegation, I would expect you all to take appropriate actions."

Whitehead half-rose. "It could be a trap." He gestured to Brent Ross, Bernstein, and Yoshi. "These are the men Rosencrance hates the most. We could lose all of them, and this would be a terrible loss to *Yonaga*." He sank back.

"Respectfully," Yoshi said. "No one is irreplaceable, Admiral Whitehead."

"On the eve of battle? Most certainly," Whitehead shot back.

Bernstein said, "I disagree, Admiral. If we are lost, we can be replaced."

The American admiral's face clouded with a mask of anger. His eyes darted from Yoshi Matsuhara to Irving Bernstein. "See here, both of you. Don't try to teach me lessons about war."

"May I respectfully remind you, Admiral Whitehead, my neck will be on the block, not yours."

"I won't take that, Bernstein!"

The slapping sound of Fujita's hand impacting his desk cut through the exchange. "That is quite enough," he said. "The matter is settled. The delegation of Commander Matsuhara, Commander Ross, and Colonel Bernstein will take off from Tokyo International Airport the day after tomorrow, Sunday, eight November at zero-eight-hundred-hours and fly to Taipei. Commander

Matsuhara will be in charge. You will be transported in one of our DC-6s painted white with green stars on the wings and fuselage. You will meet with the Arab delegation in the Taipei Hilton."

"Security?"

"It will be provided by Swiss personnel from the airport to the hotel and throughout the meetings. A Swiss diplomat will conduct and moderate the meetings." He stared at Whitehead. "All participants will be thoroughly searched before each meeting."

"I still don't trust the bastards," Whitehead grumbled.

"Who does?" Gibney said.

This time, the CIA man and Bernstein nodded in agreement.

Colonel Bernstein appeared puzzled. He said, "Switzerland does not recognize the National Government of the Republic of China, Admiral. Won't that be awkward?"

"No, Colonel. Their relations with the Taiwanese government are very cordial. They have no embassy on Taiwan, true. That is why you will meet at the hotel. Their personnel has already been flown in from the Philippines."

The admiral replaced his glasses and turned to Yoshi Matsuhara. "Commander, you will remain on board. Our negotiating team will be briefed tomorrow. Select your replacement now."

"Lieutenant Kunishi Kajikawa," the air group commander responded without hesitation.

"One of the best," Fujita said. His eyes moved from Matsuhara to Bernstein and finally came to rest on Brent Ross. He stared so long, that Brent became uncomfortable. There was sadness in the eyes. For a moment, the old man seemed to become transparent. Not only were the three members of the negotiating team valued members of his staff, they were also very close to the old man's heart. It was almost as if he were feasting his eyes

267

on his precious trio before losing them forever.

The old rummy eyes shifted to a small shrine on the far bulkhead where the most prominent icon was a statue of the powerful deity Nyoirin Kwannon. The squat little god was seated in his usual *rajalila* (regal repose). A grotesque figure, he had six arms, and in each of his six hands he carried symbols including a rosary, the jewel that grants all desires, a lotus bud, and the wheel of the law. Brent expected Fujita to call on the deity to aid their task. He was not disappointed.

"Oh, Nyoirin Kwannon," Fujita said, gesturing at the god, "help us remember the three universal truths of Confucius—intelligence, humanity, and courage—and help us to call on them in our coming trials. Let us remember intelligence is the willingness to discuss problems with others. Humanity is simply doing something for others and courage is gathering one's strength and pushing ahead, disregarding the circumstances." His eyes searched every face and found each man staring back into his eyes. He smiled. "Anything conflicting with these three truths is not worth recording."

He cleared his throat and spoke with a military timbre hardening his voice. "The negotiating team will be briefed in Flag Plot tomorrow morning at zero-nine-hundred. Mister Gibney, Admiral Whitehead, please attend. We will need your, ah—as you Americans would say, 'input.'"

Everyone chuckled.

"All members of the negotiating team have liberty tonight. You will be restricted to the ship tomorrow. You are dismissed."

The men filed out of the room.

Yoshi and Brent paused in the passageway. Instead of discussing the impending meeting with Rosencrance, Brent forced his mind into another important area. "You saw Tomoko last night, Yoshi-san."

"Yes." Yoshi smiled, pleased Brent had avoided the unpleasantness facing them in two days.

"She has brought changes in you."

The Japanese nodded. "There is a very strong affection between us, Brent-san."

"Good. Good, old friend." Brent clasped his arm. It was like iron. "You are no longer *shinigurai?*"

"I have much to live for."

"That's the best news I've heard in years, Yoshi-san."

"And you, Brent-san, you will still see Garnet tonight?"

"Yes. It's still on. I'll be at her place for dinner."

"Good. And do not forget, Brent-san—we have a date at the Taipei Hilton on Sunday."

"Glad you reminded me. Should be a most interesting soiree."

Yoshi's laugh was subdued. "Most interesting."

The two officers clasped hands before parting.

The meal was superb: Caesar salad tangy and zestful with chunks of Roquefort cheese and croutons touched with just a hint of garlic; filet mignon tender enough for the edge of a fork and broiled to just the right pink hue; au gratin potatoes mouthwatering with a delightful mix of cheese, butter, and chives; delicate, savory asparagus tips topped with melted butter; and a superb chocolate mousse to bring down the curtain on a true gourmet *tour de force*.

"A gastronomical achievement fit for Zeus, Mithras, Isis, Osiris, Amaterasu, Allah, Ahura Mazda—take your pick," Brent said, leaning back on the couch and sipping his wine.

"They weren't important enough to make my guest list. Just you," Garnet laughed back from the kitchen.

He brought the snifter to his chin, savoring the light, delicate, softly fragrant aroma of the Cabernet Sauvignon. Reminding him of the great clarets of Bordeaux that he loved, the California wine had been a perfect selection for the meal. Garnet had thought of everything. He watched her as she finally placed the last of the dishes in the washer, picked up her wine, and approached him.

She looked especially beautiful tonight. The moment she had opened the door the strength of her sexuality had struck him with a palpable force. He had seen her only once before and did not realize her hair was so long. It flowed past her shoulders and down her back like Jason's fleece, shimmering even in the penumbra of weak light behind her. There was a smile on the beautiful face and the blue eyes glowed with warmth at the sight of him. but there was sadness there—and, Brent thought, a trace of fear. She was wearing a white blouse and a tight black shirt. The skirt was short, showing her magnificent legs. This time, she wore no hose. She took both of his hands, came up on her toes, and kissed him on the lips. There was no passion. It was more like being greeted by an old friend.

He had been late because of some problems with a new computer in CIC. When he stepped into the apartment, the meal was ready with the exception of the steaks and the tossing of the salad. She poured him a double Scotch, neat, and walked into the kitchen. While broiling the meat she called out to him some small talk about traffic, weather, and Tomoko, whom she had seen that morning. "She's in love with your friend Yoshi, I'm sure of it," she laughed.

"Hope so. He needs her. There's a big void in Yoshi's life. I think she can fill it."

"She has a void, too, that needs filling."

They both laughed at the inadvertent double entendre.

"I didn't mean it that way," Garnet protested.

"I know. I know."

Now she was seating herself next to him, not close, but not at the far end of the couch, either. After pouring just the correct amount of wine into the large bowl-shaped glasses, she placed the bottle of Cabernet Sauvignon on

270

the small walnut table in front of them. She tried to circle his huge biceps with a tiny hand but failed. There was a hushed grimness in the timbre of her voice. "Policemen have been following me and Tomoko since that terrible night."

"I know. There are some concerns about the Japanese Red Army. I'm sure Admiral Fujita arranged it."

"There's a sailor with a rifle outside my door."

"And another at the end of the hall outside the elevator doors. They're with me—with all our officers who go ashore."

She shook her head. "This is no way to live."

"If they're after anyone, it's me, not you," he said with all the casualness he could muster, trying to reassure her. "And there's no sign of them."

"But they could still be out there."

"It's possible, of course."

She took a large swallow and moved closer. "I'm afraid, Brent. It's not an easy thing to say about yourself, but I'm afraid."

"You wouldn't be normal if you weren't." He took her hand. It was warm, soft. He could feel her fingers moving across his knuckles in a caressing motion.

"Are you ever afraid, Brent?"

"Of course. At times, all human beings feel fear."

"You've learned to live with it?"

"In my business, you must."

"Sounds terrible. Why don't you go home? You've been out here for eight years. Couldn't you get duty back in the States—maybe a cushy job in the Pentagon?"

"Yes, but my work, my duty, is here."

"Didn't that slaughter at *Chōjō Seiyoken* sicken you, the way that beautiful waitress was shot to pieces? And all the others . . ." Her voice trailed off. She turned away and took a large drink.

"Of course." And then, in a rare patronizing moment, "I was very frightened."

"And very angry."

271

"That's natural. Fear and rage are close neighbors. Sometimes they're roommates."

She finished her wine and Brent tossed off the rest of his. She recharged the glasses. "You were out of control, Brent."

Brent turned the wineglass in small circles so that the wine swirled and peaked as it sloshed against the curved sides. He stared at the glass. "I know."

"You blinded him, tore off his jaw."

Brent drank. "He had it coming."

"I tried to stop you."

"Oh? I don't remember."

"Even after Yoshi and the seaman pulled you off him, you tried to break free—to get back at him."

Suddenly Brent remembered through the red haze, "Yes. And you said I had no choice."

"I had to calm you. I was in shock."

"You think I'm an animal."

"No. Basically, you are very kind and gentle."

"I spent the night with you."

She smiled. "And you kept it platonic. You could have had anything you wanted."

"A visit to soapland?" He was pleased by her laughter. She moved closer, and he could feel her thigh against his.

"Not quite, but I was vulnerable."

"You wanted me?"

"Yes, Brent."

"It would have been wrong—in my mind, a violation of you, and this may sound corny, a betrayal of myself."

She looked deep into his eyes, tied his stare to hers with the force of her gaze. "You're a strange one, Brent."

"Why?"

"So violent, so—ah, brutal, and yet so considerate, gentle, even chivalrous."

He tore his eyes from hers. "No. Not chivalrous. I guess I'm really a savage."

"I didn't say that."

He ignored her. "Others have. And it's true because

272

we all are. You find that out in the business I'm in. Under this thin veneer of civilization we wear you'll still find Neanderthal Man fighting, clawing, and scratching for his life."

Her quick mind picked up the thread, "In the boardrooms, the White House, the Diet . . . ?"

"Especially. You're very perceptive."

"And you're a cynic."

"I think of myself as practical—pragmatic."

Her sigh was long and hushed, like a secret whisper. "You know, Brent, when I study history, all I find is endless wars interrupted by short periods of peace."

"True."

She rubbed her forehead. "It seems mankind is afflicted with terminal ignorance—has been trying since he first appeared on this planet to eradicate himself."

"You agree with Goethe."

She looked up in surprise. "I do. I didn't know I was a philosopher. That's pretty good company."

He took her hand and caught her eyes. "Goethe said, 'Evil is militant ignorance.' Isn't that what we're really fighting, what good men have always fought? Ignorance?"

She shook her head and then leaned against his shoulder. "I don't know, dear Brent. It's bewildering and so damned eternal."

He took her chin in his hand and turned her face to his. Strangely, the early passion he had felt for her had faded. He meant to kiss her gently. But her mouth was not gentle. Instead, it was open and she pressed her lips to his with a fierce urgency, tongue penetrating and finding his. He felt latent lust ignite and he pressed her back onto the couch. It had been a long time since Arlene Spencer—a very long time. Suddenly, he had to feel those marvelous legs. He reached down, ran his hand up under the skirt. It was like touching smooth, hot silk. She parted her legs slightly but not enough for him to reach his goal. He kissed her neck, cupped a breast and caressed the nipple.

She squirmed . . . moaned . . . then pushed him away and stood up.

"What's wrong?"

A film of moisture made the blue of her eyes even more intense. "I'm not sure. But this is only the second time I have ever seen you."

A terrible sense of frustration gripped his stomach as if he were becoming sick in the heart of a typhoon. Frustration flamed into anger. "It's time for me to leave," he said brusquely, coming to his feet.

"No. Please, don't leave."

"But you said it's too soon."

"It's not just that, Brent." She brought her knuckles to her mouth. "It's that waitress, those others, all slaughtered."

"All right. I understand." He walked toward the guest closet where she had hung his tunic. Her hand on his arm stopped him.

"I'm not a tease." He stared silently. "Believe me, I do want you, Brent."

He opened the closet, shrugged into his tunic, and walked to the door. He turned and she clutched him in a near desperate embrace. Her words shocked him: "Don't leave me."

"Don't leave you? Garnet, I don't understand. We can't just lie in bed and torture each other. I'm not that chivalrous."

She dropped her eyes and turned her lips under. "I've made up my mind."

"You have?"

"Yes." She looked up. "Stay with me. It won't be torture this time."

Brent could not comprehend the mercurial swings of this strange girl. She was bewildering. "You're sure? Just a minute ago you said you couldn't."

She took both of his hands in his. "I know, Brent. Please understand, I'm a mass of confusion and have been for days. But I've made up my mind." And then, with finality, "It's time to finish what we started two nights ago."

Brent choked back the rush of desire that thickened his voice. "He could hardly believe his own words: "You owe me nothing."

"Perhaps. But you owe *me* something."

She led him into the bedroom.

She lay in the crook of his arm, her breath coming in the long, measured tempo of the sexually sated. Gently she ran a hand over his broad back. "That was marvelous. Don't you ever get tired?"

"I've been at sea for months," he kissed her cheek, "storing it up."

She reached down, took him in her hand. "You keep it in cold storage?"

"Hot storage."

She laughed. "The girls used to make naughty jokes about sailors."

"What did they say?"

"You won't be offended?"

"No."

"They said sailors were horny—were great lays when they finally got a chance."

He laughed. "Why, that's a compliment. Were they right?"

"No."

"No!" he repeated, coming up on an elbow.

She pulled him down on top of her. "No. You're not great. You're unbelievable. Inexhaustible. Have a great body. The lover every girl dreams about, but few ever find."

Her kiss was fierce. She pulled him over her and he slid between her parted knees easily, as if he had been created to be part of her.

"Fill my void," she whispered into his ear. In a moment she was no longer capable of speaking.

*   *   *

"I must leave," he said, holding her just inside the door. He waved, "My men are out there."

"I wanted you all night, Brent."

He kissed her. "And I wanted to stay. Maybe next time."

She laughed. "Maybe it's a good thing you're leaving."

"Why?"

She kissed his cheek. "Because, if you stayed, I might not be able to walk tomorrow."

She kissed him and held him for a long moment. "When will I see you again? When I first met you, you mentioned the *Kabuki, Bunraku,* the *Noh* theater, sumo wrestlers." She leaned back, "Can't we see some of those things together?"

He held her very close. "There's nothing I could want more, but I have a special duty for several days."

"Phone me."

"I can't."

"You're going to Taipei."

He pushed her back in shock. "How did you know anything . . ."

She laughed and waved at a television set in the corner. "It was on the tube—the evening news. Kadafi announced a parley to be held in Taipei starting Sunday, and you just told me you won't be available."

"On the news, well, I'll be damned."

"You didn't know, Brent?"

He shook his head. "It came over while we were driving here. We never play the radio. It's a distracton."

"You're going?"

Brent clenched his jaw and rubbed his chin. "Since the entire world already knows, yes, I'm on the delegation."

"Will you phone me when you return?"

"Of course. As soon as we return."

The kiss was long and lingering. Finally, he pulled himself free and left.

276

Chapter Thirteen

The conference room at the Taipei Hilton was actually a banquet room. Now cleared of its tables and chairs, it was furnished only with a long conference table and ten upholstered chairs. Charts of the world had been attached to the walls. Walking down the long hallway, Commander Yoshi Matsuhara, Commander Brent Ross, and Colonel Irving Bernstein approached the room warily, adrenaline charged, like hunters close on the spoor of an elusive lion.

Brent heard Rosencrance before he saw him. The high-pitched voice reverberated down the hall long before Brent entered the room. The renegade American was laughing. He was obviously in high spirits. *Bad news*, Brent thought as he passed between rows of Nationalist soldiers in full battle kit. Security had been very tight.

When he had alighted from the DC-6 at the Taipei Airport, he had expected to be met by Swiss security guards. Instead, the big Douglas was immediately surrounded by armored personnel carriers and four trucks loaded with Nationalist troops. Facing away from the delegation, the soldiers deployed in two solid lines like living barriers, automatic rifles at port arms. The path between the troops led to a black Cadillac limousine parked at the edge of the tarmac. As the three officers began the short walk to the stretch Cadillac, a Nationalist colonel nervously fell in beside them and ushered them to the shiny automobile. Then the troops climbed back into their trucks and the entourage roared to the hotel, sirens blaring, red lights flashing.

The Colonel, Cho Tsung Tang, sat in the front seat of the limousine with the driver. "Welcome to Taipei," he said in garbled English. "The hotel is on Chung Hsiao West Road. It will only take us a few minutes."

True to his word, the drive was short. However, they were not allowed to enter the hotel until the lobby was cleared and the troops deployed in their solid ranks. Before leaving the Cadillac, Colonel Tang politely asked for their weapons. Three pistols were handed over to the Nationalist. Brent felt naked. "Give me your word as officers and gentlemen that you carry no other weapons."

The three acknowledged that they were unarmed. "You will pass through metal detectors, you know, and your attaché cases will be searched," the colonel warned.

"We know," Yoshi said. "Our word is sufficient. You are not dealing with Arabs." Bernstein and Brent snickered.

When the trio entered the room, the talking and laughter stopped as if it had been chopped off by a meat ax. There were eight men in the room. Four in gray business suits stood against the walls. All were fair, young, and powerfully built. These were the Swiss security men. Four men were seated, each with an attaché case before him. One of the four was Colonel Kenneth Rosencrance. Brent recognized him immediately.

Although Brent had not seen the American killer for three years, Rosencrance seemed to have not aged a day. Just over thirty years old, he was a big man with a huge, leonine head and a full shock of blond hair, bleached in silver-white splashes from the tropical sun, darker streaks showing beneath. His thin lips were colorless, his sunken cheeks like those of a cadaver. His pasty-white face had weathered to a honey-golden brown so that the

278

faded blue of his eyes was pale in contrast. And the narrow eyes had a strange tilt, giving them a cruel reptillian mien. When they fell on Brent they hardened and became as cold and hard as gun metal.

Brent did not recognize the other three men. One, a short dark man in an expensive black business suit, sat at the end of the long table which was at the far end of the room. It almost seemed as if the man was placing himself at a safe distance from the six enemies. With brown eyes and swarthy skin, he had a thick black mustache that drooped down over his lips. Appearing to be Latin, he wore the mustache as a symbol of his masculinity. To Brent, he looked like a young Marlon Brando made up to play a thirtyish Don Corleone. Brent chuckled to himself. If this man was the Swiss moderator, he certainly did not appear to have any ethnic ties to the blond young security men standing against the walls. But Switzerland was a diverse country with four distinct ethnic groups: German Swiss, French Swiss, Italian Swiss, and Rhaeto-Roman. Brent guessed the dark man was from the southeastern part of the country that bordered Italy. The four men rose and the security guards suddenly tensed and stood rigid.

Yoshi, Brent, and Colonel Bernstein took places at the table facing their opposite numbers. Brent's chair was directly across from Kenneth Rosencrance's. Brent placed his attaché case on the table and stared at the flyer. The renegade killer stared back, a sneer twisting the corners of the thin lips down at the corners. "Welcome, American samurai," Rosencrance whispered sarcastically.

"It's been a long time, 'Rosie,'" Brent taunted back, knowing the appellation infuriated Rosencrance.

The sneer vanished, the jaw altered into hard lines by clenched teeth. But before the flyer could lash back, he was interrupted by the dark man at the head of the table. Brent knew immediately that his guess about the man's origins had been correct, "*Signori*, I am Pietro Mercadante of the Swiss *Ministero degli Esteri.*" He was from the Foreign Office.

Brent saw Rosencrance turn to the man on his right and whisper, "A fuckin' wop! Jesus! Those greasers can't fight—can't do nothin' right. Shit!" Brent glanced at Yoshi and the Japanese shook his head resignedly as if he were the victim of a bad omen.

Mercadante asked Rosencrance to introduce his delegation. Although Mercadante's English was heavily accented and he occasionally called on an Italian word when his English vocabulary failed him, he managed to express himself well enough to be understood by all present. The American gestured to his right to a man in the uniform of the Libyan Army. "This is Major Alai Said Otaba, a special envoy from *Jihad* headquarters, Tripoli. The major is a personal representative of Colonel Moammar Kadafi."

A short slender man of about fifty, the major had the long, thin face of a weasel, riven with the scars of war and other ancient conflicts so that it was a miniature lunar landscape. His skull was shaven, the fine stubble of hair that covered it shining silver in the harsh light like glass fibers. Ominously, his cruel black eyes darted around the room in quick bursts, like those of an addict overdue for a fix. When his eyes skipped over *Yonaga*'s delegation, his lips twisted with loathing.

Rosencrance gestured to the man on his left who was garbed in a magnificent black burnoose trimmed with white silk piping. Heavy-set, dark, and very Semitic in appearance, he looked familiar to Brent. He was sure the man had been at the abortive meeting at the UN in 1989. "This is Sheik Iman Younis," Rosencrance said. "He represents the Arab League."

Brent said, "When we met before, he represented Yassir Arafat and the PLO, Hafez Assad, Abu Nidal and . . . ah."

Rosencrance picked it up, "And the Popular Front for the Liberation of Palestine, Nabih Berri, and the Shi'ite

Amal Militia." Rosencrance smiled. "True, ol' buddy."

"Don't 'ol' buddy' me, asshole."

"*Signori,*" Mercadante shouted in alarm. "*Por favore,* control yourselves! We are here to wage peace, not war."

Rosencrance tucked his lower lip under and remained silent. Brent looked at Yoshi, who nodded almost imperceptively. The young American turned to the Swiss and nodded. There were no apologies.

Hastily, Mercadante asked Yoshi to introduce himself and his delegation. Yoshi gave a brief description of Brent's and Bernstein's responsibilities and then looked expectantly at Mercadante. "*Signori,* before we seat ourselves, would you shake hands?"

Brent looked at Yoshi and then Bernstein. The Israeli's eyes were as cold and hard as carbon chips. "Mister Mercadante," Yoshi said, "let us dispense with that formality." He glared at Rosencrance. "I find the prospect revolting."

"Up yours, gook," the American shot back. Two of the security men took a step forward.

Aware of his gaffe and afraid the entire proceeding would end in a shambles before it even began, Mercadante interrupted, "*Por favore, signori.* We cannot be of any service to the prisoners if we bicker and fight before we even begin." He gestured grandly with both hands. "*Por favore,* be seated.

Grumbling, the six men found their chairs.

Speaking from his chair, Mercadante continued, "Our *primario* reason for being here is to discuss the exchange of prisoners."

The men nodded. Brent patted his attaché case and remembered Admiral Fujita's last instructions to the group. "Bargain hard, try for a one-for-one trade, but give them no more than two for one," he had said. Yoshi and Bernstein asked about other matters: the bases in the Marianas; submarine activity off the coast of Japan; the lifting of the oil embargo; the poison gasworks at Rabta; even possible negotiations for the cessation of hostilities, including attacks on Israel. The old man gave his permission to discuss whatever topics might show a possibility of progress. But no hard agreements could be reached except in the area of prisoner exchange. "And," the admiral had added, "remember, you will be dealing with Arabs—the most corrupt, disreputable people on earth." And then he had concluded, "Assure them we will not tolerate any abuse of prisoners they hold—including Israelis. We will retaliate two for one—with the blade, to the neck."

Mercadante's voice jarred Brent back to the present. "*Colonello* Rosencrance, may we see your list of prisoners?"

Rosencrance nudged Major Alai Said Otaba. The major pulled some documents from his case and began to read in perfect English, "As a consequence of your abortive raid on our pharmaceutical works at Rabta . . ."

"Pharmaceutical works!" Bernstein and Brent exclaimed in astonishment, half rising.

"Yes, pharmaceutical works," Otaba retorted hotly.

"Show me a doctor who writes prescriptions for nerve and mustard gas," Brent scoffed. Yoshi laughed. Bernstein glared.

The major waved a finger at the young American, "You would destroy anything good, anything humanitarian . . ."

"Humanitarian! Nonsense!"

Bernstein joined Brent in his rage and excitement, shouting a mixture of Yiddish and German, "*Schmuck! Arab scheisse!*"

"*Signori!*" Mercadante yelled over the uproar.

Brent began to object again, but Yoshi's firm hand on his shoulder restrained him and planted him firmly in his chair. His other hand pulled the steaming Israeli back and silenced him. Glaring at Brent, the Libyan major continued, reading from a document, "We captured Colonel Latimer Stewart, Captain Ronald Sparling, Lieutenant Jerome Hennessy, Lieutenant George Woodford, Lieutenant Terry Dunne . . ." He continued, naming five officers and seven enlisted men. The major paused, pulled another list from a dossier. "And after the battle off Gibralter, our humanitarian units at great risk to themselves rescued eight more of your pilots and crewmen." He read the list.

"That's a lie!" Bernstein spat. "You picked up twelve! It was reported to us by both Portuguese and Spanish fishermen."

"Fishermen! Ha!"

Bernstein pounded the table with both fists. "You executed four."

Major Otaba shook his head. "That is wrong, Colonel. Some died in captivity from their wounds—perhaps four." He shrugged. "In any event, we hold twenty prisoners taken after the raid on our works at Rabta and after the battle off Gibralter." He turned to Bernstein, "The Israeli prisoners are another matter."

Bernstein said, "You hold three hundred forty-two Israeli prisoners, but remember, we hold four thousand six hundred twenty-four Arabs." And then, with sarcasm, "Kill one of ours and fifty of yours die."

Mercadante said, "*Signori,* the exchange between Israel and the Arab forces is now being discussed in Geneva. We are here to discuss an exchange between the Arabs and the forces under Admiral Fujita." He gestured to Yoshi Matsuhara, "*Por favore,* Comandante. Will you read your *lista?*"

Clutching a document, Yoshi stood. "We hold forty-two of your men."

Rosencrance said, "According to our intelligence and neutral reports, you captured fifty."

Matsuhara ignored the American and stared at Major Otaba. "Eight died from their injuries and two will die for any one of the men you hold who succumbs to his injuries. So, I would suggest, Major Otaba, you keep your prisoners in good health." Brent expected an outburst, but Alai Said Otaba only muttered an oath under his

283

breath. Yoshi read the long list of names while Otaba, Rosencrance, and Iman Younis nodded and took notes. The air group commander concluded with, ". . . Major Horst Fritschmann, Lieutenant Hamoud Rogba, and Commander Henri DuCarme." He looked up. "That is all of them."

"DuCarme!" Rosencrance shouted. "Why, that fuckin' frog got his ass kicked by an old limey can." He looked around. "I saw it."

Yoshi jerked a thumb at Brent, "And he did it—sank *Abu Bakr*."

"You were on that old limey tub?"

"The *Haida*. And yes, I was in command."

"Well, I'll be goddamned," Rosencrance said in awe. And then, harshly, "You keep the snail-eating frog. We'd be better off if he was on your side, anyway." His harsh laughter filled the room. No one joined him. After regaining control, he continued, "You said you held Lieutenant Hamoud Rogba?"

"True."

"He's a fuckin' kike." Bernstein stiffened. Both Brent and Yoshi restrained him with hands to his arms. "Keep him, too. Send 'em to Jew heaven—I don't give a shit."

"And the rest, *Comandante* Rosencrance," Mercadante asked.

"We'll deal."

"Quid pro quo," Yoshi said.

"Quid pro what? Don't pull that Latin shit on me," Rosencrance snapped.

"Something for something. In this case, one for one."

Brent turned his head sharply, Yoshi's expression was flat and taciturn, but there was intense concentration in his eyes. He had been told the bottom-line exchange could be on the basis of 2-to-1. Then Brent understood; Yoshi was bargaining. *A used car salesman*, the American thought.

Sheik Iman Younis broke his long silence. With only a trace of an accent, the voice was as soft and glossy as satin, as slow as honey. There was the assurance of authority in the timbre; Eton or King's College or Harvard, too, could be there. "Ah, gentlemen, four of our men for one of yours." He was an Arab and the bargaining had begun. Surprisingly, Rosencrance held his tongue, and for a moment, at least, became a spectator.

"We do not hold enough prisoners to support that ratio," Yoshi countered.

The sheik stabbed a finger at Colonel Bernstein. "But they do."

"I thought we were to avoid discussions of Israeli prisoners."

"I am empowered to discuss any matters I consider pertinent, Commander Matsuhara." Brent eyed Iman Younis curiously. The man wore an aura of power like a king's cloak. He began to suspect the Arab spoke from considerable authority and intelligence. There was a mouth of Webster here, but not the usual Arab head of clay. Rosencrance remained tight-lipped. Brent was surprised by the ease with which Younis had taken the floor from the American pilot.

"A four-to-one ratio is not very complimentary to your side." Bernstein and Brent chuckled at Yoshi's slur.

Unperturbed, Younis drummed the table, "Four-to-one."

Yoshi whispered some incoherent nonsense into Brent's ear and then did the same to Bernstein. Both men nodded grimly as if they were mulling a profound decision. "One-to-one."

The Arab delegation huddled and went through the same ridiculous charade. "Three-to-one."

Yoshi finally arrived at the figure prescribed by Admiral Fujita. "Two-to-one," he said with finality.

Iman Younis drummed the table. "Three-to-one. We will concede no more."

Yoshi shook his head. "Sorry. Two-to-one is our final offer."

"Why not two-and-a-half-to-one," Rosencrance bellowed, voice cutting with sarcasm. He laughed boisterously at his clever quip.

"The wisdom of Solomon," Brent said scornfully.

"Up yours, ol' buddy."

"*Signori*," Pietro Mercadante begged. "*Por favore.* We are close to an agreement." He turned his hands up and shrugged, his shoulders nearly touching his ears, his expression and body language almost burlesquing the stereotype of the frustrated Italian. "A *piccolo* concession." He looked around hopefully, but was met only by unrelenting stares.

Iman Younis said to the mediator, "Mister Mercadante, I have been instructed to make no further concessions." He glanced at Yoshi. "Three-to-one."

"Two-to-one," Yoshi insisted, his face a stone wall.

Silence filled the room. Every man stared straight ahead or toyed with documents. Mercadante finally broke it, face brightening with a new idea, "Signori, another meeting. Return to your superiori, advise of the impasse and the near decisione. We will meet again. No?" He threw out both arms in an expansive gesture.

"No!" Rosencrance growled, grabbing his piece of the debate. He glared across the table. "The only place I want to meet these bastards is in the sky." He stabbed a finger at Yoshi. "This old fart should've been retired years ago to play with his grandkids. The only thing that keeps you up there is that crazy souped-up Zero, but I'm going to nail your ass yet."

Yoshi laughed, "Any time, Rosie."

The American shot out of his chair, waving a fist. "I've got something to settle with you, you son-of-a-bitch. You creamed Vatz, von Weidling, Hani Meri . . ."

Bolting to his feet, Yoshi fired back, "You murdered Willard-Smith in his parachute!"

"*Signori!*" Mercadante rose.

Rosencrance leaned forward on his clenched fists, gusts of hatred storming across his face. "I enjoyed every minute of it, 'Buddha head'. Gutted him like a fuckin' trout, didn't I?''

The security guards moved with amazing swiftness. Grabbing both pilots, they pulled them back into their chairs.

"Let go of me, assholes. I'm gonna chop that slant's ass," Rosencrance shrieked. He almost pulled free, but Younis and Otaba helped restrain him.

Brent helped the pair of Swiss guards control the struggling Yoshi Matsuhara. "Easy, old friend. Easy," Brent said, trying to placate the flyer. Yoshi was so filled with rage he gasped for breath and his eyes were tearing.

"*Signori! Signori!*" the mediator shouted. "Control yourselves. There is much to do. We are here to seek peace."

"Let go of me!" Rosencrance shouted.

"Your word that you will control yourself, *Colonello*."

The renegade American growled, hissed out pent-up anger, and finally conceded, "All right, my word."

"And you, *Comandante* Matsuhara?"

"My word, but no more insults," he said through the heavy breathing.

"Release them," Mercadante ordered.

The security men stepped back and the other men seated themselves.

"*Signori*," Mercadante said, showing surprising persistence and courage in the face of an almost impossible situation, "there are other matters that can be discussed." And then, after looking at Yoshi and Rosencrance imploringly, "Perhaps if we control ourselves, we can make *progresso* elsewhere—in other matters."

Iman Younis glanced at the Italian and then said to Bernstein, "Your line . . ."

"The Ben Gurion Line."

"Yes. Two lines of blockhouses." Younis stood, walked to a chart of the Middle East, and traced a line with a manicured fingertip. "Two lines of blockhouses extending from Gaza to Sedon in Jordan, then north to Al

287

Khushniyah and then back to the sea at Ashzib." He seated himself.

Bernstein chuckled. "It's deeper than two lines. We've piled enough Arab carcasses to prove that point. And what about it?"

A shrewd look crossed the Arab's face. Brent expected some more used-car bargaining. He was not disappointed. "What would you take to pull back from the Golan Heights and the West Bank?"

"The Golan Heights. We paid for them with blood— and the West Bank, too. Why, we'd weaken the whole line."

"Please, Colonel, I'm not asking you to abandon the Ben Gurion Line. The Golan Heights and the West Bank are of great political and religious significance to the Arab states." His restless fingers challenged the tabletop. "What would you ask in return?" The man actually sounded sincere.

Bernstein shook his head. "You ask too much."

"Too much?"

"Yes. I cannot speak for my superiors, but I'm sure they would demand that you demobilize, dismantle the poison gasworks at Rabta, pull back from the Marianas and cease your oil embargo."

"Impossible."

"What could you concede, Sheik Younis?" Mercadante asked hopefully.

"A pullback of our forces in the Middle East and a request for UN peacekeeping forces—and a possibility of UN observers on the site of the pharmaceutical works at Rabta."

"The Marianas?" Yoshi asked.

Sheik Younis shook his head, "Out of the question."

It was obvious to Brent the clever Arab was trying to drive a wedge between the Israelis and their Japanese allies. Bernstein burst the bubble before it could fly. "I'm sorry, Sheik Younis, but Israel would never accept terms that were unacceptable to our Japanese allies."

Younis was not finished. The Byzantine mind was hard at work. "We could make concessions in the Marianas and Tomonuto."

"What concessions?"

"If the forces of Admiral Fujita remain west of the one-hundred-eightieth meridian, east of the one-hundred-twentieth, and north of the tenth northern parallel, we will pull our forces back to Indonesia."

Yoshi stood and walked to a chart of the Eastern Hemisphere. He ran a finger over the Western Pacific. "You are only giving us sixty degrees of longitude and eighty degrees of latitude. You would restrict us to the Gilberts, the Marshalls, part of the Aleutians to the east, and the northern part of the Philippines, Korea, and part of the Chinese and Russian coasts to the west. Tomonuto is out of the area, and so are your bases in Indonesia. And obviously, Japan could not support Israel." He shook his head and returned to his chair.

"But there would be no threat," the sheik countered. "We would pull out of Tomonuto and the Marianas as well."

The air group commander fingered the grip on his attaché case. "I cannot speak for Admiral Fujita, but I am convinced he would never accept *any* restrictions on his operations."

"You have two carriers, Commander."

"True."

"We have two, and two cruisers."

"We are all aware of this, and Sheik Younis, I would suggest you not threaten me."

The sheik raised his hands in a placating gesture. "That was not a threat, Commander. I was merely pointing out the logistics of the contending forces."

"I do not anticipate any tactical or strategic problems that we cannot solve."

"*Signori.* We have made *progresso?*" The hollow tone of Mercadante's voice could not mask his disappointment.

"Perhaps," Younis said.

Yoshi shrugged his shoulders.

"Another *incontro*?" the mediator insisted.

There were sighs and the men looked at each other. Sheik Younis broke the silence with a surprising suggestion. "I will consult with my superiors and will be happy to meet with you in the future." He leaned toward Yoshi. "Will you do the same?" Rosencrance looked at Major Alai Said Otaba, then growled, but remained silent. Apparently, Sheik Iman Younis had enough clout to keep the American in some semblance of control.

The air group commander looked first at Bernstein and then at Brent. Neither man gave any signal. "All right," Yoshi agreed. "I will advise Admiral Fujita of your offer and suggest another meeting."

"*Bene, Signori, bene.*" Mercadante clapped his hands together in delight like a young boy at his first puppet show. "Then it is settled," he said, beaming.

Rosencrance pushed himself up, staring at Brent. "Not quite. There's something else to settle before we leave."

"What do you have on your mind?" Brent asked evenly.

Rosencrance glanced at Sheik Younis, who stared back. It was almost as if Rosencrance were looking to the sheik for a silent gesture of approval. Brent saw nothing, heard nothing pass between them. If there was a signal, it was absolutely undetectable. Maybe something had been prearranged. The renegade stabbed a finger at the seated Brent Ross. "This is personal. This has nothing to do with what we've been bull-shitin' about here. Between you and me, ol' buddy." Again, another glance at Younis. The sheik stared back wordlessly. But now an almost imperceptible hint of a smile toyed with the corners of his lips.

Brent stared back at Rosencrance, suspicion growing. Rosencrance said to Brent, "Two years ago in *Yonaga*'s sick bay, you stomped my ass when I was wounded, you

290

chicken-shit bastard."

"That's a lie," Brent hurled back, leaping to his feet. "You weren't wounded, you were in good health and you were trying to kill Lieutenant Taku Ishikawa, who *was* badly wounded." Now he knew what the renegade had on his mind.

"I'm healthy now, chicken-shit. Wanna try me?"

Brent ran his eyes over the rest of the men. Everyone stared back with the keen eyes of gamblers at a high-stakes poker game. "Don't do it," Bernstein warned. Yoshi's expression was inscrutable. He said nothing.

Mercadante said, "*Signori. Por favore,* control yourselves." He gestured to the security men. They stepped forward. "We have made *progresso,* why destroy it now?"

Sheik Iman Younis spoke. "These gentlemen have a problem to settle that is between them." He nodded at Rosencrance. "The colonel discussed this matter with me before the meeting. I feel that a settlement of this issue could actually have a beneficial effect upon these proceedings. Perhaps clear the air of at least one festering animosity." He raised his hands like a supplicant calling on a deity. "After all, we have made progress. Another meeting has been agreed upon."

Major Alai Said Otaba grunted and nodded his approval. Bernstein shook his head vigorously; Yoshi smiled his assent. "Kill the *ronin,*" the Japanese finally muttered.

Reluctantly, Mercadante waved the security men off. Brent swung to the big pilot acidly, scoffing, "All right, Rosie, do your damnedest." He waved at a small clear area to one side of the table, removed his tunic, and walked around the table. Rosencrance threw his tunic on his chair and stepped into the indicated area, holding his balled fists at his side like the street fighter he was. Approaching him slowly, Brent heard chairs scrape on the floor as the onlookers moved to better positions to watch the fight. A palpable air of anticipation filled the room.

Silently, the pair faced each other. Brent had fought many men. He disliked risking his nose, eyes, and jaw to big crashing fists. But once started, there was a strange atavistic fulfillment to each encounter, almost ritualistic in the way the dramas always unfolded. Man to man, fist to fist, cunning versus deception, and finally, pure brute strength versus all the power he could muster. This was primal, this was how men were meant to fight other men, no electronics, no automatic killing machines, just man versus man, where skill, raw courage, and strength prevailed. And Rosencrance's broad shoulders and big arms exuded strength, the strength of a man who had fought the controls of a fighter for years. Brent's stomach began to clutch and he felt the same hollow nausea he had known before each Army-Navy game. He smiled at the analogy.

"I'm going to wipe that fuckin' grin off your face, oh mighty American samurai," Rosencrance taunted, eyes flashing cold blue light like the glint of bared blades. The man was the personification of evil, but he was no coward.

Brent began to circle around his opponent, who pivoted to face him. "Well, do something about it, 'Rosie boy,'" Brent goaded back. He raised his fists and shifted his weight to the balls of his feet.

Leaping more than stepping, Rosencrance swung a fist the size of a small roast in a roundhouse swing. Surprised by the speed of the big man, Brent ducked and stepped backward too late to avoid a grazing impact to the top of his skull. The blow stung as if a handful of hair had been pulled from his scalp. The second punch came from his right and whistled past his nose.

"What's wrong, ol' buddy? I can see that yellow stripe . . ."

Before Rosencrance could complete the mockery, Brent exploded out of his crouch, leading with his left. The fist caught Rosencrance squarely in the mouth. Impacting an open mouth, there was a sharp pain as teeth

292

cut into knuckles. But Brent felt teeth give like twigs crushed by a foot. Saliva, enamel, and blood sprayed and Rosencrance staggered backward. Brent followed, swinging his right with all his power at the point of his opponent's chin. But Rosencrance dropped under the blow and leaped to the right, wiping blood from his mouth with his sleeve, cursing.

"Lucky motherfucker," he growled, spitting blood. His fists were up and his face was contorted with fury. Brent had expected the blow to the mouth to take some of the fight out of his big enemy. Most men would have been demoralized. He was mistaken. Rosencrance charged recklessly, coming after Brent like a great white rising to the smell of blood. In the confined space the barroom brawler had the advantage. Rosencrance took it.

The flurry of blows were wild, and powerful and fell on Brent like a hailstorm. He retreated, backed into a wall, and jumped to the side. For a moment, Brent was so busy defending himself he was unable to counterpunch. Most blows bounced off his shoulders, fists, arms harmlessly. But one caught the side of his head. A great gong seemed to bang and reverberate inside his skull, his teeth jarring, his head snapping to the side. His brain burst into bright colors, stabbing lights fused with areas of deep, echoing black. Another burst of sound in his skull dragged down a black curtain that almost blotted out his vision. Dumbly he licked his upper lip, and it tasted of coppery salt. His teeth had torn his cheek. He spit blood and shook his head, gave ground, swaying his head back or to the side, deflecting blows with his arms, shoulders, fists, ducking carefully under flying fists and counterpunching only with his left hand, flicking it in with deceptive lightness. He could hear shouts from the excited spectators.

Still retreating in a small circle, he wove and ducked out of the circle of wildly lashing fists which were now meeting only air. As he breathed deeply, his head cleared, and he could feel the strength flow back into his arms and legs. Sweat rolled from his brow, and his eyes stung. He spit more blood. He had been surprised. Never again.

"Come on, chicken-shit. Come on," Rosencrance spat. He was breathing heavily. Tiring.

Brent rocked from side to side, shook his head as if he were badly injured. Sensing a kill, the big man took the bait and charged like a sun-mad pit bull. Stepping gracefully to his left and dropping far down—knees almost touching the floor—Brent punched straight ahead and up with a right made more devastating by the power of his legs as he fired up from his crouch. He felt the cords of muscles of his enemy's midsection yield like power lines in a gale and the breath exploded from his lips in a whooshing sound. Blood and saliva sprayed Brent's face. Then, as Brent straightened, a left to the right eye was followed by a crushing right to the jaw. The three-blow combination hit in a quick musical rhythm, a bang; *bang-bang*.

The pilot was swatted back two or three staggering steps and then seemed to trip over his own feet and fall straight down, his knees giving way like dry reeds overweighted by the first rain. Dropping to the floor, he rolled to his back.

The wild animal was on Brent again. His mind blotted out by a red curtain of hate, he leaped on the pilot. He must destroy, obliterate. He punched down hard, once, twice. Rosencrance's head was snapped from side to side by the power of the blows.

"*Dio mio!*" Mercadante shouted. "Stop him!"

Brent felt hands grab his arms, his shoulders, and then other hands gripping his waist, pulling on his legs. Snarling and spitting blood, mucus, and saliva, he was dragged from the unconscious form.

"In the name of God," Bernstein shouted.

Then Yoshi's voice, "Brent-san—stop! Stop!"

Sheik Iman Younis's shocked voice: "What kind of wild animal is this?"

Yoshi said, "You wanted to clear the air, Sheik. Well, breathe it."

Chapter Fourteen

Delayed a full day at Taipei by engine trouble, Brent Ross, Irving Bernstein, and Yoshi Matsuhara were anxious to return to *Yonaga*. When they finally walked onto Dock B-2, preparations for putting to sea were in full swing. Stores were being loaded, fuel tanks were topped off, and seaman were busy chipping and painting, waging the sailor's perennial war with rust. Brent wondered at the activity. Yoshi Matsuhara had radioed a report of the meeting to Admiral Fujita, emphasizing the point that at least a small amount of progress had been made in the prospect of further negotiations. And the Arab delegation had released the information to the world media. Yet to all appearances, *Yonaga* was preparing for sea.

Brent had never become accustomed to the awesome size of the great vessel. Looking up from the dock at the leviathan, he felt like a man staring up at the towers of the World Trade Center: the same feeling of diminutiveness, insignificance, and a stroke of apprehension that the entire mass might topple over and crush him. How could such a Gargantuan mass of steel—which a sailor believed had a heart and soul of its own—obey the will of one man? Mounting the accommodation ladder, he smiled at his romantic ruminations.

Stepping onto the quarterdeck, the three officers

saluted the colors and then the Officer of the Deck. He directed them to Flat Plot, not Admiral Fujita's cabin.

When the trio entered Flag Plot, a staff meeting was in progress. Admiral Fujita was at his usual place at the head of the table. All heads turned as the newcomers entered. Brent gazed at the usual faces: the scribe Commander Hakuseki Katsube, Executive Officer Captain Mitake Arai, Chief Engineer Lieutenant Tasuya Yoshida, Gunnery Officer Commander Nobomitsu Atsumi, Torpedo Bomber Commander Lieutenant Shinji Hamasaki, Dive Bomber Commanding Officer Commander Takuya Iwata, Rear Admiral Whitehead, CIA Agent Alfred Gibney, Escort Commander Captain John Fite, and the captain of carrier *Bennington*, Captain Paul Treynor. Documents were scattered over the table and plastic overlays attached to charts of the Western Pacific were cluttered with red course lines, dates, and times. Especially cluttered was a chart of Tomonuto. This was a war room, no doubt about it. It was written on the walls, in the intense concentration on the faces turned toward them, in the electricity in the air. Admiral Fujita waved the trio to their seats.

The admiral held up a yellow sheet. "I have your report here." His eyes fixed on Yoshi Matsuhara. "But this brief report gives us only a bare glimpse of what transpired. Give us a complete report, Commander."

Standing, Yoshi opened his attaché case and removed some documents. He described the meeting in great detail: Rosencrance's expected belligerence; the attempts to negotiate with the intractable, hostile Major Alai Said Otaba; the clever bargaining of Sheik Iman Younis. He did not mention the fistfight.

"The authority of this Major Otaba and the Sheik Younis?"

"Otaba was sent from Jihad Headquarters, Tripoli."

CIA Agent Alfred Gibney said, "I've heard of him. He's a close aide to Kadafi—highly trusted."

"Highly trusted," Bernstein scoffed. "As much as any

Arab trusts another Arab. We at Mossad know him well. A master of duplicity, a brawler, an unconscionable killer."

Admiral Fujita halted the blooming argument before it could gather steam. "We all know this—no Arab can be trusted." He turned back to Yoshi. "Please continue, Commander."

"Major Otaba claimed the plant at Rabta manufactures pharmaceuticals."

Laughter exploded, reverberating from the steel walls in waves. Katsube toppled to the side and Arai caught him before he could crash to the deck.

After the laughter died to giggles, Yoshi continued, "Sheik Iman Younis represented the Arab League—seemed to have the greatest authority at the table. He is a politician and, I must say, spoke with great intelligence." Brent and Bernstein nodded.

Fujita chuckled. "Machiavelli said, 'In politics there is neither good nor evil.'" He laughed, actually rocked in his chair. "Obviously, Machiavelli never met an Arab." Everyone guffawed at the admiral's wit.

Yoshi continued, describing the hard bargaining over the prisoner exchange. He held up a document, "They hold twenty of our men. Here are their names." He passed the document to Admiral Fujita.

The admiral studied the list. "You told them we would kill two for one?"

"Yes, sir."

"Good." The old man shifted his eyes to the bruises on Brent's cheek and his partially swollen eye. "Apparently, at one point, your negotiations became very vigorous, Commander Ross." A giggle circled the room and the officers looked at each other knowingly.

"Ah, sir, Colonel Kenneth Rosencrance and I had a minor disagreement."

"He beat Rosencrance to a pulp," Yoshi said pridefully.

Shouts of *"Banzai!"* filled the room.

Rear Admiral Whitehead spoke for the first time.

"And this was a peace parley?"

Brent turned to the American admiral. "It was a private matter, something that begged resolution outside the scope of the meeting, and it was resolved."

"Without wrecking the meeting?"

"That's right, Admiral Whitehead." Yoshi and Bernstein nodded.

Yoshi reclaimed the floor, "They want another meeting, Admiral Fujita."

"I know, Commander." He tapped the yellow message sheet. "You informed me in your radio report." His expression changed, the little chin taking a hard line, eyes as black as smoke-fogged lamps. "Two special envoys have already been dispatched."

"Dispatched? Already? Where?"

"Tripoli! Over my objections, by the foreign office, at the insistence of those 'women' in the Diet." He slapped the tabletop. "The Minister of Foreign Affairs selected Nishio Kanji and Norio Tokumitsu. Both are career diplomats. They are empowered to negotiate only, and will report back daily through the Swiss ambassador."

"The parameters, Admiral?"

"Those idiots would give away everything. But I insisted that before we concede anything, I want a withdrawal from the Marianas and Tomonuto." His eyes found Bernstein. "Also, a standdown along the Ben Gurion Line and the establishment of a ten-kilometer neutral zone, patrolled by UN teams. Also, a UN inspection team must be posted at the gasworks at Rabta."

Yoshi shook his head. "Very difficult to negotiate those terms, sir?" He gestured at Brent and Bernstein, "We tried."

"I know, but Kanji and Tokumitsu have been instructed not to yield from them." He tapped the bony knuckles of his little fists together and his mouth became a thin, grim slash. "At least the foreign office promised me those objectives would be inflexible." He dropped his fists. "Whatever a politician's promise may be worth," he added sardonically.

The air group commander waved at the overlays and pointed at the chart of Tomonuto, "And, Admiral, you are preparing to get under way. Why, if we are negotiating at the same time? Shouldn't we delay our attack until our special envoys make their report?"

"Negative, Commander. As I informed you at our last staff meeting, we will move against Tomonuto, date of departure, plan of attack are unchanged. Our invasion of the Marianas can never succeed while an Arab force occupies that atoll. We will make our strikes while the envoys are negotiating. They have given me no alternative."

Brent's eyes widened and he looked at Rear Admiral Whitehead. They would attack while peace envoys were in Tripoli negotiating. He heard Whitehead mutter, "Just like seven December, nineteen forty-one." The American admiral turned to Fujita. "I know you were on the team that planned the Pearl Harbor attack, Admiral Fujita, and I met Kichesaburo Nomura and Saburo Kurusu, who were negotiating directly with Cordell Hull while your task force was under way for the Hawaiian Islands. They distracted us, all right. But those tactics won't work here."

The admiral avoided the distasteful topic of the events of December seventh. "My hand has been forced, Admiral Whitehead." He scratched the side of his head. "And why do you anticipate failure?"

All eyes moved from admiral to rear admiral as the two senior officers entered into one of their frequent tactical and strategic discussions. As a specialist in carrier warfare and special adviser to Admiral Fujita, Whitehead was obliged to offer his opinions. However, Fujita's steely resolve and near inflexible determination to stick to his guns usually turned these discussions into debates. Everyone enjoyed listening to the old warriors. Both were skilled in presenting their views and there was much to be learned from both. Brent suspected the two old men enjoyed these exchanges. After all, they had been mortal enemies in their youth.

Whitehead's response was quick, reflecting his vast knowledge of military events. He spoke of the Pearl Harbor attack force. "Because Kido Butai staged at Hitokappu Bay in the Kuriles, it was easy to keep their sortie a secret. But the whole world will know when *Yonaga* sorties from Tokyo Bay."

"We have spread the word that we are steaming on training exercises. Even the politicians believe this."

"It won't work, sir. The Arabs don't trust anyone. They'll suspect—and prepare for us." Whitehead shook his head. "And how long will it take the politicians, all of Japan, for that matter, to guess, to know an operation is under way?"

"Yes, Admiral Whitehead, I would expect suspicion from all quarters. But we will proceed with an attack on Tomonuto anyway. The subterfuge may gain us a slight advantage and the foreign office will be forced to maintain its silence. They will be in a very awkward, embarrassing situation." The old admiral chuckled humorlessly.

"And if this duplicity does not fool anyone—gain us the time you want?"

"I have been planning this attack for months, and you are aware of this, Admiral Whitehead. I will not allow a group of bumbling, cowardly politicians to interfere with my operations." Fujita's tiny fist punched the oak. "We must seek the enemy out and destroy him! Negotiations be damned!"

"Banzai! Banzai!"

Whitehead was not finished. "The first thing they'll notice is the absence of radio transmissions." He waved at a chart of the Western Pacific. "Why, their new listening station in North Korea can even monitor our pilots in air-to-air transmissions." There was a babble of shocked surprise.

"New listening station?" Brent and Yoshi chorused.

"Yes," Whitehead answered. "We just learned about it yesterday." He walked to a chart and pointed. "Here at Kosŏng, just north of the thirty-eighth parallel." He returned to his chair and said to Fujita, "*Yonaga* will put to sea, radio transmissions will cease," he shook his head. "They'll know, they'll know."

Fujita pushed himself to his feet with jerky, arthritic slowness. Stiffly, he walked to the same chart. Obviously, he was tiring. He gestured to the executive officer, "Captain Arai and I resolved this problem this morning. We will deal with this listening post or any other eavesdropping receivers and *Rengo Sekigun* traitors who watch our every move." He pointed at the southern tip of Kyushu. "We have two squadrons of fighters and a squadron of Aichis here." He moved his finger northeast. "And two Zero-sen fighter squadrons on Iwo." He turned to the staff. "I have ordered the squadrons on Iwo to return to Tokyo International." A confused buzzing filled the room. Fujita's raised hands silenced the men. "Their Zero-sens will be painted with the markings of *Yonaga*'s air groups, and they will continue exercising training procedures and transmit using the call signs of *Yonaga*'s air groups. It will appear that our training procedures are still under way."

Whitehead said, "But Iwo, sir—you would leave it unprotected?"

The old man turned to the captain of *Bennington*. "Captain Treynor, you report a squadron of F6Fs Hellcats and a squadron of F4Us Corsairs ready for operations."

"Yes, sir. And seven of my SBD dive bombers."

"Good. You will send the Hellcats and the SBDs to Iwo."

"To Iwo, sir?"

"Yes. Daily they will be sent on patrols to the northeast and west, transmitting air-to-air and air-to-ship signals using the call signs of *Yonaga*'s air groups. This

301

should mislead any Arab listening posts into believing *Yonaga* is exercising her air groups."

Whitehead shook his head, and Gibney joined him. "The Arabs will guess," the rear admiral said.

"They're not fools," Gibney added.

Brent broke into the discussions, "Admiral, *Bennington*'s exterior damage appears repaired."

"True."

"We're not ready for sea," Treynor said.

"I know," the young American acknowledged. "But you could appear to be ready."

"What do you mean?" Fujita asked.

"This, sir." Brent hunched forward, resting on his elbows. "Why not move *Bennington* into the roadstead—anchor her where the whole world can see her."

"But why?"

Brent's big palms began to beat a tattoo on the oak. "Because, if we were planning an attack, obviously both carriers would be under way."

The old man rubbed his shiny pate. "Good thinking, Brent-san." He turned to Treynor. "Anchor two kilometers out in the bay. See to it immediately after this meeting. Consult with Captain Arai, select your anchorage, inform the harbormaster, and then check with me."

"Aye, aye, sir."

The dive bomber commander Takuya Iwata broke his long silence. There was scorn on his face. Fixing Brent with a mocking stare, he said, "But the media knows of *Bennington*'s damage."

"Not the full extent," Brent countered.

"There are still yard workmen aboard."

"I know," Brent said, staring the pilot in the eye.

"The yard workmen will be restricted," Fujita said, closing the topic. Iwata sank back.

Whitehead still had forebodings about the entire operation. He said, "The Arabs might use the negotiations as a cover for a sneak attack of their own." He stood and walked to a chart. Tracing a wide, curving line, he said almost to himself, "Send *Al Kufra* and her two cruisers from Tomonuto on a wide, sweeping course northwest, just the reciprocal of our move—actually a mirror image of it—using an umbrella of fighters from the Marianas and strike our fields on Kyushu or even make strikes on Yokosuka—destroy our base and probably *Bennington*, too." He looked at Brent. "Which will be a glorious target sitting out there in the bay." Iwata snickered.

Fujita joined him at the chart. "Frigate *Ayase* will maintain radar picket duty here," he stabbed a point two hundred miles southeast of Tokyo Bay, "and destroyer *Yamagiri* will patrol here, midway between Kyushu and Okinawa." He looked toward Captain Treynor and explained, "These ships are the only survivors of the Maritime Self-Defense Force. Both vessels have excellent radar but weak gun power." He returned to the chart and swept a finger in a wide arc south almost to the Marianas and spoke directly to Whitehead. "Also, Admiral, keep in mind, we have seven PBYs and five PBMs making continuous sweeps."

"They could still pull it off, Admiral. Fighters from the Marianas could shoot down our reconnaissance, and bombers could take out *Yamagiri*."

"The Arabs could take heavy losses—lose their entire force, Admiral," Fujita countered.

"They're on their *jihad*, sir."

Fujita waved a tiny fist theatrically. "True, but we are driven by the spirit of *bushido*, *Yamato damashii!!*"

"*Banzai!*" boomed through the room.

Shaking his head, Whitehead returned to his chair. Fujita said to Treynor, "While we are at sea, you will be Senior Officer Present and Afloat, in command of all our forces."

The American captain sat bolt upright, eyes wide. "My orders, sir?"

Fujita gestured to Captain Mitake Arai. "My execu-

303

tive officer will give you the call signs to be used by the fighters flying out of Tokyo International and for your fighter operating out of Iwo. Your instructions contain the course for *Yonaga*'s false training cruise, position reports and dates, latitudes and longitudes, speed of advance, even the plane-to-plane exchanges and reports of casualties, rescues, names of lost pilots. Arab eavesdroppers have been recording everything—we will give them what they expect to hear." The men chuckled. "See Captain Arai after this meeting is concluded."

"Aye, aye, sir."

The old admiral turned to the whole group. "We will carry on with normal procedures." He glanced at Brent. "Even liberty for tonight only. All hands will be restricted to the ship tomorrow night and we will get under way at zero-four-thirty the next day, Sunday." He looked around. "Are there any questions?"

Matsuhara spoke immediately. "Sir, has there been an intelligence update on the forces at Tomonuto?"

The old man returned to his chair and lowered himself into it slowly, as if his joints were made of rusty metal. He sighed and replied, "Yes, Commander, as you know, the American nuclear submarine *Glenard P. Lipscomb* is on station off Tomonuto. Yesterday she reported two more depot ships, another tanker of about fifty thousand tons, and four more *Gearings*, which escorted the depot ships and the tanker. All are anchored in the atoll."

Yoshi narrowed his eyes and mulled the information for a moment. "Then, there are five depot ships, two tankers, two yard oilers, sixteen destroyers, *Al Kufra*, and cruisers *Babur* and *Umar Farooz*."

"You have an excellent memory, Commander."

Yoshi smiled. "A fine target, Admiral." There was a murmur of approval.

"Most tempting," Fujita agreed.

Brent broke into the exchange. "Barry Island, sir. Is

the strip operational?"

A new tension silenced the murmurs. "Not yet, Commander Ross." The old man's fingers found the single hair dangling from his chin and stroked it gently. "And that is another reason why we must strike hard and strike fast."

Before the shouts of "*Banzai!*" could explode, Whitehead made a sobering point. "If we attack while our special envoys, Nishio Kanji and Norio Tokumitsu, are negotiating, the Arabs will devise some inventive ways to dispatch them." He drummed the table. "And they're unaware of the danger they're in."

"True, Admiral. Would you expect me to inform them of my plans to attack Tomonuto?" There was rebuke in the voice.

Whitehead's face reddened. Even his neck took on a sunset hue. He ran his fingers through his thick white hair, clenched both fists on the table, and said, "That is an unconscionable act, sir, foreign office or not. Condemning two men to hideous deaths. We should wait . . ."

Fujita interrupted, his voice cutting like Saracen steel. "I ask for no man's approval, Admiral. The foreign office sent these men and we may gain an advantage while they negotiate. And certainly you should know commanders are often faced with sacrificing a few so that many may live." He pulled on the parchment-like skin of his chin, and the deep cut lines turned downward from the corners of his eyes and mouth as if they had been slashed by a razor. "Must I remind you of Hiroshima and Nagasaki, which were incinerated to end a war that was projected by your own planners to cost a million American casualties if it had been concluded by conventional means?"

Whitehead sputtered, "That is not an accurate analogy."

"And why not?"

"Japanese lives were saved as well."

"By immolating over a hundred thousand, including my family?"

Whitehead looked down at his clenched fists, thumped the table in frustration. "With all respect to your family, sir, we cannot continue to relive that."

"We must and I have. We must learn from the past or repeat the stupid blunders of our predecessors. Your own philosopher George Santayana sounded that warning. Kanji and Tokumitsu are career diplomats. They are aware there are risks whenever you enter a den of vipers."

"They won't be prepared for this den—for these vipers and what they'll get."

Fujita drew himself up and said, "They are Japanese."

"Banzai! Banzai!"

Fujita silenced the shouts with his raised palms. Brent expected a prayer. He was not to be disappointed. Although the old man's face was a map of fatigue, he pushed himself to his feet, faced the shrine, and clapped twice. Every man in the room rose and the Japanese and Brent Ross clapped.

Fujita opened with a low, solemn voice, combining both Shintoism and Buddhism in his invocation. "Oh, Izanagi and Izanami," he said, calling on the male and female Shinto deities who had created the islands of Japan. "Help us find the strength and compassion of Buddha and self-reliance on the path of enlightenment. And enlist Tenjin-Sama, the Heaven Spirit Lord of State, to aid our negotiators, and Hachiman-San, the god of war, when we do battle with our enemies. And as the Kurozumi teach, let us not be without constantly believing hearts, or yield to anger or grief." The tired eyes ran the length of the table and settled on Brent. "And if we die, let us die facing our enemies with a prayer for the Mikado on our lips."

The old man turned back to his staff, eyes resting on Brent Ross. Brent thought he saw the creases and furrows rearrange themselves into a hint of a smile. Fujita spoke softly, "Gentlemen, you are dismissed."

Brent fidgeted impatiently while knocking on Garnet Shaw's door. It was very late, almost 2100 hours. After phoning her, he had been delayed by a glitch in a new computer in CIC. He had phoned her again to warn her of the delay. The delay did not upset him. It had been the tone of her voice. Although she agreed to see him, there was a strange distance to her voice—an amalgam of congeniality and coldness that made no sense. She was a strange girl with unpredictable, mercurial changes in mood. He had certainly experienced these wild fluctuations the last time he saw her.

When she opened the door the sight of her washed his misgivings away. In her tight silk frock she looked lovely. She glanced at the armed seaman standing behind Brent and then pulled the young officer into the room. Her kiss was warm but not driven by the passion of their last night together. She led him to the sofa where a bottle of Scotch, ice, and glasses waited on the small table.

"Neat, Brent?"

"Please."

She poured his drink. "Hungry?"

"Negative. And you?"

"I've eaten."

"You had a successful trip, Brent?"

"It could've been worse."

"Arabs are hard to negotiate with."

He smiled. "That's the understatement of the year."

Gently, she ran a hand over his bruised face. "How do you people negotiate, with baseball bats?"

He laughed. "That was another matter."

"Did you conclude it successfully?"

He clenched his fists and raised his bruised knuckles. Cuts from Rosencrance's teeth were clearly visible.

307

"Very successfully."

She laughed, and kissed his knuckles and his bruised face soothingly. Her lips were soft, warm, moist. He wanted to grab her, kiss her passionately. But he sensed that it would be wrong, that she was not ready for a rush of emotion and would turn it back. "You're leaving," she said. "It's been on the news."

"I know. A training cruise. We have—ah, some new pilots. It takes a lot of training to develop a good carrier pilot." He avoided disclosing that almost half their pilots were new.

She nodded as though she believed him. He felt reassurance at his minor success. Then she dashed it. "You're going out to kill, aren't you, Brent?" She put her hand to her mouth and talked into her palm, "To kill and be killed."

Eyes wide, he came erect. "Why, no. It's a training mission."

She emptied her glass and poured more Scotch into both glasses. "You're not lying?"

"Of course not."

"You're important to me, Brent. I've had something with you I've never had with any other man." Her eyes suddenly moistened, and she looked away. When she spoke, her voice almost broke. "I can't stand the thought of losing you before I even ever really had you."

"You've had me."

She turned back, a slight smile quivering at the corners of her mouth. "Oh, dear boy, I wasn't talking about sex." She placed a finger on his lips before he could reply. "I've got to admit, it was the greatest, something a woman can never forget. But this is only the third time I've seen you." She dropped her hand. "I really don't know you," she waved down the hall toward the bedroom, "in spite of that. Does that make sense?"

"Of course you make sense." He sipped his drink.

"But war compresses everything—and it interferes."

She stared at her glass. The voice was suddenly serious. "I think I'll be leaving, Brent."

He tabled his drink in shock. "Leaving?"

"Yes."

"But why?"

"I have a chance to work for Worldwide Network News."

"They're in New York."

"Headquartered in New York. They have offices all over the world."

"But your novel."

"I'll let it wait."

"But why not finish it?"

She recharged their glasses. "Do you know what its like to try to work with two policemen hounding your every step? And sometimes I see your seamen following me, too."

"They get in your way?"

She looked away. "It's not just that, Brent."

"Then what?"

"You'll think I'm a coward."

"No, I won't."

"I'm afraid—just plain scared. I can't put that night at the restaurant out of my mind." She looked up. "Do you understand?"

"I told you before, I've lived with fear for years."

"I don't want to leave you, but I can't live like this."

"Do what's right for you, Garnet."

"I definitely know of one thing that's right for me, Brent." She tabled her drink.

"What?"

She turned to him and held his eyes for a long moment. "Don't you know?" She lifted her lips to his.

This time the kiss was long, intense, filled with hunger. Finally, she broke away and came to her feet slowly. The power of her look pulled him from the sofa. She led him to the bedroom.

Chapter Fifteen

The morning *Yonaga* sortied was gray and overcast. There was a sense of ominous predestiny in the air, an oppressiveness that entered through the eyes and burrowed its way into the brain, heart, and soul. Everyone felt it; the stirring of unease, of fear even, deep within.

Standing at his special sea detail on the flag bridge between Rear Admiral Whitehead and Admiral Fujita, Brent stared at the sullen sky, a dirty gray roof that matched his mood. He had lost Garnet, perhaps forever. He had phoned her Saturday morning. Her first words were tremulous, on the edge of weeping. "I'll miss you, my darling," she said.

"What do you mean?"

"I've decided to return to the States—take that job with Worldwide Network News."

Listening to her broken voice, he felt as though he were shriveling in size under the burden of loss and sorrow. He wanted to plead with her to remain, but knew her fear of the *Rengo Sekigun* was real. As all terrorists, they were completely unpredictable. She was in danger. How much, only the terrorists knew. She could spend a lifetime in Japan and never see one of the thugs, or she could be ambushed anywhere at any moment. The police could never give absolute protection against fanatical, suicidal killers. It was a maddening situation. He dared not try to persuade her to remain. He could only say, "You must make your own decision, Garnet." She was crying when she hung up.

The clack of parallel rules moving across a chart and then the voice of the navigator, Captain Mitake Arai, interrupted his musings. "Suggest course one-eight-zero. Should put us in the center of the channel, Admiral."

"Very well," Fujita said, bending over a bank of voice tubes. And then into a tube that connected to the pilothouse beneath his feet, "Right standard rudder."

"Right standard rudder," echoed up from the helmsman.

"Steady up on one-eight-zero, speed twelve."

"Steady up on one-eight-zero, speed twelve, sir." There was a pause as the bow of the great warship swung to the right and Brent felt the pulse of the four powerful engines increase their beat. Now, through the wan light, he could see the dark outline of the heavily forested Bōsō Hantō Peninsula to port. In his troubled mind, the silhouette reminded him of a leopard crouching low in the twilight, waiting for an unsuspecting morning meal to walk past. To starboard the Uraga Peninsula loomed black and equally foreboding, the lights of Uraga and Kurihama still burning weakly in the growing light. His glasses brought it all very close, the sea shaded from black to deep blue to patches of emerald in the shallows, the rind of white beaches and ranks of waves moving across it like ripples on a pond. He watched as wave after wave wasted themselves on the rocks and sand.

"Steady on one-eight-zero, speed twelve, sixty-two-revolutions, sir," came up the tube.

"Very well."

Then Arai's voice, "Quartermaster Rokokura, tangents on Uraga and Nojima Points." He gestured seaward.

Leaning against the gyro repeater, the quartermaster squinted through the peep sight of his bearing circle and

311

shouted out two bearings. Arai grunted his acknowledgement and cut in the new bearings on his chart. He turned to Admiral Fujita. "Dead in the center of Tokyo Canyon, sir."

"Very well." Fujita turned to a rating wearing the headset of a talker. "Seaman Naoyuki, radar verify."

Naoyuki spoke into his mouthpiece. "Verified, sir. In the center of the channel."

"Very well."

Brent raised his glasses and studied the sea ahead. The mists and ghostly swirls of fog were fast yielding to the onslaught of the rising sun. Three *Fletchers* were visible, breaking out into the open sea beyond Bōsō Hantō's Point Nojima. Looking astern, he could see the first three of six more destroyers following in the carrier's wake. Nine destroyers. He felt his spirits lift. Five escorts could cover all quadrants. However, with a possibility of engaging an enemy force of an *Essex*-class carrier, two cruisers, and an unknown number of *Gearings,* Admiral Fujita had taken all the firepower available. With five-inch, 38-caliber cannons, dozens of 20-millimeter and 40-millimeter guns, and ten torpedo tubes, the *Fletcher* was a formidable opponent for anything afloat.

Brent caught a glimpse of a black object bobbing in the gray chop. "Sea buoy," he shouted, "bearing three-five-zero, range two thousand!" A young lookout Brent had not seen before turned and gave the American a curious stare. Although the language of the ship was English, Brent was not sure of communication with many of the new men. Brent added, "Yards, Admiral."

"Very well, Commander," Fujita said. He glanced at the new man and then back to Brent. He chuckled. "We will proceed with English units on this operation, Commander Ross, as I indicated at our last meeting. All hands have been instructed—you know that." There was no reprimand in his voice.

"Yes, sir."

Slowly, the force moved out into the open sea. Course was changed again to avoid O Shima Island and the string of islands lying to the south and east of the channel. Speed was increased to sixteen knots and the destroyers formed a protective screen around *Yonaga*: Fite's DD-1 leading five hundred yards ahead, two destroyers off the carrier's bows, two off her beams and two trailing off her quarters. Two more ranged far ahead of the force, scouting, sonar searching for the invisible menace below. Only the upper works of the pair would be seen in clear weather.

Submarines were on everyone's mind. Byron Whitehead dropped his glasses and, waving to the south, said to Admiral Fujita, "Carrier *Shinano* was sunk less than two hundred miles south of here by submarine *Archer-Fish*."

Brent looked at the two old warriors. The destruction of the mighty *Shinano* was one of the most brilliant and tragic events in naval history. Similar to *Yonaga*, she had been built on the same hull as battleships *Yamato* and *Musashi*. Massively armored and honeycombed with compartments, *Shinano* was considered almost unsinkable. But fear of B-29s had frightened the Naval General Staff into sending her to sea on an ill-advised run to Kure on the Inland Sea before she had been completely fitted out.

Fujita nodded grimly. "Yes, November of forty-four. She was seventeen hours into her maiden voyage, sixty-five miles off Shiono Misaki." He pounded the oak rail of the wind screen. "Stupid! Stupid! She was not ready for sea—was not even commissioned. Why, some of her watertight doors had not even been fitted with gaskets, and she still had yard workmen on board."

"I know, Admiral. It only took four fish to deep-six her."

Fujita said, "Her commander, Captain Toshio Abe, was stupid. Knew nothing about handling such a huge vessel. His damage control was criminal."

"His escorts must have been poor."

"True, Admiral Whitehead. He did have three destroyers. Their sonar search was very poor."

With animosity softened by the years, and reflecting the love of ships known only to men who have spent a lifetime at sea, Whitehead said with genuine sincerity, "A tragedy, sir. A tragedy."

"Yes. Over a thousand men lost because of sheer incompetence." The old Japanese raised an eyebrow and stared at Whitehead. "She was your enemy, Admiral."

"I know, and I would have sunk her, too." He let his binoculars dangle at his waist and turned up his palms. "But that does not change the fact her loss was a waste, Admiral Fujita, such a terrible waste."

"Is that not the nature of our business?"

"Since the beginning of time," Whitehead answered.

Both officers raised their binoculars and stared to the south as if they were searching for the ghost of the long-dead carrier. After a long silence, Fujita turned to Naoyuki and said, "Secure the special sea detail, condition two of readiness, port section has the watch." He turned to Brent, who would be the officer of the deck. "Maintain course one-eight-five, speed sixteen." He examined the sky where dark patches of sky like translucent sheets of blue ice were visible through the dissipating overcast. Only Venus and a few first-magnitude stars glimmered, the rest already snuffed out by the growing light. Now, in the east, the red orb of the sun peeked over the still misty horizon. It was very red, spilling into the vault of the sky like blood. Fujita took it all in and said, "Our air groups should be rendezvousing soon." Glancing at the chart, his eyes narrowed and his lips pursed in thought. "In about two hours—when Nii Shima is broad on the starboard beam. My standard orders of the day apply, Commander."

Brent repeated his orders and said, "I relieve you, Admiral."

Fujita and Whitehead left. Soon there was the sound of boots on steel and four new ratings relieved the

314

lookouts while Brent's talker, Seaman First Class Nobunaga Oda, took the headpiece from Naoyuki. The Junior Officer of the Deck, Lieutenant J.G. Tokuma Shoten, a young, bright-eyed officer not more than twenty-five years of age, relieved Captain Arai and took his place at the chart table. With a round, fully packed face, the likable Shoten reminded Brent of a jovial toad. Officially, young Shoten was the navigator. Usually, he would stand his watch between the charthouse and pilothouse. However, while piloting and with the imminent arrival of the air groups, the junior officer of the deck reported to the flag bridge. Quartermaster First Class Hio Rokokura, who was in Brent's section, remained, taking a lookout's position at the windscreen, near the gyro repeater.

Brent missed Colonel Irving Bernstein and the CIA man, Alfred Gibney. Both men had conferred with Admiral Fujita just hours before sailing and then rushed ashore. Usually, the Mossad agent and CIA man would sail with *Yonaga*. Something was up, and whatever it was, Fujita was keeping it to himself.

Brent grasped the windscreen with both hands and stared over the bow and swept the semicircle ahead with his binoculars. Then a glance over the stern. Japan had vanished. They were in the open sea at last, *Yonaga*'s natural element, and, Brent thought, his. There was a small swell following from the northeast in serried ranks, taking the great vessel on her port quarter and causing her to roll ever so slightly as her prow cut through the sea, sluicing surging billows aside into her frothing wake. Brent lifted his eyes. Most of the sky had been flushed clean by the warm, probing rays of the sun, the timorous reds, pinks, and saffron of dawn waxing into a clear blue. Only in the north were clouds visible. Here a long squall line bruised the sky, their bellies pressing down to the sea. Beneath them gray rain drifted down to meet the sea like sheets of lead filings. Sunlight filtering through the rain-spun rainbows, and the cloud shadows moving slowly across the sea reminded Brent of a herd of grazing buffalo. He chuckled to himself at the wild flights of his imagination.

Filling his lungs with clean salt-laced air, he felt the depression ease and he was suddenly filled with a strange euphoria. He was at sea, a pristine world not yet defiled by men. True, here he was an interloper, challenging the elements, the gods, for survival. *And,* true, there were other men lurking below the surface and above the clouds, waiting for a chance to kill him. But with death waiting impatiently, a man lived life to the fullest. And he had his comrades, a bonding of men known only to those who fight, live, and die together. Nothing on earth or in heaven can weld men closer.

Brent ran his eyes over the carrier. At Condition Two, half her weapons were manned—thirty-two of the 127-millimeter (5-inch) dual-purpose cannons and thirty-one of the ship's sixty-two 25-millimeter triple-mount machine guns. He could see the helmeted heads of the gun crews huddled around their weapons. Glancing back and up, he could see two more 25-millimeter mounts on the superstructure and another pair on platforms attached to the tilted stack. The ship's forest of antiaircraft guns could deliver a blizzard of shells. But on several occasions he had seen determined pilots—perhaps fanatical pilots high on hashish—penetrate the flaming shield and deliver their bombs. Over the years, more than one hundred twenty crewmen had been killed and another three hundred wounded. His euphoria began to wane.

Almost an hour later radar reported its first contact with the air groups. "Many aircraft bearing zero-one-zero true, range one-six-two, and they are at a low altitude, Commander Ross," the talker, Nobunaga Oda, reported.

"IFF?"

"Friendlies, sir."

"Very well. Notify the admiral."

Thirty minutes later, Admiral Fujita and Rear Admiral Whitehead walked onto the bridge. "Steaming as before,

Admiral," Brent said.

"Very well, Commander. You still have the deck."

"Aye, aye, sir." Brent turned to the talker. "Range and bearing on aircraft."

"Bearing zero-zero-five true, range ninety-six."

"Very well. Radar, I want a reading on Nii Shima."

Oda spoke into his mouthpiece, listened, and reported, "Nii Shima bearing two-two-zero true, range thirty-eight miles."

"Very well."

Rear Admiral Whitehead said to Fujita, "Your DR was very accurate, Admiral."

"Thank you, Admiral Whitehead. I have been practicing for over eighty years." Everyone produced his obligatory chuckle.

Fifteen minutes later the first rumbles were heard. Brent focused his magnificent Zeiss lenses astern. A swarm of insects was visible in the far distance. "I have them, sir. Bearing one-nine-zero relative, low on the water."

Fujita spoke as he raised his glasses. "That is why they got so close before our radar picked them up." He said to Brent, "I relieve you, Commander." And then, to Oda, "Pass the word, aircraft handling party stand by to receive aircraft." Oda threw a switch, and spoke into his mouthpiece, and the command blared through the ship's PA system. A rush of boots was heard and men began to stream across the flight deck.

Fujita shifted his eyes to young Shoten. "Mister Shoten, a Beaufort reading?"

"Force three from the northeast, Admiral."

The old man rubbed his chin thoughtfully. "Eight to twelve knots," he mused.

The rumble had turned to thunder, and Brent could make out individual aircraft. The first formations were Aichi D3A dive bombers. Slowly the bombers banked toward the carrier's starboard side to begin their counterclockwise orbit. Behind them streamed the

Nakajima B5N torpedo bombers and last of all, the fighters. Although all the aircraft bore Japanese markings, it was truly an international force, especially the fighters. Six Englishmen, twelve Americans, two Frenchmen, a German, a Greek, and a Dutchman flew fighters. A Turk, a Pole, a Russian, and a second Frenchman flew bombers. All the remaining bombers were piloted by Japanese. However, two Spaniards, two Englishmen, and a Frenchman manned guns.

Oda reported to Admiral Fujita, "All stations manned and ready. Ready to receive aircraft, sir."

"Very well. Signal bridge, make the hoist at the dip, Course zero-four-five, speed twenty-four."

Brent scanned the escorts. The answering hoists raced up their halyards almost as fast as *Yonaga*'s signalmen could bend on their flags and pennants. Obviously, all of the escorts had the aircraft in sight and were waiting for the flagship's signal. "All escorts answer at the dip, Admiral," he said.

"Very well. Two block!"

Immediately, the carrier's hoists were snugged close up to the yardarm. "All hoists two-blocked, sir," Brent said.

"Very well. Execute!"

The hoists were whipped down and the admiral spoke into the voice tube. "Left standard rudder, steady up on zero-four-five, speed twenty-four." The commands rang back up the tube and the carrier heeled into her turn. Again, Brent could feel the beat of the engines seven decks below increase through the soles of his shoes and the slight vibrations in the windscreen. Like a *daimyo* accompanied by fawning courtiers, the force turned as one, not a single escort slipping out of station. Brent felt the ship steady on her new heading.

A voice in the tube, "Steady on zero-four-five, speed twenty-four, one hundred twenty-eight revolutions."

"Very well."

With a breeze of at least twenty-eight knots whipping

over the deck, the aircraft would land into an adequate head wind. Brent had seen the carrier from the sky. When making a landing, the leviathan looked like a child's toy boat floating in a bathtub. It took more than skill to land on a speeding carrier: it took luck and courage.

Oda said, "Flight deck crew standby, barrier up." Running from beam to beam, the barrier was cranked out of its well amidships. Made of fearsome steel mesh, the barrier would snag any aircraft that missed the cables or overshot the landing area. It could crush a plane like a swatted housefly.

Fujita said to Oda, "Signal, bridge, hoist Pennant Two."

"Pennant Two two blocked, sir."

Seeing the pennant at the yardarm—a white ellipse on a blue background—the first Aichi made its approach. Hook extended, the big plane sank as it neared the stern. Brent could see the yellow-clad landing officer on his platform extending his yellow paddles and tilting from side to side like a stiff-winged bird riding a thermal. Suddenly, the paddles were crossed at the knees, the throttle cut, and the plane dropped, catching the second cable. It bounced on its two big tires while handlers in yellow and green rushed out, disconnected the hook, and wheeled it forward over the retracted barrier to the forward elevator, where it was struck below. Then, bomber after bomber roared over the stern, caught a cable, pounded to a stop, and was wheeled forward.

Overhead, the fighters wheeled gracefully and blasted their power as they swung in wide arcs over the bombers. Yoshi's red, green, and white fighter with two Seafires riding his elevators was unmistakable. Flying Officer Hooperman was there along with Pilot Officer York. Hooperman was a good one, an outstanding pilot in every respect. However, only the crucible of combat could prove his true mettle; whether he was an adequate replacement for Captain Colin Willard-Smith. Vic after vic of white Mitsubishi A6M2 Zero-sens followed Yoshi's three. And four more Vickers-Supermarine Seafire F.47s were to be seen, flying in their usual RAF pairs.

But the most spectacular were the twelve F6F Hellcats, which roared in their elements of two behind the Mitsubishis and the Seafires. Led by their new Commanding Officer, Steve Elkins—the replacement for the injured Lieutenant James Bender—the blue American fighters seemed to be loafing along. And indeed, they were. With their new 3,100-horsepower Double Wasp Pratt and Whitney R-2900-12W engines, they were faster than the *Bennington*'s Vought F4U Corsair, which was the first American fighter to achieve level flight of over 400 miles per hour. And astonishingly, this was done in 1942. Now the F6F had been clocked at 480 in level flight. In an all-out dive, one test pilot had flirted with the speed of sound. The tremendous buffeting had forced him to throttle back. No one knew just how fast this plane could dive, and no one was eager to find out.

The honk of the emergency klaxon jerked Brent's eyes to the deck. A Nakajima had been waved off. But the engine refused its throttle and the plane dropped ponderously to the deck, bounced high, crashed down on its port wing, ground-looped, and crashed sideways into the barrier. Its starboard wing bent up as if it were made of wet cardboard, shattered Plexiglas flew in clouds, and ripped aluminum scattered across the deck. All three members of the crew were hurled to the side of the cockpit despite their restraints. Frantically, the next bomber was waved off.

Dozens of men rushed to the wrecked torpedo plane, a half dozen in the white fire-retardant suits of firefighters. White foam was sprayed on the wreck. Luckily, there was no fire and the crew was pulled from the cockpit. One was able to walk with support, the other two were removed on stretchers.

Fujita was furious. "Drag that junk off my deck," he screamed at Naoyuki.

The command was unnecessary, a small rubber-tired vehicle acquired from the U.S. Navy dragged the bomber to the side. Within four minutes, the bomber had been pushed over the side, deck cleaned of wreckage and the landings resumed. The rest of the aircraft were recovered without incident.

"Only one casualty," Whitehead commented to Fujita.

"One too many," Fujita grumbled.

Whitehead shook his head. "Very good, Sir, when you consider that about half those pilots had never landed on a carrier before."

Fujita ignored the remark. He turned to Captain Mitake Arai, who had relieved Shoten of the navigation duties. "I want a standard combat air patrol of six fighters."

"Aye, aye, sir."

"And standard scout patrols by four bombers—immediately."

"We will fuel them, arm them, and have them airborne within forty minutes."

"Make it thirty."

Arai gulped. "Aye, aye, sir."

On strict radio silence, the force cut a course almost due east. All communications between ships was done by flashing light and flag. Aircraft maintained radio silence. After five days of steaming, and with Midway Island 500 miles to the east and Wake Island the same distance to the southwest, course was changed to due south. This wide swing took the force out of range of Saipan and Tinian's prowling Constellations and Douglas DC-6s. The southerly heading was held for two days until the battle group was southeast of Wake and north of the Marshall Islands. Then, still cruising at 16 knots to conserve fuel, the force swung to the west and south for the run-in on Tomonuto.

Steaming at latitude twelve degrees north, the ships were deep in the tropics. The weather had changed dramatically since leaving Tokyo's thirty-seventh parallel. There it had been cold and damp. Now, 1,500 miles closer to the equator, it was still damp, but hot. There was no overhead to shield a man on the flag bridge, and the sun would beat down on exposed weather decks mercilessly. Flurries of squalls trooped past. Billowing into the sky like miniature thunderstorms, they dumped water into the sea in opaque gray sheets, sometimes soaking the men on watch and sending water streaming out of the scuppers. In minutes they would pass, the pitiless sun returning to send steam boiling from the decks like swamp fog.

In the radio room, radiomen copied news reports from all of the world's major services. Negotiations between Japan's special envoys Nishio Kanji and Norio Tokumitsu and the Arab leaders headed by Sheik Iman Younis were in full swing in Tripoli. But there was an ominous tone to the reports. From the very beginning, the Japanese were faced with almost impossible demands. However, the talks continued.

Two days from launch point, Brent was called to CIC by an excited cryptographer second class, Stan Fleishman. Handing Brent a printout, the young man said, "First group five Ys and then four groups of numbers and the Greenwich Civil Time of transmission in plain language. A CISRA transmission, sir—right?"

"Right."

Anxiously, Brent took the signal to his cabin. He placed an NEC laptop computer on his small desk and went to work. First he typed in the eight-figure subroutine which masked the alphabet. Then he entered the ten-figure digital control code which was predicated on the phase of the moon and the Greenwich Civil Time of the message plus three. With the NEC formatted for decoding, Brent struck the "Enter" key. The message READY TO DECODE flashed across the screen. Brent took a deep breath, said a short prayer, and began to type in the groups from the signal. Almost miraculously, the message appeared letter by letter across the screen in plain language. It was from the *Glenard P. Lipscomb*, transmitting from just off Tomonuto:

TOP SECRET
061391—0855
FM COMLIPSCOMB—TO COMYONAGA
INFO—CINC—COMPAC

ONE ESSEX CLASS CARRIER, TWO CRUISERS, TEN DESTROYERS SORTIED TOMONUTO THIS DATE AT 0850. COURSE NORTHWESTERLY.

After printing out the message, Brent rushed to Admiral Fujita's cabin. While Brent stood, the old man scanned the message. His jaw altered into a hard line and he bit down on his thin lip. He said, "I wanted to kill the vermin in their lair." He waved the message, "Now, we will kill them on the high seas." He dropped the message to the desk top and slapped it with an open palm. "I expected this, Brent-san."

"You did, sir?"

"Yes." He sighed. "Our subterfuge did buy us nine days—nine days that will prove fatal for the enemy. They know we departed Tokyo, and, as Admiral Whitehead suggested, the Arabs are on a northwesterly heading to make a strike of their own. But they have waited too long—should have sortied immediately." He waved Brent to a chair. Obviously, he wanted to talk.

After seating himself, Brent said, "Sir, they couldn't suspect we are so close to Tomonuto."

"The supply ships?"

"Of course, Admiral. They would've bugged out—ah, sorry, I meant they would be under way, headed for Indonesia."

"You are very perceptive, Brent-san. At this moment,

I am convinced they are confused, but believe their anchorage is safe."

"Their battle group could double back, make for Indonesia."

"That is not consistent with their mentality. By now they have obviously confirmed that the radio signals they are monitoring to the east of Japan are false. They believe *Yonaga* is far to the east, leaving our rear open, and they can inflict punishment without receiving it in return." He rubbed his wrinkled chin. "No, they will head north at high speed."

"You expected this from the beginning?"

"Of course, Commander. I have planned on it, but of course, I hoped to catch them at anchor."

"You said they would expect *Yonaga* to be far to the east."

"Correct."

"How can you be so sure? After all, there are only two Arab targets in the Western Pacific worthy of an all-out attack—the Marianas and Tomonuto."

The old man pinched his tiny nose. "Remember, just before sailing, I detached Colonel Bernstein and Alfred Gibney?"

"Yes."

"I gave them several tasks. One was to contact Mossad and the CIA by *Yellow Oscar* and arrange for a tanker to move to a position off the west coast of South America and another just south and west of the Azores."

Brent scratched his head. "Those are refueling positions for our battle group when we make for North Africa. And sir, *Yellow Oscar* is compromised."

The old man laughed. "The tankers are under way and the Arabs know it."

"But we'll never refuel from those tankers. We're not headed for the Atlantic—North Africa."

"Correct. But the enemy does not know this. Remember, Brent-san, we have made attacks on North Africa twice, using the same route around Cape Horn.

With the tankers steaming to what appear to be rendezvous positions, they must consider this possibility again." He ran a single finger over the desk top while his forehead furrowed in thought. "Nine days of steaming would put us east of Palmyra and north of the Marquesas—almost four thousand miles to the east and south of Japan."

"More confusion."

"A smokescreen, Brent-san."

"But Sir, smokescreen or not, they may strike our fields in southern Kyushu or Iwo Jima. Even Yokosuka and *Bennington*. Take out our graving dock before we can engage them. Admiral Whitehead warned of this, too."

"Sometimes a rat will devour some of the cheese before the trap snaps shut. It makes no difference. We will trap them with their backs to our own islands." He crossed his arms over his bony chest and rubbed his arms. "There is little chance they will hit targets in Tokyo Bay."

"We have too much fighter strength at Tokyo International and Iwo."

"Correct. Two squadrons of Zero-sens and a squadron of Corsairs at Tokyo International and a squadron of Hellcats and seven dive bombers on Iwo." He rested his chin on a tiny fist and pondered for a moment. He seemed to contradict himself with his next thought. "But the Arab mind is devious and completely unpredictable. You know, my young friend, you have fought them for years. They can be fanatically brave and make suicidal attacks or run like whipped curs at the first shot." He shook his head.

"Then Tokyo Bay is not safe."

"True."

"We are completely out of position to intercept, sir."

"Not if we steam south of the Marianas and north into the Philippine Sea."

"Abandon the attack on Tomonuto?"

"Yes, remember, *Al Kufra* is only a day ahead of us."

Brent still felt pangs of doubt. "But, sir, *Al Kufra* can still make her attack and race back to the protection of her aircraft based in the Marianas."

"That is what I hope they will believe, Brent-san."

"But her bunkers are full and she can steam at thirty knots while we must reduce speed to conserve fuel. She'll pull away, sir."

"I know. But we will be between her and her bases and our reconnaissance aircraft out of Kyushu should pick her up."

"And if they don't?"

"*Yonaga*'s scouts will be out and we know for once what corner of this ocean to search." He hunched forward, the scent of blood raising his spirits, eyes gleaming as if backlit. "I want *Al Kufra*. She is the most dangerous enemy target in the Pacific." The admiral's little fist came down hard on the desk. He spit out his words, "I want her, Brent-san."

"Of course, sir. But we'll come within range of their bombers in the Marianas."

Fujita gestured at a chart, "True, but if we steam west-south-west we will pass six-hundred-miles south of Tinian and Saipan and at their extreme range."

"I see, Admiral. Then, as you said, turn north into the Philippine Sea and head for home."

"Yes. Pass west of the Marianas and then engage *Al Kufra*."

Brent walked to the chart. "Respectfully, sir, that is a big gamble." His finger traced a line south along the Asian coast. "Their battle group could attack our bases in Japan and then slip by to the south—through here." The finger traced a line just off the coast of China through the East China Sea and the Straits of Formosa and moved into the South China Sea to a point west of the Philippines and north of Indonesia. "Once here, they can either head for Surabaya or, with refueling, head back to Tripoli." He scratched his head while Fujita watched silently. "Or, Admiral, they could hit Iwo and then run directly south, hoping to pull us into a pursuit that would take us within range of their squadrons based in the Marianas." He returned to his chair.

"Good thinking, Brent-san, and distinct possibilities. A good commander always tries to anticipate all contingencies." He tugged on his chin. "We will maintain a continuous reconnaisance to the west and east—cover all escape routes."

"They can still evade us. It's a big ocean, sir."

"I know. I know, Brent-san. He sighed and sank back into his chair. "But remember, war is based on rolling dice."

Troubled by a new thought, Brent stared into Fujita's eyes. "Sir, this plan is so complex—depends on so many contingencies falling into place—why did you not discuss it with the staff, which is your usual procedure?" He waved his hands. "Give and take, search for opinions, debate? It works."

The old man nodded. "True, Brent-san." His eyes found the bulkhead above Brent's head. "Remember our attack on Rabta?" Struck by horrifying memories, Brent shot erect, as though his spine had been replaced by a steel rod. "Remember the traitors and spies Horace Mayfield, Lia Mandel, and Arlene Spencer?"

Brent rubbed his temple, spoke from deep in his throat. "Of course, Admiral. How could I forget? But surely you don't think . . ."

"No, Brent-san, I do not think I have traitors on my staff. However, this plan you and I discussed was conceived on the basis of many factors falling into place like a game of *Go*. And obviously the smaller the number of people privy to plans, the smaller the chance of a leak, or betrayal." He waved a hand in an encompassing gesture. "All of you knew enough."

Brent's reflected on the Admiral's use of the game of *Go* as a simile. Played on a checkerboard with nineteen vertical and nineteen horizontal lines, two players tried to enclose the larger area on the board. It was war without blood being spilled.

But something was wrong with the admiral's logic—his sudden change in attitude. He trusted his staff, but did not seek their input in this most critical phase of planning. He was aging, true. And he had shown shocking lapses of memory—sometimes remembering distant events with crystal clarity while forgetting yesterday's conversations. But many old people showed these traits. But now Brent detected a trace of paranoia—an unreasonable fear of betrayal and distrust of those closest to him. Although his face showed control, Brent felt the cold grip of apprehension clamp down on his stomach. He managed a calm, "Yes, Admiral, the secret was certainly safe."

"Good, Brent-san. I am pleased that you agree." The old man smiled as broadly as the wrinkled parchment would permit. Slowly he pulled a microphone across the desk and threw the "All Stations" switch nested among a dozen mounted on a black baked-enamel plate. Glancing at Brent, he spoke into the microphone with a new youthful vigor he always showed before battle. "All hands, this is Admiral Fujita. All of you are aware of my plans to attack Tomonuto. However, it has been reported that carrier *Al Kufra*, the cruisers *Babur* and *Umar Farooz*, and at least ten destroyers put to sea less than an hour ago. This was expected, and the enemy believes we are unaware of his departure." He paused and rubbed his chin thoughtfully, and his voice took on new power. "The enemy intends to attack our sacred homeland. We will abandon our attack on the atoll, change course, and increase speed. We will trap him with his back to our squadrons on our home islands and destroy him." A great cheer rang through the ship and Brent could hear the thunder of thousands of boots stomping steel. Fujita began to sing the old anthem that Brent had heard so many times on the eve of battle. With the first word thousands of voices, including Brent's, joined the old man's. *"Corpses drifting swollen in the sea depths. Corpses rotting in the mountain grass. We shall die, we shall die for the Emperor. We shall never look back."*

"*Banzai! Banzai!*" cannonaded through the ship. Brent added his. The look on Fujita's face was one of complete satisfaction. He said, "Come, commander, accompany me to the flag bridge. We have a war to fight."

Brent followed the old man out of the cabin.

Speed was increased to twenty knots. A day later the battle group passed south of Guam and entered the Philippine Sea without sighting a single enemy aircraft. Course was changed to three-four-five—a heading that would open the range on the Marianas and point the bows of the force at the southern tip of Kyushu. The impatient Fujita wished to move at flank speed, but the destroyers' bunkers were running low and flank speed was out of the question. The *Fletchers* must be nursed and enough fuel conserved for the battle. Battle devoured fuel as greedily as it claimed men and machines. Captain Arai calculated *Al Kufra* must be nearly 400 miles ahead of them.

Seven hundred miles west of the Marianas, an enemy Constellation was sighted. Immediately the klaxons were sounded and the men rushed to general quarters. Painted blue to hinder detection from above and flying at only two hundred feet to evade radar, the four-engined aircraft roared over the horizon from the east and made a big sweeping turn toward the north, coming so close to the ships the two starboard escorts and DD-1 opened fire with their five-inch guns.

Cursing, Admiral Fujita pounded the windscreen. "He is transmitting!" he screamed. "Shoot him down!"

Four Grumman F6Fs of the CAP poured out of the sun and caught the big Lockheed before it could complete its turn. Forming in a single line, they ripped the four-engined aircraft from tail to cockpit. The Lockheed was not helpless. A dorsal power tureet mounting twin 13-

millimeter guns and a jerry-rigged single mount in the tail returned fire. One Hellcat was hit. Trailing brown smoke from a ruptured oil tank, it rolled out of the fighter stream and turned toward the *Fletcher* off *Yonaga*'s port beam. The Hellcat pancaked into the sea with a great splash that sent spray flying in sheets. The pilot bobbed away in his tiny inflatable dinghy.

The blue fighters pressed their attack with new fury. Quickly, they killed the enemy gunners and shot out the Lockheed's Number One engine. Yellow-orange flames blowtorched into the slipstream from the starboard wing tanks and from both engines. Then laying a thick black carpet of smoke, the great aircraft did a slow roll and plunged like an arrow into the sea. Both wings were ripped off by the impact and within seconds the giant had vanished, its grave marked only by spreading flames. Cheers were raised from thousands of throats, but not Fujita's.

The old admiral turned to Captain Arai, who was standing next to the chart table. "Now they know where we are, Captain," Fujita said.

"Yes, sir." The navigator tapped the chart with a pointed end of a pair of compasses. "Six hundred miles west of the enemy's fields in the Marianas." He looked up from the chart. "We could make a preemptive strike, sir."

Fujita rubbed his chin. "I know. We would have to close the range. I cannot spare the time." He waved to the north. "*Al Kufra* is up there. She should be sighted by our PBYs and PBMs at any time." He licked his lips. "I want to be in her wake when she attacks."

Arai waved at the diminishing cloud of smoke quickly fading astern. "Now that they know our position, they may abort and try to escape."

"I know. Double the number of scouts." He glanced at Brent Ross, who was leaning against the windscreen. "Especially, search to the west, along the China coast."

"Extreme range."

"Our Nakajimas can do it with auxiliary fuel tanks, and we are shortening the range on this heading."

"Aye, aye, sir."

Fujita said, "We will remain at General Quarters." He waved to the east. "If a big Constellation can sneak in under our radar and not be detected by our CAP, so might bombers."

The old man took a place at the windscreen between Brent Ross and Admiral Whitehead. Brent knew they were sailing over a great graveyard of the old Imperial Navy. He wondered if the old warriors were dwelling on it, would relive it. His wait was short.

Admiral Fujita said to Rear Admiral Whitehead, "These waters are cursed, Admiral."

"Because we were spotted?"

"No, Admiral Whitehead. Not just that."

"The Battle of the Philippine Sea?"

"Yes. Thousands of brave samurai sleep beneath our keel." He looked at the American admiral, who stared at the horizon. "You were there, Admiral Whitehead?"

The two old men stared at each other. "Yes. I was on Admiral Marc Mitscher's staff."

Fujita drummed the oak rail of the windscreen. "He was a brilliant commander."

"I agree."

"Admiral Jisaburo Ozawa was stupid—threw away over four hundred planes and three carriers."

Whitehead waved at the CAP. Trying to alleviate Fujita's depression, he said, "He faced the Hellcat, an aircraft far superior to anything he had. Ozawa's pilots were inexperienced."

Fujita's voice was uncommonly thick and a film of moisture turned his eyes into black slits. "You called it the 'Marianas Turkey Shoot.'"

Whitehead fidgeted with his binoculars but remained silent. Everyone shifted uneasily.

Fujita continued, "Our gallant eagles, slaughtered like turkeys, Admiral Whitehead. Was that it?"

Whitehead looked up, his unflinching eyes finding the admiral's. "It was a battle, a fair exchange, and it went our way."

Fujita seemed not to hear. "And the gallant crew of carrier *Taiho* fell into ranks on her sloping flight deck and sang our anthem until she capsized and hurled them into the sea."

"Brave men all, Admiral Fujita."

"We Japanese know how to die."

"No one can argue with that, sir."

"Sir," Naoyuki interrupted. "A signal in plain language from Iwo Jima."

"Iwo Jima!"

"Yes, Admiral. The airfield is under attack by aircraft and they are being shelled by cruisers and destroyers."

"Sacred Buddha!" Fujita said, the dead sleeping fathoms deep forgotten. He moved to the chart table.

Naoyuki said, "Admiral, Radio Iwo Jima is off the air. We cannot contact them."

Brent heard Byron Whitehead mutter, "The curtain's going up."

Fujita thumped on the table in frustration and said to Arai, "Captain, strike a three-hundred-mile circle around Iwo. *Al Kufra* should be somewhere on that perimeter."

"With respect, sir," Whitehead said. "The enemy's aircraft don't have the range of our aircraft." He stabbed a finger at the chart. "I would suggest a two-hundred-fifty-mile circle."

For an instant Fujita looked confused. Brent felt concern again. The old man knew the enemy's aircraft had shorter ranges than *Yonaga*'s. Yet this critical fact had slipped his mind.

"Why, yes, of course. A two-hundred-fifty-mile circle, Captain Arai."

The circle was struck and the men huddled over the chart. Fujita, now all military and intensely cognitive, pointed and said, "She's somewhere here, in the southern semicircle or within it. Captain Arai, give me a bearing and range to this point." His finger struck the semicircle at its southern extremity.

Arai lay his parallel rules on a line from *Yonaga*'s position to the point, worked the rules across the chart to the compass rose at the bottom of the chart, and announced, "She bears about zero-four-three." And then he measured the distance between *Yonaga* and the semicircle with his compasses and touched the two points of the instrument to his latitude scale. He announced, "Range five hundred to five hundred fifty miles, Admiral."

Taking in all in over Fujita's shoulder, Brent said, "Respectfully, Admiral, he should be to the east of that point."

Fujita turned from the chart. There was a challenge in his eyes. "Why, Commander. You believed they would run to the China coast."

Brent felt heat on his cheeks. "They may still do that, sir. And, Admiral, I did suggest an attack on Iwo, too."

"Go ahead Commander—out with it," Fujita said impatiently.

"I believe they will turn and head south on this heading." His finger traced a line to the east of the Marianas Islands.

Whitehead joined the exchange. "Force us to fight both his carrier planes and the land-based squadrons."

Fujita nodded. "Yes. That would be a good plan."

"That's what I'd do if I were the enemy commander," Whitehead said.

Fujita rubbed his pate and braced himself on the chart table as the ship rolled gently. "Then let us not disappoint him."

"What do you mean, sir?" Whitehead asked, concern rippling his brow. "It's a trap."

"Let it be. We will set a course of zero-six-five, speed twenty-four."

Arai said, "That course will take us just north of the Farallons."

"Yes. We should be able to engage *Al Kufra* just north of the twentieth parallel and west of the one-hundred-fiftieth meridian." He stabbed the chart.

Whitehead said, "That position puts us about four hundred miles north of their fields on Saipan and Tinian."

"Yes, Admiral Whitehead—two fighter squadrons and perhaps a dozen bombers."

"That's what our latest intelligence tells us."

"And *Al Kufra*, an *Essex*, operates about eighty-five aircraft."

"Yes, sir."

"And *Yonaga* operates over one hundred fifty aircraft, Admiral Whitehead."

"True, sir. But the enemy operates from three airfields, two of which cannot be sunk." The American turned his palms up and shrugged his shoulders. "*Al Kufra*'s planes can overfly and land in the Marianas. One hit on our flight deck and all of our air strength would be put out of the battle."

"What would you suggest?"

Whitehead pinched his nose and licked his lips. He nodded at Brent Ross. "This enemy strike is obviously an attempt to lure *Yonaga* into just the attack mode Commander Ross suggests." He ran a finger across the chart. "I would suggest different tactics—a run to the north, pick up the protection of the squadrons on Kyushu and return to Tokyo Bay. Return to fight another day on our terms, not theirs."

Fujita said, "As usual, Admiral, you are logical and make good military sense." He tapped the chart and his small jaw took on a familiar hard set. Brent knew what was coming before the words were uttered. The old man threw his head back and squared his narrow bony shoulders. "An attack on Iwo Jima is an attack on our sacred soil. To allow a desecration of this sacred island on which so many Japanese soldiers and American marines bled is a sacrilege beyond comprehension. We will pick

334

up the gauntlet, fight the enemy on his terms, our terms, anyone's terms, and destroy him."

Arai, Brent and the lookouts, who had been eavesdropping, all shouted, *"Banzai!"*

"A mistake," Whitehead persisted.

"But an unexpected tactic."

"Yes. Probably."

"Well, Admiral Whitehead, remember, Gebhard von Blücher's charge at Waterloo was unexpected, too. He only defeated Napoleon and changed the course of history." Fujita turned to Talker Naoyuki and shouted a command, "Signal bridge, make the hoist, course zero-six-zero, speed twenty-four."

The signal shot up the halyards, and then were jerked down. As one, the ten-ship battle group swung to the new course and increased speed.

"We're in God's hands," Brent heard Rear Admiral Whitehead mutter.

Chapter Sixteen

At dawn the next morning the first report from a scouting PBY, "Wild Goose Number Three," was received. "Enemy carrier and escorts sighted at latitude twenty-one, longitude . . ." The message ended abruptly.

Standing on the flag bridge, Admiral Fujita read the message and cursed. "'Wild Goose Number Three' must have been shot down." With Brent Ross, Rear Admiral Whitehead, and Captain Arai all crowding close around the chart table and Lieutenant J. G. Tokuma Shoten, who was the duty navigator, Fujita pointed at the twenty-first parallel. "She must be out here, steaming about one-zero-zero." He drummed his temple with the fingers of his right hand. "She would hold that heading until she reaches the one hundred forty-ninth meridian. And then steam one-eight-zero due south to her umbrella from the Marianas. She has no other options. We block her escape route to Indonesia and can interdict her route to Tomonuto and she does not have the fuel to steam all the way back to the Mediterranean." He turned to his executive officer. "Captain Arai, have we heard from Scout Number Three? He took off three hours ago." He tapped the chart. "This is his sector."

"Nothing, sir. Either he has not sighted the enemy battle group or he has been shot down."

Talker Naoyuki's high-pitched voice interrupted,

"Admiral Fujita, the radio room reports Iwo Jima radio is back on the air. They report that the enemy attack ended at eighteen hundred hours yesterday. All of Iwo's fighters have been destroyed, and five of their seven dive bombers. The strip is pitted with bomb craters, but they are filling them. Should be operable within four hours. The control tower has been destroyed. They claim one hit on an enemy cruiser."

"Sacred Buddha. They should have done better than that." Fujita slapped the table. He seemed to be thinking out loud. "If they broke off their attack at eighteen hundred hours, they have been steaming for at most ten hours." He drummed both fists on the table and looked at Captain Arai. "*Al Kufra* must be closer than we thought—under four hundred miles to the northeast." He studied the chart. "And the fields on Saipan and Tinian are about the same distance to the southeast." He asked Captain Arai, "All air groups ready to take off, Captain?"

"Commander Matsuhara reports all aircrews have been briefed as per your orders, aircraft armed and fueled. All pilots and crews are in their briefing rooms awaiting their mission assignments." He gestured at the flight deck, which was crowded with fighters. "As you ordered, sir, Fighter Squadrons One and Two are on the flight deck."

Rear Admiral Whitehead said, "We'd be attacking at a long range, Admiral."

"I know, Admiral Whitehead. We have the range and we have the aircraft that can do it."

"If our groups fail to make contact, they won't have much time to search, and enemy squadrons based in the Marianas could take us on the flank, sir."

"I am aware of this, the trap you warned about, Admiral Whitehead." Fujita pinched his tiny nose and pulled down on his nostrils.

Brent knew there would be no grand strategy here, no carefully crafted tactics. This was a commander caught

337

on the jaws of a dilemma laid by a clever enemy; driven to the wall by the force of circumstances that demanded a solution now—at this moment. Every man knew there would be a battle today. Only where he would fight and probably die were the unknowns. The pistol was cocked, primed, and ready. The worst thing a commander could do under these circumstances would be to call for a stand-down. However, such a decision did not honor the dictates of *bushido* or the persona of the samurai. Staring at the old admiral, Brent could tell by the expression on his face that the decision had been made—a decision that could spell death for perhaps thousands of young men on this glorious day in the tropics.

Fujita's jaw quivered for a moment and then he spat out the fateful words, "Fighter Four will provide CAP for the battle group. Fighters One and Two will escort Bomber One in an attack on the enemy fields on Saipan and Tinian." He glanced at Rear Admiral Whitehead. "This will cover our flank. Fighter Three and four British Seafires will escort all dive bomber and torpedo bomber squadrons on a heading of zero-eight-zero until they intercept the enemy battle group." He waved a tiny fist in the air. "Kill them!"

"*Banzai! Banzai!*"

"Sir," Whitehead exclaimed through the shouts anxiously, "Admiral Isoroku Yamamoto split his forces at Midway, too. Attacked both Dutch Harbor and Midway. He should have concentrated on Midway. Lost the battle and the war. I believe your tactics are flawed, Admiral."

"Flawed or not, we have two enemies, and we will kill them both or one of them will kill us. It is the way of the samurai!"

More shouts of "*Banzai!*" Whitehead turned up his hands in a gesture of futility.

Fujita shouted at Naoyuki, "Crew chiefs, start engines. Prepare to launch. Pennant One at the dip." And then, to Arai, "Notify all pilots and aircrews of their assignments and prepare their point option data."

"Aye, aye, sir." Captain Arai hurried from the bridge. There was the whine of energizers and cough of cold engines coming to life. Then, with the force of an artillery barrage, the sound of warming Sakaes ripped open the peace of the morning with disciplined savagery.

With a final thought, Fujita turned to Rear Admiral Whitehead and said over the din, "Send the following signal to Captain Treynor in CISRA, Admiral. Addressee, SOPA TOKYO, detach Corsair squadron to Iwo Jima immediately receipt this message. Use caution. Airstrip damaged. COMYONAGA."

Scribbling on a pad, Whitehead said, "Fighter Six to Iwo Jima. That is a good idea, sir." He hurried from the bridge.

Commander Yoshi Matsuhara's Zero was the first fighter to leap off the flight deck. Immediately, he pulled up his gear and slammed his canopy shut and locked it. A little left rudder brought the fighter into its counter-clockwise turn, which allowed the remainder of Fighter One, Fighter Two, and the dive bombers to form up behind him before they set a course for the Marianas. It was a good day for flying. Overhead, there was a light four-tenths cloud cover; cirrus clumped like lamb's tails, stratus like faint chalkmarks all going in the same direction.

He smiled to himself as he first felt his hachimachi headband and then his belt of a thousand stitches. When he'd first entered flight training, his old aunt, Shikiko, had stood on a Tokyo street corner and collected a thousand stitches and a thousand prayers from strange women who passed by. Running his hand over the belt, he felt the miniature icons sewn into the material: a talisman of the "Eight Myriads of Deities," and a "Buddha from Three Thousand Worlds." And some-where, near his spine, was an image of the Buddha only millimeters in height, fashioned of gold and exquisitely carved. When his Aunt Shikiko had given him the belt she had said, "No bullet can ever touch the man who wears this. The gods will ward them off, bend them from their path." Thus far, over five decades, she had been right. But when the belt was made, Kenneth Rosencrance had not yet been born. The American was evil incarnate, could call on all the forces of the black underground. He was sure he would need all the power of the belt this day.

The vision of the gutted Willard-Smith drifting into the sea flashed before the commander's eyes, then Rosencrance's leering face. He was probably up there, leading his *Vierter Jagerstaffel* on an interception. After all, the enemy knew where they were. Yoshi actually salivated, thinking of meeting the renegade. "I will kill you!" he screamed into the roar of the engine. His hands were trembling on the control column. Taking several deep breaths, he calmed himself. Another troubling thought intruded. He did not like Admiral Fujita's tactics; splitting his forces and attacking in two different directions.

Now calm again, he licked his lips. The taste of saké was still strong. Before taking off, he had led his Japanese pilots—oh, Amaterasu, they were so young—in the traditional drink and the eating of two chestnuts. Flying Officer Claude Hooperman, Pilot Officer Elwyn York, and a young German, Ensign Stefan Schafter, gulped down the saké but refused the old, hard chestnuts. York asked for more saké, but was refused. Everyone laughed nervously. Then, the Japanese solemnly cut their fingernails and snippets of hair and placed them in envelopes. In the event they were killed and vanished into the depths of the Pacific, the hair and fingernails could be cremated by relatives. This would assist in polishing a man's karma and assure his spirit of an honored place in the Yasakuni Shrine. Yoshi had addressed his envelope to Tomoko Ozumori.

On a lean mixture and with his propeller on coarse

pitch to save petrol, Yoshi slowly flew around the carrier at his long-range cruise speed of one hundred thirty knots. In fact, he was moving so slowly he was forced to push his throttle ahead a notch when making his turns to maintain lift. Within minutes, Hooperman was off his port elevator and York off his starboard. But the bombers were maddeningly slow in taking off and forming up. As he began his third turn around the carrier, his stomach churned with frustration. Then, after what seemed an infinite waste of time, all thirty-six aircraft were airborne and Yoshi set a course for the southeast, the fighters climbing to twenty-four thousand feet, the bombers flying at nine thousand.

Commander Takuya Iwata settled his Aichi D3A dive bomber onto a heading of zero-eight-zero. Turning the control knob of the new Sumitomo-Hamilton constant speed propeller, he changed the fine pitch of takeoff to the coarser pitch of cruising, causing a slight vibration as the blades rotated and bit more deeply into the air. The effect of the variable-pitch propeller was remarkable. It was like shifting gears in a car. "Overdrive," he said to himself. "That is what the Americans call it."

The whole performance of the Aichi improved without any greater effort by the engine. Easing his throttle forward and at the same time thinning his mixture, he watched his airspeed indicator creep up to 140 knots. A backfire told him his Sakae 42 would take no more. A hairlike movement of the mixture control soothed the rebelling engine and the backfires ceased. RPMs 1,350, oil pressure 34 kilograms, oil temperature 98 degrees centigrade, cylinder head temperature 110 degrees, manifold pressure 140 millimeters of mercury.

He snickered. At least Fujita's insistence on using English units had not changed the metric calibrations on his reliable old instruments. With the growing number of foreign pilots, the old man had insisted on switching to

NATO terminology. He had even abandoned the old simple international phonetic alphabet for the new clumsy multisyllabled NATO system. In fact, he even called *Yonaga*'s "task force" a "battle group" as a sop to the large number of Americans.

Pulling his stick back gently, he began to climb slowly to his assigned altitude of 9,000 feet. The engine coughed once, but made no more objections to the increased load.

Iwata looked around. Trailing him in three echelons were thirty-two more dive bombers. He grunted with irritation. Senile old Fujita had kept eight of his bombers for scouting. In fact, two were patrolling 150 miles apart and over 100 miles ahead of the force. At their cruising altitude of 8,000 feet they would have a horizon of over 100 miles. It was a good idea, but the old man should have used Nakajima D3As. He had more of them and the Aichi was a far more potent weapon.

No one could deny the lethality of the Aichi. During the Greater East Asia War it sank more Allied ships than any other Axis aircraft, including the Stuka. And in the war against the Arabs, the Aichi had sunk three enemy carriers, two cruisers, and four destroyers. Greedy, glory-seeking D3A commanders had claimed the same ships, but they were either liars or had trouble with their vision. Now, on this most critical day in the war against Kadafi, he was attacking with only 33 Aichis, while far below 47 Nakajima D3As lumbered along with their 1,760-pound torpedoes slung under their fuselages. Three more of the big planes had to be left on *Yonaga* with sundry engine and control problems.

He liked the Aichi. True, it was slow and poorly armed. But it was easy to fly and forgave errors. With its low wing loading it was capable of carrying a bomb load of 1,100 pounds and deliver it with devastating accuracy. He glanced at the big 47-foot elliptical wings, felt the lever control for the narrow dive brakes mounted beneath the wings. With excellent visibility from its high canopy, it was the easiest airplane he had ever landed on a carrier. Its loss rate through accident was the lowest of all their aircraft.

He craned his neck back and stared overhead. Ten thousand feet above, glinting like bright bits of mica in the sun, he saw the twelve Zero-sens of Fighter Three flying in four vics of three. Trailing were four Seafires flying in the usual British elements of two. Only sixteen fighters. *Al Kufra* could probably launch more than twice that number. It could be a very difficult day—a day in which the Yasakuni Shrine could welcome a host of newcomers.

Settling down into his cockpit, he stretched both legs against the stirrups of his rudder pedals and shrugged his shoulders, which were already bunching and beginning to ache against the restraints of the cramped cockpit. He tugged on the straps of his six-point military harness to assure himself all was tight and the locks were secure. There was an itching and a hand to his oxygen mask moved it slightly. He hated the way the mask stuck to his skin and caused perspiration to form even in freezing temperatures. He checked his radio's six-switch control panel. Channel Four, the bomber frequency, was open, but all he heard in his earphones was the hiss of the carrier wave. His stomach was tight, his heart thumping against his ribs like a tiny animal trying to fight its way out. He always felt like this before battle. Were all men this way? A hand to his hachimachi headband and the feel of his belt of a thousand stitches brought a brief moment of comfort. He wondered if other pilots were finding confidence in the same way.

A new thought turned his stomach. His gunner was that inept twenty-year-old Spaniard Pablo De Luna. No other pilot would take him, and as squadron leader, he felt compelled to accept the young man from Barcelona. No one else was available. Just the sight of him turned his stomach. The man always looked as if he were layered with grease, and he stank of garlic. Rumor had it the Spaniard bought his garlic at a Korean grocery store near

Dock B-2 and stored it in his locker. He nipped on it like most drunks sneak drinks of saké. He was a terrible shot. Maybe his own fumes clouded his vision.

Iwata squirmed again in the tight cockpit. He hated the arrogant American, Lieutenant Commander Brent Ross, but at this moment he wished the American was in his rear cockpit. The man was an uncanny shot. Two years ago, he and Ross had planted a bomb in the center of carrier *Ramli al Kabir*'s flight deck. The American had shot down an Me 109 that day and saved both their lives and made the destruction of the carrier possible. Yes, at this moment, he would happily welcome the despicable American aboard. But he was Fujita's favorite—some said he was a replacement for the old admiral's long-dead son Kazuo. Perhaps. Sometimes, the workings of the admiral's twisted old mind were beyond logic, beyond comprehension.

He glanced at his watch. If the old admiral's geriatric brain had managed to crank out a reasonable solution to their complex problems, they should make contact in less than two hours. The engine droned on, the slipstream rushed past his canopy with the sound of water hissing out of a fire hose, and the fan turned in front of him. It was all hypnotic, dulling, and it could be fatal. He forced himself to search the skies in the usual jerky movements. He snapped on the intercom. "Pablo, keep a weather eye out."

"*Si, señor.*"

"English, you blockhead!"

"Yes, sir," came back contritely.

"Lock your canopy open, unlock your Nambu and clear it—six rounds only."

"Yes, sir."

"And Pablo, try not to shoot down any of our planes."

There was no answer. Iwata felt a rush of air against the back of his head as Pablo locked his canopy open, and then there was a burst of gunfire, the young Spaniard squeezing off a few rounds. The commander pushed the safety cover from his red button, checked ahead through his range finder, and pressed the red button. The airframe vibrated as two wing-mounted 7.7 machine guns fired a short burst. Soon, every plane in the formation followed their leader's example, dozens of tracers arcing down to the sea.

"Very good," Takuya Iwata said to himself. "No one was shot down." He laughed uproariously. Pablo stared with wonder in his eyes.

A voice on the bomber frequency brought Iwata erect, senses tuned. "This is Scout Seven. Main enemy force in sight. One carrier, two cruisers, ten destroyers. One cruiser burning. Latitude twenty-two, longitude one hundred forty-seven degrees, thirty minutes. Speed twenty to twenty-four. Many aircraft headed two-six-zero. I am under fighter attack." The radio went silent.

Iwata checked the chart strapped to his knee. The enemy was much closer than they had expected, and his air groups were flying the reciprocal of his own course. They knew where *Yonaga* was, and they were headed for her. He unsnapped his binocular case and studied the air and sea ahead. He sighted a swarm of insects to the north and then a cloud of smoke on the far horizon, enemy air groups to their north and ships on the horizon. He saw the battle group clearly. One was burning. He opened both the bomber frequency and the fighter frequency. "Enemy ships bearing zero-two-zero relative, range sixty. Our new course is zero-nine-zero. All bombers attack. Fighters, give us cover. Be alert for their CAP." He paused and then shouted, "Get the carrier!"

Following Iwata's lead, the armada banked to the new heading.

Elwyn York's voice crackled in Yoshi's earphones. "Me cock's up. Them bloody buggers' about!"

Hooperman's voice, "Balderdash! You randy Cockneys always have hard-ons. Anyway, you've probably confused your prick for your stick."

"Up your bloody kilt. Quit playing wid your pisser an' open your eyes."

"Edo Flight!" Yoshi roared. "Maintain radio discipline!"

"They'se about, guv'nor." And then, with great excitement, "There they is, Hooperman, your nibs, dead ahead, bandits, thick as 'ores at Soho."

Yoshi saw them, like a horde of bees swarming on the horizon. He was shocked. Far too close. They were only two hundred miles out from *Yonaga*. And there were too many. Intelligence had counted far fewer enemy aircraft in the Marianas. He raised his glasses. Maybe thirty fighters flying over at least a full squadron of Ju 87 Stukas and perhaps a dozen Heinkel 111s. He turned on his electric gunsight and flicked the cover from the red button.

With both fighter and bomber frequencies open, Yoshi spoke into his microphone, "This is Edo Leader. On my command, Edo Flight (Fighter One) will engage enemy fighters, Okami Flight (Fighter Two) will attack enemy bombers, Kobura Flight (Bomber One) will continue on to the enemy fields."

Lieutenant Kunishi Kajikawa's voice rasped back, "Edo Leader, this is Okami Leader. Okami Flight will attack enemy bombers."

Then, the voice of Lieutenant Kyozo Makino, the young commander of Bomber One. "Roger, Edo Leader. *Kobura* Flight will attack enemy fields as per your briefing."

The enemy formations were at a lower altitude and closing fast. A squadron of black fighters pulled up sharply in an attempt to gain altitude. They were flying in their usual *Schwarm*—six elements of twos. Then Yoshi saw it: the blood-red Messerschmitt of Kenneth Rosencrance with an insanely painted Me off his right rudder and below. There were shark's teeth in front of the oil cooler intake and yellow splotches smeared at random

346

over the black of the rest of the aircraft. It was Rudolf "Tiger Shark" Stoltz. Rosencrance and Stoltz. Yoshi's blood seemed to turn to lava, and for a moment he was incapable of breathing. Then he gulped down pure oxygen until his throat ached on the rancid, metallic taste and he coughed into his oxygen mask. Keying his microphone, he shouted, "This is Edo Leader. Attack! Attack! *Banzai!*"

Following Lieutenant Kunishi Kajikawa, Fighter Two split-essed into a dive and streaked for the enemy bombers. But at least twelve enemy 109s raced to intercept. Yoshi did not have time to watch Kajikawa's attack. Instead, he shouted into his microphone, "This is Edo Leader. Edo Flight, follow my lead. Hold your sections until I release you to individual combat. *Banzai!*"

Pulling his stick back and then to the side, he punched the throttle into overboost. The acceleration pressed him back and the engine made a monstrous roaring sound like an untamed beast unleashed. The torque of the 3,350 horsepower *Taifu* whipped the light fighter into a tight half-roll and then, with the stick forward, into a screaming dive. The usual apprehensive glance at his instruments. Cylinder head temperature two-seven-five. Still in the green.

Rosencrance had pulled up sharply, bringing his guns to bear on the hell roaring down on his squadron. His men held perfect formation. They would meet the attack with the discipline of veteran fighter pilots.

Yoshi pulled back on the stick and felt the usual light-headedness that came with pulling out of a dive. And his sinuses were complaining. It must be age—they had become very sensitive to changes in pressure. Now they felt as if they had been blown up with a bicycle pump and his hard breathing seemed to send little fireflies dancing across his eyes. A hard shake of the head sent the flies fleeing. Now, with his head cleared, a slight touch of rudder brought the 100-millimeter yellow-orange reticle of his gunsight to the knifelike wings and round engine of the red Messerschmitt. But the monster in the nose was accelerating the Zero too quickly. The engine seemed to be trying to shake itself free of its mounts. Everything vibrated. Even the red Me 109 was blurred and bouncing all over the reticle.

York's voice, "Slow 'er a bit, guv'nor. Your arse's as wide open as a Lambeth 'ore's pussy."

Hooperman's calm voice, "You're uncovering your backside, Edo Leader. We can't cover you, old boy."

Yoshi eased the throttle back and the vibrations eased. Now the red Me steadied in the sight. The two formations closed with incredible speed, the combined rate almost a thousand knots. The enemy was no longer undistinguished specks. They had developed high Galland-type canopies, filigree gun barrels, oil cooler intakes like dust pans, radio masts, D/F loops, insignia, numbers, letters, the shining discs of propellers, red and black spinners, wisps of blue smoke fleeing exhausts. His enemy's wings reached the second sight bars.

Five hundred yards. Zero deflection. Wing tips touching the first sight bars. The pip was on Rosencrance's spinner. Lips pulled back over clamped white teeth, Yoshi thumbed the red button. The fighter bucked and slowed with the recoil of two 20-millimeter cannons and two 7.7-millimeter machine guns. And most of his sections were firing, adding their armament to his. But the Messerschmitts blossomed with jots of red fire like the blooms of deadly roses. Tracers met and whipped past each other like a mad December blizzard.

An Me off Rosencrance's port side lost a wing and whipped over into an impossibly tight roll and was tearing itself to pieces as it dropped from Yoshi's view. Another Me suddenly lay down a runner of black smoke and dropped out of formation. Yoshi cursed, his tracers seemingly disappearing into the red machine or whipping past. There was a thump and a series of bangs, and two holes appeared in his starboard wing. The renegade

American ruddered to his right and shot past Yoshi's port side so fast and so close the Zero bounced in the Me's turbulence.

Matsuhara heard a distinct Teutonic voice agonize in his earphones, "*Gott im Himmel!* This is Schafter. *Ich bin tot!*" Glancing into his rearview mirror and then craning his neck, Yoshi saw a zero gracefully curve off to the right and down. Schafter was hit. Blood was splattered over the inside of the Plexiglas and the engine was belching black smoke in puffs and streaks as if the pilot were skywriting his own epitaph. He was slumped over his controls. Ensign Stefan Schafter had found his *Götterdämerung*. There was no time to mourn. Many more fine young men would die this day.

With Rosencrance far behind, Yoshi led the eleven survivors of his Fighter One down on a sprawling dogfight below. Kajikawa's squadron was completely engaged in a savage dogfight with a swarm of enemy fighters. Within seconds he saw a Messerschmitt with its cockpit blown to pieces by cannon shells roll into a vertical power dive and scream for its grave far below in the sea. Another enemy fighter turned south, leaving a gray haze of coolant in its slipstream. A Zero flamed and then exploded in a blinding nova of burning, smoking bits.

Yoshi called on Hachiman-San (the God of War) and pounded his padded combing. The enemy bombers were proceeding unmolested on their northerly heading. To the south, Kyozo Makino's Bomber One was under heavy attack from at least six Me 109s. Yoshi cursed again. He counted only seven Aichis left. He weighed his priorities. The greatest danger was to *Yonaga*. He must attack the enemy bombers and take his chances with Rosencrance and his fighters. Makino's bombers would be on their own.

He keyed his microphone. "This is Edo Leader. Edo Flight, attack the enemy bombers." He glanced to the south, where Rosencrance was leading his squadron in a wide, sweeping turn. Yoshi knew his men could inflict punishment on the enemy bombers. But the ten survivors of *Vierter Jagerstaffel* would be on them soon. They would have time for one pass on the bombers.

The plan was basic and simple. His section, Edo Yellow, and the Green Section would attack the bombers to port, and he would send his two other sections to attack the bombers to starboard. "Edo Red and Edo Blue, take starboard. Edo Yellow and Edo Green will take port. Stay alert for enemy fighters. Follow my lead and then individual combat."

"Edo Red wilco." "Edo Green wilco." "Edo Blue wilco," came back from his section leaders.

Jamming the stick forward, Yoshi kicked rudder and turned to the north in the wake of the enemy bombers. He set his jaw and sucked in his stomach. Caressing the red button, he muttered, "Hachiman-San, be with us." He brought the first bomber on the left into the glowing reticle.

Commander Takuya Iwata could not believe his eyes. The sky was raining Messerschmitts. According to intelligence, an *Essex*-class carrier could operate eighty-five aircraft, maximum. Yet *Al Kufra* must have launched at least ninety, perhaps one hundred. The enemy CAP had torn through their cover of twelve Zeros and four Seafires and were shooting down bombers and torpedo planes like game birds.

On the first pass, he had lost thirteen bombers and he was sure the lumbering Nakajima torpedo bombers had suffered even more heavily. The entire well-organized attack had turnd into chaos, an orgy of killing. Flying in pairs, the enemy fighters wove through the slow bomber formations, almost casually shooting down the big slow planes. The two 20-millimeter cannons and the pair of 13-millimeter machine guns mounted by the 109s struck with devastating effect.

All three aircraft to his starboard side had been shot down, two burning, the third diving into the sea with a dead crew. Far to the left, an Aichi and its executioner vanished in a great yellow luminescent ball of flame as the bomber's bomb exploded. Pablo had been firing, frantically, swinging the Nambu and firing long bursts. "Short burst, you stupid 'greaser.' You will burn up your gun!"

"*Si! Si!*"

"And watch out for our own fighters!"

"*Si!*"

Zeros and Seafires were mixed into the maelstrom, flying hard on the tails of the Mes. The sky was a moving stitchery of tracers, incendiaries, and cannon shells. But there were very few friendly fighters left. Perhaps six Zeros and three Seafires. Nine against an enemy reduced to about forty. But they must sink *Al Kufra*. There could be no turning back.

He saw a great black bat in his rear vision mirror. "Five o'clock, Pablo. On our tail."

"I see him, *Señor*."

The Me was so close Commander Iwata could see the goggled face of the pilot hunched forward and staring through his 90-millimeter antiglare gunsight screen. The Aichi shook as Pablo fired. Then flame leaped from the enemy's wings and hood. Tracers and shells hummed and ripped by. Iwata kicked left rudder and jammed the stick to the left and down, rolling out of the stream. There was a spine-tingling screech followed by "*Dio mio!*" and Pablo collapsed.

Two 13-millimeter rounds had punctured the belly of the fuselage and pounded up through the gunner's seat. One struck Pablo's pelvis, ripping off most of his genitals before passing through his bladder and severing the abdominal aorta. It exited through his liver. The other shattered his upper left femur, pierced the ilium neatly, and severed the spinal column between the two lower lumbar vertebrae. With the severed aorta pumping blood

351

into the abdominal cavity and the severed spinal column paralyzing his respiratory and cardiovascular centers, death was almost instantaneous.

The black bird of death whipped past, seeking easier game below and Iwata pulled the big plane up and regained his position in what was left of his squadrons. He squeezed off a few rounds from his twin 7.7-millimeter machine guns, but the Me was already out of range. He cursed and punched his instrument panel, and shouted into the intercom, "Pablo! Pablo!" No answer. He looked around, saw the corpse. Inexplicably, he felt a great sorrow, a great feeling of loss he did not expect. His gunner was dead—perhaps a fool, but his ally. His brother-in-arms. And the Spaniard had died nobly, like a samurai.

In the mysterious way of air battles, the sky was suddenly empty of fighters. Iwata keyed his microphone, "*Mukade* Leader to *Mukade* aircraft. Close on me. Attack formation. Single-up."

Only eleven Aichis moved in, forming ragged echelons behind Iwata. Then the commander looked down and discovered why the fighters had disappeared. They were ripping through the torpedo bombers. The Zeros and Seafires were still fighting valiantly, but they were hopelessly outnumbered, although there were fewer Messerschmitts still flying. Iwata watched in horror as bomber after bomber plunged into the sea. Some fell in flames, others lost wings or tails or exploded, while yet others with dead pilots simply plunged into the sea. He thought he saw three more enemy fighters crash, but he could not be sure. Another Zero spun into the sea.

Then Iwata realized the enemy preoccupation with the torpedo bombers might give the Aichis an advantage. They were very close to the enemy battle group. In fact, most of the *Gearings* to the starboard of the carrier were firing. Patches of shaggy black blobs like the foul pustules of a loathsome disease soiled the sky ahead and above. Almost immediately they were flying through the hanging shaggy blobs and bounding on the turbulence.

He could see the entire enemy battle group quite clearly. *Al Kufra* with her big rectangular flight deck, the pyramidal stacking of four twin-mount 5-inch guns fore and aft of her island, gun galleries with scores of 40-millimeter and 20-millimeter guns waiting for him to come into range. Ten of her cannons were firing at the approaching torpedo bombers. And then he noticed most of her machine guns on her starboard side were depressed and pointed at the approaching Nakajimas, which were very close to launch point. Cruiser *Babur*, steaming ahead of the carrier, and cruiser *Umar Farooz*, astern, added their 5.25-inch and 4.5-inch fire. Flames and black smoke roiled from *Umar Farooz* amidships. Iwo Jima's SBDs had hit her heavily.

The first Nakajima bounded over an outlying destroyer. Then another and another. One, its wing blown off, spun around in a flat trajectory and slapped the water like a flat stone, skipped, and then disappeared in a great geyser of spray and debris. Another struck a tower of water thrown up by a 127-millimeter shell. Its engine drowned and one wing twisted up at a queer angle, it flipped over onto its back and dived into the sea. And the Messerschmitts and Japanese fighters still clung on in hot pursuit, despite the storm of AA. Counting the torpedo bombers, Iwata almost sobbed. There were less than a dozen. But they bored in, converging on *Al Kufra*. Sheets of 20-millimeter and 40-millimeter fire flashed across the sea to meet them. Three were hit immediately and crashed. Then two Messerschmitts and a Seafire were shot out of the sky. Most of the Nakajimas had been destroyed. The torpedo attack would most certainly fail. Dead men cannot harm anyone.

Iwata looked to the left and down. The carrier was sliding past his left side and beginning to disappear beneath his port wing. It was time to dive. He glanced at his instruments and grunted with satisfaction. "He shouted into his microphone, "This is *Kobura* Leader.

Kobura flight attack. Follow my lead!"

He set his dive indicator for 85 degrees, reduced manifold pressure to dive speed, dropped his dive brakes, set the propeller on full course, glanced at the carrier, which was almost obscured by his wing, and pushed the stick forward.

Immediately, the sky shot upward and was replaced by the sea. The enemy was spread beneath him—the carrier, cruisers, and destroyers—all alert to the doom rushing down on them. All firing. Perhaps four torpedo planes had released their torpedoes and were curving toward the north. And through the corner of his eye he could see black fighters racing up through the AA, frantically trying to intercept *Kobura.*

The carrier was traveling at flank speed and turning toward the white tracks of two torpedoes. Two other torpedo tracks were visible far astern of *Al Kufra.* The torpedoes would miss. All that sacrifice and not one hit. Over forty Nakajimas destroyed. He gripped the stick more tightly as gusts of wind caught the dive brakes and skewed the big bomber. Balancing with rudder, he brought his sight to the center of the carrier's deck. A black form rising from his right suddenly sprouted flame. Holes stitched his port wing and he felt his controls vibrate, more slugs ripping through the Aichi. Then he was past the Messerschmitt and the vast deck loomed beneath him. His altimeter showed 1,200 meters. The ship was twisting. He worked his controls calmly. He was at work. This was his destiny. The whole purpose of his training, his life.

The carrier was aflame with muzzle blasts. Shells and bullets sleeted past. A thousand meters. A piece of aluminum flew from the top of his port wing. Five-hundred meters. The cross-hairs of his sight were dead center on the flight deck. Three hundred meters. His judgment. *Now!*

He pulled back hard on the manual bomb release. He felt the peculiar motion of the bomb trapeze flinging the bomb clear of the propeller and then the nose came up slightly. Pulling back on the control column, he cranked his trim wheel to compensate for a loss in weight of 1,100 pounds. Plunging down only a few meters from the water, he pulled up his dive brakes, set his propeller on fine pitch, and punched his throttle to the wall. Surprisingly, he found cruiser *Umar Farooz* in his sights. He squeezed the red button and raked the warship from stem to stern as he flashed over. More holes appeared in his wings and fuselage.

Looking back, he saw a Vesuvian blast erupt in the center of the carrier's flight deck. And more Aichis poured down, bombs plummeting like tiny black flechettes. A second bomb hit her forward, a third was a near miss, a fourth struck in the middle of the holocaust amidships. Then two more plunged into her stern in quick succession. Steel plates, men, guns were hurled into the air. A 5-inch magazine exploded, blowing her two after-gunhouses from their mounts and enveloping her island in flames. Then a tungsten-uranium-tipped bomb penetrated forward and exploded in gasoline and bomb stores on the hangar deck. The result was cataclysmic, a hundred feet of flight deck ripped open and flung aside by a gigantic blast that appeared to be in the kiloton range. A great roiling, twisting cloud of smoke flashing red and orange shot into the sky and the Aichi was buffeted like a leaf by the shock wave. *"Banzai!"* Iwata shouted, fighting his controls. But there was no time to watch the carrier die.

Messerschmitts, Zeros, and Seafires raced after the bombers. Maddened enemy pilots shot three more bombers down. But the Japanese fighters clung tenaciously, destroying the enemy with a killing madness of their own.

After glancing at his point option data. Iwata brought his bomber onto a heading of two-six-zero, a course that would take him back to *Yonaga*. Then another huge blast turned his head. He expected to see the doomed carrier blown to pieces. But instead, *Umar Farooz* leaped from the water, a great explosion ripping her bow and sending her Number One turret flying high into the sky.

Seven-point-seven bullets could not do that. No chance at all. Then he saw a faint line in the sea. A torpedo passing astern. One of the immolated B5Ns errant torpedoes must have hit the cruiser. She was sinking fast, her great speed scooping up water, smashing bulkheads and driving her into her grave. *"Banzai!"*

He spoke into his microphone, "This is *Mukade* Leader. *Mukade* Flight, form up on me." Hugging the sea, only four Aichi D3As followed to the southwest. Then three Nakajima B5Ns climbed up from nowhere and joined the formation. A miracle. Some of the torpedo bombers had survived. He choked back a sob and felt tears pooling in his eyes. He raised his goggles and rubbed them.

He was past the last enemy escort now, and he began to gain altitude. Then he saw the fighters. Three Zero-sens and two Seafires, flying above them. Where were the Messerschmitts? He looked back. He saw perhaps twenty black fighters circling over the battle group and the carrier which had stopped and was burning from stem to stern. She already had a list to port and men were leaping into the sea. *Umar Farooz* had vanished and three *Gearings* were picking up survivors. Maybe the enemy expected more dive bombers. They had been attacked by only thirty-three, and the enemy knew *Yonaga* carried over forty. Or perhaps they would remain for a few minutes and then head for the Marianas. They probably had enough fuel to make Saipan and Tinian.

Then he saw a black Me 109 with three white stripes on the rear of its fuselage turn to the south. Soon, the entire force was flying south toward the Marianas. "Petrol! That's it," Iwata said to himself. "They don't have our range! It is either the Marianas or crash."

His laughter was wild, came in gusts like wind before a storm. He was hoarse and could feel his heart barging against his ribs. The earlier sensation of control was slipping away. Twisting his neck, he glanced at his dead gunner. "Did you hear that, Pablo?" The dead man rocked with the plane, seemingly nodding approval. "They are leaving, Pablo, and we've won." He looked at the handful of bombers now arrayed to both sides and to the rear. "A great victory—great glory for all!" He chuckled and spittle ran down his chin.

Suddenly, he seemed to be detached from himself, as if he were part of the instrument panel staring back at himself. He was an instrument. That was it! A samurai was an instrument of war, an instrument of death—was he not? Why not a part of the panel? That was where all the other instruments were. It was very logical. It made great sense.

Laughter seized him again. "I am an instrument," he gasped through the spasms. His whole frame shook like a man with convulsions. He doubled over and tears ran down his cheeks and his nose ran. He shook his head like a drunk trying to restore sobriety. Gripped the stick with all his strength. Gulped oxygen and finally brought himself under a semblance of control. He was back, restored. He glanced at his instruments. He still had more than half his fuel left. "We'll make it, Pablo. I will take you back. And Pablo, you're not a 'Greaser.'"

Pulling back on his stick, he gradually gained altitude and speed. But something seemed to be tugging on his port wing. The hits. Chunks of aluminum had been blown off the wing and trapped air was destroying his trim. He pushed on the right rudder pedal and cranked his trim wheel. The big bomber skewed to the side and flew as though a side wind were twisting it. The damage was much more serious than he had first realized. The entire wing was weakened and could rip off. Reducing throttle, he said, "Amaterasu, be with me."

The endless blue sky ahead glared back silently.

*　　*　　*

Commander Yoshi Matsuhara led Fighter One through the enemy bombers like piranhas on a feeding frenzy. The twelve Heinkels were echeloned above the Stukas so that their superior firepower would protect the slow, vulnerable Junkers. Lieutenant Kunishi Kajikawa's Fighter Two had drifted far to the west in its sprawling battle with enemy fighters. Kajikawa would be of no help.

Diving through the Heinkels, Matsuhara gave the last bomber on the left a half-length for deflection and then hammered it with a two-second burst. Every bullet and shell struck the cockpit. The bit bomber slowly turned to the west and began its final descent.

He was past the Heinkels in a blink and streaking down on the Stukas. Tracers raced up to greet him. Again, he picked a trailing bomber to avoid covering fire. The lumbering bomber expanded steadily until its bulk filled his reflector sight. He pushed down on the red button. A short burst of shells and bullets blew off the Junkers' hood and turned the big Jumo engine into flaming junk. It rolled into a spin and a single white parachute opened behind it. There were shouts of *"Banzai!"* in his earphones as other pilots scored.

York's voice: "Smoked the bugger!"

Hooperman: "Tally-ho. Scratch another Heinkel."

Ensign Hitoshi Kitajima's excited shout: "Sent one to Allah. Burn! Burn!"

Pulling up from his dive, Yoshi could see four Heinkels and five Stukas tumbling toward the sea. Incredible shooting. But Rosencrance was leading his fighters in a screeching attack like avenging black angels.

The fighter circuit buzzed with a warning, "Edo Leader, fighters to the south and high."

"See them," Matsuhara shouted. "Edo Flight, regroup. Engage enemy fighters!"

The sections reformed and turned as one toward the Mes plunging down on them. Yoshi looked for the red Messerschmitt but a black fighter to starboard veered in toward him. Punching the Sakae into overboost, he rocketed upward. Kicking rudder and horsing the stick back brought the pip in the center of the yellow-orange circle to the enemy's spinner. The enemy pilot was completely fooled by the Zero's speed and maneuverability. A short burst ripped off the oil cooler intake, smashed into the underside, and destroyed the landing gear locking device. Streaming black oil and smoke and with its gear down, the 109 tipped up on one wing, rolled past, and began its final spin into the sea.

All semblance of disciplined unit fighting vanished. The dogfight became a brawl. Every man fought desperately for his own life. Fighters twisted, turned, burned, disintegrated, exploded. The fighter circuit was alive with shouts of warning, victory whoops:

"Rubin, behind you."

"I see him, Sago."

"Break left, Rubin. Left!"

Yoshi caught a glimpse of Marvin Rubin's Zero turning brutally in an attempt to shake the madly painted Messerschmitt of Rudolph Stoltz. But the Me rolled gracefully into a perfect killing angle, behind and above the fleeing Zero. A short burst of cannon fire blew off the Japanese fighter's hood, smashed the canopy, and shattered the likable young American's skull. Flipping over and gyrating wildly like a falling leaf, the Zero plunged toward the sea.

A Seafire charged after Stoltz. Then the sound of gunfire turned Yoshi's head. The old adage "If you can hear machine guns, they are probably being fired at you" ran through his head. Then he saw it—the red Messerschmitt in his rearview mirror. There were thumps and holes appeared magically in his wing. Still in overboost, he pointed the nose of the Zero at the sky. The 3,350-horsepower engine pulled him upward, as if a rocket had been fired in his tail. He glanced at his instruments. Cylinder head temperature had crept up to 275. It was too close to the red.

Rosencrance fell off and Yoshi eased his throttle as he

rolled into a dive. Hell was spread beneath him. At least four Zeros and five Me 109s had been shot down. Columns of smoke marked three graves and four parachutes were drifting down. And the bombers had vanished to the north. Yoshi cursed. He wanted the bombers, but Rosencrance would not let go. Then he saw the red Me with the tiger-shark fighter off its starboard side. Rosencrance and Stoltz were on the tail of a Seafire.

York's voice, "Hooperman, you've got two of the buggers on your arse. Break to your right, toward me."

"See them, old boy. Breaking!"

Hooperman broke sharply to his right, but the Mes turned with him. Stoltz fired a burst and then Rosencrance. The Seafire seemed to stagger. Again, with the Sakae in overboost, Yoshi hurled his fighter across the sky. He and York were converging on Hooperman and his pursuers from opposite directions.

A shout of death filled Yoshi's earphones. "I'm hit. In the name of the gods, I'm hit!"

A burning Zero rolled wildly, making three snap rolls before shedding a wing and then exploding. The numbers on the vertical tail fin identified the pilot as Naval Air Pilot Yuiji Akamatsu—a youngster not more than twenty years old.

Yoshi put the horror out of his mind and brought his sight to the red Me. Rosencrance, intent on his kill, did not see him. In mere seconds Hooperman would be a dead man. Yoshi had a poor shot. He had no choice. At least 800 yards, with three-quarters deflection from the right and slightly above. Allowing a length and a half for deflection and aiming above the enemy's line of flight to allow for bullet drop, he squeezed the button. The tracers arced up and then dropped down, striking the red fighter in small flashes like tiny lights blinking on and off.

York was firing at very long range, too. His tracers whipped into the tiger shark fighter. The two enemy flyers immediately pushed their sticks forward and plunged toward the south. Rosencrance was trailing glycol and wisps of brown smoke. Stoltz hung back protectively. Then the sky was suddenly cleared of enemy fighters, peaceful. A miracle.

Yoshi wanted to follow the enemy—kill Rosencrance and his butcher wingman. He still had nearly sixteen seconds of fire power left and perhaps 500 miles of petrol. He ruddered to the north in the wake of the bombers. "Edo Flight. Reform on me."

Slowly, two Seafires pulled up off his elevators and two Zeros flew in tandem above and behind his section.

A voice in his earphones said, "This is Edo Red Leader." It was Kazuo Kubota one of his veteran pilots. "I have Red Two with me. His radio must be damaged. He cannot transmit but signals he is all right."

Then the voice of Lieutenant Kyozo Makino, the leader of Fighter Two: "This is Okami Leader. Have you in sight!"

Pivoting his head, Yoshi saw four specks closing fast from low and to the southwest. "Form up on me, Okami Leader," Yoshi said. "Give me top cover."

"Wilco, Edo Leader." The white specks began to climb.

Yoshi opened his microphone. "All pilots, we will return to *Yonaga*. Enemy bombers are vectoring in on her."

Makino's voice, "This is Okami Leader. I have no ammunition, Edo Leader."

"Then ram!"

There was no hesitation. "Wilco, Edo Leader."

Yoshi Matshuhara looked around at his pitifully weak force. Nine fighters. And then he noticed. An almost imperceptible trail of glycol was streaking in Hooperman's wake. "Edo Two," Yoshi said. "You are losing coolant."

"Just a trifle, Edo Leader. Let's chop the bloody bastards."

Yoshi was not satisfied. Using RAF terminology, he said, "Edo Two, do not go to War Emergency Power. We

361

will cover you and if you overheat, try to ditch near a friendly destroyer."

"There's nothing friendly out here, old boy."

"We should sight some of our *Fletchers* in less than an hour."

"Roger, Edo Leader. I'll try to keep the old girl in the air."

At almost full throttle, the nine fighters droned to the north. Looking to the northwest horizon, Yoshi saw a gathering storm, dark clouds rearing up ominously like great threatening monsters. All rolling blackness and flashing lightning. Susano, the god of storms, was upset. Perhaps he was irritated by the slaughter with which men had fouled his realm. But there would be more, much more.

Chapter Seventeen

Yonaga's crew went wild with joy when Commander Takuya Iwata radioed a cruiser sunk and carrier *Al Kufra* burning and sinking. On the bridge, Brent Ross shook hands with Rear Admiral Whitehead while Fujita smiled and nodded. Captain Arai, too, exchanged hand clasps with Brent and Byron Whitehead. Then radar broke the euphoria.

Air search had lighted up with dozens of blips. Large flights of aircraft were approaching from the east and south. IFF showed a confusing mix of both friendly and enemy aircraft. From the east, large formations of unidentified aircraft were trailed by a handful of friendlies. From the south, a dozen unidentified blips were very close, with nine friendlies closing from the rear. All of Commander Steve Elkins Fighter 411 Grumman F6F Hellcats had been launched. Flying high above the battle group, the rugged fighters circled protectively. And two of the Nakajima D3As had been repaired and were flying as part of the CAP.

On a heading of three-five-five, the battle group was steaming at high speed for Tokyo Bay. And the course shortened the range on Iwo Jima, where the twelve F4Us of Fighter Six were based. To concentrate the power of their massive AA fire with *Yonaga*'s, the nine *Fletchers* pulled in close to the carrier.

"Admiral Whitehead," Fujita said. "You radioed Iwo Jima—I want those Corsairs."

"Yes, sir. No response, sir. Their radio must be out again—at least their transmitter."

"Sacred Buddha," Fujita said, slapping the windscreen. "I had planned on using them." He waved a hand. "Two big raids are closing on us. Try again."

"My operators are trying to make contact continuously, sir."

"Very well."

Lieutenant Commander Brent Ross adjusted the chin strap of his helmet and brought his glasses to his eyes. Something had glinted high in the sky to the east. Then his lenses brought a cloud of aircraft into focus: perhaps twenty Stukas and a dozen North American Texans. The Texans had torpedoes slung beneath their bellies. And high above, twenty black Messerschmitts loafed along, giving top cover.

Before he could report, a lookout on the foretop screamed, "Many aircraft to starboard!"

"Give me a bearing, elevation, *tsumaranu!*" Fujita demanded.

"One-one-zero, relative, elevation angle thirty, Admiral," Brent said, before the flustered lookout could reply.

"Number? Types?"

"About thirty bombers, Stukas, and Texans with torpedoes and about twenty fighters," Brent replied.

Talker Naoyuki, looking tiny under his huge helmet said, "Radar reports raid to the east at thirty miles."

"Very well. Raid approaching from the south?"

"Range one hundred."

Fujita said to Naoyuki, "CAP intercept raid approaching from the east. All batteries stand by to engage. Fire when in range."

"That will leave us with no fighters to deal with the raid from the south ," Whitehead said.

"I know. We must give priority to the nearest threat."

Whitehead nodded.

Fujita glanced through his binoculars and then to Naoyuki, "All ahead flank!"

The talker repeated the order and the power of the great engines surged the carrier ahead at over thirty-three knots. Brent held onto the rail of the windscreen as 84,000 tons of steel brutally smashed into the seas and sent spray and blue water flying in sheets. Astern, the wake boiled white.

Now Brent could hear the rumble of approaching engines. Then thunder boomed. There was a storm brewing to the west and north, but the thunder came from the east. It was the drumfire of 5-inch, 38-caliber cannons firing as fast as they could be loaded. Four *Fletchers* off the starboard side had opened fire. With each ship firing over a hundred rounds a minute, a carpet of black puffs seemed to march through the enemy formations.

Radar-directed and using proximity fuses, the fire was devastating. Within a minute, a half-dozen enemy bombers had been shot out of the sky. Then Commander Steve Elkins led his eleven F6Fs in a plunging attack on the bombers, the two D3As trailing like lumbering albatrosses with clipped wings. Four more bombers were shot down before the escort dived down and began dogfighting the Hellcats. Now the bombers were free of attack and they bored on like messengers of doom.

With a report that rattled Brent's eardrums and stabbed pain into his skull like needles, the sixteen cannons of the starboard 127-millimeter battery opened fire. He grabbed his ears and then, following Fujita's angry gesture, raised his binoculars. Through his lenses, Brent could count eleven Stukas and six AT-6s. Then he saw another group of aircraft diving in from the east, but south of the enemy attack. They were friendlies. He counted: five Aichi D3As, three Nakajima B5Ns, three Zero-sens, and two Seafires. "Friendly aircraft, Admiral," he shouted over the thunder. "Eleven of them, bombers and fighters, bearing one-three-zero, range twenty."

Fujita, Whitehead, and Arai raised their glasses. "Thank Amaterasu. It is Iwata's and Hamasaki's returning bombers and Fighter Three." He dropped his glasses. "You said eleven, Commander?"

"Yes, sir."

"Sacred Buddha!" His voice shook, "Only eleven left out of ninety-six?"

"That's all I see, sir."

The ripping sounds of 25-millimeter guns on full trigger tore through the bedlam of the barrage. Whipped by the wind, the pungent smell of cordite washed over the bridge. Five AT-6s carrying torpedoes were making their runs on the starboard side while high overhead six Stukas were stacking up in their usual oblique stepladder attack formation. Now all of the *Fletchers* were firing. The assault on Brent's eardrums was overwhelming. He felt like a man trapped inside a steel barrel pounded by lunatics armed with sledgehammers. He groaned, but kept his hands on his glasses.

A Texan was hit, lost its torpedo, and crashed. Another, leapfrogging over a *Fletcher*, was shot into three pieces, its torpedo arcing into the sea gracefully like a glistening dolphin. The three survivors bored in. Then the tail of one was blown off and it swung wildly to port and flipped over on its back and was lost in a tower of water and debris. Daunted by the murderous fire, the two survivors dropped their torpedoes at long range and banked sharply away.

"Right full rudder!" Fujita screamed into the voice tube.

The carrier swung hard and was heeled far to port by the force of her turn. The two tracks approached while Fujita hunched over the tube. When the bow swung precisely between the tracks, the old man shouted, "Meet her! Steady as she goes!"

"Meet her! Steady as she goes!" A pause. "Steady on zero-seven-zero!"

"Very well."

Fascinated, every man watched as the white tracks streaked by to port and starboard and passed astern.

"Left to three-five-five!" Fujita shouted. The ship started its turn back to its base course.

A change in sound brought Brent's eyes back to the Stukas. They had closed their cooling gills and were dropping their dive brakes, and their propellers rumbled in coarse pitch. Far to the east, the Hellcats of Fighter Four were fully embroiled with the Messerschmitts. The pair of Nakajimas had vanished and only eight Hellcats were still flying. Sixteen Messerschmitts were visible. *Yonaga* could expect no help from Fighter Four.

Now Iwata's assortment of fighters and bombers charged in from the east. Three Zeros and two Seafires led. In the first sweep, the fighters shot down two Stukas. But only the Seafires fired short bursts, and then their armament fell silent. Fujita slapped the windscreen. "Sacred Buddha, the Zero-sens must be out of ammunition!"

"And so are the Seafires," Whitehead said, pointing. "That was the last of it. They're just making dry runs—trying to disrupt the Stukas' aim."

And the American rear admiral was right. With only sixteen seconds of firepower, the Zeros had expended their last rounds in the dogfight over *Al Kufra*. The heavier, more powerful Seafires had had a short burst left. But now they too had empty magazines.

Guns silent, the Zeros and Seafires wove through the dive bombers, braving fire from the tail gunners and the tremendous barrage from the battle group. A Zero was blown to bits by a direct hit and a Seafire limped off to the north trailing smoke. The four remaining Stukas plowed on serenely, seemingly immune. The surviving friendly fighters dove out of the AA.

"Here comes Iwata!" Captain Arai shouted, pointing.

Streaking far ahead of his four Aichis and three Nakajimas, Commander Iwata led the big, clumsy planes

367

in a desperate attempt to head off the Stukas. But it would be futile. There were too many enemy fighters for Fighter Four to contain. Six Me 109s dived out of the dogfight onto Iwata's pitiful assortment and shot down two Aichis and all three Nakajimas in a single pass.

Two of the surviving Aichis banked sharply and zoomed down close to the water where their bellies were protected. Tail gunners and AA blew two of the Arab fighters to pieces and damaged a third. The three surviving 109s pulled up sharply and headed back to the dogfight where the Americans had taken advantage of the enemy's reduced numbers and shot down three more black fighters.

In the melee and heavy AA, the Mes had missed Iwata's Aichi. Plodding on unscathed, he brought his sights to bear on a Stuka. The first bomber was already tipping over into its dive when Iwata opened fire on the second bomber.

Brent prayed and he could hear Rear Admiral Whitehead calling on Jesus Christ.

"We will kill them, Pablo," Commander Takuya Iwata said into the intercom while pressing the red button. The Stuka filled his gunsight. Silently, Pablo rolled from side to side, chin touching his chest, arms outspread, blood seeping from the huge holes in his buttocks, genitals, and abdomen.

The first Junkers had already screamed into its dive and was out of range. Iwata was firing on the second bomber from only three hundred yards, the tracers from his two fixed machine guns stitching through the enemy's tail surfaces and fuselage. The Arab rear gunner fired back with his own twin MG81 guns. Frustrated, Iwata spit out an oath: "Why don't you burn? Why don't you crash?"

The enemy had slowed to about 120 knots for his dive, and Iwata closed fast at almost twice that speed, despite his damaged wing. So much of the skin had peeled off he could see the main spar, the dive brake actuating mechanism, stringers and ribs. The breech of a machine gun and part of an ammunition box were visible. The drag forced him to use still more right rudder and he knew the wing could break loose at any instant. He ignored it. *Yonaga* was in mortal danger.

"Die, damn you, die!" he cried, his tracers hosing the big plane. The Stuka began to nose over and Iwata pushed his stick forward to keep the bomber in his sights. The pilot was so intent on *Yonaga* he was ignoring Iwata. He had actually given him the Stuka's blind spot. The commander could not believe his eyes.

Now he was firing up through the fuselage. Frantically, the gunner pushed up hard on his grips to depress as much as possible. His tracers smoked over the Aichi's canopy and passed to his right. Three rounds punched through his starboard wing, paint flaking from the rents and leaving halos of shiny aluminum. Iwata could see the huge bomb snugged up close to the belly. Pushing the stick forward, he released the red button and dived with the Stuka, beneath its fuselage and just behind the tail.

Shoving everything into a corner, he dragged the Aichi through a turn that made the rivets creak and the port wing bend. The Junkers slid into his sights again. He pressed the red button. There was a hiss of compressed air and the clank of breech blocks. He was out of ammunition. He slugged the instrument panel in frustration. "We must kill them! Kill them, Pablo."

There was something red on the floor plates. Blood. Blood seeping forward from the rear cockpit and coagulating under his feet. "You are bleeding, Pablo."

No answer. "We will kill him together, Pablo. We will ram them, show the world how samurai can die!"

Filled with a sudden inexplicable joy, Commander Takuya Iwata pulled back on the stick, kicked rudder, and watched fascinated as the belly of the Stuka loomed large. Then it filled his windshield. Blotted out everything. *"Banzai!"* He had aimed for the bomb, but the port wing bent up suddenly, taking control of the aircraft and causing it to half-roll to the left. He hit the Stuka's great Jumo engine squarely from the front and below, directly on the oil cooler intake.

"Tenno heika . . ." He never finished his salute to the Emperor.

Although death came in an instant, time seemed to slow, and he was surprisingly aware of the sequence of his immolation. There was a shock, as if the aircraft had suddenly struck a wall of masonry, and he was hurled forward against his restraints. Pain shot through his stomach and abdomen and air mixed with mucus and blood exploded from his lungs. Then a brief shriek as the engine ran wild for a millisecond. The Stuka seemed to envelop the universe and petrol burst in a torrent from its wing tanks and the Aichi's reserve tank. He actually smelled it. The 33-foot Aichi compressed down to 27 feet, the wings ripped off, and the propeller blade whirled off behind the tail. Plexiglas flew.

Crashing back through the fire wall and instrument panel, the Sakae became a battering ram, crushing his ribs, sternum, lungs, and heart and snapping his spine like a toothpick. Commander Takuya Iwata died so quickly he did not even have time to scream. His last sensation was that of being enveloped by something darker than black and as big as infinity.

Mashed backward by the engine, his mangled corpse met that of his gunner's, which was still moving forward with the momentum of the disintegrating aircraft. Splintered bones, pulverized flesh, torn organs mixed with metal and each other, all blended into one bloody mass.

Thousands of fragments whirled like a flaming tornado and the two aircraft showered from the sky, followed by a rain of burning petrol, smoking debris, and what was left of Commander Takuya Iwata and Gunner Pablo DeLuna. The largest pieces were the two engines and a slice of the

Stuka's starboard wing, which fell slowly, oscillating from side to side like a dead leaf in autumn.

The bomb fell harmlessly into the sea.

"Left full rudder!" Fujita screamed as the first Stuka shrieked down. No one had time to mourn or even comment on Iwata's sacrifice. Every eye was on the Stuka that seemed to be descending on the tip of a cone of tracers. Then the bomb separated and the plane pulled up and ran headlong into a flurry of 25-millimeter shells. Molting aluminum, it continued in a shallow dive and plunged into the sea.

Brent Ross watched as the 1,100-pound bomb plummeted down. As usual, it seemed to be dropping directly on his head. However, at the last instant, it gave the illusion of veering and exploded with a towering blast that ripped the sea just off the starboard bow. The tower hung in the air for a moment as if frozen and then collapsed back into the sea.

Two more of the bombers were diving. "Right full rudder!" Fujita screamed.

The third plane dropped its bomb and turned sharply toward the east. While the bomb fell, the last bomber released its bomb and made the same turn to the east. This time, there was a concussion to the port side so close that shrapnel clanged and ricocheted off the island and funnel.

"Two misses!" Whitehead exulted.

"But not three," Fujita said in a funereal tone.

The prediction was tragically accurate. The black missile shrieked down, and just before it hit, Brent pulled Admiral Fujita down and sheltered the old man with his own body. The bomb struck the carrier's flight deck squarely amidships. Tipped with depleted uranium, it penetrated the 3.75 inches of steel of her armored flight deck and exploded on the hangar deck. Yellow flames, choking acrid smoke, steel plate, cement, sawdust, and latex, erupted. Tremors warped through the ship like the convulsions of a mortally wounded man.

The shock threw Brent Ross and Fujita against the legs of the chart table. Tumbling over them, Captain Arai grunted as he hit the deck. Whitehead had ducked into a corner. Flames, smoke, and debris shot into the sky. Shrapnel and ripped steel plates clanged and bounded from the steel windscreen. A port lookout, frozen by terror and standing erect, lost his left arm and most of the left side of his chest to a whizzing blade of shrapnel the size of a serving tray. Hurled across the deck, his ripped lung, arteries, and veins spilled blood and gore on the deck. High in the foretop, a gunner and a lookout were hit and knocked from their stations. Both bodies tumbled past the flag bridge streaming blood and disappeared into the devil's cauldron below. One man, with no legs, was screaming as he passed.

"My feet! Help me to my feet, Brent-san," Fujita yelled into Brent's ear.

"You all right?" Brent asked as he pulled the little man up.

"Fine! Fine!" Fujita answered, gripping the voice tube. "Left full rudder. Steady on three-five-five!" he shouted in a strong voice of command. The old man was unbelievable. He seemed completely composed and in charge of himself.

Then to Naoyuki, who was struggling to his feet: "Damage Control! I want a report!" Stunned, Naoyuki spoke into his mouthpiece like an automaton.

Fujita called a lookout. He gestured at the corpse, which was still bleeding. "Drag this man off my deck." In a moment, the dead man was pulled from the flag bridge.

Every man stared down at the flight deck. Flames were leaping up through the giant hole and streaming aft. Whitehead said to Fujita, "I suggest you reduce speed, Admiral. The wind is spreading the flames and making it more difficult for Damage Control."

Fujita said into the tube, "Speed twelve."

The beat of the engines slowed and a voice answered, "Speed twelve, sir. Sixty-two revolutions."

Naoyuki said to Fujita, "Lieutenant Yoshida reports no damage to the engineering department."

"Damage Control! I want a report from Commander Atsumi!"

Naoyuki said, "Commander Atsumi reports two petrol tanks ruptured on the hangar deck and ignited. His men are fighting the fires with the new American foam."

"Gasoline fumes, sir," Whitehead said. "Gas could leak below and make a bomb of the ship. That's how *Lexington* and *Taiho* were lost. They filled with vapors and exploded."

Fujita nodded and shouted at Naoyuki, "All hands! Do not ventilate ship—I repeat, do not ventilate ship."

"Good. Good, sir," Whitehead said.

Fujita said to the talker, "Ordinance?"

"Commander Atsumi reports all bombs and torpedoes are still in their ready racks fore and aft. They are being jettisoned."

"Very well." He turned to Captain Arai. "Go below. Take personal charge and keep me informed."

"Aye, aye, sir." The executive officer rushed off the bridge.

"It's not as bad as it looks, Admiral," Whitehead said.

"I know, Admiral Whitehead." Fujita waved at the sky. "But at twelve knots we are an easy target."

As if to punctuate the admiral's warning, Naoyuki shouted, "Radar reports raid from the south closing fast, sir. Nine friendlies are trailing."

Immediately every pair of binoculars on the bridge swung astern. Brent saw them on the far horizon. "Six Stukas, Admiral, and six Heinkel 111s."

"I see them. Can you see the friendlies?"

"No, sir."

Fujita pounded the windscreen in frustration. "All ahead flank!" he shouted down the voice tube.

"The fires?"

"We have no choice, Admiral Whitehead. It is a choice of dying by fire or water." Then, to the talker, "All guns that bear, stand by to engage raid approaching from the south!"

Brent raised his glasses wearily. His hands were trembling. He had never been under such continuous attack. *Yonaga* had been heavily damaged and was burning, and still another enemy attack was approaching. The Arabs had gambled everything to kill the great carrier. A trap within a trap. Phony negotiations, a clever ruse and sweep by *Al Kufra*, and now more bombers attacking from his fields in the Marianas. And he was sure Fujita had suspected it, charged into it like a samurai astride his warhorse, seeking the decisive battle; the quick solution so dear to *bushido*.

Six survivors of Fighter Four had been drawn far to the east, fighting for their lives against twice their number of Messerschmitts. *Yonaga* needed fighters. Where was Yoshi Matsuhara? Friendlies had been reported to the south, but he had not picked them up yet. He would give his life to see that souped-up red, green, and white Zero. He winced at the thought. He would probably give his life anyway.

There was something peculiar about three of the Heinkels. Each plane had large missiles slung beneath its wings. "Admiral," Brent said, controlling his voice with an effort. "Three of the Heinkels are carrying torpedoes."

"Sacred Buddha!"

Whitehead said, "Must be the Model H-6. They were equipped to carry two torpedoes."

Brent noticed the smoke had diminished. Looking down on the flight deck, he could see men in white fire-resistant suits crowding around the huge hole and pouring foam and water into it.

Naoyuki reported, "Captain Arai reports fires on the hangar deck under control. There is no damage lower than the hangar deck. Water tight integrity is secure."

"Amazing," Whitehead said. "Such efficiency."

"And armor helps, too," Fujita said. He glanced at the approaching bombers, which had split into two groups and were moving to port and starboard.

The escorts began to fire. Staring at the sky as though he were searching for a diety, Brent's lips moved ever so slightly, "Come on, Yoshi. In the name of the gods, we need you."

Commander Yoshi Matsuhara saw the smoke long before he saw the battle group. His stomach clenched into a solid ball of acid. *Yonaga* was burning. He was sure of it. And twelve more enemy bombers were ahead of him, barely perceptible in the distance. He punched his throttle into overboost. The engine howled like a demented spirit and the fighter surged ahead.

Hooperman's voice: "You're showing us your tail feathers, Edo Leader."

York's voice: "You'll burn 'er up, guv'nor."

Yoshi threw the transmission switch on his oxygen mask. "I will take the chance. Go to war emergency."

"I already am," Hooperman said. "I'm burning her up."

Yoshi answered, "We must take the chance."

Quickly the red, green, and white Zero pulled away from the two Zeros and two Seafires of Fighter One and the four Zeros of Lieutenant Kyozo Makino's Fighter Four. Hunched over his controls, Commander Yoshi Matsuhara held his jaw hardened in a rictus of determination. The cylinder head temperature was creeping toward the red, but he ignored it.

"*Yonaga*, Brent-san, I am coming," he said.

Brent watched the three Heinkels climb high for their level bombing run while the three Heinkels with torpedoes circled far to port and dropped low on the water. The Stukas began to stack up in preparation for their dive. AA began to crash and thunder. Then Brent saw them, first a speck in the clear sky to the south, and then a group of specks—Zeros and two Seafires closing fast. But the bombers would have time for one run before the fighters arrived. Brent cursed.

A shout from the foretop and Brent swung his glasses to the north: twelve fighters diving out of a light cirrus cloud cover on the edge of the storm. They had bent wings and huge engines and were closing at about 500 miles an hour.

"Corsairs!" Brent shouted. "Bearing zero-one-zero—high."

"I'll be goddamned," Whitehead said. "The calvary arriving in the nick of time—they're even wearing blue."

Fujita said to Naoyuki, "The fighter frequency." The talker threw a switch.

A speaker hissed and a voice popped in the speaker. "This is Carousel Leader joining the party. Out of my way, everyone, we're coming through like a dose of salts."

Every man on the bridge whooped with joy. It was Commander Harrison Giles, the flamboyant commanding officer of Fighter Six based on Iwo Jima. His timely arrival off Morocco had saved a damaged *Yonaga* a year earlier. And now Giles was back.

Breaking up into elements of two, the twelve big fighters swept over the task force and dived on the enemy bombers. With each F4U armed with four 20-millimeter cannons, the destruction was catastrophic. Six of the enemy were shot down on the first pass and then the six survivors, two Heinkels and four Stukas, turned south in a futile effort to escape. They all jettisoned their bombs and torpedoes. The Corsairs pulled up high and regrouped for a second pass.

"Cease fire!" Cease fire!" Fujita shouted.

The guns fell silent and then Brent noticed the red, green, and white Zero closing fast from the south, far ahead of eight trailing fighters.

376

"Yoshi! Thank God," he said.

"Kill them! Kill them!" Fujita shouted, waving a tiny fist. And then, to Brent and Byron Whitehead, "Who trapped whom?" The old man laughed. Brent had never seen the old man so gripped by laughter. He bent over, clung to the windscreen, and almost gagged before he regained control.

Yoshi's attack was head on. He throttled back and took the leading Heinkel, which had dived down low on the water. Its forward gunner panicked and took hopeful squirts at him far too soon. The gunner in the dorsal power turret added his fire. Yoshi laughed, waited until the wingspan filled his reflector sight, and then pressed the gun button while he counted, "One, two, three."

His shells and bullet stream ripped the length of the fuselage, killing the forward gunner, demolishing the bulbous cockpit, and shattering the dorsal turret. Shards of glass made a sparkling trail, glinting in the wash. Only a hundred feet off the water, the big bomber dropped its nose and bored into the sea with so much force both wings flew high into the air and the fuselage shot fathoms deep with its own momentum.

Giles's voice: "Edo Leader, this is Carousel Leader. Leave some for us. Don't be a hog."

"Be my guest, Carousel Leader," Yoshi said, caught up by the American's jovial demeanor.

Caught between nine fighters from the south and twelve from the north, the hapless bombers were easily shot down. Then, with the red, green, and white Zero leading, the fighters made a triumphant sweep around the battle group. They were joined by four survivors of Elkins's Fighter Four. Five black enemy fighters were visible fleeing to the east and south.

"Edo Leader, this is Carousel Leader. Should I clobber those four Mes hauling ass to the southeast? I could cream 'em."

"Negative, Carousel Leader," Yoshi said. "Stay with the battle group."

Hooperman's voice: "I say, Edo Leader. It looks like our home took a bit of a pasting."

York's voice: "Crikey, she's takin' a real bullockin', guv'nor."

Looking down, Yoshi was shocked and dismayed by the gaping, smoking hole in the center of *Yonaga*'s deck. There was no chance of landing on the carrier. His spirits, sent soaring by the arrival of the garrulous Harrison Giles and his Fighter Six, sank. And there was no more whimsical humor from Giles, who was grimly studying the terrible damage to the carrier's flight deck.

A new voice from *Yonaga* broke into the fighter frequency. "All air groups, this is *Saihyosen*. Your vector to Iwo Jima is zero-one-zero. You are to proceed to Iwo Jima and land. I am sending two PBMs and three PBYs to patrol your route. Also, three destroyers frigate *Ayase* will provide lifeguard patrol. Good luck." It was Icebreaker.

Yoshi spoke into his microphone. "Edo Flight and Okami Flight, do you have sufficient fuel to reach Iwo Jima?"

One pilot replied that he was losing petrol from a damaged fuel connection, and another reported an overheating engine. Hooperman's engine was running hot, but he felt he could make the island. "I have a definite antipathy for cold seawater, old boy" the Englishman said blandly.

Yoshi ordered the two damaged Zeros to ditch near destroyers and then turned north with twelve F4Us Corsairs, four F6F Hellcats, nine Zeros, and two Seafires trailing him. It would be a nervous flight.

Chapter Eighteen

The voyage home was grim. Despite the destruction of *Al Kufra* and *Umar Farooz*, the losses to the Japanese air groups had been devastating. The dive bomber and torpedo bomber groups had been wiped out and most of the fighters lost. Most of the group commanders—key officers in *Yonaga*'s offensive punch—had been killed. Lieutenant Shinji Hamasaki had died in the massacre of his torpedo planes in his attack on *Al Kufra*. Lieutenant Kyozo Makino had vanished with his Bomber One in its gallant but hopeless attack on the enemy fields in the Marianas. Radio transmissions from the tiny island of Aguijan reported attacks on the enemy field on Tinian by three Aichi D3As. All were shot down by fighters.

Commander Takuya Iwata had died like a true samurai, ramming an enemy Stuka in full view of thousands. Truly a glorious demise for the samurai. Fujita had delivered his epitaph succinctly, "His karma will glow like polished steel for all time."

The fighter group had fared better. Commander Yoshi Matsuhara, Commander Steve Elkins, and Commander Harrison Giles had made Iwo Jima. In all, nine Zeros, twelve F4U Corsairs, four F6F Hellcats, and one Seafire had landed on the strip on the volcanic little island. Flying Officer Claude Hooperman had ditched and been picked up by frigate *Ayase*. Twelve fighter pilots, eleven bomber pilots, and fourteen gunners and radiomen had been picked up by destroyers and patrol craft. Many more must have died lonely deaths in the thousands of square miles of frigid water over which the great battle had been fought.

The damage to *Yonaga* was serious and would require at least five months to repair. Forty-seven men had been killed and sixty-one wounded. They could be replaced quickly, but the training of pilots and aircrews took time. Also depressing had been the fanatical bravery shown by the enemy bomber pilots. "It must be the spirit of *jihad*," Rear Admiral Whitehead had commented. "Arabs are their most dangerous when they are gripped by religious fervor. This bunch had it."

Brent stood his watches silently, leaning on the windscreen. Giles's Corsairs provided CAP at the beginning of their return to Tokyo Bay and then the Corsairs were joined by Zeroes flying from Tokyo International. Then, two days from landfall and with Brent Ross on watch, Yoshi Matsuhara's red, green, and white Zero, followed by a Seafire, four Hellcats, and eight more Mitsubishis, roared over the battle group. They all wore *Yonaga*'s identifying blue stripe back of their canopies. Turning smartly, they circled and then dropped so low they had to hop over the carrier. Everyone shouted and waved. Brent cheered until he was hoarse. Feeling a dampness on his cheeks, he turned away from the lookouts and blew his nose. No one looked at him. On a heading for Tokyo, the fighters disappeared to the north.

One day out from Tokyo Bay, Brent was called to Admiral Fujita's cabin. The old man waved the American to a chair. "You served me well, Brent-san," he said.

"Thank you, sir."

"The Yasakuni Shrine is crowded with the brave spirits of our men."

"The price was high, sir."

"Many years ago your father told me the price of glory was never too high."

"My father was not always right, Admiral."

"We bought more than glory, Brent-san."

"Of course, Admiral. We bought time for Japan—the entire free world. Stopped the terrorists."

The old man pinched his tiny nose. "Do you ever wonder if this war will ever end, Brent-san?"

"It seems to feed on itself."

"That is true of all wars." Fujita dropped his hand to the desk and rubbed his withered fingertips together. "You did not answer my question, Brent-san."

The answer came from deep within the young American, "It will end when we destroy them utterly and completely."

"And then?"

"Hopefully, peace."

The old man shook his head. "No, Brent-san, Kadafi will be replaced by another monster."

Brent sighed with resignation. "And it will go on?"

"On and on, Brent-san. That is the way of mankind. Endless monsters and good men must fight them." He leaned back in his chair and spoke through tight lips. "That is why ours is the oldest profession."

Brent chuckled.

"Why do you laugh, Brent-san?"

"Because Commander Yoshi Matsuhara said exactly the same thing."

"He was right."

"Yes, he was right, sir."

The old man fingered a dispatch on his desk. Another matter had entered his mind. "I have just received word about our envoys in Tripoli."

Brent came erect with new interest. "Nishio Kanji and Norio Tokumitsu, they've been murdered?"

"Negative. We hold too many of their men—important people like Major Horst Fritschmann and Captain Henri DuCarme. I warned Kadafi if our envoys were harmed, I would gouge Fritschmann's eyes out and force DuCarme to eat them." Brent rubbed his chin and stared into the black eyes. It was like staring into the bottom of a grave. Fujita was not bluffing. The old man would have carried out his threat. Fujita continued, "Kanji and Tokumitsu have been declared *persona non grata* and expelled."

"Then the negotiations are off?"

"As you Americans would say, 'the understatement of the year.'" He drummed the desk as his quick mind moved to another thought. "We have spent eight years fighting evil all over this planet, Brent-san, and we both agree it will continue."

"True, sir."

"For most of your professional life, you have known nothing but war."

Brent wondered at the old man's point. He was preparing the ground for a trenchant topic. True to his Oriental genesis, he approached his points obliquely. "It is my destiny, sir," Brent acknowledged matter-of-factly.

"You are a samurai." It was a statement, not a question. "The American samurai."

"The media have attached that name to me, Admiral."

"I know. But does it please you?"

"Of course, sir. It's a compliment." The old man nodded and smiled. Brent continued, "You know I've studied *bushido,* the *Hagakure.*"

"Then do you feel you fit the Confucian ideal of the complete man who is both warrior and scholar?"

Brent was confused. "What do you mean, sir?"

The old man laced his fingers over his chest and stared at the overhead. "Long ago a Chinese poet, Li Po, wrote, 'A man should stir himself with poetry, stand firm in ritual, and complete himself with art and music.'"

"I have tried to fit the Confucian ideal, Admiral. I have studied the great thinkers of both East and West. You know that. Have I failed?"

"No, Brent-san, you have never failed me or any of our traditions." He rubbed his withered chin and tugged on the single white hair. Brent knew the old man was still troubled by a thought he had not yet broached. "That is not really the question, Brent-san," Fujita said. "It is your future that concerns me. You could have a brilliant future back in Washington—would rise high in rank."

Brent laughed. "In that warren they call the 'Pentagon'?"

Fujita nodded. "It is your place—with your countrymen. And there, perhaps, you could attain the ideal Li Po exalts." He tapped the report. "And there is a woman—a woman for whom you have great affection."

"Garnet Shaw. She's gone, Admiral. Back to the States." Brent was not surprised by the old man's knowledge. He had learned years ago that he seemed to know everything about his subordinates' private lives.

However, the old man managed to shock Brent with his insight. "Because you chose *Yonaga* over her."

"You could say that, sir."

"Think about your choices, Brent-san. I can only offer you interminable warfare, danger, and possibly a hideous death."

"Have I ever complained, sir?"

The old man smiled. "No, Brent-san, you have not."

Wiping the frown from his forehead, the young American spoke slowly and deliberately. "Arnold Toynbee said, 'Any civilization that does not run to seize the future, and shape it, is doomed to die with the past.'"

"And *Yonaga* runs to seize the future?"

"She is from the past and should have been doomed to die there, but refused."

"And now she shapes the future, Brent-san?"

"Yes, and there is no future for me without her, Admiral."

"Our enemies are strong, wealthy, and vicious, and you know the ordeal will continue."

"I know, sir."

"You will not return to Washington?"

"To search for Li Po? To be chained to a desk?"

The old man shrugged. "Some very valuable men fight

383

their wars from a desk."

"Discard my sword, Admiral?"

Fujita chuckled at the symbolism. "Perhaps put it aside temporarily."

Brent nodded at the *Hagakure* on the admiral's desk. "It is written in your—our sacred volume, 'If a sword is always sheathed, it will become rusty and the blade will dull.'"

"Then, Brent-san, you will not sheath your sword?"

"Not until this evil blight is stamped out."

"Spoken like a samurai, Brent-san."

The two men sat silently, complete understanding reflected in their eyes, which were tied together for moment. Admiral Fujita spoke softly. "Commander Ross, you are dismissed."

Brent stood, bowed deeply, and left the room.